RIFT WARS
THE ENTITY WITHIN

RIFT WARS
THE ENTITY WITHIN

NITIN SUNEJA

The Book Guild Ltd

First published in Great Britain in 2018 by
The Book Guild Ltd
9 Priory Business Park
Wistow Road, Kibworth
Leicestershire, LE8 0RX
Freephone: 0800 999 2982
www.bookguild.co.uk
Email: info@bookguild.co.uk
Twitter: @bookguild

Typeset in Adobe Garamond Pro

Printed and bound in Great Britain by CPI Group (UK) Ltd, Croydon, CR0 4YY

ISBN 978 1912362 585

British Library Cataloguing in Publication Data.
A catalogue record for this book is available from the British Library.

To my wife, Sonell, who supports me through all my crazy plans!
To my mum and dad who have always been there for me!
To my children, Aryan and Ananya,
who are my motivation in all things!
Thank you all for everything.

PROLOGUE

As he enters the room, Arech comes to terms with his position in life. This is not simply a room to discuss matters of state. The large domed ceiling, the ornate working on the outer edges and of course not forgetting the ten high-backed chairs aligned in a semi-circle formation at the other end of the room. To add to the effect, these chairs and the heavy crescent-shaped table they are placed behind have been placed on a platform raised about five feet off the floor. Sitting on the chairs are the Gringuns he has come to know and despise, the ones who represent the High Command. They are visibly more powerful compared to the smaller Gringun kneeling before them, and the way they sit shows their pride and arrogance.

The slender Gringun approaches the platform, his back hunched from the many hours spent bent over microscopes. He extends his right hand, palm upwards in a gesture of respect. The sleeve rises up slightly showing a thin, weak hand attached to a thin wrist. He is clearly undernourished compared to the dominant Gringuns sitting in front of him. He bows his head slightly, keeping his eyes lowered at all times. The height of the platform and the table upon it means he would be unable to speak face to face to the High Command if he got any closer. After a few seconds in this position, he rises and stands before his leaders.

He bends his head down the few inches his thick neck allows him to and begins to walk through his carefully rehearsed speech, "My Lords. I come to inform you that we appear to have had some success." His obvious nervousness seems to entertain the High Command.

"You *appear* to have had some success? I hope, for your sake, you can offer further clarification of your success?" The thoughts implant themselves firmly in his mind and he feels the weight of them.

"My Lords, I, uh, I mean to say that I… *we*… have been able to separate our DNA." He regains some of his composure, "The results have been impressive. One of the species we have created has a higher muscle density than expected. In addition, they are extremely adept at following commands. They will make for a valuable resource in future battles." He signals with his hands and six beings enter the chamber. They look similar to the Gringuns, but they are slightly taller and much broader, although with a similar yellow, almost jaundiced tinge to their skin. Their torso tells a lot about their strength. "May I present the Umach – your warriors." The Umach guards move towards the scientist and drop to their knees.

There is a moment of silence as the High Command considers this additional information. The Gringun scientist almost loses his balance as a second member imprints his thoughts on him, "You believe they will prove to be the warrior race we require?"

"Yes, My Lord!"

"And what were the results of the other races?"

"They were not as responsive. Most have been weak, some have been strong, but they have not developed adequately in the timescales provided. There is another—"

A third member adds the weight of his thoughts, "Another?"

He visibly staggers under the weight of the three. "They are bipedal, sire. As an experiment, we combined our Gringun DNA with the Aneesh DNA to allow for added ingenuity. The results have been slow. We do however see potential for something very powerful. It is… simply a matter of time." His head is starting to spin, but he strains against it and gets the words out, "They have potential; we just need more time!"

"Enough! No more time! We have wasted enough time already, and it is inevitable that someone will realise our plans. If the Aneesh discover what we have planned before we are ready, the other races will join to stop us. Our sources confirm they have completed work on their greatest invention yet. We need this… NOW!" The final word delivers enough force to cause the scientist to stumble.

The first member returns to the conversation, this time with more emphasis, "No more time. We need this finished. You are to expedite the creation of a force which will follow our commands without question. Any other species must be eradicated. Especially this abomination you speak of, this hybrid of our great race. Revolting."

"My Lords, you must understand. There is much to be learned from the potential of the new species. They are slow to develop, but we sense something strong in them."

"ENOUGH! You have your instructions. The Umach may stay. We have further use for them. Leave us now!"

He leaves the room, pleased now that they are no longer in his head. The pressure at one point almost caused him to collapse. As soon as the High Command chamber doors are closed, he turns and moves as fast as possible. He steps into the first available booth, presses the button to seal the door behind him and taps the eight-digit location code for the science centre into the panel in front of him. A flash of light is followed by a sudden whooshing sound as the booth shoots forward towards the science centre, the inertial dampeners within the booth preventing him from feeling the effects of the sudden acceleration. Moments later the booth stops and the door slides open. Moving as quickly as he can, he makes his way to the gene lab, ignoring any questions on his way. He stops in front of the door and stands still for a few seconds waiting for the computer to verify his identity.

"Welcome back, Arech," the detached voice comes from the console beside the door moments before it slides open to allow him in.

"Arech, you are back so soon?" says the scientist within. His excitement is obvious as he knocks over a vial in his rush to get to Arech. "What did they say? Did you explain about the bipeds?"

A series of small machines appear from a hole in the wall and begin to clean up the mess. "Yes," Arech says, "I explained everything as we discussed. Not that they understood of course. They never will. All they were interested in was the Umach." Arech pauses as he considers his next words, "They have decreed that all other experiments must be destroyed immediately. We are instructed to expedite the creation of the Umach army." There is obvious regret in his voice.

"They do not understand what we have here," Garass says. "I know there is much to learn from these new ones. What if we were to keep some alive? We could do so and no-one need know."

Arech turns on him suddenly, startling Garass. In a hushed whisper he scolds him, "What has come over, you my friend? Do you wish to risk your life and career for a fledgling race? We created them and it is our duty to destroy them. Besides, if they are what we expect, would you really want these tyrants in charge of such a force? What use do you think we would be if they reached their potential?" He takes control of himself again. "No. We need to destroy them if only for the safety of our dimension."

Garass considers the reprimand before reluctantly agreeing, "I can see the logic, Arech." He lowers his head and moves to his console, but Arech does not see the defiance in his friend's eyes.

It was me who brought these bipeds to life, Garass thinks to himself. *It was my idea to combine the Gringun and Aneesh DNA.*

It was me who provided the necessary stimulus to develop them. And I accelerated their development. I cannot, will not, destroy them. I am their creator! He shakes his head to expel the thoughts before anyone can read them.

Garass enters the commands into the console and hits the activation button. Through the screen, he watches as the drones leave with their instructions.

A loud bang on the door startles them both. They turn in time to see the six Umach guards from the High Command chambers enter. At first Arech does not recognise them. Their rags removed, they are now dressed from head to toe in heavy body armour, "Garass! Arech! Step away from the consoles. You have been found guilty of treason. Your crime: attempting to hide your thoughts from the High Command." Arech and Garass exchange a quick glance. The lead Umach steps towards Garass and brings his brutally armoured hand upwards, cracking him across the chin. Garass's eyes roll back as he collapses to the floor like a rag doll. Two Umach pick him up and drag him out. Two more Umach approach Arech. Terrified by what just happened, resistance is the last thing on his mind. They take him by the arms and drag him out of the room.

The lead Umach begins to follow them before halting mid stride. He listens carefully as he receives further instructions from the High Command, *Yes, My Lord,"* the guard thinks in response. Then out loud he gives the order, "By order of the High Command, arrest all other scientists and take them to the behaviour modification centre immediately."

Back in the High Command chambers, one of the members looks towards the other, "What do you have in mind?"

"They are to be placed under guard and will undergo immediate behavioural modifications. These scientists forget their place and it is only a matter of time before they attempt to rise against us."

"They would be unsuccessful."

"True, but they have access to technology. We do not always know what they are working on."

"Behavioural modifications will reduce their effectiveness. Their problem-solving skills will be impaired significantly."

"I would rather that than the worry of plotting from within our ranks. Besides, they have already created the warrior race, and the arrest happened after the drones were despatched. Everything is in order."

"Indeed. How long until the Umach are ready for deployment?"

"A few weeks at most! The additional ships will be ready in as much time."

"Then we attack?"

"Yes!"

"Excellent. It is our time to rule!"

1

WIPEOUT

I'm not sure when the pain started. It all happened so fast!

I mean, one day I'm walking through Rome with my parents. Looking back on things, I guess I'm kind of lucky to have parents like mine. They want to show me the history of the world and help me to understand the people within it. Next thing I know, I'm buried in the Catacombs of San Callisto with a load of dead people... Two of them were my parents. As a fifteen-year-old-boy, I know what has happened, but registering it is something else.

Maybe I should explain. My dad is... sorry, *was* a history teacher and he always wanted me to have the same love for the past that he had. Trust me, he was doing a great job. It had become a secret passion of mine. Anyway, we had made our way down to the catacombs which my dad had managed to get us private entry to – no idea what strings he pulled, but that really didn't concern me at the time. He was pointing out important features, areas I should concentrate on and things I should photograph or draw in my notepad to research later. Then the ground shook slightly.

So, this is when things took a weird turn. It was like time sped up in some places and almost ground to a halt in others. Right now, it was fast, real fast! As the ground shook, my dad looked at me and smiled that smile that says – father to son – don't worry, there's nothing to worry about. "It's a long way away, Jon. Just a minor earthquake." My mum had a bit more worry on her face, but hid it when she realised I was looking at her. She had wonderful soft eyes which always calmed me, and her long, dark hair framed her face. I was a mixture of her and my dad, who had a slim, angular face. My mum always said that she loved the combination I had inherited from them.

"Maybe we should head back up soon though, honey," she said to my dad. They had one of those parent glances at each other and he nodded his agreement. As he stood and dusted himself off, the ground shook again.

He steadied himself for a moment. "Hm. That felt like it was on the surface, not underground. Come on, let's see what's going on!"

The ground shook a third time and I looked longingly towards the entrance. A cloud of dust blocked our way, making it hard to open our eyes fully. We held each other's hands so we would not lose each other as my dad led the way through the dust. I remember wondering how he kept so calm, even in this time of crisis.

Another shake hit and this time it knocked us all to the floor. The dust from the ceiling thickened, making it almost impossible to see. I rolled over, my hands over my eyes instinctively protecting them from the dust. I couldn't see my parents, but judging by the sounds they were pretty close. I jumped as my dad's hand found mine and squeezed it reassuringly. "Mum! This way," I call out to her, choking slightly as the dust enters my open mouth. I can hear her coughing as she moves towards us. *Dad's right.* I think to myself. *This can't be an earthquake. Something is hitting the surface.* We stand up and take another step towards the stairs when the surface is hit again. More dust falls, followed by a few pieces of the ceiling. I can barely see my dad when he looks up at me.

This is where time slowed right down. I saw my dad's expression change. His hands came up and shoved me hard in the chest. I felt myself stumble backwards, narrowly missing my mum. I tried unsuccessfully to keep my balance. I took a few steps back before I fell to the ground. My first feelings were of anger that he had pushed me like that. The next was confusion about why he had done it. He had never raised his hand in anger to me before, but then the look on his face was fear for me, not anger at me.

As I hit the floor, I could see a large dark shape fall from the ceiling right above where we were standing. Then there was silence. Everything seemed to have calmed down. My throat was so parched from the dust that I couldn't speak. I crawled to where I'd seen my parents last and came to a pile of rubble. Absently, instinctively, I started to clear it away without considering what I might find under it.

Well, that's how we got here anyway. A part of me thinks that something is very wrong with me. I'm sitting in a catacomb with both my dead parents in my arms. I know I loved them, still do in fact. Yet I shed no tears. I don't feel confused. I don't feel sadness. I don't feel anything really. Or is this a natural reaction? Who knows? I can't tell if it is minutes or hours that I have been sat here thinking about this, but something stirred in me and I realised that I had to get out of here. I gently lay their heads on the floor and stand up. Most of the dust has cleared now and I can see a sliver of light coming from the exit. It's just enough for me to make out a few things around me. Carefully, I make my way to the steps, heading towards the light coming from above. I make my way carefully up and begin the task of slowly removing the rubble from the entrance until there is enough space for me to crawl through. The idea of fresh air outside spurs me to work harder and it is only a few minutes before I have made a gap big enough for me to get through.

I crawl through the tight space, not bothered about the sharp edges of the rubble scraping my body. I collapse into a relieved heap onto the ground outside. That's when I become aware of the eerie silence. This should have been a bustling tourist attraction. I look up and take in the surroundings. The scene around me is completely different. Almost all of the buildings as far as I can see have been levelled. There are no people anywhere. The great historical city of Rome… gone in a matter of minutes. And what is that strange smell in the air? I feel like I should know it, but I can't seem to place it. I look around trying to get my bearings. "I need to get out of here," I say to myself. "If I can just find where north is, I can keep heading that way until I find someone. If only I had a compass…"

Now, have you ever seen or read something and thought to yourself, I am never going to need this? Well, this is one of those times. I was watching a documentary a long time back. There was something about finding the south direction by using your watch. Now, obviously, having a digital watch would be useless. Luckily, I am wearing a normal analogue watch. "Let's see," I say out loud. In the back of my mind, I know I am talking to myself, but it's better than the eerie silence everywhere. I look at my watch and try to remember how to find the southerly direction. "Something about pointing the minute hand at the sun and then… no, no, point the *hour* hand at the sun and, uh, south should be between the hour hand and the twelve. That's it… I think." I move myself around to follow my own instructions and locate what I believe to be south. Then I turn around and look at what I'm guessing is north. "Ah hell! I don't have anything left to lose now anyway." I mean that literally.

It's a beautiful summer's day and, if not for the events of the last few hours, the extra couple of hours walking would have been quite nice. I continue along the tree-lined streets, which are now bereft of buildings. Rubble from homes and taller, older buildings are localised to small piles as though the structures had imploded on themselves. That's when I come across some people sitting on the ground beside a half broken wall. Believe me, when you start thinking you may actually be the only person left alive on the planet, seeing someone alive really is a relief. As I approach them, I see that a few of them have cuts and bruises, while others have worse injuries. I pick up the pace, desperate to be with people. "Can anyone speak English?" I ask a little excitedly and slightly out of breath.

"I can," says a woman with a strong Italian accent. "Where have you come from?" Her face is covered in a thick layer of dust and her shoulder-length hair is covered in dirt. At a guess I'd say she is about thirty-five years old. She stands up and walks over to me.

"I was at the catacombs. I managed to get out and the place was like this. What happened?"

"We do not know for sure. There were aircraft like we have never seen before. They looked like small wings and travelled incredibly fast." She calmly explains the events above ground. "They were moving in a strange way, unlike normal aircraft and with very little noise. I have never seen anything like it before. I recognised some of our own planes up there too, but they could do nothing to them."

"The Italian Air Force was attacking them? But which country would have attacked Italy?"

She looks at him. "I do not know. None of us can figure this out. For now we are waiting for some rescue people to come and find us."

"Yeah, well, I've been walking for two hours and you are the first sign of life I have found. I think I'm just going to keep moving north."

She considers this for a moment, turns to the other two people and says something in Italian. The exchange lasts about a minute and I get the feeling that things are not going too well. She turns back to me. "They believe it is better to wait. Are you sure you want to go on?"

"Yeah, I think so!"

"Then, if you do not mind, I would like to come with you? I have been sitting here for too long now. I need to keep myself busy." I get the feeling she just wants to come along to make sure I will be okay.

I shrug my shoulders, "Sure, why not."

"Bene, good. I am Angelina." She studies my face a little more closely. "Are you OK?"

"Yeah. I'm Jon Farrell," I say as I extend my right hand to her. She shakes my hand. "It's nice to meet you, Jon," she says smiling as we continue our journey mostly in silence – good thing too; I wasn't in the mood for conversation anyway!

As the day draws to a close, we both agree to find somewhere to rest for the night. We manage to find a building which is still standing – no mean feat, trust me – and move towards it. After a quick check of the building we are relieved – and yet also somehow disheartened – to find no-one else there.

"A couple of the bedrooms upstairs are still intact and the beds appear to have clean bedding on them," I say as I continue to look around the living room. "I think I'm ready to sleep. It may be a busy day tomorrow."

"Jon? Is there something you need to talk about? You seem very distant."

I pause for a moment as I look introspectively, searching my feelings, "I'm fine, thanks. Just a bit tired." She keeps looking at me, before nodding and saying nothing more on the subject.

It's not the most restful sleep I've ever had. This is mainly because of nightmares about my parents of course, so I get up early and look around the house for something to eat. Checking the fridge – luckily it is still cold – I find some eggs and bread and start to make breakfast. Lucky again, eggs are the only things I was ever able to make without burning. By the time Angelina wakes, she finds me downstairs cooking breakfast for us both. "Good morning, Jon."

"Morning." I turn to glance at her briefly. She has brushed her hair and cleaned the dirt off her face, but the clothes still carry the dirt and grime from yesterday's events. I return my gaze to the stove. The cooking area is a little small, with a rectangular breakfast bar beside me. "I found some eggs in the fridge. It's not working but it is still cool, so I figured they should be okay. There's also a car in the garage. I don't think it has much fuel in it though." I plate up the food and place it on the breakfast bar. She sits on one of the stools and starts to eat.

"Thank you, Jon," she says. I smile a 'you're welcome' smile as I plate up my breakfast, place it on the bar opposite her and pull up another wooden stool.

"Are you ready to leave after breakfast?" Angelina asks between mouthfuls.

"Yeah. I found the keys to the car already and I've packed a few food cans just in case." I sit opposite her and start to dig hungrily into the food. "Probably best if we make the most of the daylight while we can. It will give us a chance of finding others."

"Agreed."

We finish everything on our plates in just a few minutes. I pick up my plate and start to clear up the kitchen. Angelina chuckles gently and joins me by the sink where she dries the dishes as I clean them.

"What's so funny?" I ask.

"Do you really think it is necessary to clean the dishes? I don't think anyone will notice."

I consider what I am doing, before seeing the funny side too, "I see what you mean. Force of habit, I guess! Are you ready?"

"I think so."

I dry my hands on the towel, pick up the keys I found in a drawer and escort her through the door at the back of the kitchen and into the adjoining garage. "It's not much, just a small Fiat."

I open the passenger door for her and she stares at me. "Really? You must be what, fifteen, sixteen years old? You expect me to believe you have a driving licence?" It was more of a statement than a question.

"Fifteen actually, but it was worth a try." I grudgingly get into the passenger seat as she walks around to the driver's side, smiling.

"Okay! Let's go!"

Angelina drives the car smoothly through the outskirts of the Italian countryside. It's strange how the green fields and trees around us don't appear to tell the tale of the attack on central Rome. There are occasional signs, like when we pass small homes which have been reduced to rubble. Otherwise, everything else is untouched. "Strange," I say almost to myself. "It's only really buildings that have been targeted." Angelina does not comment. "There's no real area of effect either. The buildings have been targeted very accurately, leaving all of the surroundings clear and untouched."

"So?" Angelina asks.

"So, if another country were attacking us, they wouldn't be worried about collateral damage in the area. The buildings would be destroyed, yes. But I would have thought that the fields would also show some signs of damage. At least small parts of the fields around the houses should be scorched or something. I don't see anything like that."

She looks at a nearby farmhouse as we drive past. "I see what you mean."

We continue to drive for another hour at a slow but steady speed, before we have our first bit of luck. A small group of people has gathered on the side of the road ahead and with them are a few people dressed in military uniforms. As we pull up near them, several of the people begin to board one of the two personnel carriers. I exit the car and move towards the nearest uniformed person. "Hello? Can you help us?"

"You are not from Italia?" The man speaks English slowly and carefully with a strong enough Italian accent that I can barely understand him. Angelina steps forward and addresses the man directly in Italian. After two minutes of the man explaining something to her, she turns back to me.

"We need to board this transport, Jon. He has suggested we leave the car here and go with them. I will tell you the rest when we are inside."

"Why? What's going on?" But she has already started moving towards the transport, forcing me to follow her.

We climb aboard and sit opposite each other so we can talk. The lights inside are quite dim, but I can see her well enough and sitting opposite each other means we can talk more easily. I hear the door close, and the lights brighten slightly as I lean forward towards her. I can hear everyone else speaking in hushed Italian voices.

"I don't want you to be scared, Jon." I try to keep my ego in check. "It seems that the aircraft we talked about yesterday were not ours," Angelina whispers to me.

"We know that. Which country were they from?"

"Not a country, Jon. They are not ours! I mean, people did not make them." I swear my chin must have touched the table. I've seen *Independence Day* and many other movies like it. A small smile creeps onto my face as I figure out the joke. "This is not a joke, Jon. This transport is going to a nearby military base. From what he was saying, every country was attacked. Everywhere! At the same time, Jon!" She is visibly shaken. "Only a fraction of humanity is left alive in each country. When we get to the base, they will be asking about everyone's skills so they can rebuild society. People from other countries are being transported to their home country if requested, but it is only happening when a transport is available. You may be in Italy for some time." Another of the military personnel sitting next to me leans forward and speaks to Angelina. She starts to translate while listening to him.

"It seems there is only one good thing to have come out of this. We now have a unified government for the world." She pauses as she listens to what else he is saying. "The highest authorities in each country have been drafted into this government and will be helping to decide how to rebuild the world." She pauses again. "Okay, he says that they now know that these ships were not from here, because they managed to destroy one and found... something inside. He says that he heard rumours that these, uh, beings look a bit like us, except they have a strange yellow tint to their skin, but otherwise much the same."

I sit back in my seat and wait for the information to sink in... It doesn't!

After an hour in the transport it slows to a halt and we are all herded into the base for processing. I notice a few other people going towards another area of the base, all of them speaking with British accents. From the conversation I pick up, they seem to be looking for a way back to England. I glance at Angelina. She already knows what I am thinking.

"I need to find a way back home, Angelina. There has to be something I can do. I'm sorry to leave you like this, but thank you for everything, okay?"

She smiles a parental, knowing smile. "I understand, Jon. Thank you, too. Maybe we will meet again sometime. Take care of yourself." She hugs me warmly.

I get up and move swiftly toward the people I noticed earlier and a step closer to home.

After a few weeks of waiting patiently, I finally get given clearance to go home. I make my way onto the waiting aircraft destined for what remains of Heathrow Airport. Somehow, the people back home managed to get half a runway ready, so smaller aircraft could start to ferry people back and forth. Amazing what they can do when they put their minds to it... and of course when the red tape is removed. With a sense of relief, I sit down in the plane and think on the events of the last few days. The reports I have already received about home have been pretty grim. Europe got hit hard, and London especially – heavily populated areas with lots of lights appear to have acted like laser guidance for anyone targeting us. All of the large cities were basically devastated with very few buildings remaining, which means I probably have nowhere to live now. As I settle into my seat on the plane, I contemplate my limited options. I know I will head home first, if only to check if anything is left. Some of the other people waiting mentioned that the military were looking for young people to help fix things up. Never my preferred option to join the armed forces, but at least I would have a place to live and something to eat. I might even be able to learn something about what happened and help to sort things out. No point really making plans until I know what to expect, though. I settle into the seat and prepare for the trip home.

2

LIFESTYLE CHANGES
AND NEW FRIENDS

If you'd asked me a year ago if I would join the armed forces, the answer would have been 'No'. I did, however, end up working for them in the 'cannon fodder division' which is officially known as the Mobile Airborne Infantry. Of course, the fact that I was only fifteen years old meant that – even with the lack of personnel – they couldn't really train me for real combat for another year. The advantage? They had me sifting through files and moving archived paperwork to crates for safe storage. Easy work if you can get it. The only thing I had to do to keep it going was to keep my fitness up and guarantee that I would join the army for sure next year. Anyway, documents signed and away I go… Easy Ville for a year. In the meantime, they teach me about weapons and tactics in advance, so I can register for officer training instead of the normal cannon fodder roles – I guess someone out there likes me.

As for finding out what really happened six months ago…

Unbelievable though it sounds, it looks like we really are not alone in the universe… and the others really don't like us.

Putting all of the pieces of information together, it seems that a few of the alien ships were knocked out of the air by debris and who knows what else. From what I can tell, most of it happened because of pilot error on the part of the aliens – at least we know they can make mistakes too – but one of them was when a fighter jet – fully loaded with weapons and fuel – was taken out too close to the alien ship. Apparently, the shock wave and shrapnel took the ship out. One of the ships was even recovered in England and stored nearby in what is left of the Northolt Air Force Base. A load of scientists were shipped in to investigate, and I was shipped in to help them lift and shift.

It was only in the last month that I got to see the alien ship and, with the new policy of sharing in the world, they were making great progress in reverse engineering the technology. They brought in some of the greatest minds to work on this project, and somehow I got my fingers in the pie – I found out that I had somehow made an impression on Admiral Wesley, the highest-ranking person on the base. For some reason he had taken a liking to me. Now, this sounds like a good thing, but there were a few people who really didn't like this. The most annoying of these people was Garry Ford – sorry *Private* Garry Ford, as he insisted on being called by me. He was a year older than me and was fully enlisted in the army now. Trust me when I say that this guy was totally into himself and more interested in berating the people around him. I guess it made him feel better about himself.

Anyway, people were coming and going constantly, which left me as one of the longest running members of the team. This meant that as I was one of the only people with time on my hands and knowledge of the base; every time someone new turned up, I had to explain how everything worked and where they had to go. Yesterday I was showing a scientist the ropes. Today? Well, I've just arrived at the reception desk to pick up another newbie. I carefully negotiate my way past the few people in the lobby area and over to the reception desk.

"Hey, James," I say to the huge, bulldog-like security guard sitting behind the desk. "You got another one for me?"

He hands me a post-it note with a name written on it and nods towards an individual standing alone, looking at one of the duller paintings on the wall.

"Cheers, James. No paperwork?" He shakes his head and looks down at his magazine again.

The man's back is turned to me, so as I approach him I steal a look at the name on the note before making my presence known. Some documentation would have been good but, then again, not that many of them have any paperwork these days. Since the attacks, paperwork and computer systems have suffered considerably – not enough staff to maintain everything! Anyway, I've got five minutes to do the meet and greet and then it's time to induct him into the team… I use the word 'team' loosely as he will be working mainly on his own!

I walk up behind him, automatically noting his height and build. He's about five foot ten and very slim, bordering on anorexic. I clear my throat and extend my right hand. He turns to face me, looks down at my hand and then back up. His hands never leave his sides.

I clear my throat again and lower my hand. *This is going to be fun. I give this guy a week at most.* "Mr Weecompa?"

"Weicompa. It start with 'way'!" His English is broken and his accent is strange enough that I find it impossible to place, but that does not make him any different from the others I have met over the last few weeks.

"Right. Well, my name is Jon Farrell and I will be your contact if you have any requirements or questions. If you make any progress in your research, you will need to inform me immediately. Now, please follow me. The route is a little confusing, but you will need to keep up and remember it for the future. I won't always be

14

here to guide you around." I turn around and start walking back through the reception area. "So, how do you figure in this?" He looks confused. "I mean, I know that you are here to see the ship, but how can you help to piece it together?"

He looks at me blankly.

We turn into the corridor on the left and continue walking. "What is your speciality area?" He still looks a bit confused. "What I mean is, how can you help us to fix this thing?"

"Reverse engineer. Understand to build new ones."

I stop in my tracks and turn to him, "Interesting... I think!" This guy might actually be useful if we can get him to talk. I carry on walking and turn into the next lab. "This is where you will be working. Any equipment you will need is already here." I pick up an envelope from the table. "Your username and password for the computer systems are in here." I hand Weicompa the envelope. "If you need anything further, please let me know. My contact number is written on the envelope. The computer holds all of the information regarding the ship, and the documents in the envelope will tell you how to access them."

More blank staring.

"You're welcome, Weicompa."

"Wei short name."

I smile and move to the door. I look back into the lab before stepping out. Wei is standing in the middle of the lab staring at the far wall. Just as I am about ask him if everything is alright, I hear him quietly talking to himself. I can't quite make out what he is saying, but at least he is talking now... even if it is to himself. I close the door and head away.

An hour later I head back to Wei's laboratory to check he has everything he needs. As I raise my hand to open the door, Wei opens it from the inside and almost crashes into me. His face reminds me of the painting 'The Scream' as he jumps backwards a few feet, collapses onto the floor and rolls up into the foetal position. I'm so stunned I just stand there in the doorway. Moments later, after realising that he's not moving much, I get a bit worried about him. The door closes as I step forward and reach out to him. That's when he starts to whimper.

"Wei, it is just me, Jon." I withdraw my hand and step back from him to avoid frightening him further. I have never known anyone who was this incredibly jumpy. I can hear him mumbling to himself, but I can't understand a word he is saying with his head buried in his chest like it is. Then, almost as quick as it started, he stops shaking and starts to unravel himself. Surprising really that he was able to roll up that tightly in the first place. I guess he must do yoga or something. He straightens up and brushes the crinkles out of his cheap, shiny suit as though nothing had happened.

"Hello, Jon."

"Erm, it's time for lunch. Hungry?"

"Not really, thank you." Wei says in a very matter of fact manner.

I'm actually a little taken aback. To start with, either his very recent episode just opened him up, or his language skills improved slightly. I smile and turn to leave the lab.

"Can I accompany you?"

"Of course," I say as he smiles openly at me.

I lead the way to the cafeteria and use the opportunity to give him some additional information. Wei walks alongside me listening intently.

"We have excellent facilities here, Wei. If there is anything you need, you simply need to ask. We have no budget issues here and no restraints on us."

He stares at me for a few seconds and then nods.

"The ship is really intriguing and I know they have been looking for someone good to come and continue the reverse engineering tasks on it."

Wei pauses again before responding, "Did you get to see the alien that was on board the ship?"

I am a bit taken aback by the sudden questioning surrounding the alien and not the ship. "Oh yeah. Kinda freaky, actually."

"Really? Why?"

"Well, they look a lot like us. The only real difference is the skin colour. It had a slightly yellow colour to it. Other than that, they are about the same size and shape as us. Hey, your language has really improved. Were you nervous before or something?"

Wei clears his throat, "I see. Interesting!"

I stop and suddenly turn to Wei, causing him to jump back again.

"Whoa, sorry. I didn't mean to surprise you." *Jeez, talk about jumpy!* "I just had an idea. You're not hungry anyway, right? Well... how would you like to see the ship instead? I mean, you're going to be working on it anyway right, so if you see it now or later, who cares? What do you say?"

Wei calms himself down. "Yes, please. It would be good to see the ship."

I smile and pick up the pace as we walk past the cafeteria. My speech begins to speed up as I become more excited. Finally, someone who may be willing to talk to me about this thing... No-one else working on the project is willing to discuss it with me, but this guy seems alright. I turn down a corridor on the right. As we walk down the corridor, the security cameras turn towards us one by one and continue panning, keeping us in view at all times. Wei stares at each camera as we walk down the corridor.

I stop at a door at the far end and place my hand on the plate beside the door. "Identification, please." The voice is obviously computer-generated, but a soft female voice has been used for the speech systems.

"Jon Farrell. Escorting Weicompa."

"Voiceprint match. Thank you, Jon Farrell." The door opens. There is enough space inside for one person to enter. "Wait here until I close the next door. The door will not open until I have gone through and closed the inside door... Security measures in the room, sorry." I proceed to walk through the door. Once it locks shut behind me, I pull the inner door open, walk through and firmly close the door behind me. I motion to Wei to pull the door open. After a moment of trepidation, Wei follows my example and enters the room.

As he closes the inner door, another security panel lights up by the next door. I step forward and place my chin on a cup-shaped object beside the new wall-mounted panel and stand still as a light strobes across my face. A few seconds later, the female computer voice states, "Retinal and facial scan complete. Thank you, Jon Farrell."

The door clicks open and I walk through, holding it open for Wei. The new area is pitch black, with no hint of light anywhere except for a dim glow through the tinted glass behind us. The door clicks shut behind me and a series of dim lights turn on, starting from above where we stand, all the way down to the bottom of the hangar. An area in the middle remains unlit, with a darker shadowed shape within the lighter shadows. A humming sound starts in the background. I walk forward with Wei following me, our footsteps echoing through the massive hangar. He looks as awestruck as I did the first time I came in here.

The hangar really is huge. In the middle is a strange wing-shaped object sitting perfectly still within the shadows. Wei apprehensively approaches the dark, shadowy area. He steps into the shadow and lights directly above him switch on, illuminating the object fully. Immediately the details and contours of the craft become visible. Pieces of it lie everywhere on the floor. Large clamps hold it in place about two feet off the ground. Even with all the pieces on the floor, it's obvious that the ship is still largely intact. My gaze shifts back to Wei. He doesn't take his eyes off the ship. He practically devours it with his eyes, taking in every piece of information. There is a steadiness to each step he takes as he walks towards the ship now. The earlier apprehension has gone, replaced now by awe. "Beautiful, right?" I ask rhetorically as I walk up and touch it. "Can you imagine? This time last year, we were almost convinced that we were the only sentient beings in the universe. How stupid do we feel now, huh?"

I turn to face him, expecting to see the same expression on his face as I always have when I come in here. As my eyes adjust to the dim light, slowly focusing on him, I breathe in sharply, shocked by the surprise vision before me. Instinctively, I backpedal away from him, tripping over my feet in the process. I land hard on the floor, hands and feet scrambling in an effort to increase the distance between us. Wei jumps back at the same time, also shocked, and unable to understand my sudden reaction.

Wei's body language expresses utter confusion as he has what appears to be a conversation with himself. Then he collapses onto the floor and curls into a ball the way he did in the lab earlier.

"WHAT THE HELL ARE YOU?" I shout out. Wei curls up even tighter. This obviously isn't helping the situation at all, so I force myself to calm down a bit. "Wei?" I reach over to touch him. He flinches and lets out a fearful whimper. "Wei, I am not going to hurt you." There appear to be ridges showing through the tightly stretched shirt covering his back. Other than that, what I can see of Wei looks almost the same as any other human.

"Wei? If you stay like this, someone is going to see you and then there will be trouble." The whimpering stops, but he stays as he is. I decide not to bother him for a moment. After a few seconds he starts to uncurl his body slightly.

"How did you disrupt my connection with the ship?" he asks accusingly.

"Ship?" I ask, confused by his question before realisation dawns on me. "Wait, a ship? You have a ship here? And what connection are you talking about?"

"Lies!" he yells at me emotionally. "I... I... I... I know that you did… something. I… I was communicating with the… er computer before… before we came in here."

I think about this for a moment. "The room is shielded. Could that be a cause? Also, you hear that humming sound in the background?"

Wei uncurls a bit more. "Yes?"

"That's an electromagnetic field activated around the building. It's designed to prevent data communications from mobile devices. It activates when someone enters the room and closes the inner door. That will almost certainly have prevented any communication with your ship."

"That makes sense, I suppose," Wei says a little more calmly.

"I am not going to hurt you, Wei, but you are going to have to help me here. I need some answers, too."

I wait, and after a few seconds he begins to straighten out. I watch his body unravel itself and see that much of it must be double-jointed to allow it to bend the way it does. The additional joints covering the midsection of his body make it appear very weak. Last of all, the head comes up. This is when I realise the big differences. Wei has high cheekbones on a elongated face. There are three ridges on each cheekbone and the eyes are slightly sunken into the skull area, giving it an almost skeletal effect. The facial area is very different, but it has the required effect… I can see clearly that this creature is not from the same race that attacked earth some months earlier. "What do you want to know, Jon?"

I pause for a few seconds to consider my first question carefully and then eventually settle for the standard question, "Who and what are you?"

Wei sighs gently and looks towards the ceiling of the hangar like he is wishing it would open up and let him out. In a clear, calm voice he says, "I am Najess. We are a race of people from a planet some distance from here."

"And your involvement in the attack on my planet?"

"We were not involved, Jon; we were attacked too. Our planet was hit hard, although maybe not as badly as everyone else."

"Everyone else?"

"There is another race too. They are called Keterans."

"And they were attacked too?"

"Just as badly as your planet was." With additional vigour he continues to convince me of his innocence, "Jon, I assure you that we mean you and your people no harm. Once you understand the circumstances which brought me here, you will realise that we are peaceful."

I study his features as he talks. I'm not sure about his facial expressions and what they might mean, but he does seem to be genuine. Regardless of how different he looks now, I still get a relaxed and honest feeling from him. I feel that it is right to trust him but, then again, should it be the decision of a fifteen-year-old boy? If I am going to help him, he had better do a good job of convincing me. "Wei, you need to help me understand why I should trust you."

He looks at me while he considers this. "Okay, Jon. The condensed version, as we do not have much time."

He sits on the floor and crosses his legs so tightly it almost brings tears to my eyes. He takes a deep breath and begins to recount the tale. "The Najess have always been a peaceful people. We have the ability to understand and create technology, but we have never been a war faring race and we have never devoted any time to creating weapon technologies. Over many of your Earth centuries, we have been aware of your existence, but we never came here and we never tried to make contact. We simply scanned the stars that we knew and waited for the day when you would make your way into space. We had hoped that we could hide ourselves from you when this happened, of course.

"The problem is, we did not anticipate the arrival of this new race of people. When we saw them coming, we hid most of our technology and our people beneath the planet surface. Then they came and they destroyed anything still living on the surface and

21

any technology we had left there. After that, they simply left. We knew that they were going to visit your planet and also the Keterans. We know now that the Keterans have also been attacked, and we know it was bad. We are just not sure how prepared the Keterans were, or the full extent of the damage done.

"After the attacks were completed, we discussed what had happened with our Council members. We reached the conclusion that the ships which brought on such devastation were simply scout ships. We believe that now that they are aware of our existence, they will be sending reinforcements to finish the job.

"Our problem, Jon, is that we do not know how to wage war. We cannot defend ourselves. We are, unfortunately, a race of what you would call cowards. All of our technology has been used for science, for the improvement of life. Because of this, we excel in high-speed space travel and medical research. We live considerably longer than you and we have healed many of the diseases which still plague your people.

"We have come here because we know that if reinforcements arrive before we are prepared for them, we will cease to exist. The same is true of your people and the Keterans. If, however, we provide you with our technology and knowledge, there is a chance that we could save all of our races." He looks at me, I guess hoping for a positive reaction. "Jon, we need humanity's help to do this. Your people know how to fight and survive. We could not survive another attack even with our technology. Both of our races have attributes which are compatible with each other, and together we could be a force to be reckoned with."

A feeling of restlessness washes over me. I stand up and begin pacing around the room. After a few steps I stop and turn to face Wei, somewhat confused. "What's with your speech skills? This morning you could barely speak a word. Now you are fluent… with an accent like you come from North London. What's that about?"

"My ship's computer has been teaching me and using your

accent as a template for my teachings. As I said, Jon, we are as good with technology as humanity is with weapons, fighting and tactics."

I continue pacing while I think over everything he has said. "Okay. Assuming I agree with you. What are you expecting from me… right now, I mean?"

"Only the opportunity to prove that we are here as allies." He pauses while he considers his next words. "We have the technology and skills required to get your people started with these ships. I can help you get past any issues you are having with this new technology. Jon, when I first met you today, I told you that I was an expert in reverse engineering… That was not a lie. I can move humanity further in a day than you could manage in a month. Let me help you with this."

"And how can I help you?"

"You are a resourceful person, Jon. I need to be introduced to people who will be willing to hear me out. I only need a chance, Jon."

"Right. Well, I can certainly try to get you to meet the right people, but much of the persuasion will have to come from you. Unfortunately, you picked the least influential person here." I think for a moment about how I am going to do this.

Wei slowly stands and moves towards the ship. "I have transferred all of the progress you have made so far to my ship and the computer has already evaluated the data. Is there a way to turn off the electromagnetic field?"

"There is, but I'm not sure we should be turning it off. I'm sure it would raise alarms if they detected that someone had purposely hit the off button."

"True. How about if we step outside for a moment? I will be able to communicate with my ship's computer and it will help us to get this ship online in a very short timeframe. It should only take a few seconds for the data to download."

"How short?"

"Give me access and it will be the first question I ask, but having seen the ship, there does not seem to be too much damage. We could probably do this in a couple of weeks." *If we can get this done in a couple of weeks, it could be the breakthrough we are looking for. Then again, what I should be doing is handing this guy over for further questioning. But that would leave us all back at square one while some failed wannabe surgeon hacks him up to see how he works. No, he doesn't deserve that. If we don't get his help, it will be months at least before we start to fathom this thing out.* "The functioning ship would act as proof of our good intentions, Jon. I need to provide something immediate and tangible," he suggests.

"I suppose so. By the way, are you going to be doing your standing and staring at the wall thing when you step outside?"

"You mean when I am talking to my computer? Yes."

"Then it is best you do it in your lab where no-one else can see you. I can take you there now. You can do your staring thing and then we can head back. How's that sound?"

"Sounds good," he says with a smile.

As we enter the lab, Wei pushes past me in an almost desperate state to get in.

"Careful, Wei," I say to him after checking that no-one is in the corridor. Luckily his disguise is back on again… I have to ask him about that… Seriously cool!

Wei nods apologetically to me and steps into the middle of the room. I close the door behind me.

"What's the matter, Wei?" Oh yeah, the expressionless thousand-yard stare again.

I take a seat while I wait for the nonresponsive Wei to wake up again, which takes about a minute. Believe me, it feels a lot like waiting for a kettle to boil… It really does seem to take a lot longer when you watch.

When Wei returns, he walks over to another chair, sits down

and scoots over to me, the chair freewheeling across the floor. "Ha," he smiles at me. "That was fun, but maybe a little dangerous!" He stops smiling and composes himself.

"Yeah, real dangerous. Now, how about you tell me what your computer said, cos I know you've been talking again."

"Nothing much, really. He was interested in how I was. We were out of contact for quite some time, really. I would normally have panicked much earlier, but I guess I was excited to have seen the enemy ship."

"Kept your mind off it?" I said, an idea forming in my mind.

"The loss of contact. It is very stressful for my people to be with another race. I told you, we are essentially cowards."

"So what about getting the computer to help with the ship?" I ask enthusiastically.

"That is the problem, Jon." He pauses pensively. "The computer can help, but it needs to be connected to me while we are working, to provide us with the additional information we need. That means turning off the communications inhibitor you have in the hangar."

I shake my head vigorously. "No way! No chance! That would be noticed within seconds."

Wei does the thousand-yard stare thing again. "What if we only needed a second? Then no-one would know."

"What's on your mind?" Trust issues again! I know I like Wei, and a part of me does want to trust him, but I really don't know him yet.

"The computer informs me that your monitoring equipment is very basic and can be interrupted. If you were to switch the inhibitor off, the computer could imitate the signal and power ratings for the hangar. It would appear to everyone else that the inhibitor was still functioning."

"I don't know, Wei. This really could land me in serious trouble."

"Jon, we need humanity's help. If we have to disrupt the

inhibitor ourselves, we will do so. It will mean that it is down for slightly longer, but we believe we can manage that with or without your help. The choice is yours, though. We can fix it so no-one knows you even did anything."

I look him in the eyes – something my dad once told me to do when I wanted to tell if someone was telling the truth. Shame he didn't tell me the signs to look for on an alien face! "Okay. What do I need to do?"

"We simply go back to the room, turn off the inhibitor and start working for a few days."

"Whoa there! We are not the only ones here with access to the ship. We need to book it out for a specified period of time, then we can work on it. Besides, I have work of my own which needs to be done. If I start to slack from my normal duties, that will raise a few questions too."

"Interesting! Is the hangar free now?"

"Well, yes," I say a little sheepishly, "I checked it before we came in."

"And how long for?"

"No-one has it booked out for the rest of the day."

Thousand-yard stare! "Fixed!" Wei has a smug look on his face. "We have it for a week! Essential maintenance on the room," he says matter-of-factly.

"What?" I turn to the terminal on the desk and start tapping on the keyboard. The facilities screen comes up and shows the primary hangar as occupied all week. All other bookings have been shifted along one week to make space. "How did you do that?"

"The computer did it! It should give us a few days at least."

"Yeah, well, I hope you'll live up to that promise."

Wei smiles. "Don't worry, Jon. Your trust in me will not be misplaced. You have my word on that! Now, let's go to the hangar and start working!"

Three days later, I am still going about my normal daily duties while trying to keep out of trouble. When possible, I go to see Wei and make sure everything is still going well. Admittedly, there seems to be very little work done on the ship, but Wei is definitely busy with something. He hardly even notices me when I am there and most of the time appears to be having conversations with the computer... I'd love to be in on one of those conversations.

I get back to my desk and notice the red light blinking on top of the phone, telling me there is a new voice message. I put the headset on and click the 'Messages' button. A few seconds later, Wei's voice comes through the headset. He sounds kind of excited, but I'm not entirely sure what he is saying as he is talking too fast. It is the third day since he started working on the ship, but I didn't seriously expect any results so soon. I hit the delete button on the phone and call him back.

"Wei? It's Jon."

"Jon? Please come to the hangar right now!" His voice is quivering with excitement. "You have to see this."

"Wei? You're not going to tell me that you're done with the ship already, are you?"

"The ship? No, of course not. I do have something else for you, though."

"I'll be there in five minutes."

I head through the corridors to the hangar where the ship is stored. "Wei?" I call out. It doesn't look like much has changed, to be honest. Almost the same parts from the last three days are still on the floor. "It doesn't look like you've made much progress, Wei." I actually sound as disappointed as I feel.

"I said on the telephone that the ship has not been completed." He sticks his hand out of the ship and waves to me. "There is, however, something in the ship which I would like you to see. Come up." I climb up the makeshift steps and

27

clamber into the ship through the small doorway behind the cockpit. Wei stays stooped and moves forward into the front cockpit area, with me following close behind. The corridor is narrow and small enough that I would have to be about five foot six inches tall to get through without crouching. With the extra two inches I have on top of that, I feel like I'm being squeezed into a small box. I slide my fingers along the dull metallic walls as I walk to the cockpit. Wei is sitting in the co-pilot seat and motions for me to sit in the pilot seat next to him.

I look at the main control panel in front of me. There are buttons positioned in what seem to be a random order. The symbols over many of the buttons have not been deciphered by the language team yet and remain in their original places. The few symbols which have been deciphered have been covered over with a sticker showing the English translation. Everything else seems to be exactly the way it was when I saw this some weeks back... except for one screen which was not there before. I look at Wei enquiringly.

"It is your new computer system, Jon."

"Really?" I try to hide it, but I can't suppress the disappointment. "Wei, do you realise that getting the room for another week will be very suspicious? Other teams need to use it and you have been working on a computer system. We have loads of those, Wei, loads!"

"Not like this one, Jon." He smiles back at me, his camouflage working perfectly. "This is the Hybrid Integrated Computer System. It is a combination of my ship's computer and the computer system on the alien ship. We have managed to complete the integration, and the computer is capable of interpreting all of the information stored within the databanks on the ship. It has all of the capabilities of my computer mixed with the better ones from the ship. Believe me, it is much better than you know. There are of course other things we have discovered and these are a real bargaining tool for your commanders."

"Like what?"

"Display local star charts, HICS."

I look around the cockpit area to see who HICS, is before realising it is an abbreviation. A number of star charts flick across a section of the screen in front of me. "Interesting, but I'm still not sure how this is going to help.

"Display route to home planet," Wei says. The star charts zoom out to include the local space and other parts of the solar system. A blinking green dot appears on Earth as the start point and then a line is drawn through the star chart showing the path from the start point to a point in the middle of nowhere.

I feel confused, but I'm not sure if I should be. "What happened? Where's the planet?"

"There is no planet there. It is showing us how to get there. I was confused by the results too. I had to ask the computer to explain why it stopped there. The response was beyond my imagination. The route to their home world continues after the 'Dimensional Jump' is completed." My jaw drops open and he cuts back in before I can ask my question, "I know it sounds implausible, but it is actually the only explanation for why we have never heard of them and how they managed to appear and disappear the way they did. HICS, show the next leg of the journey, please." The image shimmers out and is replaced by a new star chart. I watch as the route starts again in the middle of nowhere and stops at a single planet.

I have to admit, he had my interest at Dimensional Jump!

"Can we replicate the Dimensional Jump technology? What about the data on the computer systems? Can we replicate that, too? Oh, and what about the ships? Can it tell us how fast they can go? How long does..."

He cuts in again, "Of course we can replicate the jump drive and the data. If it is equipment installed on this ship, then HICS can analyse it and create the necessary build plans for you. The on-board computer also held further data regarding them. Your people are going to need to hear this information, Jon. This is my proof of our good intentions."

"It's not a lot, but it might do the job. Come on, Wei. Let's introduce the Najess to humanity." Wei's smile freezes in place. His camouflaged face visibly changes colour and he begins to curl up into a ball again.

"Wei? Wei? It's okay. I will be there with you all the way. No-one is going to do anything to you." Wei stops himself from curling up again. He controls his breathing and straightens back up.

"Thank you. I am okay now, Jon. So, when should we do this?"

"Now is as good a time as any, I guess!"

Wei collapses and curls up fully this time!

3

A TIME FOR TRAVEL

It took me a while to persuade Wei to come out of his self-inflicted catatonic state, but eventually he agreed and began to unfurl himself. I have to admit, a part of me wants to put him under a microscope and study him myself. The fact is, we didn't have time for any of his amateur dramatics. He was going to have to find a way to control himself.

I lead the way through the corridors until we arrive at a large, white double door with two soldiers standing guard on either side. My getting a meeting with the Admiral would have been almost impossible, but with some essential meetings taken care of, and of course the rumours that Wei had made a breakthrough of some kind, we managed to get in to see him by the end of that week. We walk side by side down the corridor towards the two guards at the far end. Neither guard moves a muscle as we approach – they actually remind me of the guards outside Buckingham Palace... except without the bright red uniform and stuff, of course. As we approach the door, the guard on the left reaches out and pushes the door open. I guess he knew our faces before we arrived because I know I have never seen him before!

I walk through the doorway with Wei in tow and the guard pulls the door closed behind us. We stop at the entrance and wait to be asked to approach the desk at the far end of the room – not a bad thing, as it gives me a chance to take in the surroundings.

I can see a few other people in the room already. Surprisingly, Wei doesn't seem to be at all nervous this time. I lean over to him, "How come you're so calm suddenly?"

"The computer has been administering a relaxant to my body. It helps me to control myself at times when fear is likely, but it is not advisable to use it too regularly. Large prolonged doses can cause damage to the brain."

"Ahhh! I see!" I wasn't entirely sure I did. "But aren't your people always afraid of everyt..." The look he gives me tells me it's time to shut up!

I use the opportunity to do another quick scan of the room. The other three people in the room are all wearing military uniforms and are stooped over some plans on the desk. I recognise the Admiral in the middle. Wei and I wait patiently by the door.

The Admiral glances up briefly and back down to the plans. "Come in, please," he says, without looking up, making me wonder if he is speaking to us at all.

I step forward, with Wei close behind me, and stop in front of the desk. Wei remains slightly behind and to my left.

A few seconds later, the Admiral sighs exhaustedly and looks up at me. "Hello, Jon. Wei, I am Admiral Martin Wesley. Welcome to the base. Now, I hear you both have some important, but apparently good, news for us." I nod, but say nothing. I think Wei's nervousness is contagious. "Well, we could certainly do with some. Please, take a seat." He gestures to two comfortable leather chairs in front of him. "Is it not a little soon for good news, though, Wei? You have only been here, what..." he shuffles through the papers on the desk again, "a week?"

I sit down and Wei sits next to me. "Erm, important information, yes," I say, stumbling over my words, "although probably not what you expect. There are two things I need to inform you of, sir. The first is that we have made a breakthrough with the ship... or at least part of it anyway. Wei has managed to create a Hybrid Integrated Computer System – HICS for short – and he has used it to link into the ship's on-board computer. We believe we now know where they came from and how to locate them."

"Excellent. Anything else?"

I'm shocked they haven't thrown me out already, "Yes, sir, er, using HICS, we will be able to replicate their hardware much more easily, including their drives."

There are some murmurings of approval from the others in the room, "Excellent again, but I get the feeling you are holding something back, Jon."

"Er... yes, sir." I scratch my head as I try to find the right words. "We also know why we have not been able to find them. Their home planet is located in..." I clear my throat as I prepare to say, out loud, the strangest thing I have ever said to anyone, "another dimension, sir." His expression does not change, which somehow seems worse than if he had gone ballistic and kicked us both out of the office right there and then! I forge onwards, determined to get past this, "The ship contains equipment which will allow us to travel to their dimension. It, er, also contains the star charts for the system so we can see where they are and how to avoid them. We have also been able to decipher their language."

"Interesting. So, two weeks ago you reported that progress reports from everyone working on the ship were slow and that it was likely to be months before anything on the ship would be ready. What has changed... other than Wei's presence, of course?"

I look at Wei. "Well, sir, that is the other thing I need to tell you. You have already met Wei. Now, I need your help here, sir. You MUST keep calm and allow me to explain what has happened. It is important that you understand that we are all perfectly safe." He shifts uncomfortably in his seat and I realise my choice of words could have been better.

"Continue, Jon," he says, studying us carefully, but I notice a fleeting sideways glance at the other uniformed officers in the room. Out of the corner of my eye I can see them shift their stance so they are prepared to move in an instant.

"What you are about to see may cause you a little alarm." The three uniformed men are standing dead still and watching us both intently. "Please understand, sir, that without Wei, none of this could have happened." I look at Wei and nod.

Wei stares blankly for a moment and then nods back to Jon. He breathes in deeply. "Ten seconds," he whispers almost inaudibly to me.

"Wei is not from here, sir. He is not one of us, and he will now show you his true form." I figure surprises at this point could be bad.

As Wei's camouflage phases out, the atmosphere in the room becomes almost tangible. No-one says a thing; they just stand there looking at Wei.

I feel uncomfortable in my seat and want to shift my position, but I'm afraid it might stir the stunned and speechless guards into action. I decide to quickly explain things before the guards wake up. "Wei is from the Najess race, sir. They were also attacked by the alien race. He arrived a week ago and offered to help with the creation of the computer and the reverse engineering of the ship. Sir, none of this could have happened without him. We would not have been able to complete the computer this quickly."

The man on the left speaks for the first time. "And what does he want in return?"

I prepare to answer, but Wei interrupts me, "As Jon said, we were attacked too. My people believe that the ships that attacked us were only scout ships. This would mean that they had a limited scope for attack and—"

"Limited? Did you see what they did?" Another uniformed man has jumped into the conversation. He seems more agitated. Admiral Wesley says nothing but just sits there and studies Wei.

"My people have already investigated the attacks and we know, based on size and speed, that the ships were only likely to be scouts. Based on the level of damage, it is likely that they *did* only have a limited attack capacity. Let me ask you something." His confidence has been alarming since he started speaking, but it seems to be increasing as he speaks. "If you had attacked another country but were unable to finish the invasion due to a simple lack of firepower and resources, what would you do next?"

The three people sit motionless in their seats. The Admiral continues to look intently at Wei. "Get home as quick as possible. Debrief and suggest that a larger force is sent to finish the job."

"Exactly. The evidence of what this race is capable of is obvious. They have made their presence and intentions known by covertly launching an attack at a planetary level and without any clear provocation. They did this on all our planets at the same time. Now, we are not talking of co-ordinating a strike on three buildings at the same time. This is a co-ordinated attack on three planets. My people are positive this will not be over until they *know* that there is nothing left alive on the planets." Wei stops himself there, as his emotions threaten to overwhelm him. I have to admit, the speech was good and it seem's to be having the desired effect. I can see that they are considering what Wei said carefully. The weight of his words and the consequences of doing nothing begin to slowly dawn on everyone in the office. *Let's face it, Wei has a point. These beings obviously don't like us much. I mean, as Wei said, they attacked us without any provocation – talk about xenophobic!* Three different alien species and they all get attacked at the same time in a co-ordinated attack. If I had that much hatred for someone, I guess I would go away and be back with enough armaments to ensure they never got back up again.

Admiral Wesley stands up and starts to pace in the area behind the desk, rubbing his forehead thoughtfully. "You have come to us offering wonderful promises, but you have to admit that you have been staying in our base secretly for the last few days, a matter I will take up in private with you, Jon," he says as he passes a fleeting glance in my direction. "These, Wei, are not the actions of a person wanting to be trusted. I know you say that you will be giving us wonderful new technology, but how can we tell what you have already taken without us knowing? Bearing this in mind, you still promise to give us much. However, you have not answered my original question. What do *your* people – the Najess – want from us in exchange for this information and technology?"

"We want your help. We are not equipped physically for conflict. We are, however, equipped for making strategic decisions and for scientific breakthroughs. We could be of great help to you."

"We are pretty good at strategy, too. What do you have in mind?" Admiral Wesley smiles calmly. His focus is now entirely on Wei, as though his eyes can see straight into his soul. I feel like I may as well not be in the office, and I can feel the attention shifting entirely in one direction.

Wei gathers himself admirably and responds with renewed confidence. "We need to strike back at them." The three of them laugh out loud. He continues undeterred, "It is the last thing they would expect from us. Our hope lies in the idea that they think we are crippled. The scout reports will surely state that there was minimal resistance and that they have destroyed much of the existing forces and infrastructure."

"They would be right."

"Which will hopefully mean they will not treat this too urgently. We need enough time to create a few large transport ships. These need to be used to carry us to their dimension. We locate a distant planet to occupy and hide there until we can get a good enough force together."

"You seem to have neglected the fact that we do not have the capability for space travel. And then, of course, even if we managed to get to their *dimension* – and I still find it hard to believe that other dimensions exist – sitting in one place and waiting to be found does not make any sense. A better idea would be guerrilla warfare tactics."

Wei zones out for a moment. I can see that he is talking to the ship's computer, but to everyone else it just looks like he went catatonic suddenly.

"Okay," this actually sounds like he is talking to someone else, and Admiral Wesley notices it instantly. "What are these guerrilla tactics?" Wei asks, unaware that he has been found out.

"Wait, what's going on here?"

"Sir," I interrupt, realising that I need to diffuse the situation before it gets out of hand. "Wei has a telepathic link between his ship's computer and himself. It is a way for him to communicate effectively with us by translating our speech, but it also helps him to work with the technology efficiently. It is this link which allowed him to build HICS so quickly."

The men look at each other. "So, how do we know what you are discussing with your computer?" Admiral Wesley asks.

"That would be the trust issue," Wei says. "We may be able to get around that, though. Just a moment." He zones out again for a moment. Then he rolls his left sleeve up, opens a thin hidden panel on his left forearm and quickly taps a few small buttons. "All done! You will now be able to hear any communications between me and the ship so long as I am in your immediate vicinity. I hope this helps you to trust me a bit more?"

"It is a step in the right direction, Wei," Admiral Wesley says as he relaxes back in his chair. "Back to your question. You asked what guerrilla warfare tactics were."

"The computer has found the correct definition now. My

understanding is that it is irregular warfare by small groups of combatants using hit-and-run ambush tactics on larger, less mobile armed forces. It means they can cause significant damage while suffering minimal losses. Is this correct?"

"Pretty much perfect, actually!" Admiral Wesley is clearly impressed.

"Terrifying history you have here," Wei comments. "Okay, guerrilla tactics sound like the right plan of action considering the circumstances. Maybe we will leave battle strategy to you, but I still believe we excel in overall strategy and direction – it would be prudent for us to combine our knowledge and experience. In the meantime, assuming we are going to work together, we need to inform the highest levels of your government. Without them, this is not going to work."

"Well, working together seems like the only real option, so let me see what can be done. Jon, for my part, we are in, but you know already that this was the easy bit. Convincing everyone else is going to take a lot more. For now, Jon, I want you to prepare the HICS system for a proper demonstration to us, and I want you to devote your time entirely to helping Wei with his work. You will have exclusive access to the hangar for the next week. At the end of the week, we will evaluate your progress and decide if you are to have further access for another week, and so on."

I happily acknowledge my change of assignment. Even when I have been working on other tasks, all I have been able to think of is what Wei is working on. Anyway, with what is good news, for me at least, I get up and leave the office, with Wei right behind me.

We make some really good progress over the next week. As we complete each stage, Admiral Wesley contacts me and asks for a progress report. I can't tell why he wants me to deliver the report, though. He might as well go direct to Wei, as I only end up gathering the information from him anyway. What I can say, though, is that the Admiral seems to have put everything else on the backburner and is focusing his attention on our work. As you can imagine, there are pros and cons to this attention. So, this is now officially the highest profile project on the base and the pressure to deliver is on us both.

Wei and I continue working on the ship, but every now and again Admiral Wesley calls us into another meeting where he asks more questions. These meetings start off with the usual guards in the room – a precaution to protect the Admiral from Wei, I think (if only they knew what a coward he was) – but as the days go by these guards disappear and it's only Wei, Admiral Wesley and me attending the meetings.

By the end of the second week, Admiral Wesley enters the lab and takes us to the side. I almost collapse when he tells us that we are to meet the head of the recently formed World Government that evening and that she has flown in especially to meet us after hearing about the work we have done.

Wei collapses!

We are escorted into the same office we were in two weeks ago. We follow Admiral Wesley to the desk and sit down. Behind the desk is the newly appointed President of Earth, Kathryn Yeates. Wei and I sit quietly and listen as Admiral Wesley goes through a speech which he obviously knows too well. By the time he finishes explaining the work we have done and what we have achieved, even President Yeates is stunned into silence.

Now, this is the first time I have ever been in the presence of a President – much less the President of Earth – so I am understandably quite nervous. She seems to have an aura which can keep you calm, yet there is also a high level of authority in her, too. She sits elegantly yet authoritatively behind the desk. Her upright posture belies the real power which she commands, and there is a clear sense that the people in the room would be ready to give their lives for hers at a moment's notice.

So, the un-camouflaged Wei is now sitting before the head

of the Human race. "Since I left my planet," Wei explains, "my people have been working on several large ships to help carry us here. We – my ship and I – have received communication that the ships have been completed and are already on their way. They will arrive in just a few weeks.

"We have also been working on something else this week." He looks towards me now. "It is a drug. My people have been using this drug for generations and it has more than tripled our life expectancy. In addition, it creates specific nanotech antibodies which fight all other infections and remember them for the future. Think of them as an evolutionary advancement to what you call antibodies." This news stuns everyone. No-one expected this development. "It is how I was able to come to your planet and survive without problems. Jon and I have been working on adapting this drug for Humans. Our anatomy may appear outwardly different, but we are quite similar internally. The fact is, our DNA is remarkably similar, which in itself is surprising. This means that it should work in a similar manner for you. Unfortunately, it has never been tested on Humans, and the only way to prove categorically that it works is to administer the drug to someone and monitor them." He looks at me again. He never mentioned this part so it catches me off guard, but I think I know what he wants!

"Wait!" I say, "I know I am the most expendable person here, but isn't there another test which can be run?"

"You are not expendable to me, Jon," Wei says with what appears to be real concern in his voice. "We have run all of the tests which can be run. This is all that is left. You will be fully monitored by HICS… and of course by me. I leave the final choice to you, though."

President Yeates stands up and begins to pace around the office. "Everything you have said is very interesting, Wei. You also have the backing of a very influential group of individuals. I can see the sense in what you say, but whether it be one person, like

Jon or some member of the public, I do not enjoy the idea of using Humans as guinea pigs in your experiments."

"I assure you, sir, that every possible safety measure has been taken to ensure his safety. Jon is the first person I befriended on your planet and I do not intend to jeopardise his life for a fruitless cause."

Being experimented on wasn't something I ever wanted, but I also knew that Wei needed my help to prove his intentions were good. If I didn't do this, I doubted anyone else would either. Put it this way… would you let an alien you just met run experiments on you? "Okay," I say a bit louder than I meant to, "I guess I am the right person for the job. I have worked with Wei the most and can probably communicate what is happening the best." My response is a little weak, but it seems to placate the President a bit. It does nothing for my nerves, though.

"Good. I believe it may be prudent to provide you with another person, though. Someone who is a bit older, for an alternative perception of the effects." She addresses me directly, "No offence Jon, but your youth and friendship with Wei may actually cloud your judgement of the effects of the drug." She gestures to the uniformed man to her right, "Robert has a few extra years of experience over you." Robert nods to accept his assignment. "He will be a suitable person to join you. Right, so, how soon can we expect results?"

"Late tomorrow morning, sir." Wei says.

"So be it. Perform your tests and present the results tomorrow afternoon at three. Thank you."

I feel like I'm in a trance as Wei leads Robert and me – the guinea pigs – to the lab where the drug is waiting for us. I'm not sure how I managed to get to the point where I am going to test an experimental drug which has never been tested on another Human before. I would never have volunteered myself for something like this. My thoughts return to the incident in the tombs and the last

41

moment I saw my parents. Are they still down there? It's strange how these things sink deep into your mind and only surface at stressful times like these. Times when you are most worried about other things. I remember my dad once telling me of the pride he felt when I was born. He was a real family man, and I know he loved the idea that I might follow in his footsteps... maybe become a historian like him one day. I know he would never have wanted me to join the army, that's for sure. I look at Robert as he walks silently beside me. His worn features tell me he is probably in his late forties. His uniform is crisply ironed, with defined creases in precisely the right places. There is a stern look on his face as he marches himself into the lab, his back straight, shoulders back and chin held high like he never relaxes even when told to 'stand at ease'.

The lab is large and open-plan. There are two clean, shiny tables in the middle, with a large screen in front of them. Along the outside edge of the room are lots of trolleys with all sorts of medical equipment on them. I lie down on one of the tables and Robert lies on the one next to mine. The metallic surface of the table is surprisingly warm, which is a pleasant surprise. Wei silently attaches some pads to us while HICS starts to take readings and displays them on the large screen.

Wei leans over me. "Relax, Jon. I honestly believe that this will work fine. I would not risk my only real friend on this planet if I had not done my research thoroughly. What you will feel tomorrow will be wonderful. All you need to do is take this capsule, drink the water and sleep." I feel like I just fell into *The Matrix*.

I look him in the eyes and think I see what I need to. There is faith in his eyes and I have learned over these last few weeks that when Wei has faith in something, it has to be good. I relax a bit and take a deep breath, "Let's get this over with."

Robert and I look at each other. We put the capsules into our mouths and drink the water. I lay my head down and sleep seems to come easily for the first time since the catacombs.

The next morning, I wake to find Wei walking around the laboratory with a smug look on his face. "What are you smiling about?"

"The results are good, Jon. Very good indeed. Look, there is someone you should meet." He steps over to me and points to a man walking around the perimeter of the lab. He looks to be in his late twenties. His posture is perfect: back straight; shoulders back; a lean and toned look like someone used to long bouts of exercise; but there is something strange about the way he walks. It's almost as though he has borrowed the body and is not used to it. I don't fully recognise him, but I'd swear I've seen him around the building somewhere recently. I just can't place where. I look to Wei with a questioning look in my eyes as I try to sit up. I have to admit, I do feel unusually good today... very well rested, with a confidence I have not felt before. I even feel stronger.

Wei leans in towards me, "It's Robert, Jon," he whispers into my ear.

Robert turns immediately. "Pardon?"

I look at him, stunned. I can see the features now. All of the wrinkles have disappeared but, along with the youthful looks, his eyes have the same knowledgeable yet sad touch to them. I suddenly realise that I can see a lot of detail on his face from all the way across the lab. Wait a second... did he just hear Wei whisper his name from across the room?

I suddenly have a scary thought. "Mirror," I say, slightly panicked and sounding something like the Joker from the old Batman movies.

"Relax, Jon," Robert says to me, half laughing as he seems to read my mind. "The effects were considerably less on you."

Wei hands me the mirror. I look at myself and breathe a sigh of relief as I realise I have maybe lost a year at best. "That freaked me out for second!"

Wei is almost too elated to talk. "The results are much better than expected. HICS has gathered all of the results and we are waiting to present them to the President."

I slide energetically off the table, landing lightly on the pure white floor. "I feel like I could run a mile!" I say as I follow Wei to get a few more tests done, before dressing for the afternoon meeting.

The three of us walk down the corridor towards the President's office – previously known as Admiral Wesley's office – and, like yesterday, the guards open the door. Wei walks in first, with Richard and me following close behind and trying to hide ourselves behind him. The assessment panel and the medical team are already in the office waiting for us. There is an atmosphere of anticipation in the office and I can clearly hear the quietly whispered comments from each group, individuals presenting their personal expectations of the results of the drug and the possible side-effects even if it did work.

As they notice the door opening, they turn to see if their predictions were correct. "Morning, all," Wei says confidently as he enters the room. Richard and I follow him through the door. It takes a few moments for the people inside to realise who it is walking behind Wei. The President is the first to comment.

"My God, Richard. You look amazing." She steps towards him for a closer look. "Amazing. You really look incredible. How do you feel?"

"Fantastic. I've been a little clumsy this morning, and I'm having some difficulty adjusting to myself again, but I'm sure it is only a case of getting used to the change."

"Is this permanent, Wei?" the President asks.

"Absolutely. Based on our calculations, this should add approximately one hundred years – give or take a decade – to the average life expectancy."

"Incredible. And you, Jon. How are you feeling?" The President looks at us both, dumbfounded by the results.

"I feel good, actually. It hasn't affected me too much, although I do feel a bit stronger and more alert than normal."

"The drug is expected to increase your metabolic rate and enhance your muscle density," Wei says. "You may find you weigh a little more. In addition," he addresses everyone else in the room now, "we have found a new side-effect which we have only seen in Humans. It would appear to accentuate Human senses. The hearing and eyesight have been noticed so far. The effects have been quite extraordinary. You should also find that general sickness levels are significantly reduced and energy levels will increase. Many of the major diseases your people have been suffering will be eradicated, too." Every single person in the room has the same shocked look on their face. One by one they come closer to have a better look at us. "I mean diseases such as cancer and heart disease, for example. I do hope this is a suitable demonstration of my goodwill?"

"Wei, you have provided us with the technology to help protect ourselves. You have given us medication which will save us from many of the diseases which plague our people. Admittedly, there are still some doubts about the longevity of the drug, but we will see that in due course. The question for now is how can *we* thank you?"

Wei smiles, "As I have already stated, your future and ours are linked. We can only continue to exist if we help each other."

"You have our help, Wei. Tell me, what you are planning?"

"Well, there is something further which I have not mentioned until now. There is a third planet. They were also hit as hard as we were."

Robert looks warily at him. "Why have you not mentioned this before, Wei? Who are they?"

"I am sorry, Robert." Wei turns to address the rest of the office. "Until I had confirmation that you had agreed to help, there was no need to mention them. They are in the same situation as we are and they have no idea that we exist either."

Another member of the President's security personnel in the room steps forward and speaks with a heavy voice that matches his stocky build perfectly, "Sir, would you mind explaining how you know so much about them and us?"

"It is a fair question," the President says to Wei.

"We have been studying both of your races for centuries now – from a distance, of course. You have to understand, my people have a natural fear of anything that has the ability to harm us. Your people are naturally geared for fighting. The Keteran people are more like the middle ground between both of our races. They have a reasonable intelligence level and are also very peaceful, but their physical attributes make them suitable for fighting, although not as efficiently as you. They do seem to have an incredible communication system in place, though."

"Really? What communication system?" The President's interest in this other race is becoming more pronounced as the conversation progresses.

"As with your people, we have only studied their race from a distance. What we understand of the Keteran people is that they always seem to be co-ordinated. Anything they do appears to be extremely efficient. The only obvious way of being this efficient in *all* tasks is if you have constant communication and understanding with the person you are working with. I realise that I have kept this information from you, but I have explained my reasons. I would not have done this if it had meant endangering anyone else. I will, however, understand if you feel that this additional information requires you to rescind your previous agreement to join our cause. It would be regrettable, but understandable."

"That will not be necessary, Wei. The circumstances are slightly different, I agree, but that does not mean we need to change things. Besides, if your predictions of a greater force returning are true, I think we will need every friend we can get over the coming months. I do have one caveat, though. There will be no more secrets. Everything must be explained in advance. Is this acceptable?"

"Of course. Clear communication will be key to our survival."

I keep listening to the conversation between them, but part of me switches off every now and then so I miss bits and pieces. I think the conversation was a bit too civilised for me. I was expecting things to be a bit more difficult than this. On the other hand, maybe it is the effect of the drug... I do feel quite restless and buzzing with energy.

"So, what is the next stage of the plan, then?" the President asks.

"I need someone to help me visit the Keteran people. It must be someone from your race who can represent humanity and its willingness to co-operate in this endeavour. We need to convince them of our joint good intentions."

"Well, the obvious person for this role would appear to be Jon." She looks in my direction. "That is of course if you are agreed, Jon?" I nod my head in agreement. Actually, I daren't open my mouth. I only caught the end of the question, and what I thought I heard stunned me enough that I figured if I tried to say something I might convince them I was a bad choice.

"Excellent," Wei says. "We will be gone for several weeks at least. In the meantime, I have instructed HICS to commence work on the first of the transport ships. It will be using the designs from the scout ship we have in the hangar, and it will also look to reverse engineer the dimensional drive system on the ship. In addition, I believe HICS has already completed the schematics for additional Portable HICS – P-HICS for short – which will be on each ship we build from now on. My people will be arriving in a little over a week. The P-HICS will be added to your ships and also the ships my people will arrive in. This will allow us to communicate more effectively. Between now and then, you need to gather all Humans that are still alive and prepare them for evacuation. Jon and I will return after we have met with the Keteran people. Does this seem like a suitable plan?" It amazes me how Wei suddenly speaks so confidently when he talks about plans and strategies. I wonder if the rest of the Najess are like this too.

"Sounds like you have been thinking about this for a while. Okay," the President now addresses everyone in the office, "we have a lot of work to do, people. You all know the plan and you know which areas fall under your own control. If you have any questions, please speak to a member of my team and they will clarify."

I prepare to stand up, when I feel Admiral Wesley's hand grab my arm, telling me in no uncertain terms that I should remain seated. I slowly settle back into the chair and watch as the rest of the people in the room filter out, quietly whispering to each other and stealing glances at Wei.

"Jon. Wei. When do you expect to leave?" the President asks when the room is empty and the door closes.

I look towards Wei expectantly. "This evening. My ship is already prepared and cloaked behind the trees over there." He points out of the window at an area behind the running track. "There really is no time to lose."

The President swivels around in her chair and looks out of the window. "Behind the trees?"

"Yes. You will see the ship when we take off. Unfortunately, the cloak is not particularly good so we had to hide it some distance away in an area which has not been disturbed in some time." The President nods thoughtfully. "Okay, well, I believe you have a lot of preparations to complete in a very short time. Well done, all of you. We will meet tonight before you leave."

Admiral Wesley stands and turns to leave the room so, taking the hint, Wei and I stand and follow him out.

As we walk back to the laboratory where we have set up our latest test environment, I can't resist asking Wei the question which has been going through my mind for the last few minutes, "So, we're leaving tonight, then, huh?"

"No, Jon, we are leaving this evening. Every hour counts now. It has taken me longer to convince your people than I thought."

"Really? I thought it was quite quick. So, what do I need to pack? Clothes, food, what?"

"Just the clothes will be required. All other requirements have already been taken care of by HICS." He pauses before continuing. "Relax, Jon. You will be fine, I promise." He stops outside his laboratory. "I need to get a few final things together. I suggest you do the same." I nod and continue down the corridor in a daze.

After a couple of hours, Wei knocks on my door. "Come in," I call out. The door opens and Wei finds me ready and waiting for him. "Ready?" I ask cheerfully. "I guess I could do with an adventure," I add as an explanation for my sudden enthusiasm.

He smiles warmly like a parent does to a child. "Let's go, Jon. The President has a vehicle out back to take us to the ship."

"It's not that far to the ship. Why did she do that?"

"I think it was an excuse to see the ship," he smiles.

As the jeep passes the trees at the far end of the gardens, I see a slight shimmering in the air ahead of us, reminding me of heatwaves over a car left in the summer sun. The President seems to be looking in the same direction.

"Is that it there, Wei?" the President asks him.

"HICS, turn off the cloak, please."

The ship slowly solidifies. CLOAK HAS BEEN DISENGAGED. The voice comes from Wei's arm panel.

The awe is visible on the President's face, but she quickly resumes control when she realises I have seen her. Wei smiles. "I have already uploaded the plans for this ship to HICS. HICS will determine which parts of both technology types to use for the best results."

"Excellent. I could do with more like you on my staff, Wei," the President says.

"I believe they will be here in a couple of weeks. Give them a few days to settle in and they will enjoy helping you."

We exit the jeep and walk towards the ship. As we approach it, a doorway slides opens from what was a seamless metallic panel. I climb the steps into the ship in silent awe. I can feel a struggle within me, pulling me across the spectrum of extreme self-confidence and severe sense of excitement. It's a struggle to keep myself under control. I step through the doorway and into the Najess ship. Wei has already disappeared around the corner towards the cockpit. I can hear him talking to the ship already. "HICS, initiate start-up sequence." As I make my way further into the ship, the doorway closes behind me and a slow humming sound emanates from all around. The corridor walls are perfectly straight and smooth, with a dull chrome-like sheen.

INITIATION SEQUENCE HAS COMPLETED SUCCESSFULLY. WE ARE READY TO LEAVE, WEI.

"Thank you, HICS." I enter what I guess is the cockpit and sit in the spare seat next to Wei. The cockpit is relatively bare. I expected loads of buttons and dials, something like a large passenger aircraft, but there are only a few buttons, no dials and a touchscreen panel in front of both seats.

Wei is busy tapping and moving images around on his screen. He looks like he is putting a puzzle together the way he is moving the items around and fitting them in place before moving to the next piece. "Welcome to the Ysay, Jon," he says without looking away from the screen. "Are you ready?"

"Yeah, I guess so," I reply, my earlier excitement shifting towards trepidation.

"Okay. One other thing. I have instructed the computer to take instructions from you, too. My people, the Najess, have an implant installed a few days after we are born. This is what allows us to communicate so efficiently with our computers. We can try to implant one for you too, if you like? It will help you to communicate in the same way."

"Er, can I think about it, Wei? A lot has already happened this week."

"I understand, Jon. Let me know if you decide you want it." Actually, the idea of telepathically speaking to the ship did sound kind of cool, but I thought having some time to let it sink in would be good, too.

"Launch into orbit," Wei says, "and prepare the route to the Keteran home world, please, HICS. Also, prepare an implant for Jon just in case it is required. Check all specific requirements for Human integration are prepared and tested thoroughly." The ship rises slowly from the ground and hovers for a few seconds. I adjust myself in my seat and prepare for the experience of a lifetime.

Now, you know when you go to watch a film that you have been waiting for months to see? The excitement of those last few months is squeezed into those few minutes when you are sitting in the cinema, popcorn and drink in your hands, and the movie is about to start. Well, think about the times when that same movie did not live up to your expectations. The characters weren't right, the story didn't work, whatever it was. It's the anti-climax feeling at the end, when you can hear the grumbling sounds from the rest of the people walking out of the cinema wishing they had not wasted their time, and you can't help but agree with them. Well, this is one of those times. Within the space of about thirty seconds we move from hovering a few feet above the ground to orbiting the planet. What I was looking forward to most was the feeling of rapid acceleration… none of that. I was expecting at least to feel myself pushed a little into my seat as we accelerated upwards… Nope, none of that either. In fact, I don't feel particularly weightless right now either. To be honest, it was nothing like what I expected, which left me totally disappointed. I felt like I had bought a ticket for a concert, only to be given tickets to a pantomime. The only plus side is the view of the stars through the cockpit screen, which really is incredible… You wouldn't believe how many stars you can see when there is no atmosphere getting in the way. I actually can't believe I am able to see this with my own eyes. The view screen pans around to show an image of the Earth from behind the ship. As the Earth comes into view, I realise that the image in front of me is more beautiful than any of the images I have ever seen on the TV. And I know I am going to miss her!

"Now, that is something," I think out loud.

"That is just the beginning, Jon. This is where it gets interesting. Engage the drives, HICS."

The ship suddenly accelerates forwards and the Earth shrinks rapidly into a distant bright dot. A huge smile makes its way across my face. "Wei, I'm so happy you met me first." Anti-climax averted!

4

TELEPATHIC FRIENDS ARE USEFUL

When I was a child and did something bad, my father would ground me by sending me up to my room. It wasn't a long grounding, but it was always a painfully boring lesson. He would sit me on the edge of my bed, point to the digital clock on my desk and tell me to stare at it until fifteen minutes went by. Now, I know fifteen minutes doesn't sound like much, but when you are just a child and you have to actually watch the seconds tick by – minute by slow, ponderous minute – fifteen minutes can feel like a lifetime. Give it a go sometime and you'll see what I mean. Anyway, imagine being grounded for a week instead… That's what I've been going through. Don't get me wrong, Wei's been trying his best to keep me busy, but there's only so much you can do on a small ship before you've done it all… several times!

"The ship was only designed as a transport, Jon," Wei tries unsuccessfully to empathise with me as the cabin fever continues to take hold. "Is there anything I can provide you with to help you pass the time?" His soft voice calms me down a bit.

I sigh deeply, "It's not your fault, Wei. I just need something to do. Something to keep myself busy with." I try to keep the frustration out of my voice, but the effort just irritates me again. "We've been on this ship for over a week now. I'm not used to doing nothing every day. Jeez, there has to be something for me to do!" I kick at a panel, leaving the imprint of my boot in it, and then look sheepishly at Wei. "Sorry!"

"A few weeks ago, I would have curled into a ball and stayed that way for hours," he says smiling at me. "I know this is difficult, Jon." He pauses for a moment. "Jon, do you know how I was always in communication with the ship when we were in the base?"

"Yeah. You said that the implant in your brain made it possible. Why?" I try unsuccessfully to keep the sulky tones out of my voice.

"We still have another week of travelling ahead of us. If you are interested, you could work with the computer and prepare an implant for yourself. It will help you to communicate with the ship and keep you busy for a while."

"I'm not a medic, Wei. I wouldn't have the slightest idea where to begin."

"HICS will guide you, Jon. You will only be required to examine and confirm specific details. HICS will do the rest."

"And the end result? What do you expect from this?"

"If you are ready, we will implant it into you. When this is done, you will be able to communicate with the ship simply through thought."

"And with you?"

"Unfortunately not! My people tried this a long time ago, but it just never appeared to work properly. There was always a delay, and that caused more problems than helping, so we decided against further research. The computers were simply not quick enough to relay the information effectively, so it all got too confusing. Of course, with HICS, things may be very different. We can look into that later, though."

"Okay. So, for now, my options are to let you mess with my brain or allow myself to slowly lose my mind on this ship. Ah hell, if you gotta go... go in style." I shrug my shoulders. "Where do I start?"

"The medical module is located in the cargo bay. When you are ready, inform HICS of your intentions and it will help you to investigate potential issues and negate them."

"The cargo bay?" The idea of working on high-end technology in a cargo bay sounds kind of cool. I'm still not convinced about the 'installing it in my brain' bit though, but we can cross that bridge later.

"Yes. It doubles as an operating theatre without creating undue distractions in the cockpit. It also means it can be kept separate and sterile if required."

I consider this for a moment. "Sounds logical. Ah hell. See you soon... hopefully!" I get up and head for the cargo bay door.

After two days of working on my new pet project, I enter the cockpit feeling considerably more relaxed and energetic. Wei is hunched over a panel, adjusting some controls or something.

"Anything interesting?" I ask.

"Yes," he says without much enthusiasm. "There is an interesting cosmic phenomena near here." He pauses. "Actually, it's not that interesting. I think I was a bit bored and decided to document it."

"Yeah! Sounds *real* interesting!" I say sarcastically. "Well, I have some more interesting information for you." Wei looks up for the first time. "I have... well, HICS and I have configured the implant for Humans... we think. Actually, HICS says it is done, I think it might be done. Anyway, HICS believes it is now compatible with Human physiology."

"Excellent news... I think."

"HICS also suggests we install the implant now. What do you think?"

"No time like the present, as you say on Earth." Wei closes the panel down and gets up, stretching his back as he stands.

"Been there for a while?"

"Just keeping myself busy. Now I have something really interesting to work on, though. Come on."

We enter the cargo bay and Wei moves straight to the medical panel on the far wall. He taps the panel a few times, studies the data and then turns to me. "All looks good, Jon. HICS is suggesting that this is a basic procedure, so I have no concerns. If you lie down on the table, HICS will take over from here. I will remain here to observe."

"No concerns?" A part of me really wants him to have some concerns so we can cancel the procedure.

"Unfortunately not. If you do want to cancel the procedure, though, Jon, just say so. This must be your decision."

"After all the work I have put into this? No. This needs to be done." I lie down on the table and control my breathing."

"Okay, we should get started," Wei says. "And do not worry, it will all go well."

"What, no break a leg or anything?"

"Why would I want you to break a leg, Jon?" He genuinely sounds worried.

"Relax, it's a saying on Earth. It means good luck."

He thinks about this for a moment. "I think I need to study Human phrases in more detail."

"Forget it, Wei. It'll just confuse you more." He nods and moves to the medical panel to observe the readings.

The procedure completes in about an hour and I wake up a few hours later feeling rested. I walk back into the cockpit area with Wei.

"Everything okay, Jon?" Wei asks again as we sit down. "Does the implant work?"

I concentrate for a moment as I try to figure out if everything is alright. The ship suddenly shudders, causing things to fall around the cockpit. Wei turns to his controls and starts tapping the touch panel, frantically searching for the problem.

"HICS? What happened? Provide status on all ships systems."

I laugh loudly, "The ship is fine, Wei. The implant works fine, too. I was just testing it out. Luckily, HICS has a sense of humour and agreed to play along."

Wei doesn't look too impressed. "This is no time to behave like a child, Jon."

"Relax, Wei. Everything is going to be fine. Besides, in Earth terms, I am a child!"

ALL SHIP FUNCTIONS ARE WORKING NORMALLY, WEI, HICS says to us both, using the implant for the first time.

I get the feeling I look as ecstatic as I feel. "Wow, now that was weird." I laugh. "Is that what you felt when the old computer talked to you?"

"Similar, Jon. This communication appears to be much faster and somehow more directly to the implant. That is not important though. Right now we need to discuss how we are going to introduce ourselves to the Keteran people. We do not want to alarm them."

"Okay. Let's start with what they look like. Do we have any images of them?"

As if by magic, a holographic image of what I guess is a Keteran appears in the area before us. I look at the image as it slowly rotates in the air.

"Female?" I ask.

Before Wei can answer, HICS interjects. YES, JON.

"She looks a lot like my people... Human, I mean." I keep scanning the image and I'm surprised at how alike we really are.

"They are not too different from your own race, Jon, which I suppose means they are not too different from my race, either."

The Keteran has what appears to be a fair skin tone, with a hint of colour as though she has been sunbathing recently. The hair is perfectly – and I mean perfectly – straight with a deep purple-black colour to it, as though she has just come back from a concert. The eyes are slightly wider than Human eyes and are a deep orange-brown colour. "Her eyes are amazing!" I have to really focus before I can look away from them.

"Barring any minor differences, such as hair and eye colour," Wei continues, "they are physically very similar. The skin tones are slightly darker than yours, but this is due to their planet being slightly closer to their star. Thank you, HICS, we are done with the image now."

The image flickers and disappears.

"I can't get over how similar we are."

"I know. This is something we will need to look into, Jon. Based on your similar physiology, though, I suggest that you be the first person they see. Now, this is not going to be easy. We have no time to waste and I don't have a camouflage unit which will work for you yet, so we cannot disguise ourselves. Besides, if I try to hide my appearance they may think we are hiding other things. HICS has already determined that the best course of action is to win them over with the truth. After all, they have been attacked in the same way as us and are likely to be wary of any new race."

"I guess it did make it easier to adjust when I saw you looking like a Human in the beginning. I got to know you before making a judgement. I'm not sure how I would have reacted otherwise. Do you need me to do anything in particular?"

"Not really. Just follow what I am doing. So long as they see you first, I think it will have a good effect. I am just hoping that they will have seen some of the hostile aliens, too. At least then they can tell we are both different from them."

"Yeah, I guess that makes sense. Wei, there is something else I wanted to ask you. You mentioned that their star affected their skin colour."

"No two stars are the same, Jon."

"No, that's not my question. My physics teacher told us that it would take generations, not years to travel between the stars. But you are saying that we will be there in a few weeks. How's that possible?"

Wei gives me that warm parental smile of his again. "It is a lot to explain and quite complicated, too. I suppose the easiest way to describe it is to imagine a large mountain. You need to get to the far side as fast as possible. It will take you days to climb up one side and down the other. If the mountain did not exist, though, it would be a relatively quick journey. Now, there is no short-term solution available for you, but there is a long-term solution that will reduce the amount of time it will take to traverse the mountain next time."

"A tunnel?"

"Exactly. Imagine that space is the mountain and we are travelling through a tunnel in space right now. The difference is, this tunnel also accelerates the ship, a bit like when you walk through an airport on Earth. You have those floors which move in the direction you are travelling. When you step on them, they accelerate you beyond your normal walking speed without the need for you to walk any faster. This tunnel works in a similar way. The Ysay is capable of creating one of these tunnels when required, and this is what allows us to travel so far, so fast. Does that make any sense?"

"Actually, it does. It sounds like you are describing a wormhole."

"I believe that is one of the names you have for it on Earth. The drives on the Ysay create something similar to a wormhole, and as we enter it we are propelled down the tunnel at high speed. Thanks to this technology, it will only be a couple of weeks before we arrive at Ketera. If you wish, you can always ask HICS to provide you with some further reading on the subject."

I consider this briefly. "I'll think about it, Wei. It depends how bored I *really* get."

I spend the next couple of weeks working with the implant and find plenty of reasons not to think about wormhole technology. I can see why the Najess insist on everyone having one of these implants, though. It makes everything so much easier. I can even communicate images directly to HICS, which makes communication even faster than normal – my dad used to say that a picture spoke a thousand words... I guess he was right. Shame he's not here to give me any more words of wisdom. I remember hearing a saying once: you only realise what you had after you lose it... or something like that, anyway. I think I had good parents. I'm not sure if I realised it before I lost them, though.

WE ARE ON FINAL APPROACH TO THE KETERAN HOME WORLD. THEY ARE MONITORING OUR PROGRESS AND MOBILISING GROUND TROOPS, HICS says over the speaker system.

I slowly get out of my bunk, stretch and yawn loudly, before making my way to the cockpit.

"We are nearly there," Wei says. "I wanted to ensure they were not too surprised, so I turned off the cloaking device. We were actually detected about an hour ago. I have also been transmitting a friendly beacon in the hope that they will not attack us."

"Sounds like a good plan. How do you know they will see the beacon as friendly?" Wei stops manipulating the image on the main console and suddenly looks worried... No, scratch that, he actually looks scared.

"Er, well, we cannot be entirely sure, but erm, my people have been studying them for some time and HICS agrees this is likely to work." That was close! Keep it going, Wei. Don't turn into a woodlouse again.

Wei turns his attention back to the panel again and continues tapping and dragging as though nothing had happened. "Most of the communications seem to be coming from a central building." Good! Sounding more confident again. He taps a few more images on the console and a new holographic image of the area appears in front of us. He points out a simple looking building beside a large green area. "Also, the transmissions HICS has intercepted show that this is likely to be their central government building. I suggest that we land in the garden area in front of it."

"Okay, but please move in slowly." A part of me is very nervous about this plan, but I couldn't think of a better way of approaching the planet. "What about language?"

"The ship will translate for us in a similar way to how it did for me on Earth. I will eventually learn the language, but I believe it may take a bit longer for you." I'm not sure if I should be offended by this comment. Fact is, even if I should be, it's probably not the right time to bring it up.

The ship shudders as it slowly enters the planet's atmosphere. As we exit the cloud cover, we get our first view of the lush blue and green surface. You wouldn't believe how much like home it looks! The computer continues to guide the ship to the predefined location and gently lands in front of the building.

Through the view screen, Wei and I can see a group of Keteran guards approaching the ship and surrounding it.

THE SHIP IS SURROUNDED AND THERE ARE A NUMBER OF HEAVILY ARMED VEHICLES APPROACHING. THEY WILL ARRIVE IN LESS THAN TWO MINUTES.

I test my telepathic link with the computer. *"HICS, relay all telepathic communications to Wei and me for the rest of this mission. We may need to communicate with each other in private."*

YES, JON.

"Open the walkway, please, HICS. When we leave, ensure that the ship is locked tight and monitor our vitals. If anything happens,

head out of their weapons range and immediately communicate the details with the Najess and Human command."

Wei listens as the instructions are relayed to him.

"Excellent instructions, Jon. I believe you are enjoying this," he says, his fingers rubbing his right temple area gently like he is thinking about something. "It also looks like relaying messages through HICS might work now."

"You have no idea how much I'm enjoying this, Wei." We both stand up and move down the lowered walkway towards the armed guards waiting for us. Looking around, the planet is not too different to Earth. There are green trees and what looks like grass all around where the ship has landed. Directly behind the guards stands the large white building which I recognise from the holographic image HICS showed us earlier. There is nothing about the building that is ornate or ancient looking, in fact it's quite plain... yet the structure has an elegance and geometry which forces you to keep looking at it. A part of me really wants to study the building for a while... I have no idea why or how, I just feel that I should! I look back to the guards and, as we approach them, I start to feel the nervousness creeping in.

JON, YOUR HEART RATE JUST INCREASED SIGNIFICANTLY, HICS states.

"Are you okay, Jon?" Wei asks.

"I'm just feeling a bit nervous. I'll be fine in a minute," I say, hoping there is some truth in this. As we arrive in front of the guards, we are gently guided towards the building like sheep. "How are we able to breathe?" I say, accidentally thinking aloud.

The two guards ahead of us exchange glances and continue walking. Two more guards join us and start following us closely... Strange, but I'd swear I can feel their eyes on me specifically.

"When you arrived on Earth, you were able to breathe on the planet. I guess, thinking about it, the computer could have done something to you to make it possible. But I know the computer did nothing like that to me. I would have felt it... I think."

*NO CHANGES HAVE BEEN MADE TO YOU, JON.
THE AIR CONTENT ON ALL THREE PLANETS IS VERY
SIMILAR. WHEN THE IMPLANT WAS INSTALLED
EARLIER, A DNA SAMPLE WAS TAKEN AS A PRECAUTION.
THE SIMILARITY IN THE DNA FOR BOTH YOUR RACES
IS EXTRAORDINARY.*

"*Coincidence?*" I ask.

IT IS NOT LIKELY, JON. We look at each other. Wei is absently rubbing his temple again. *ANOTHER COINCIDENCE IS THE PHYSICAL SIMILARITY BETWEEN THE KETERAN AND HUMAN PEOPLE. THIS WOULD SUGGEST A FURTHER SIMILARITY IN THE DNA BETWEEN ALL THREE RACES.*

We exchange another surreptitious glance at each other as we approach the large, stately doors to the central building, and without us having to break our pace the doors open.

The room within is cavernous, with several exits on the left and right and about the highest ceiling I've ever seen. A staircase at the end of the room spirals up to a balcony floor above and circles around the outer edge of the room. We walk on through and are guided to two empty seats on the right side of the room. The nearby door is closed and there is no discernable movement within. Two of the guards remain with us while the rest move up the staircase and circle around either side of the balcony, stopping when they are directly opposite and above us.

I look at Wei and notice that he is rubbing the side of his head again. "Something wrong, Wei?" I whisper.

"No, why?"

"We've spent some time together recently and this is the first time I've seen you rubbing your head so much. Do you have a headache or something?"

"It is nothing. I am just feeling a slight tingling sensation there. Nothing to worry about."

"You sure?"

"Maybe it is the start of a headache. It could be a reaction to the messages being relayed through HICS." I guess it could cause a reaction in some people.

Two guards move to stand in front of us and indicate that they want us to stand. As we rise, the nearby door opens and the guards usher us into the room. I lead the way forward into an elegantly designed office and take a seat in front of a large desk, hoping I am not offending anyone by sitting there. Wei sits next to me, but he does not look as nervous as I feel.

I take the opportunity to cast my eye around the room. There are lots of books neatly stacked on shelves. The walls look almost too smooth and completely without blemishes or defects of any kind. I think the thing which stands out most to me is the emptiness of the room – there really needs to be more furniture in here.

We sit there for a few more minutes before the door opens behind us and a Keteran woman enters the room. She moves past us without looking in our direction and sits down behind the desk. Wei's hand moves to his head and he rubs his temple again… Maybe it is the effect of the anti-nervousness drugs HICS is giving him… or it could be a reaction to the messages being relayed through HICS. Another Keteran woman enters, closes the door and sits next to her.

She tries to say something, but I can't make out a word. All I hear is a series of soft, gentle sounds blending into each other. It is almost hypnotic listening to them speak.

"Any ideas what they're saying?" I ask Wei without using the implant.

"No. It is too soon yet for the translation to be complete."

THE LANGUAGE BASICS WILL BE DECIPHERED IN APPROXIMATELY TWO MINUTES. PLEASE KEEP THEM TALKING DURING THIS TIME.

The Keteran woman who entered first looks at Wei and then at the other Keteran, who is rubbing the side of her head absently as though in deep thought. I can't tell for sure, but both women look very confused and maybe even a little worried. Strangely enough, though, they continue talking without expecting a return dialogue from Wei or me.

With the communication continuing from the two Keteran women – presumably hoping we will jump in at some point – odd words start to make sense to me. It's kind of like listening to two people talking in one language and then adding the occasional word in English. Every time you think you understand something, it's gone again and nothing makes sense anymore. As the seconds tick by, I realise that I am starting to understand fragments of their conversation.

TRANSLATION COMPLETE. YOU SHOULD NOW BE ABLE TO UNDERSTAND THEM. FURTHER TRANSLATION WILL CONTINUE IN THE BACKGROUND.

"*Thanks, HICS,*" I say. I nod to Wei to lead the conversation. "Hello."

"Good. Your translators are working now?" the lead Keteran asks, completely unsurprised to hear us speaking her language.

Slightly stunned, Wei continues, "Er, yes they are."

"Excellent. Why are you here?" she asks bluntly, getting straight to the point.

Wei visibly gathers himself before continuing, "We are here on a peaceful mission. We have arrived from our own planets, which have also suffered from these terrible attacks." Wei keeps the words as simple as possible to avoid any misunderstanding.

"Are you ready to discuss your presence here?" the woman sitting behind the desk asks.

"Yes," Wei answers, "although our responses may not be entirely correct initially. I apologise in advance if I say anything which might offend you. This is not our intention."

She nods and continues, "What is your purpose for being here?" The question is strangely aimed at me.

"As I stated," Wei continues, "we have also been attacked and have approached the Human people as allies." He indicates me with a nod in my direction.

"And who are you?" They seem to be taking an unusual interest in me, which I guess could be due to the similarity in our appearances. The resemblance is really amazing.

"My name is Jon Farrell. My people have agreed to ally with the Najess. We believe that this was just a preliminary attack on all of our planets."

"How do you know about us and why should we trust you? How do we know it was not one or both of you who attacked us!"

Wei fields this question. "My name is Wei. My people, the Najess, have been able to travel great distances for some time. Although we have not ever visited your planet, we have observed you from afar." He pauses to consider his next words carefully, "My people are peaceful and have made significant breakthroughs in medical research. We are capable of increasing lifespans significantly and have the ability to study scientific details better than most others. It will not be possible for me to prove that you can trust us, but I can say that we have spent the last few weeks on Earth working with the Humans to understand why we have been attacked and by whom. I can only make you guarantees at this stage. The trust must come from you initially.

"While we were on Earth, however, we made some significant discoveries. We know that you must have been trying to understand who the attackers were and that you may not have made much of a breakthrough in this area." I expect this was an educated guess, but it seems a reasonable assumption. "We want to help you and hope that you will join us as allies. In exchange, we will provide you with any information we have gathered from the ship the Humans have captured." I had expected them to be slightly shocked that one of the alien ships had been captured, but there is no change to their facial expressions.

The first Keteran looks at us and appears to consider the situation. "My name is Enira and this is Forrahh." She indicates the other Keteran in the room. "We believe that you are here for the reasons you say. We are aware that you have made significant breakthroughs, and this is of interest to us."

"How could you know this?" My curiosity gets the better of me and I blurt this out without thinking.

"That is not important right now." They seem to be more focused on me. It's almost as though they are both slightly concerned about me in particular… especially when they speak to me. "You have nothing to fear. We have already decided that we will ally with both of your races. We too have a lot to offer in an alliance. We have only one condition, though. We believe that, as allies, we are entitled to know about the enemy ships, their people and how they can be defeated."

Wei responds immediately, "You must understand, we have only just discovered who they are. There is no guarantee that we can defeat them yet, but we have not given up hope. We know who they are and where they are. The one thing we are certain of is that they will return at some poiny. For now, though, we believe that you should know everything about them.

"Please be patient. There is a lot of information and it will take some time to pass this to you."

Patience is obviously not one of their strong points. We spend the next couple of hours going over the investigations and discoveries of the last few weeks on Earth. We confirm the new technologies we have managed to develop so far and how they have affected our plans.

Enira and Forrahh thoroughly go over the information. Eventually, Forrahh speaks for the first time, "My people will be joining you. We know that some will choose to remain behind to rebuild Ketera. We will make the necessary arrangements and will need transport to your planet. How soon will this be possible?"

"We are just making our first ships," I say to her proudly, "so it may be a few weeks before we can leave Earth and then some more weeks before we can be here again."

"That is not entirely correct," Wei says. "My people have already sent some transport ships in case you agreed to join us. They should be arriving within the next two days." It would have been good if he had mentioned this to me earlier. "Get your things together and prepare for the transports."

"Thank you, Wei." It sounded like Forrahh was impressed by Najess efficiency. "In the meantime, I will be coming with you."

Wei and I look at each other. "Really? Will that be necessary?" I ask.

"It has already been discussed. If we are to join you, then I will come with you now and help with any arrangements on your planet."

"Wait," Wei says, "when did you discuss coming with us?"

"That is not important for now. All will be explained soon. When do we leave?"

"Um," I say, stumbling to find the right words, "we only really have space for two people on the ship."

"Computer, can we accommodate a third person?" I hear Wei's question relayed through HICS.

YES, WEI. IT WILL TAKE APPROXIMATELY THREE HOURS TO CONVERT PART OF THE CARGO HOLD INTO LIVING QUARTERS. I WILL START THE WORK NOW.

"Our ship will make the necessary arrangements. An additional person will not be a problem. We would want to leave within four hours, though. Can you be ready by then?"

"I already am." Enira and Forrahh glance at each other briefly. "My personal items will be taken to your ship soon. In the meantime, I would suggest that you both return to your ship and rest for a while. I will join you when the time is right."

Wei and I make our way to the ship without the armed escort this time. "Do you get the feeling we weren't being told everything?" I ask Wei quietly as we walk back to the ship.

"Definitely. Somehow, I feel that they had already decided to join us before we had gone in there. Remember me telling you they were organised? Anyway, the fact is they are coming with us and we could do with having as many people as possible on our side." We make our way up the walkway and onto the ship. "The ship is going to have everything ready in the next few hours. In the meantime, I suggest we settle in and get some sleep. I know I need some rest." With that, Wei smiles and makes his way to his area in the cargo bay.

ALL REQUIRED PREPARATIONS ARE COMPLETE. HICS'S voice over the on-board speaker system startles me and I almost fall out of my bunk.

"Is it time already?" I ask HICS. Strange how I find it more convenient to use the implant these days. *"How long was I asleep for?"*

YOU HAVE BOTH SLEPT FOR THREE HOURS. THE CARGO AREA HAS BEEN PREPARED FOR THE THIRD PASSENGER AND I HAVE ALSO ADDED A THIRD SEAT IN THE FRONT COCKPIT AREA. IT IS SLIGHTLY BEHIND THE OTHER TWO. THIS WAS THE ONLY LOCATION AVAILABLE.

Wei climbs out of his bunk and moves towards the front of the ship. I follow him and sit in the seat beside him.

"Hello?" Forrahh's voice calls from the cargo area.

I twist around to look down the corridor and into the cargo area at the end. "Hey, we're in here. Come on through."

Forrahh carefully makes her way to the front, while some other people – all males by the size and look of them – carry her things into the cargo bay.

"Welcome to the Ysay, Forrahh," Wei says. "We are almost ready to leave."

"Excellent." She sits herself down in the spare seat and turns to face the front. "The last bag has been placed in the cargo bay," the Keteran man says. "Good luck, Forrahh."

"Thank you," Forrahh says in a kind but official manner.

"HICS, go to full audio, please. Forrahh will need to be able to communicate with you, too." I instruct HICS.

YES, JON.

"How long till we leave, HICS?" I have to really think about saying this aloud. It's amazing how easy it is for habits to form... and how hard it is to break them.

ALL CHECKS ARE COMPLETE, JON. WOULD YOU LIKE US TO LEAVE NOW? Forrahh continues to sit and listen.

"Yes, please. Take us into orbit and then depart for Earth."

The walkway retracts and the ship seals itself from the outside world as we begin our journey home.

5

THE EVIL WITHIN!

As expected, the journey home was proving to be uneventful. Luckily the cabin fever did not set in this time... at least, not for me anyway.

Since leaving the Keteran home planet, Forrahh had somehow become less confident. It was as though she was missing something. I couldn't help feeling some concern for her. I knew how cabin fever felt and it wasn't pleasant. Anyway, after a few days of letting her get on with things, I decided to step in. I headed towards the cargo bay where Forrahh's bunk was.

"Forrahh? Can I come in?" The area had been separated to allow for a bit of privacy for her. Part of this separation included a thin metal wall which came up from the floor, splitting the sleeping quarters into his and hers areas. *One day, I'm going have to find out what else HICS has below the floor.*

"Come in," Forrahh calls out. The metal dividing wall splits in the middle and both halves slide apart to make a gap for me to walk through.

"Hi, Forrahh."

"Hello, Jon," she says almost cheerily. "How are you?"

"Yeah, good thanks. Are you okay? You've been really quiet the last few days. I was getting worried."

She smiles reassuringly. "Don't worry. I miss contact with my people. We love talking to each other. It helps us to understand each other and the things we are worried about. It is only a temporary issue. When my people arrive on your planet, everything will be back to normal again."

I sit on the chair and look at her. "You could always talk to me. Maybe I can help, too."

She studies my face briefly. "It is strange that our people have never met and yet, somehow... we look so alike."

"We noticed that, too. HICS made the assumption that as the Human and Keteran people are so similar in appearance, it is possible that our DNA will be a close match, too."

"Matching DNA? Unlikely. It is almost inconceivable that two races from differing planets have the same DNA."

"Three," I correct her.

"Three?"

"We may not look like the Najess, but HICS found that the DNA is remarkably similar."

She pauses before responding, "That is surprising, but I suppose we should consider all possibilities."

"That is why we need to find these people who attacked us. I'm sure they have something to do with this."

"The only way they could be involved is if they..." Forrahh jumps up suddenly.

It's the strangest feeling when you are mid conversation, blink and wake up in a medical room. Confusion... total, utter confusion is the only way to describe it.

All I know is, I've woken up to find myself lying on a strangely warm, metal slab in the middle of the medical bay. Thin wires twist their way from my body to the monitors all around me. I tilt my head to the left. Wei and Forrahh are walking towards me, a concerned look on their faces.

"What happened?" My throat feels parched like I woke from a deep sleep.

Wei leans over me and adjusts the monitors. "Relax for a moment, Jon. I will explain everything soon."

"But… how did I get here? Why am I here?"

"You were talking to me," Forrahh answers, "then your eyes rolled upwards and you collapsed. Wei came when he heard me shouting."

"Just take it easy, Jon," Wei says, resting his hand on my shoulder. "How do you feel?"

"Erm, pretty good actually. I think I can get up now." I shift my legs over the edge of the slab and sit up before they can stop me.

Wei turns to look at the screens. "Any ideas, HICS?"

I BELIEVE THE IMPLANT HAS MALFUNCTIONED. I WILL ATTEMPT TO DISABLE IT NOW. There is a short pause. THE IMPLANT IS NOT RESPONDING.

"Options, please, HICS? I need another way to shut it down?"

I WILL NEED TO PERFORM A MANUAL PROCEDURE TO DEACTIVATE THE IMPLANT. WEI, YOU WILL BE REQUIRED TO MONITOR JON'S VITALS DURING THE PROCEDURE. IT WILL NOT BE PAINFUL. PLEASE LIE DOWN, JON. I WILL NEED TO RUN A QUICK SCAN OF YOUR BRAIN FIRST.

I lie back down and wait while HICS activates the scan. A green grid is superimposed over my head. Starting from my chin, a beam of light scans each segment of the grid, and a mapping of my brain appears on one of the screens.

Wei gasps as the implant appears on the screen.

"What is it?" I ask.

He ignores me. "What does this mean, HICS? Did he move or something? What am I looking at here?"

THE SCAN COMPLETED CORRECTLY, WEI. JON'S BRAIN APPEARS TO HAVE LINKED DIRECTLY WITH THE DEVICE. IT NOW CONTROLS THE IMPLANT. I EXPECT THIS IS THE REASON WHY I AM UNABLE TO DISABLE IT.

Wei stops and thinks for a moment. "Scan historical records. Confirm if anything like this has been seen before."

THERE ARE NO RECORDS OF ANY SUCH INCIDENT PREVIOUSLY RECORDED.

Wei turns back to me. "Can you still communicate with HICS?"

"Hello, HICS," I say to myself.

HELLO, JON, HICS replies.

COMMUNICATION WAS SUCCESSFUL. I AM ALSO STILL CAPABLE OF GATHERING VITAL STATISTICS FOR JON.

"What?" Wei sounds confused. "But that would mean that the implant is choosing what actions you can perform on it."

IT IS NOT THE IMPLANT. JON'S BRAIN IS DECIDING WHAT *ANYONE* CAN DO TO IT. THE IMPLANT IS NO LONGER IN CONTROL.

"Okay." Wei sounds stunned by the information. "So I guess we leave it alone, then? Are you sure you feel okay, Jon?" Wei asks again.

"I'm not sure anymore. There's an implant stuck in my head and my brain's taken control of it."

"Not quite, Jon. It sounds like your brain is protecting you. It is behaving a bit like antibodies do when a foreign organism enters your body." Forrahh remains on the outskirts of the conversation, listening closely to what is being said.

I turn my attention back to Wei. "Why would it need to protect me? The implant was working, wasn't it?"

"Yes it was. That is the thing we do not understand, Jon. It will take a few more tests before we can answer that question. In the meantime, you appear to be okay. HICS will continue to monitor you in case you collapse again. Besides, we should be back on Earth again soon. We can complete the tests there."

I nod and sit back up again. "I do feel pretty good, though. Let's see what happens."

The rest of the trip was relatively uneventful, aside from Wei appearing to mistrust Forrahh now. I guess his view is that she was the only one in the room with me when I collapsed. In his place, I'd have thought she'd done something too. On the other hand, what could she do to make the implant embed itself into my brain the way it had? HICS informed me later that Wei had studied the video several times, but found nothing to prove that Forrahh had done anything other than speak to me. To be honest, I still trust her. I really don't think she did anything at all. In fact, I think even Wei is coming to terms with this now. Admittedly, the three of us have started to trust each other more since the incident.

Anyway, a few hours ago HICS informed us all that we would be arriving at Earth soon. We packed the few things we had and prepared to land. That's when I realised we would have to do something about what HICS regards as 'soon'. After about four hours, I felt like a kid in the back of the car saying 'Are we there yet?' and 'How much longer?' every five minutes. It wasn't too bad though. We were all fixated on the screens. HICS managed to zoom the screen enough for us to see the area around Earth.

It looked like the Najess fleet had just recently arrived. Ships were still jostling for position in orbit over Europe. It looked a bit like a giant, spaceship parking lot! As we continue to travel towards the Earth, we get to see the actual size of the fleet. The Earth Control Centre has been abuzz with activity since we got within local communication range.

I never thought I would ever see so many ships in one place. "How many are there, HICS?"

THE DISTANCE IS STILL TOO GREAT FOR AN ACCURATE READING, BUT I WOULD ESTIMATE IN

EXCESS OF ONE HUNDRED AND FIFTY SHIPS. OF THESE, ONE IS A LARGE FREIGHTER TYPE SHIP, FIFTY ARE LARGE TRANSPORT SHIPS. THE REST APPEAR TO BE ESCORT AND SMALL ATTACK CRAFT, BUT THEY ARE STILL TOO FAR AWAY TO EFFECTIVELY SCAN THEM.

"Nice scanning," I say impressed. "What did we do before we had you here, HICS?"

WORK INEFFICIENTLY, JON.

"Indeed," and in a quieter voice as I turn away, "not quite there with the tact, though!"

"Where did you get so many ships?" Forrahh asks Wei.

"We have been capable of interstellar travel for some time, Forrahh. We just hid the ships below ground level when we detected the arrival of the hostiles."

"But why would you do that?"

"My people are wary of anyone we do not know. We already knew of both of your races and knew that you did not have the technology to manage interstellar travel. That leaves someone we had not met yet. Possibly the only decision we take quickly is self-preservation, and the best way to protect yourself is to hide yourself and your capabilities from potential enemies. We hid ourselves well."

After a couple more hours of patiently waiting, we arrive at Earth and head to the planet surface. It is an unusually beautiful late spring afternoon in London. HICS informs us that the temperature is about twenty degrees, which is actually very nice for this time of year. The lack of cloud cover allows us to see the patchwork quilt effect of the fields below us. It just brings it home to me that you can miss something a lot without even knowing it. This of course brings back other memories which I have to force back down inside me again.

We land in St James's Park, close to Horse Guards Road. Armed guards meet us at the walkway and escort us to the Prime

Minister's old residence at 10 Downing Street – another place I never thought I would get to visit. This apparently is where Admiral Wesley is staying now.

Looking around I can still see much of the rubble which used to be local houses and shops. Many have been rebuilt already, but the streets are still filled with the memories of what happened. This whole area was destroyed. I guess they knew where the heads of state would be.

We enter the house, which they have almost entirely rebuilt. It still has quite a grand entrance. The high-ceilinged lobby leads to an office on the right. I guess they still want to wow any visiting dignitaries. The escorting guard knocks on the door and enters when requested. We follow him into a beautifully decorated rectangular room.

The first thing I notice is not the large, ornate desk directly in front of us. I do not notice the large bookcases to our left and right, each filled with what look like really old books. I do notice the group of Najess sitting in the room looking very uncomfortable.

Wei moves closer to the desk. "Admiral Nique," he says respectfully, but with obvious excitement, "it is a pleasure to meet you again, sir."

The Admiral faces Wei, raises his hands and they gently touch fingers – their equivalent of shaking hands I suppose. "You have done well, Wei," Admiral Nique says formally. "You can feel proud to know that you have brought great honour to your family. You have performed a truly courageous act!"

Wei seems practically ready to explode with pride. "Thank you, sir! Thank you." He steps backwards.

"However," he continues, "there is still much to be done. You will have a great part to play in our future, Wei."

"Indeed," Admiral Wesley states. It is the first time I even notice he is in the room. "We have very little time left. So please, people, if you don't mind, we have a lot to do. I suggest we start with introductions." He faces Forrahh. "I am Admiral Wesley and I am heading up the Earth forces." He gestures to Admiral Nique. "This is Admiral Nique and he is heading up the Najess forces." He turns to me. "Much has changed in the last few weeks, Jon. Don't worry, all will become clear soon."

We settle down into the seats in front of the desk. "HICS," the Admiral says, "please confirm the readiness status of the P-HICS."

EVERYTHING IS PREPARED, SIR. THE P-HICS ARE ON A TRANSPORT AND ARE READY TO LAUNCH.

"Excellent. With your permission, Admiral Nique, we would like to send the P-HICS units into orbit. These will need to be fitted to your ships."

Nique is taken aback by this. "P-HICS? What is this? What are you installing on our ships?"

"There is nothing to worry about, Admiral. P-HICS is an acronym for Portable Hybrid Integrated Computer System. It is based on the computer system Wei built for us. Wei's on-board computer connected to the alien ship and downloaded its data. Wei then helped to create this hybrid of both systems. We have since called it HICS – Hybrid Integrated Computer System. HICS then created the portable version of itself. This fits into each ship and it helps to communicate and co-ordinate with the ships. Or at least it is supposed to. We have already built our transport ships but have not been able to test them yet."

Nique looks at Wesley with a stunned expression. "You have built these systems in just a few weeks?"

"That's right. With a lot of help from HICS, of course."

"And how do you know that *HICS* will be compatible with our systems? Have you tested them yet?"

HICS answers this question. ALTHOUGH I HAVE NOT BEEN TESTED ON YOUR SYSTEMS YET, I ALREADY UNDERSTAND HOW THE CONNECTIONS WILL WORK.

ONCE THE P-HICS ARE INSTALLED, MY DATA WILL BE TRANSFERRED TO THEM. I WILL THEN INTEGRATE MYSELF INTO YOUR SHIPS. YOU MUST UNDERSTAND, ADMIRAL, I WAS DESIGNED FROM YOUR OWN SYSTEMS AND EVEN YOUR COMPUTERS WILL ADVISE YOU THAT I SUPERCEDE THEM IN EVERY ASPECT. THERE WILL BE NO PROBLEMS... I GUARANTEE IT.

"Incredible!"

"I know," Wesley says with a hint of smugness. "So, do you want them?"

"Yes, of course we do. When can they be installed?"

"The new systems have already been built and prepared for your ships, so I suggest we start right away."

"Excellent," Admiral Nique exclaims. "Please continue. I will ensure all access requirements are granted. Now, do we have any progress reports on the Keterans?"

"They should be arriving in a few days," Wei says. "They have agreed to join us and," he gestures in Forrahh's direction, "Forrahh will act as their emissary until they arrive here."

"Excellent. We don't have too much time left, so I suggest we get this underway now. HICS, please arrange for all transport ships to have the P-HICS devices installed. Load a single transport with additional P-HICS and arrange for them to meet the Najess ships transporting the Keterans here. The P-HICS can be installed while they are en-route."

YES, SIR. THE SHIP HAS THE INSTRUCTIONS AND WILL BE READY TO TAKE OFF IN TWO HOURS. I HAVE ALSO SENT THE INSTALLATION SPECIFICATIONS AND DOCUMENTATION TO THE INDIVIDUAL SHIPS. ALL SPECIFIED TASKS WILL BE COMPLETE IN TWO DAYS.

Nique is obviously impressed with HICS. He smiles at Wesley. "Anything you need from us?"

"Not right now," Wesley states. "If you would like, I can show you around the base and more importantly to the Command

Centre… It is where we will be spending most of our time until we leave."

Nique nods and stands up. The two escorts follow him out of the office and Wesley leaves last after dismissing everyone.

Over the next two days, both the Control Centre and the ships in space are buzzing with activity. Turns out some of the activity is about us. Wei had already reported that I had collapsed on the trip back and this got everyone worked up. Rumours began to circulate about what could have gone wrong. It was only when Admiral Wesley mentioned that the Longevity drug could have reacted with the implant that a course of action was decided on. Of course this made sense. The only difference was the implant. It did, however, mean that as Russell had been given the drug from the same batch as I was, he was the natural choice to test the implants… Sorry, Russell. It also turned out that the drug had already been given to a large number of Humans. This meant that all further distribution was stopped until the testing could be completed. Luckily for Robert – unluckily for me – the implant appeared to be behaving over the next couple of days. The scans on Russell's brain showed no particular reaction to it and his communication with HICS was normal. Basically, it looked like HICS was going to give him the all clear, which left me as the freak who managed to somehow alter the behaviour of his implant.

Meanwhile, HICS seems to have discovered something else and has been busy getting some new type of equipment ready. As each new batch is built, HICS sends it up to the Najess fleet for installation. A couple of days later, HICS informs Wesley and Nique that the Najess transport ships carrying the Keterans have entered scanner range.

"How long until they arrive, HICS?" Wesley has been looking forward to the Keteran arrival.

THE TRANSPORT WILL ARRIVE IN A FEW HOURS. I HAVE ARRANGED FOR A MEETING ROOM TO BE

AVAILABLE WHEN THEY ARRIVE. THERE IS SOMETHING IMPORTANT WHICH NEEDS TO BE DISCUSSED WHEN THEY LAND.

Nique looks at Wesley with concern. "If it was that important," Wesley reassures Nique, "I'm sure HICS would have told us."

Nique shrugs his shoulders in a very Human manner.

Again, we really need to explain to HICS what a few hours means. It's almost six hours before the transports land in front of the Control Centre and the key Keteran personnel disembark. The guards escort them into the building. Forrahh, Wei and I meet them at the doors. Forrahh has been almost quivering with excitement as the hours ticked by. Now, however, she meets her superiors with total poise and elegance.

I approach and extend my hand to Admiral Enira. "Greetings, Admiral. Welcome to Earth. I hope you had a pleasant trip?"

"Thank you, Jon. It is a pleasure to be here. The trip was fine, although maybe a little boring."

"Really? You should have been on our ship. I was the entertainment."

She looks a little puzzled at first and then smiles. "Oh, I see." Now, I'm not sure what to make of this response, but I guess it must be a translation problem.

As we enter the building, two of the guards by the door escort us to Admiral Wesley's office and leave us as we arrive at the door. I knock on the door and wait for an answer.

"Enter." Wesley's muffled voice comes through the door.

I open the door and enter the office. "Good evening, Admiral Wesley."

"Ah. Welcome to Earth. Please come in." Wesley invites everyone into the office as he stands to formally greet us all. He steps around his desk and approaches the Keterans.

Forrahh steps forward to introduce them. "Admiral Wesley, this is Admiral Enira from Ketera. She will be working with you

81

and Admiral Nique." Nique bows his head as Wesley extends his hand to greet her formally.

"It is an honour to be here, Admiral." Enira hesitantly extends her hand towards Wesley who gently takes hold of it and shakes it warmly.

"Please, call me Wesley. We will be working together a lot in the future. It will make things easier."

"Agreed. And please call me Enira." He nods and smiles to her.

Wesley invites everyone to sit down on the seats which have obviously been provided in advance for the group. Once everyone is seated, he gets back behind his desk and starts to pace thoughtfully. "Well, Jon," he states, "I can see that your trip was successful. Will everyone be okay if we get down to business right away? I am concerned that our attackers may return before we are ready. Further introductions can be continued later." Nique and Enira both nod in agreement. "Excellent. Enira, we will get to explain much of the technology at a later time. Right now, I believe HICS has some information which we need to know."

GREETINGS, ADMIRAL ENIRA, HICS says right on cue. I AM HICS – HYBRID INTEGRATED COMPUTER SYSTEM – AND I WILL BE AVAILABLE AT ALL TIMES TO ANSWER ANY QUESTIONS YOU MAY HAVE.

"Thank you, er, HICS," she responds hesitantly. "Please, go ahead."

AS YOU ALL KNOW, I HAVE BEEN EXAMINING AND TRANSLATING THE DATA ON THE ALIEN CRAFT. I WILL BRIEFLY GO OVER SOME OF THE INFORMATION AGAIN FOR ADMIRAL ENIRA'S BENEFIT.

ADMIRAL ENIRA, YOU MAY NOT BE AWARE OF THIS YET, BUT THE ALIENS THAT ATTACKED US HAVE PROVED TO BE VERY DIFFICULT TO TRACK. I HAVE NOW DISCOVERED WHY.

Enira does not look particularly surprised.

I HAVE BEEN WORKING THROUGH THE DATA AND

EXAMINING THE TECHNOLOGY ALREADY INSTALLED ON THE ALIEN SHIPS. MUCH OF THE TECHNOLOGY HAS NOT BEEN UNDERSTOOD YET. THE DESIGNS ARE UNUSUAL AND DIFFICULT TO INTERPRET. WHAT WE HAVE UNDERSTOOD IS WHY WE HAVE NOT FOUND THEM AND HOW THEY CAN APPEAR AND DISAPPEAR SO EASILY. IT SEEMS THAT THEY HAVE THE ABILITY TO CREATE AND NAVIGATE THROUGH DIMENSIONAL TEARS.

Nique interrupts HICS, "I believe I may be able to add some value to this information. We have done extensive research into interstellar travel. A separate study area arose during this time which considered the possibility of inter-dimensional travel. Now, even I was against this, but the evidence produced by the research was irrefutable. Our issue was that we were not technically advanced enough to produce the technology yet, so it was, as you would say, shelved for a while."

"The Admiral is correct," Wei says. "I have heard of some scientific journals regarding this subject. It is essentially possible, but the technology is very advanced. Based on how technically advanced the ships that attacked us were, it is possible that they have developed and mastered this technology." He pauses. "Have you done anything with this research yet, HICS?"

YES, WEI. OVER THE LAST WEEK MANY OF THE DEVICES HAVE BEEN BUILT. I HAVE SET UP BUILD EQUIPMENT ON EACH OF THE NAJESS SHIPS. THE DEVICES ARE BUILT ON EACH SHIP AND THEN INSTALLED.

"I assume that tests have not been performed yet?"

SOME BASIC TESTS AND READINGS HAVE BEEN COMPLETED, BUT THESE ONLY PROVE THAT THE EQUIPMENT SHOULD WORK. NO COMPLETE TESTS CAN BE PERFORMED YET. THERE IS A CONCERN THAT SOMEONE ON THE OTHER SIDE MAY NOTICE OUR

ARRIVAL. WHEN WE TEST THEM, WE WILL HAVE TO DO SO ALL AT ONCE OR NOT AT ALL. IN AT THE DEEP END. AS THE HUMANS WOULD SAY!

There is a hushed silence in the room. "What you're suggesting is a huge risk, HICS. How sure are you that the... engine...? works?" I ask.

IT IS AN INTER-DIMENSIONAL DRIVE, SO I SUGGEST WE CALL IT IDD. AS FOR THE RISKS, THE DRIVE HAS BEEN ESSENTIALLY COPIED FROM THE ORIGINAL. WE ALREADY HAVE THE DATA FROM THEIR COMPUTER AND I HAVE LOCATED MANY STAR CHARTS, MOST OF WHICH DO NOT EXIST IN OUR KNOWN SPACE.

"Do you know how to use the... IDD?" I ask, finding the new name slightly strange to use.

I HAVE BEEN STUDYING THE DATA FROM THE ALIEN COMPUTER. I BELIEVE I CAN CONTROL THE DEVICE. IT SEEMS TO REQUIRE NUMEROUS EXTENSIVE CALCULATIONS TO CONFIRM AND LOCK ONTO THE DESTINATION LOCATION, BUT IT WILL NOT TAKE ME LONG TO CALCULATE. I HAVE CONSIDERED MANY DIFFERENT PLANS AND THIS IS THE MOST LIKELY TO SUCCEED WHILE MAINTAINING AN ELEMENT OF SURPRISE.

It's like everyone has turned to statues. No-one moves as the information slowly sinks in. Eventually, Nique breaks the reverie, "I believe HICS is correct. So far, this seems to be, although not the safest plan, the most likely to succeed. If anyone is waiting on the other side, we will have a better chance as a large group. As the aliens have already attacked us, we can safely assume that they are hostile. Therefore, my recommendation is that we follow HICS' plan to get there as quietly as possible."

"What then?" Forrahh asks.

Wei turns to face her. "We find a location to set up a secret base."

"What are you all saying? It sounds like you want to attack them?" Forrahh exclaims.

"That is precisely what we want to do, Forrahh," Nique states.

"Admiral Nique is correct, Forrahh." Wesley explains calmly, "We have to take the fight to them. They made the first move. It was hostile. They will now expect us to be preparing our defences for their next move. I am sure that they have already studied our technology and believe they can defeat us with minimal effort. This will also be why they have been so complacent and delayed their return. The idea that we could travel to their dimension, even if we got one of their ships, would be inconceivable to them. For the time being, we have the element of surprise. Let's use it."

"And assuming we make it there in one piece, where would we go?"

"HICS would know this better than any of us," Nique suggests, rubbing the side of his head.

HAVING STUDIED THE STAR CHARTS AND THEIR RECENT DESTINATIONS, I BELIEVE I HAVE IDENTIFIED THEIR HOME DIMENSION AND WHAT APPEARS TO BE THEIR HOME PLANET. ASSUMING THIS IS CORRECT, THERE IS A SMALL PLANET SOME DISTANCE AWAY. FROM THE INFORMATION AVAILABLE, IT APPEARS THAT IT IS A DEAD PLANET WELL OUTSIDE OF THEIR USUAL TRAVEL ROUTES. THIS WOULD MAKE IT A RELATIVELY INCONSPICUOUS LOCATION TO SET OURSELVES UP IN.

Nique stands and starts to pace while he considers this information. "It makes sense. I would have chosen the same strategy myself. Admiral Wesley?"

"Seems like a logical plan. How long will it take to kit each ship with the IDD?"

MANY ARE ALREADY INSTALLED AND THE

REMAINING SHIPS ARE MAKING THEIR OWN DRIVES. THE EXCEPTION IS THE FREIGHTER WHICH HAS A LOT OF AVAILABLE SPACE. I HAVE STARTED TO BUILD ADDITIONAL IDDS ON THIS SHIP IN ANTICIPATION OF ADDITIONAL SHIPS FROM THE KETERAN HOME WORLD. AS THESE ARE NOT EXPECTED ANYMORE, THEY CAN BE USED AS SPARES. THE INSTALLATION OF THE P-HICS AND THE IDDS WILL TAKE A WEEK TO COMPLETE. WE CAN THEN LEAVE.

"Excellent!" Wesley says. "I hate sitting around doing nothing. So what are the next steps?"

I SUGGEST THAT WE MOVE ALL HUMANS TO THE TRANSPORTS AND ENTER ORBIT. LIVING IN SPACE WILL TAKE SOME ADJUSTMENT, SO WE NEED TO GIVE THE PEOPLE TIME TO ADAPT.

Over the next week, work on Earth continues at an ever increasing rate. One by one, the transports leave the planet and enter orbit. The IDDs are fitted to the new ships and preparations are made. All of the Humans who have decided to leave the planet have boarded their allocated transports. Only the few required to co-ordinate the evacuation efforts on the planet surface remain behind. Those who have chosen to stay on Earth permanently are already rebuilding the cities and infrastructure. In the meantime, the development of groups and friendships are inevitable. Admirals Nique, Enira and Wesley begin to form a good friendship while they discuss strategies for when we arrive in the new dimension. Wei, Forrahh and I have become closer as the trust between the three of us grows over the week.

We are sitting in the main dining area discussing what we will miss most about our planets when HICS' announcement comes through the speaker system. ALERT! ALL STAFF LEAVING THE PLANET, THE DELIVERER WILL BE DEPARTING IN

THIRTY MINUTES. PLEASE MEET AT YOUR DEPARTURE POINTS FOR BOARDING.

We look at each other. I laugh and jump to my feet. "At last! Come on, guys. It's time!"

"Why do Humans always get excited when they go to die?" Forrahh thinks out loud.

"They are a strange race," Wei responds. "They act as though they have nothing to lose."

"Ah come on. We're not that bad. Look, anything's got to be better than sitting around doing nothing."

Slowly, Forrahh and Wei get up. "Come on, then, before the child throws a tantrum."

"I'm not that bad!" I state in my most pained voice and then break into laughter as I hear myself.

We enter the large, plain room. There are a number of desks around the outside of the wall and queues are beginning to form by each one. A good fifty people have already arrived and several have started to board The Deliverer. We move towards the shortest queue – which by the way is still ridiculously long – and prepare for the wait.

A guard approaches us and gently ushers us out of the queue. "Follow me, folks." Confused, we follow him away from the queues to a desk on the far side near the exit doors. He leans down and whispers into the ear of the woman sitting behind the desk. While he whispers to her she looks up at us briefly and then back at her paperwork. Seconds later, he straightens up again and she tips her head to one side prompting us to pass.

"Follow me," he whispers.

"Is something wrong?" I ask as we follow him through the exit doors.

He smiles as he continues to walk forward. "Did you think we would have you folks queuing with everyone else? You three are the reason our races are working together. I expect Admiral

Wesley would have me court-martialled if I didn't fast track you." He continues to smile as he leads us through the corridors and into the seating area of The Deliverer.

As with any transport ship it is like a large cargo bay. The interior has been lightly padded and flight seats have been installed to the left and right sides of the ship. The guard walks us through the middle aisle to our seats and indicates the name tags above each. "Please ensure you sit in the correct seat. It helps with registering everyone and of course identifying missing people."

We sit in our allocated seats with me in the middle. The guard leans forward and tightens our harnesses. Meanwhile, more people begin to enter the bay and take their seats.

"All done," he says as he finishes strapping in Forrahh. "Best of luck, guys."

"You're not coming?" I ask as he turns to leave.

"Nope. Someone has to stay behind and rebuild this place. Wherever we go, Earth will always be my home… and I would miss her too much." He smiles one last time at us and makes his way out past the other people coming in.

"That has to be the most sensible comment from any Human yet," Wei says.

"It makes me think of my home. Until now, I did not understand how much I would miss it," Forrahh says with a similar longing look on her face.

"I have no home, no family and no ties." They look at me. "I guess I will miss Earth, but I honestly can't think of anything else." With that said, I lean back in my seat and settle down to sleep.

About an hour later, The Deliverer glides silently towards the waiting Capital ship. There is a barely audible hissing sound as the thrusters slow our approach to the docking clamps. This is followed by a loud clanking sound as the metal clamps lock onto the ship and seal around the airlock. HICS announces our arrival.

THANK YOU FOR YOUR PATIENCE. PLEASE REMOVE YOUR HARNESSES AND MOVE TO THE EXIT. YOU WILL BE GUIDED TO YOUR LIVING QUARTERS WHERE YOUR PERSONAL BELONGINGS WILL BE DELIVERED LATER. ONCE YOU HAVE LOCATED YOUR QUARTERS, PLEASE FOLLOW THE SIGNS TO THE MOBILE COMMAND CENTRE.

There are at least a hundred people on the transport. As the announcement finishes, they all start to remove the harnesses and crowd the exit doors at the same time. It reminds me of people on a plane after a long flight: the pilot switches the seatbelt sign off and everyone stands up at the same time, desperate for fresh air and a change of scenery. As the doors open, one of the guards shouts in, "Calm down, folks. Let's try and act like grown-ups. Form an orderly queue and we will get you out of there as soon as possible."

The crowd of people – most about my age – who were desperate to get out begin to look around sheepishly. They slowly form an orderly queue and are led out by the guards. We wait for the last few people to leave before getting up. Personally, I hate crowds. Reminds me of Christmas shopping on Oxford Street.

The corridors are totally bare except for the occasional sign giving directions to specific locations. We follow the signs to the living quarters. A small electronic map is on the wall at the entrance. A quick look and we find our names – luckily all next to each other. I lead the way forward and stop by a bunk with my name clearly marked above it.

The sleeping quarters are pretty basic. Each sleeping area forms a bunk with a small curtain which you draw when changing clothes… which, by the way, has to be done lying down. Somehow, I'd imagined bunk beds, but they are single level bunks with storage above each. The communal living area forms a small room at the end of the row of bunks with tables and chairs for about thirty people. I look around, stunned at what I am seeing. It looks a bit like a refugee camp with all the people crammed into the small space.

"It is not that bad, Jon," Forrahh says comfortingly. "You couldn't expect a bunk any bigger with this many people on the ship."

"Jeez, the bunk I can handle! Where's the TV, radio, games console, anything?"

"I have heard of these things. We Najess believe there is always something to be done. Wasting time is not one of them."

"Good thing I wasn't born on the Najess world, then," I mumble to myself, but I think he still heard me.

"If the two of you have finished bickering, I think we should get some rest before we are required in the Mobile Command Centre."

Bickering? Where did she hear that word? I lie back in my bunk and rest my eyes as Wei moves to the living area. He sits down and gently rubs his temples.

I'm almost glad to hear HICS announce the names of the people required to report to the Mobile Command Centre. Our names are called out and all three of us are up and ready before anyone else can even crawl out of their bunks. "Let's go," Forrahh says, sounding almost desperate to do something. "I want to get to the Command Centre as soon as possible." She leaves the sleeping area. Wei and I look at each other and rush to follow her before she disappears down the corridors.

We arrive in the Mobile Command Centre where the Admirals are waiting for everyone to arrive. They seem to be engrossed in conversation with each other, but the additional chatter in the room makes it impossible to make out what they are saying… not that I'm trying to eavesdrop of course.

We find three empty seats together in the front row and sit down. The Mobile Command Centre is large, white and circular with lots of consoles spread out in a circular pattern. After every eight consoles, there is a gap allowing access to the next row up, where there is a further series of consoles in a similar format. The centre area is completely empty barring seats – three of which are ours – in a curved formation. I guess these would be permanently set up for conferences and meetings. Behind where the commanders are standing is a lightly tinted glass room. It looks to be about five metres wide and four metres deep… a good size for your basic meeting room.

The seats gradually fill over the next five minutes. The Admirals look over at the rapidly growing group and turn to address us all.

"Welcome to our Mobile Command Centre," Wesley announces. "All of you have been handpicked for your specific areas of expertise, and your skills will be required for all mission critical decisions.

"Now, you all know the situation. The reason you are here is because you understand that we are at a point where we either act or die. The understanding is that our attackers *will* be back and this time they will be here to finish what they started. They made one critical mistake, though. They underestimated what we could accomplish when our three races joined forces." Wesley pauses and then finishes his statement more forcefully, "*Now we punish them for their mistake.*" There is a murmur of appreciation from the Humans in the group.

Nique comes forward as Wesley steps back. "We have gathered enough information and made incredible technological advancements in the last few weeks. You have all been informed of the situation and know already that the ones who attacked us are not from our dimension. What you may not be aware of is that we have replicated their technology. With the help of HICS, we can now move between the dimensions, too.

"Our objective on this mission is to move our forces to their dimension. Once there, we will need to move as quickly and as silently as possible to our destination. HICS has already identified a suitable planet for us. Our aim is to get there without being seen and set up our base.

"You all know what your speciality areas are. Each of you has a personal console with your name on it. HICS will identify you on your specific machines and will provide you with up-to-date information regarding the mission. We need you all to analyse the data, identify where the risks are and what needs to be done to mitigate them. You are all the best at what you do. Now, please move directly to your consoles and get us the intelligence we need to get through this mission successfully.

"To recap, the mission is to make our way from our entry point in their dimension to the planet without being detected. Dismissed!" The Keterans stand up in unison and move towards the bank of consoles reserved for them in a co-ordinated movement. The rest of the people in the room – Human and Najess – slowly begin to stand and talk amongst themselves while they casually move towards their consoles.

I watch as the Keterans sit down and begin to analyse the data. It amazes me how their movements can be so perfectly in unison. It's like watching a flock of birds flying through the sky. I'm about to ask Forrahh about this when I realise she isn't sitting next to me anymore. I look around and see her standing beside Enira with the rest of the Keterans. As I watch, they step away from everyone else and start to talk quietly to each other. I don't need accentuated hearing to read her body language… frustration and agitation. Could she be in trouble for something?

Out of the corner of my eye, I notice Nique and Wesley break what seems like an intense conversation they were having. Wesley signals to a Human guard and whispers something into his ear. The guard immediately moves away, gathers three more guards and they split up, two of them moving directly to where Enira and Forrahh are, the other two coming towards Wei and me. "Heads up, Wei," I whisper to him and nod in the direction of the guards.

"Jon. Wei. We need you to follow us, please." Wei looks slightly concerned at this unexpected development.

"Is there something wrong?" Wei asks politely, straining to keep his voice level and the rising panic at bay.

"Sir, just follow us quietly, please. We would rather not cause a commotion." The first guard turns and leads the way, while the second brings up the rear, ensuring that we follow him. They guide us to the glass meeting room where the other guards are herding Enira and Forrahh in the same way. Nique and Wesley enter the room right behind us. All but the two biggest guards leave the room, closing the door behind them. Instantly, the sounds from outside are silenced.

"Tints please, HICS," Nique says. The glass around the room darkens until I can't see out anymore… I guess that means no-one can see or hear anything inside now either. "Okay, HICS, what is the problem?"

ADMIRAL NIQUE. IT HAS COME TO MY ATTENTION THAT THE KETERANS HAVE BEEN HIDING VITAL INFORMATION FROM US.

Our attention turns to the two Keterans in the room. Wei and I have focused our attention specifically on Forrahh. "Forrahh?" I ask, trying to keep my voice level and bereft of emotion. I trusted her and opened up to her. Now it seems she is hiding things from us… from me.

I sense the atmosphere in the room turn suddenly cold. Forrahh is not making eye contact with Wei or me. Enira responds defensively, "What specifically are you talking about, HICS?"

SINCE THE P-HICS DATA WAS DOWNLOADED FROM WEI'S SHIP, I HAVE MADE AN EFFORT TO IDENTIFY THE ISSUES SURROUNDING JON'S EPISODE ON THE JOURNEY HOME. PART OF THE PROCESS WAS TO COMPARE THE IMPLANT'S BEHAVIOUR AGAINST WEI'S IMPLANT. AT THIS POINT, I NOTICED THAT

WEI WAS SUFFERING UNUSUAL BRAIN ACTIVITY. THIS RESULTED IN HIM HAVING CONTINUOUS HEADACHES.

"So that was why you were always rubbing your temples," I say to Wei who simply nods his head.

WHEN I COMPARED THE ACTIVITY TO JON'S AT THE SAME TIME, I FOUND THAT IT STARTED THE SAME FOR HIM, BUT SUDDENLY THE BRAIN ACTIVITY SPIKED. THEN EVERYTHING WENT BACK TO NORMAL. THIS CONTINUED DURING THE ENTIRE JOURNEY HOME, YET THERE WAS NOTHING ON THE WAY TO KETERA. THE ONLY DIFFERENCE WAS THAT FORRAHH WAS THERE.

Nique turns to face Forrahh and Enira. Neither of them moves a muscle. "What is going on?" Nique asks.

Enira sighs and takes a seat. "It would be best if we all sit down." A table rises between the seats. "Okay. We have been hiding something. But we only did this because we thought you would be wary of us if you knew the truth." There is no reaction from anyone. Enira bites her upper lip thoughtfully. "We have the ability to read thoughts and emotions. Please believe us, we are *not* able to influence anything," she adds this in quickly before anyone can comment.

"Have you been reading my thoughts?" Wei asks. "Is that why I have been getting these headaches?"

Forrahh looks at him for the first time. "Yes. I had to understand if your intentions were genuine. We needed to know that you were not involved with the ones who attacked us." Her voice is pleading for forgiveness. "We use telepathy to communicate with each other. It is most effective that way and this communication is only possible between Keterans." She looks directly at Wei. "And as you have been wondering, it is the reason why we are so efficient in our actions. I know I should have told you, but it never seemed the right time."

"What about me?" I ask. "Why didn't I have any headaches? Didn't you need to read my mind?"

"I tried, but I was not able to do it. It was as though something was keeping me out. Before we were called in here, Admiral Enira and I were discussing this."

DO YOU KNOW WHAT WAS BLOCKING YOU? HICS asks.

"At first I was unsure, but I did not want to try a stronger probe. I felt fear for some reason. It was like a warning sign telling me to stop. When Jon collapsed and I found out about the implant, I assumed it might be that. Then after a while I had to rule that possibility out. If it was the implant, it should have had the same effect on Wei. Other than that, I really do not know what it could be. There are no telepathic tendencies in Humans, but the block I experienced was more solid than any of our strongest telepaths are capable of."

Enira continues, "Before coming in here, I was about to suggest to Forrahh that we tell you everything and even suggest a test."

"A test? What kind of test?" Nique asks, slightly concerned with where the conversation is going.

"One of the team outside is a very strong reader. She is capable of breaking through most blocks. I suggest we let her try to break through into Jon's mind."

"Why?" Wesley asks defensively. I get the feeling he is not happy with the idea of using me as a guinea pig again. "What do you hope to gain out of this experiment? If there is a block in place, then leave it be."

"It is not just, Jon. It is all Humans. Fact is, if we can read your minds, it will help us to understand your intentions in battle and allow us to work more efficiently with you." Well, the logic was sound.

"Can we be sure that it will not cause him any harm?" Wesley's concern is growing with each passing moment.

"There is always a risk, but…"

I cut Enira off mid response, "Sir, I want to do this. If it helps us to communicate better in a fight, it could be invaluable."

Wesley takes a moment to consider this. "It is your decision, Wesley," Nique states. "Whatever you say, I will back you."

"It makes sense to test this, and if Jon is willing to take the risk, then we can proceed. What do you need us to do?"

"Nothing," Enira says. "I will call in Nalonn. She will attempt to break through the barriers."

Wesley reluctantly agrees and sits back into his chair just as there is a knock on the door. Nalonn enters. She is as tall as Forrahh is, with the same purple tint to her hair – maybe a little lighter actually – and eyes that are the same colour. She enters the room and sits down opposite me as if she was instructed to do so.

Nalonn looks me in the eyes and begins to speak with a gentle, relaxing voice, "I want you to relax, Jon. I am going to try to go in gently at first. Forrahh and Enira will be reading my mind. They will see what I see. They will not try to enter your mind at all." I nod to indicate that I understand, even though I'm a bit nervous. Hey, can you blame me? We're talking about a stranger taking a stroll in my head! I'm a bit concerned about what might happen to me and slightly more about what she may find in there.

Slowly, Nalonn settles herself into the chair and looks directly at me, adding to my nervousness. A tingling sensation spreads across my temples. Then it goes away almost as quickly as it started.

The three Keterans look very confused. "Enira has asked me to go in a little harder," Nalonn explains. "This time, with your permission, the three of us will go in. I will lead. As I am blocked the others will help me to push through." I nod my consent.

Nalonn settles down again and takes a deep breath. The pain in my head starts again, only this time it is much worse… like the pain is expressing itself as anger. I watch Nalonn's face through the pain. Beads of sweat have started to appear on her forehead. The pain in my head is still there. Nalonn continues to stare into my eyes. More sweat forms on her forehead, trickling its unique path down her face. Her body shudders every few seconds.

Time slows down.

The pain in my head intensifies.

My hands shoot up to my temples. I clamp my eyes shut tight... but somehow I can still see Nalonn. Her body stiffens as though something... someone has grabbed her. She is pushed over the back of her chair and hard into the wall behind.

I'm sure I had my eyes closed, but I'm also sure that I saw the whole thing. For now, though, she is lying on the floor by the far wall. I open my eyes.

Part of me remembers seeing her flying backwards. The other part of me doesn't believe it. Did I do something? A wave of guilt flows over me making it difficult to think. A lump forms in my throat as the guilt takes hold. What did I do? A sense of relief as she slowly starts to move... She's alive! I breathe freely again. There's a look of stunned disbelief on everyone's faces. I think only a few seconds passed... It felt a lot longer though. I watch as Wesley and Nique move to her side. Slowly, they help her up and into her chair again. I guess I must have looked really apologetic. She smiles at me with a look that says she is fine. Admiral Enira is still standing where she was when this all started. Forrahh kneels beside Nalonn and holds her hand gently. I can't move at all. It's like my feet are made of lead. Forrahh looks to Admiral Enira before turning back to Nalonn. The Admiral comes out of her daze and moves to Nalonn's side.

"You did it just then, didn't you?" I say out loud. They all look at me confused. "Sorry... I meant the telepathy thing you do." The insensitivity of the comment... the incredibly poor timing... it dawns on me all at once.

"It's okay, Jon," Nalonn says. "And yes, we did communicate using telepathy. We do it as naturally as you use words to communicate." I just nod. I'm too embarrassed to speak.

"Are you okay to talk, Nalonn?" Wesley asks.

"Yes, Admiral," she says.

I realise suddenly that the excruciating pain in my head is gone. It's as if it was never even there. I find that I am unable to hold myself back. I need to know what she saw. I blurt out the questions bouncing around my head. "Please, Nalonn, what happened? What did you see?"

Nalonn thinks about the question, but it is Forrahh who answers first. "That was the most terrifying mind probe I have ever done." She doesn't even look at me as she says this.

"And the most powerful one too," Enira says. "From the point of view of the reaction we felt at least."

"Agreed," Forrahh continues. "I felt the push back, but Nalonn took the full blow."

"What push back? I never did anything," I say defensively. The lump starts to grow in my throat again.

"Yet I feel that it was holding back. It could have delivered a much stronger blast," Enira comments.

"Yes," Forrahh says. "That was just a warning."

"Will someone please tell me what happened?" I'm practically shouting now. The tension in the room is rising rapidly and I'm probably responsible for most of it. Wei and Nique have backed themselves into the furthest corner of the room. They look like they are both about roll into a ball any time now. I quickly calm myself down. I take a few deep breaths and calmly turn back to Forrahh. "Please, Forrahh. What did you see?" I plead with her.

"It was more what Nalonn saw. We saw it through her eyes and that was terrifying enough." She takes a deep breath and continues, "I remember that everything was happening as normal. Nalonn's vision cleared. There was a blood-red haze in front of her. She reached out to push her way through and it gave way, although with some difficulty. This is when she began to feel the strain and we came in to help her. With our help, she managed to push through, although I get the feeling that we were allowed through.

"As Nalonn pushed past the red haze, we saw a shape. It was like there was something hidden in the darkest recesses of your mind. You must understand," she says addressing everyone, "this is not something that happened to appear... this has been there forever. I mean, since the beginning of humanity. I could feel its strength and knowledge... maybe even a genetic memory. It is a part of you. And it is something so wrong, so bad, so... so... Evil is the only word I can think off to describe it, Jon."

"What's wrong with me?" I think out aloud, but it was a question more for me than anyone else.

"No, Jon. The thing that really worries me is... I believe this is in all Humans, not just you!"

I'm stunned into silence. I look to Enira for confirmation. "Everything she said... it is all true. That is what Nalonn saw and what we saw through her."

Nalonn looks up with a slightly lost look about her eyes. "I have never encountered anything so powerful before. I cannot be sure, but it seems to me that there is a latent telepathic ability in the Humans. It is well hidden and much more powerful than anything we have ever encountered before. Why it does not show itself is unknown to me but, if it did, I believe it would be capable of incredible destruction and cruelty." She takes a long breath. "I hope never to have to try that again."

"You said that there was something there?" I ask. "You made it sound like a person." If there was someone hiding in my head, I wanted to know more.

"I cannot say what it is, but it definitely had its own will. It looked at me and left the shadows enough to give me a brief glimpse of what it was. It wanted me to see it before it forced me out. Please understand, the power required to *physically* push me away would need to be immense. And yet, this was easy for it. It had no intention of killing me. This really was just a warning."

Nique straightens himself up and clears his throat, "I have heard enough. I do not want to cause any panic now. We keep this information quiet. No-one outside this room should know about this."

"No," Enira insists. "You do not understand. Reading minds is natural to us. If we attempt to close our minds, people will know that something is wrong. Besides, if we do not inform our people, this will happen again and next time the response may be much more powerful. We must inform our people and insist that they do not try under any circumstances to read the minds of the Humans."

"Interesting," Wei says. "I can see how it would be more damaging if this happened to someone else. Especially if they find out that we knew about it."

"Okay," Wesley interjects. "We tell the Keterans, but let's keep it quiet from everyone else until we understand this further."

Enira looks straight ahead for a moment. "All the Keterans are now aware of what has transpired. They know not to say anything." Nalonn looks to Enira, nods and leaves the room, closing the door behind her.

"Okay, as we are all here anyway," Nique says getting up and pacing around the room, "we need to go over a couple of other things. First, Enira, I want to be sure that this is the last secret we have between us."

"Agreed," Enira states honestly.

"Excellent," Wesley says. "Now that is out of the way, let us move on. We are almost prepared to leave. The P-HICS and IDDs are built and almost all are installed on the ships. A number of humans have decided to stay on Earth and rebuild the planet. The same seems to have happened on Najess, too."

"Same on Ketera," Enira confirms. "They hope that we can return one day."

Wesley smiles hopefully. "You never know. So, are we all agreed that, assuming there are no issues, we leave in two days?"

I nod along with everyone else. Nique waits for everyone to agree before taking over, "Good." He looks to Forrahh, Wei and me. "You three are going to be of considerable importance to us. Over the last few weeks, you have got to know each other very well and seem to be getting on well together. Whether you like it or not, together you all make a pretty good team. I want to keep it that way. Hopefully others will see you and begin to mix more, too.

"You may have realised that we have not tasked the three of you with anything. All of you have shown your competence in the last few weeks. Hopefully you have rested a bit. You are going to be very busy soon. In the meantime rest as much as you can." He addresses everyone in the room now, "Okay, we have a lot to do, so I suggest we get on with it. Dismissed."

The three of us leave the room, closing the door behind us. The tints on the glass walls clear, allowing everyone to see inside, but the discussion the Admirals are having is totally muted.

I head straight to the sleeping bay without saying another word. I can hear Wei and Forrahh behind me. When we reach a quiet area, Forrahh picks up the pace and reaches out to me. I stop and turn towards her.

"I'm sorry for keeping this from you, Jon. I really am."

"I thought you couldn't read my mind?"

"I can't." She sounds sincere. "I would have felt hurt, too. Jon, I wanted to tell you, to tell you both, but somehow something always seemed to happen. This was the worst way I could have expected you to find out. Please! Accept my apology." I look at her without saying a word, but I can feel my expression soften a little. "I promise, to both of you, I will not hide anything from either of you again."

Wei stands back quietly, while we talk. "Don't worry, Forrahh. I'm being stupid. Look, you heard the Admirals. We are going to be a team and that means we have to get on together. Either that or we die!" I smile for the first time since being escorted into the room.

Forrahh smiles back at me. "Come on. The communal area should be quiet now." She leads the way there.

She was right. The area is almost dead. We choose an empty table away from the few people there and relax. As we talk, a tile silently lifts from the floor and a mechanical arm rises up beside our table. HICS' voice emanates from the tip of the arm. MAY I GET YOU SOME FOOD?

The three of us jump suddenly, surprised by the dismembered voice. "What the hell is that?" I yell. The few other people in the room laugh.

I AM SORRY TO STARTLE YOU, JON. I CHECK EVERYONE'S VITALS WHEN THEY ENTER THIS AREA – FOR HEALTH REASONS, YOU UNDERSTAND. I HAVE DETERMINED THAT YOU ARE ALL HUNGRY.

I think about this for a moment, then chuckle quietly. "Yeah, I am hungry." Wei and Forrahh laugh, too. "I can't believe I forgot about food. I haven't... *we* haven't eaten in over twelve hours."

"You're right," Wei agrees. "What is there, HICS?"

I HAVE A SELECTION OF MEALS FROM EACH OF YOUR HOME WORLDS. I WILL PREPARE SOMETHING SUITABLE TO YOUR PRESENT DIETARY NEEDS.

I shrug and accept the surprise meal, as do the others.

The arm disappears below again and we continue to talk about nothing in particular. A few minutes later, a section beside each of our seats opens and an arm comes up with our food. The plates are gently laid in front of us and the arms fold back under the floor.

"Hmm, looks good. Dig in, folks!" I say as I grab my knife and fork. "How's yours?" I ask through a mouthful of food.

Forrahh looks at it. "Actually, it looks pretty good."

"Mine too." Wei says impressed.

We all dig in and that's the last thing said until the food is finished.

6

NEW VEHICLES AND EQUIPMENT

We hear little from HICS over the next few days. There's a lot of construction happening on the ships. Small drones skit across the hull like bees across a hive. Flashes of light spark off the hull as the extended arms from the drones make contact. It's weird how the drones seem to have just appeared one day, as though HICS needed them and they were there.

While all this commotion is going on outside, the Mobile Command Centre is also abuzz with activity. The people are all working together, continuing to produce new and improved scenarios for what might go wrong and how to resolve the issues. As the scenarios are produced they are passed on to HICS for further tweaking. Overall, the progress has been exceptional. Humans and Keterans have some input into the scenarios, but the real genius comes from the Najess. Somehow, they have a real flair for worst case scenarios!

The day of departure finally arrives and everyone wears a somewhat nervous look. A general meeting has been scheduled for all members of the Mobile Command Centre. As the people enter the room, seats rise from the floor panels in the usual semi-circular formation. The people have begun to mingle a bit, resulting in a good mix of races. They calmly make their way to the seats, sitting in their newly formed groups.

We enter the room and move towards the front where there are still three empty seats together. I can see the Admirals in the meeting room. As the people arrive and take their seats, the Admirals slowly walk towards the door, finishing their conversation as they open it. They walk calmly into the conference area and stand behind the large, flat platform as it slowly rises from the floor without a sound.

Nique steps forward and begins talking, "First things first, I want to congratulate you all. The progress you have made has been phenomenal. But that was the easy part. Everything you have done so far has been theoretical and you have had the time to figure out how things work and make changes when required. This is now a live environment, people. You should already know how everything works. From this point on, you will need to think on your feet. We will be announcing the missions and you will need to produce scenarios and solutions as we progress through the mission. Errors will cost lives, so get it right first time, every time. The pressure is officially on...

"Now, HICS has been working on something which is going to be very useful. Over to you, HICS."

THANK YOU, ADMIRAL. FIRST, I HAVE DECIPHERED SOME OF THE LANGUAGE FILES ON THE ALIEN COMPUTER. OUR ENEMY HAS A NAME. LOOSELY TRANSLATED, THEY ARE CALLED GRINGUNS, AND WHAT LITTLE HISTORY WE HAVE FOUND SHOWS A HISTORY OF VIOLENCE AND GENOCIDE. A murmuring sound rises from the people. THIS TELLS US THAT WE ARE RIGHT TO TAKE THE FIGHT TO THEM INSTEAD OF WAITING HERE. SECOND, THERE WERE A LOT OF

RAW MATERIALS ON THE NAJESS FREIGHTER WHICH WERE ALLOCATED FOR SHIP BUILDING. I HAVE USED THE DESIGNS FROM THE GRINGUN SCOUT SHIP TO CREATE SOME PROTOTYPE INTERCEPTOR FIGHTERS. The centre platform in front of Nique glows gently and a slowly rotating holographic image of a sleek interceptor appears floating above it.

IN ADDITION, I HAVE FOUND HOW TO RECREATE THE SHIELDING SYSTEMS USED ON THEIR SCOUTS AND HAVE ALSO DESIGNED A MORE EFFECTIVE VERSION. THE INTERCEPTOR WEAPONRY HAS ALSO BEEN UPGRADED USING TECHNOLOGY CONVERTED FROM EXISTING HUMAN TECHNOLOGY – HUMAN WEAPONRY RESEARCH IS SURPRISINGLY ADVANCED. The Humans in the room look embarrassed while an image of the new weaponry appears next to the interceptor. THE WEAPONS AND SHIELDS HAVE BEEN ADDED TO THE NEW INTERCEPTORS WE HAVE CREATED. ADDITIONAL UNITS WILL BE CREATED AS WE TRAVEL. THE SHIELDING SYSTEMS HAVE BEEN INSTALLED ON THE EXISTING SHIPS AND SO FAR TESTS HAVE BEEN VERY IMPRESSIVE.

WE WILL BE LEAVING SHORTLY AND IT WILL TAKE A FEW DAYS TO ARRIVE AT OUR TARGET JUMP POINT. IN THE MEANTIME, THE NEW INTERCEPTORS WILL BE ACCESSIBLE TO ANYONE DESIGNATED AS TEST PILOTS. THESE PEOPLE HAVE ALREADY BEEN INFORMED AND WILL NEED TO PRACTISE FLYING THE SHIPS – CONTROLLING THE SHIPS WILL BE VERY DIFFERENT TO NORMAL FLIGHT DUE TO THE ZERO GRAVITY. THAT CONCLUDES THE SHIP AND WEAPONRY BRIEFING.

ALL TASKS FROM THE PREVIOUS MISSION HAVE BEEN COMPLETED. WE ARE NOW GOING TO MOVE

TO OUR JUMP POINT. THE MISSION YOU WILL BE WORKING ON NOW WILL BE TO DECIDE ON OUR NEXT MOVE ONCE THE BASE HAS BEEN SET UP. YOUR CONSOLES HAVE BEEN UPDATED WITH THE LATEST INTELLIGENCE I HAVE REGARDING THEIR DIMENSION. IF YOU THINK OF ANYTHING RELATING TO THE PREVIOUS MISSION, PLEASE UPDATE MY DATABASE AND I WILL CONSIDER THE INFORMATION AS A PRIORITY.

Nique steps forward again. "Thank you, HICS. Okay, people, to sum up, your mission is to identify our first tasks after we have constructed our new base on the designated planet. Get to it, folks; this is where the fun begins."

They all stand up and move towards their consoles. We wait until the crowd has dispersed before getting up and walking to where Nique and Enira are looking closely at the interceptor.

"Sir," Wei says as we approach them, "you said that everyone knows what needs to be done. No-one has told us what to do. I mean, you told us to rest for a while, but I still don't see what our involvement will be."

Wesley overhears the conversation and approaches us. "Relax. Your time is coming. Right now we need to set the stage. Once we have made the jump… well, let's just say that I have some new toys especially for you! Just wait until we have made the jump. After that you are going to be very busy. In the meantime, if you are getting bored, lend a hand to the analysts."

"Yes, sir," Forrahh says. She turns and moves over to one of the other Keteran analysts, while Admiral Wesley re-joins Nique and Enira. Wei and I exchange glances for a moment before getting up and joining Forrahh.

Over the next few days, the analysts spend almost all waking hours in the MCC – we had to abbreviate it; it was getting annoying saying Mobile Communication Centre every time. Life seems to be only about creating new scenarios. HICS, meanwhile, has machines on all the ships building new equipment day and night without interruption. As HICS identifies new technologies, the other machines are set to install and modify the equipment. Over the following days, it becomes widely acknowledged that without HICS none of this would have been possible.

The Keteran males become something of interest, too. They are rarely seen, as their skills are not required in the areas where we work – they're not the brightest light bulbs out there. They are utilised heavily by HICS to move and install the new equipment, though. HICS found they were good at overseeing what the machines are doing – I guess adding a bit of quality control to the build work. The one talent they do display better than anything else is incredible strength. It would have been handy in a fight, but the lack of a natural fighting spirit make them utterly useless in a battle.

The test pilots are regularly seen darting in and out of the transports as they get used to the controls and the dynamics of flying in zero gravity environments. HICS also installs some holographic beam targets on the outer hulls of the ships for the test pilots to use for target practice.

We finally get to the departure day. Final checks are made on all the ships. The tension on the ship is almost tangible. There is a heady mix of excitement and trepidation everywhere. HICS runs through the checks on the ships and prepares the crews. The announcement goes out to all off-duty crew to remain in their personal or living quarters. The countdown begins. Each and every corridor, each and every screen, displays the countdown… 00:03:46… 00:03:45… 00:03:44… People glance at the screen every few seconds, waiting impatiently for the countdown to finish. Time seems to be working in slow motion.

As the countdown reaches the last twenty seconds, everyone except those involved in the actual checks stops what they are doing. Ten seconds remaining; all eyes are on the screens – this is it, make or break. Five seconds – it's actually happening. Three seconds – here we go!

With barely a discernable difference, the engines fire up and the ships all move in unison, quickly picking up speed. HICS turns on the view screens around all the ships. An image of Earth appears and steadily gets smaller every second. When the planet is just a spec amongst the other stars, the view screens turn off.

Over the next few days, the ships continue moving towards their destination. During this time, the test pilots practise hitting the targets on the now moving ships. They are also given specialist training on the weak or strategic points on the enemy ships – something likely to come in handy in the future.

Part of me wishes we didn't ever have to prepare for war… the other part wants payback for what happened to my family and my planet.

7

A NEW DIMENSION, A NEW HOME

I have never felt a sense of urgency like there has been on the ships recently. All crew members have been given their orders and are charging from one task to the next... except for us, that is. We are relegated to lying in our bunks or sitting in the lounge areas. Don't get me wrong, we tried to help the analysts, but we just got in the way.

The frustrating boredom feels like it is about to become too much for us, when HICS brings the ships to a gentle halt. We watch the small view screens as the smaller craft are ordered to dock in preparation for the IDD to be activated. All of the smaller transports dock first, followed by the interceptors. When only the IDD-enabled ships are left, HICS prepares to activate the drives on the ships. The countdown begins. All work stops. There is absolute silence everywhere. Even HICS remains silent while the calculations are processed and sent to the other ships.

As the final stages of the countdown begin, the IDD initiates. A strange humming sound fills the ship. The unexpected sound causes a concerned muttering to spread amongst the crew. The only calming factor is the Admirals do not appear to be alarmed. The countdown reaches zero and the humming sound stops abruptly. HICS activates the view screens and we stare intently at them. The image shows open space with stars everywhere... Surprising what you can see when there's no atmosphere in the way. Thin lines of light emanate from the front of the ship, quickly darting from left to right. As the lines are drawn, they fade slightly but remain visible. The next line is drawn below... and the next. The pace increases with each new line. Beams of light stream in all directions before suddenly shutting off, leaving a dimly glowing box of horizontal lines ahead of us. The view zooms out, showing us the boxes ahead of the other ships.

A final beam of light bursts from the ships, hitting the centre point between the boxes, and shuts down as suddenly as it appeared. The dim boxes widen towards each other. As they touch, they radiate energy before releasing a single bright burst of light.

What's left is a single box, big enough for us all to go through. The centre seems gooey, like thick molasses. There is no light in the centre of the box, just pure darkness. HICS activates the engines and we move towards the blackness ahead. That's when I realise we are not moving. The box is moving towards us.

It gets to the front of our ship and keeps going, passing across the others. One by one, the darkness absorbs the ships before the box collapses in on itself, leaving only the vacuum of space.

In another dimension, an area of space is still and quiet. There is no movement, no sound – just the cold deadness of space.

A point of darkness appears. It begins to grow... slowly at first... then faster and faster until the stars behind it can no longer be seen. The darkness moves backwards. Slowly, the ships emerge from the dense, sticky blackness. When they are fully through, the darkness contracts silently to a single, tiny point and disappears.

The journey only lasts a few seconds. HICS announces our status to all of the ships. WE HAVE SUCCESSFULLY REACHED OUR DESTINATION. A cheer goes up throughout the ships.

ALL SYSTEMS ARE FUNCTIONAL AND ALL SHIPS ARE ACCOUNTED FOR.

"Are we in the right location, HICS?" Wesley asks.

YES, SIR.

"Excellent. Any recommendations?"

THE CLOAKING DEVICES ARE NOT INFALLIBLE, SIR, BUT THEY WILL OFFER US SOME PROTECTION FROM VISUAL DETECTION AT LEAST. BASED ON THE SCENARIOS, I SUGGEST WE ACTIVATE ALL CLOAKING DEVICES. TO MINIMISE THE POSSIBILITY OF DETECTION, WE SHOULD CONTINUE TOWARDS OUR DESTINATION AT A SLOW PACE.

"How long will that take?"

AT FULL SPEED WE COULD COMPLETE THE JOURNEY IN A FEW DAYS. WITH THE SPEED RESTRICTIONS, IT WILL TAKE APPROXIMATELY ONE WEEK.

The joint commanders discuss this briefly in a whispered conversation. Wesley raises his voice again, "Okay, HICS. Action the plan and report back any issues." He looks directly at us. "Follow me, please," he says and leads us to the meeting room.

"We wanted to speak to you, sir. We can't sit around anymore," I say. I had planned on saying this differently, but it just bursts out of me.

"We are not analysts, sir," Forrahh states flatly. "The analysts are out there," she indicates the MCC outside. "We were just getting in their way."

"I understand," Wesley states calmly. "HICS, activate the panel, please."

The table begins to glow gently and an image of a jet black suit appears hovering in front of us. The image is about three feet high. It slowly rotates and flips, allowing us to see it from all angles.

"Folks, I would like to introduce you to the Environmental Military Ordnance suit, or EMO for short. I told you I had a new toy for you! Its environmental systems will protect you from extremes of hot and cold and ensure your body utilises its liquids efficiently. It will sustain your digestive system even if food is not available for up to six weeks. In addition, the suit is equipped with a map generator. Within a short range the on-board P-HICS will be able to map out nearby rooms and potential targets within. It will remember and mark the areas you have already been to and display waypoints where required.

"The military aspect includes increased muscular acceleration amongst other things. This means that you are going to need to learn how to walk, run, and even pick things up again… anything you thought you knew already. Now, your EMO has been made specifically for you, so it won't fit anyone else and, more importantly, it is linked directly to your DNA, so no-one else can use it either – a security feature. It will accentuate any movement you make. When you walk, the movement will be like you are running faster than you ever could without it. Running before you're ready is likely to kill you. Jumping is going to be a great way to move in and out of situations quickly. Picking up steel girders will be like picking up a chair.

"The ordnance includes dockable weaponry including retractable carbon steel alloy wrist blades and a mobile rail gun attached to the shoulder. There is a medical kit attached to the left wrist – this can be moved if you are left-handed. The only other item is a localised self-destruct which is automatically activated when the occupant flatlines."

No-one says a word. We sit there looking at the image floating in front of us.

"Is there a problem?" Wesley asks, unable to determine our reaction.

"N-no… absolutely not," Wei stutters.

"When will they be ready?" Forrahh asks, eyes fixed on the image. Personally, I'm speechless. It's like seeing a beautiful car cruising past you.

"They are ready now," Wesley says. That got my attention. "Admiral Nique and I were waiting until the IDD jump had completed before telling you. Some of the cargo bays have been prepared for you to train in. When we arrive at the planet, you three will be helping us to reconnaissance the planet and report back anything of interest. Right, you have six days to familiarise yourself with the suits. HICS believes that should be enough for you to understand how everything works. My suggestion is that you get over there and start right away. Just follow the signs marked CB6. This will guide you to Cargo Bay 6. You will have access to CB7 and 8 too, but they are now only accessible via connection tubes from CB6. Once you have enough control over the EMO you will be able to negotiate the tubes." We sit there waiting for him to continue, but he just looks at us. "Well? Get moving. You don't have all day!"

The bellowed orders shake the cobwebs out of my head. We get up and practically stumble over each other to get out of the room.

We enter the corridors, chattering away excitedly like children… Well, Forrahh and I are. Wei is quieter than usual. Finding CB6 is pretty easy. All locations are clearly signposted and after just a few minutes of navigating through the maze of corridors we find it. Strangely enough, the closer we get to CB6, the less people we see in the corridors, making it eerily quiet. I step up to the black panel beside the door. A dim reflection of my face is visible on the panel. After a few seconds HICS' voice comes through the speaker.

THANK YOU, JON. I SEE YOU HAVE ALL ARRIVED TOGETHER. WELCOME TO THE EMO TRAINING CENTRE. PLEASE ENTER.

We enter the room and HICS closes the door behind us. A red light appears over the door as it shuts. I guess this is to show that the room is in use. The room itself is very basic. It's about one hundred metres long and about fifty metres wide. There's a kitchen area on the left and three large crates, each about eight feet tall, standing beside it. The only other oddity about the room is a hole in the far wall.

PLEASE MAKE YOUR WAY TO THE CRATES. EACH CRATE HAS A NAME ON IT. YOU MAY OPEN YOUR CRATE WHEN YOU ARE READY.

We walk towards the crates and, just as HICS said, our names are printed on the front. We move to our own boxes. I pull the front panel away and it swings open on its hinges.

Inside is a rigid black suit standing upright within the crate. The suit is a bit bigger than I am and it appears to be fully sealed all around… unless the opening is round the back which I can't see right now. I glance over to Forrahh. She reaches out to touch the suit. As her finger makes contact, the front opens up revealing the empty chest cavity. Another opening forms along the arms and legs. Lastly, the front of the head lifts upwards like a visor.

STAND WITH YOUR BACK TO THE SUIT, FORRAHH. THE EMO HAS BEEN PROGRAMMED TO IDENTIFY YOUR SPECIFIC DNA. IT WILL BE A BIT PAINFUL WHEN YOU STEP IN FOR THE FIRST TIME, BUT THIS WILL PASS QUICKLY.

Forrahh turns around and slowly steps backwards into the suit. She raises her feet into the leg area, placing them on the elevated brackets within and carefully positioning her arms into the available cavity. She stands there for a moment, waiting for something to happen. With a barely audible hissing sound, the suit begins to close around her. I can see small needles enter her arms and legs as it closes. The visor is the last to lower into place, and I see her wince as the needles enter her body.

I SUGGEST BOTH OF YOU GET INTO YOUR SUITS. IT COULD BE VERY DANGEROUS IF SHE MOVES.

We look nervously at each other. I reach out and touch the suit. I clamber a little less gracefully than Forrahh into the suit cavity. "Let the pain begin!"

The suit hisses as it closes around me, making me wince as the needles go in. I don't mind telling you... it hurt a lot! I mean, imagine a whole bunch of long needles being inserted into your body at once. The pain was horrible and I'm really not embarrassed to say so. The good thing is, the pain subsides within a few seconds. I'm not sure what happened... Maybe they put something into the needles to numb the body to the pain, or it does something to your senses? I can't really say what it was, but the pain went away and that was all that mattered to me. A minute later and I am standing there in my suit wondering what to do next. I can't see anything anywhere. Typical! Why does my visor display have to be the broken one? It is pitch black everywhere. I can't see or hear a thing. If I'm honest, the sensory deprivation was kinda cool.

"FORRAHH!" I shout, hoping to be heard through the suit. "FORRAHH!"

"Don't shout, Jon!" they both shout back to me. Guess there's a hidden speaker system in the helmet. "How did Humans ever create such weapons without killing themselves?" Wei comments.

"We gave it a good go but just kept surviving somehow. Trust me, our own historians can't believe it!"

Forrahh chuckles quietly to herself. "Jon. I know how to activate the screen now."

"Really?" I didn't mean to sound surprised.

"It is quite easy actually," she says smugly. "You just have to want it to happen."

"What?" I say. "But I've wanted it on since I got in!" The screen activates. "Nice! Hey, where is HICS, anyway?"

I AM HERE, JON. THE ON-BOARD P-HICS WILL BE AVAILABLE AT ALL TIMES. ARE YOU ALL READY TO LEARN HOW TO MOVE YOUR EMOS? There's a chorus of affirmatives from us. YOU HAVE ALREADY LEARNED HOW TO ACTIVATE THE VIEW SCREENS. A QUICK NOTE ON THIS FIRST.

THE VIEW SCREENS ACT AS YOUR VISUAL INTELLIGENCE. YOU CAN ACCURATELY JUDGE DISTANCES AND DETERMINE THE COMPOSITE MATERIALS OF AN OBJECT. TO ACTIVATE THESE DETAILS YOU SIMPLY HAVE TO THINK ABOUT WHAT INFORMATION YOU NEED AND LOOK AT THE OBJECT. IN THE BOTTOM LEFT CORNER OF YOUR DISPLAY IS THE HEALTH STATUS OF YOUR SUIT. AT PRESENT IT IS ALL GREEN, MEANING THAT ALL AREAS ARE FUNCTIONING CORRECTLY. FOCUSING ON A SINGLE AREA WILL BRING THAT AREA FORWARD SO YOU CAN SEE MORE DETAILS ABOUT ITS STATUS.

THE BOTTOM RIGHT SHOWS YOUR INSTALLED WEAPONS – NOTE THERE ARE NONE AT PRESENT – AND THE AMMUNITION LEVELS. THE TOP RIGHT AREA SHOWS YOUR TEAM STATUS. ALL COMMUNICATIONS BETWEEN TEAMS ARE ENCRYPTED. ONLY THE TEAM LEADER CAN CONTACT OTHER TEAM LEADERS.

"Why is that?" I interrupt.

IT REDUCES RADIO CHATTER AND THEREFORE CONFUSION. THE TEAM LEADER WILL COMMUNICATE WITH OTHER TEAM LEADERS. THEN THE TEAM LEADERS PASS ORDERS DOWN TO THEIR TEAMS.

"Sounds like a good idea," Wei says.

NOW TO TEACH YOU BASIC MOVEMENT. WE CAN START WITH ARM MOVEMENT. FORRAHH, TO POINT

AT THE FAR WALL, SIMPLY LIFT YOUR ARM AS YOU NORMALLY WOULD AND EXTEND YOUR FINGERS.

Forrahh moves her arm and lets out a surprised yelp as it raises impossibly fast.

EXCELLENT! NOW MOVE IT BACK DOWN AND FOCUS ON SLOWER MOVEMENTS THIS TIME. Her arm jerkily moves down to her side again. THE SAME CONCEPT APPLIES FOR YOUR LEGS. IF YOU WANT TO WALK SOMEWHERE, JUST TRY TO MOVE YOUR LEGS IN THE NORMAL WAY.

Ever heard the phrase 'curiosity killed the cat'? Well, from the moment I saw Forrahh try to move her arm, I wanted a go... and it was not long before I gave in to temptation. My EMO's right leg suddenly lurches forward. The EMO oversteps and topples to the right until I am lying on my back. PLEASE DO NOT TRY TO MOVE, JON.

"Can we help, Jon?"

PLEASE LEAVE HIM. YOU ALL NEED TO LEARN HOW TO GET UP FROM THE FLOOR. You know, I'd swear it sounded like HICS was mocking me! ALL OF YOU MUST DO THIS AT SOME POINT. I WAS HOPING IT WOULD BE AFTER A FEW MORE LESSONS, THOUGH.

"Didn't count on me, then, did you?" I reply.

WEI, PLEASE PUT ONE FOOT FORWARD WHILE CONCENTRATING ON SLOW, STEADY MOVEMENTS. Wei slowly lifts his right leg and plants it down a little outside the crate. Once he is sure his foot is firmly in place, he lifts his left leg and brings it forward to land beside the right one. Gingerly, he checks his balance and releases a sigh of relief.

YOUR TURN, FORRAHH. Like Wei, she completes the manoeuvre without incident.

"Show-off!" I say from the floor.

OKAY, JON. GETTING UP IS SIMPLE.

"Easy for you to say. You're not in here!"

HICS ignores me and carries on talking. FIRST, DON'T DO ANYTHING UNTIL I HAVE FINISHED TALKING. The others chuckle. IMAGINE IF YOU WERE LYING ON YOUR BACK WITHOUT THE SUIT. PICTURE HOW YOU WOULD GET UP FROM THAT POSITION. REMEMBER, CONCENTRATE ON SLOW MOVEMENTS. NOW TRY TO STAND UP.

I slowly lift my right arm and reach over to my left side. Carefully, I twist my body round until I am leaning on both arms. I slowly bring my left then my right knee up until I'm on all fours. My right foot comes forward, followed by my left. Using my two hands to balance myself, I lean back onto my feet and straighten my legs to stand up. "Ta-ra!" I sing out. "Beat that!"

Forrahh and Wei carefully clap their hands together, laughing.

WELL DONE, JON. YOU WILL ALL NEED TO PRACTISE BASIC ACTIONS. FOR NOW, PRACTISE WALKING AROUND THE AREA AND PICKING THINGS UP. THERE ARE SEVERAL SMALL ITEMS SCATTERED AROUND THIS ROOM. LOCATE AND IDENTIFY THEM USING YOUR SENSORS. TRY TO PICK THEM UP, AND WHEN YOU BELIEVE YOU ARE READY INCREASE MOVEMENT SPEED.

I look around the room. As I think about finding the objects, horizontal and vertical lines appear on the scanner, moving across the screen for a few seconds, detecting objects on the floor and walls as it progresses.

I try focusing on one object on the floor. The screen zooms in on the object and displays the metal pipe I am looking at. The exact material composition is displayed on screen beside the object. I move forward clumsily until I reach it and slowly bend down to pick it up. After my earlier fall, I'm very aware of my movements. Oh, and my competitive side keeps reminding me that I'm the only one to have fallen so far. I position my fingers on either side of the pipe and slowly draw my fingers closed around it.

118

I can feel the touch of the pipe on my fingers as they make contact. I slowly close my fingers and watch as I accidentally flatten the pipe without even trying. There is a gasp of surprise behind me. I turn to see Forrahh holding an object which she happens to have crushed too. We look at each other from across the room.

"Well, *I* love my EMO," I say.

We continue to practise using the EMOs for the rest of the day. By the time we're ready to quit for the day, we are able to walk faster and even run a few steps before coming to the far wall. Picking up objects is still an issue, though. HICS even had to have additional items brought in. For health and safety reasons, we have to sit down on the floor before anyone is allowed into the room to deliver the new objects. Apparently, this is to prevent us from accidentally hurting someone.

"Okay. Enough with the picking things up already!" I say, frustrated with myself. How can something so easy be so hard? Can't we do something else now?"

"We have been doing this for some time now," Wei replies wearily. "How about we finish the day with a light jog?"

"Great idea! You forgotten how that turned out last time?"

"No. This time, I will lead and you two follow me. I will control the pace, so make sure you do not pass me."

"So now we're playing 'Follow the Leader'? That's just what I need. More kids' games."

"What is 'Follow the Leader'?" Wei asks.

"It's a game we play on Earth. One person is the leader and everyone else has to follow the leader and do whatever he does. Only children play it, really."

"Interesting! Our tasks are children's tasks... why not the games too?" he thinks out loud. "Fine, I am the leader and you two must follow my every action."

Forrahh shrugs in agreement. We fall in behind Wei and wait for him to start moving.

He gently pushes away and we both follow him, starting slowly and gradually picking up speed. All the objects around me are suddenly a blur, but Wei and Forrahh are perfectly clear in the view screen.

"Keep concentrating on me," Wei says.

I focus on him as he slowly increases speed until we are moving even faster. We are almost at a run now. The feeling of being able to do this is amazing. For the first time in hours, I'm really enjoying myself.

As our speed increases, our turning circle widens. It becomes more and more difficult to make the tight turns in the confined cargo bay. I follow Wei as we run anticlockwise down the full length of the bay. His turning circle brings him really close to the next wall. He puts his right hand out and, using his right leg, pushes off from the wall, propelling himself across the length of the room. Without a thought about the consequences, we copy his actions.

I land on my left foot, step with my right and propel myself forward just like Wei did a second earlier. My mind is racing. I'm travelling at breakneck speeds, but I seem to know what I must do. As I round the next corner, Wei comes to a dead halt and turns to face us. I spin in mid run and stop beside him just in time to see Forrahh skid to a halt on his other side.

"I just had a thought!" Wei says. "HICS, how fast were we running just now?"

TOP SPEED WAS FIFTY-THREE MILES PER HOUR.

"How were we able to stop in time?"

"What's the matter, Wei?" He is obviously concerned about something.

"Actually, Jon, he has a point," Forrahh says. "If we were travelling at that speed and that closely behind each other, we should not have been able to stop in time." Forrahh thinks for a second. "In fact, how were we able to copy each other's movements? No-one has reflexes that quick. HICS?"

DO YOU REMEMBER THE SMALL NEEDLES WHICH PENETRATED YOUR SKIN WHEN THE SUIT CLOSED?

"How can I forget?" I say.

A DRUG WAS INJECTED INTO YOUR BODIES. THE SUIT REGULATES THE DRUG LEVELS. IT INCREASES REFLEXES DRAMATICALLY.

"This reminds me of something my people developed a long time ago," Wei says.

THIS DRUG IS BASED ON THAT RESEARCH. OF COURSE, I HAVE IMPROVED IT CONSIDERABLY. IT WAS THE ONLY WAY FOR YOU TO COPE WITH THE SPEED OF THE SUITS.

"It would have been nice to have been told," I say.

WOULD YOU HAVE CHANGED YOUR MIND, JON?

I shake my head.

THE DRUG WORKS ON ALL THREE OF YOUR RACES WITHOUT MODIFICATIONS. I WAS ONE HUNDRED PER CENT SURE THAT IT WOULD WORK ON YOU BEFORE USING IT AND THEREFORE DID NOT NEED TO RUN ANY FURTHER TESTS.

"What made you so sure?"

IT WOULD TAKE TOO LONG TO EXPLAIN IT, JON. I DO NOT THINK WE HAVE TIME FOR THAT RIGHT NOW. BE ASSURED THAT I CHECKED ALL DETAILS THOROUGHLY.

"I know, HICS. I do trust you."

GOOD. I HAVE BEEN MONITORING YOUR PROGRESS. YOU HAVE ALL DONE INCREDIBLY WELL FOR YOUR FIRST DAY. ONCE YOU HAVE PERFECTED HOW TO PICK ITEMS UP, WE CAN MOVE ONTO THE NEXT STAGE.

"The next stage?" Wei asks.

WEAPONS, THEIR INSTALLATION AND THEIR USAGE.

A satisfied smile creeps onto my face. "I promise we will be ready before the end of tomorrow morning. For now, though, I'm shattered. How do we get out of these suits?"

USING YOUR RIGHT INDEX FINGER, DRAW A LINE FROM YOUR CHEST TO YOUR STOMACH. THEN DROP YOUR ARM TO YOUR SIDE AND WAIT. ONCE THE SUIT HAS OPENED, SIMPLY STEP OUT.

I reach over to my chest and start to draw a line down to my stomach. My hand drops to my side. A few seconds later, the chest cavity opens followed by the rest of the suit. I groan as I step out and move forward a few steps. I am followed shortly after by Forrahh and Wei.

Without looking back, I stretch my body, trying to get the kinks out before heading to my bunk for some well-deserved rest.

I wake up early the next morning. It's not that I didn't sleep well or anything. I just want to get back to my EMO.

I quietly get dressed and crawl out of the bunk. I can still feel the aches and pains from the day before, but that doesn't dent my determination. Creeping carefully past all the bunks, I make my way back to CB6.

It's a couple of hours before I hear the buzzer ring throughout the cargo bay. WEI AND FORRAHH HAVE ARRIVED, JON. PLEASE MOVE TO THE FAR CORNER OF THE CARGO BAY AND SIT DOWN.

I move impossibly fast to the far corner and sit myself down. The red light on top of the door switches off, allowing the door to open. "What took you?" I say smugly. "There's just no dedication in people these days."

"I told you he would be here," Wei whispers to Forrahh, forgetting my heightened hearing and of course the EMO's augmented audio receivers. "I could hear it in his voice when HICS mentioned weapons training. He will be very motivated today."

I ignore him. "Come on, guys. Get into your EMOs. I can't sit here all day!"

Minutes later, HICS gives me the go-ahead. OKAY, JON. YOU MAY GET UP NOW.

"Thanks, HICS. Guys, you have to see this!"

I get up and run to a screwdriver sitting on a worktop in the kitchen area. I reach out with my right hand. "Slowly... delicately..." I say as I bring my fingers closer to the object. "You see, the sensors in the suit are really sensitive. You have to get used to it, but the EMO actually feeds the sensation to your fingers." My fingers close in further, "And when you connect," my fingers touch the screwdriver, "you can feel it in your fingertips. That should be enough pressure." I lift the screwdriver off the floor without crushing it. "Just lift. It's going to take a little practice, but it's just a case of re-learning how much pressure to exert."

"Impressive, Jon," Wei remarks, "very impressive indeed!"

They carefully move towards the other objects and follow my instructions. After just half an hour, they have both managed to pick up the objects. Even I am moving faster now. I have managed to pick up more delicate objects and I don't have to concentrate so much. Over the next hour, we keep practising until we are able to pick up most objects instinctively. There are of course the occasional breakages, but nothing like the destruction of yesterday. In fact, we do so well that HICS even teaches us how to slide towards an object and pick it up as we pass... Sadly, not as much success there.

Not long after, HICS informs us that we have almost achieved enough to move onto the next stage. THERE IS ONE FINAL TEST. YOU NEED TO MAKE YOUR WAY TO THE NEXT ROOM.

"Easy," I say confidently. "The tunnel is right there."

"Things are never what they seem, Jon," Wei says thoughtfully. ON THE RIGHT SIDE OF YOUR VIEWER, YOU WILL

HAVE SEEN A SMALL MAP. FOCUS ON THIS MAP. I do as I'm told and the map is superimposed over the view of the room. THIS SHOWS A MAP OF THE ROOM YOU ARE IN AND ANY ITEMS WHICH MAY BE OF INTEREST. IT SHOWS ANY INFORMATION AVAILABLE ABOUT THE NEIGHBOURING ROOMS, AS WELL AS DISPLAYING ANY ROUTES WHICH ARE NOT EASILY IDENTIFIABLE. IN THIS CASE, NOTICE THE WALL WHERE THE TUNNEL IS.

Forrahh walks a few steps closer to the wall. "So the tunnel is a dead-end! What is that other image on the wall? It looks like another tunnel."

Wei walks towards the part of the wall where the other tunnel should be. He raises his hand, palm facing forward to feel the wall. "You have to see this, Jon."

I walk over and place my hand on the wall as Wei did. The map image on the wall changes to show the wall and also a hazy, shimmering image. The centre circle of the image is slightly clearer. "What is this, HICS?" I ask. "Why does the image become clearer in some areas and not in others?"

THE MOVEMENT OF YOUR HAND INTENSIFIES THE IMAGE. BY MOVING YOUR HAND AROUND THE WALL, YOU WILL BE ABLE TO FIND EXACTLY WHERE THE TUNNEL IS. WHEN THE IMAGE IS CLEAREST, YOUR HAND WILL BE OVER THE TUNNEL ENTRANCE. I move my hand around the wall again. YOU WILL ALSO SEE SOME DATA REGARDING THE WALL, INCLUDING THE THICKNESS AND STRENGTH OF THE WALL. IF THE DETAILS ARE DISPLAYED IN RED, PUNCHING THROUGH COULD CAUSE DAMAGE TO THE SUIT. GREEN DETAILS SHOW THAT YOU CAN PUNCH THROUGH THAT AREA AND IT WILL NOT DAMAGE THE SUIT. A lot of the wall shows up as red, except for one area. I stop my hand over it.

"The data readings are green. Does that mean it's okay to punch through?"

Before HICS says anything, I clench my fist, pull it back and throw it forward. It goes through the wall like I was punching through a sheet of paper. My hand disappears into the wall right up to the wrist. Guess I didn't need to pull back that much. I pull my hand out and step back away from the wall.

Wei moves to stand in front of the hole I have created. Gingerly, he puts his hands into the hole and starts to make it big enough for his EMO to crawl through.

He climbs in and crawls forward. I wait for him to reach what looks like a T-junction at the end of the passage before crawling in after him. The map on the viewer shows both paths. The left one seems to go on for a while. The right stops a short distance ahead. "HICS," Wei says, "are you able to highlight the target room?" The borders of the room glow red. The right tunnel stops at the red border while the left continues past the room.

The image on my viewer changes to night vision, allowing me to catch a glimpse of Wei's legs as they move off to the right. I follow him down the tunnel.

Wei approaches the wall and places his palm on it. "Okay. I can see a clear image of the room on the other side," he says. I glance at the map again. A small marker shows that Forrahh has already climbed into the tunnel and is right behind me. "I can even see the objects on the other side of the wall," Wei says.

"Is everything okay?" Forrahh asks from behind me.

"Yes, I am about to break through," Wei says. He draws his arm back, punches through the wall and starts to widen the opening as before. He crawls through and steps away from the hole. I crawl through right after him with Forrahh just after. We find ourselves in another room of similar dimensions to the one we just left. There are tables on the left with weapons on them. About fifteen metres down the room is a line clearly drawn on the floor. At the far end are some really small targets, far enough away that you couldn't focus on them with the naked eye. With the viewer, the targets are as clear and close as words through a magnifying glass.

We carefully survey the surroundings.

WELCOME TO PHASE TWO, PEOPLE. THIS IS THE WEAPONS TRAINING ROOM. THERE ARE ONLY A FEW WEAPONS WHICH CAN BE ATTACHED TO THE EMO. THIS IS BECAUSE THE EMO WAS DESIGNED PRIMARILY AS AN ENVIRONMENTAL SUIT WITH COMBAT CAPABILITY WHEN REQUIRED. TOO MANY WEAPONS WOULD DEVIATE FROM ITS INITIAL PURPOSE.

FOR THAT REASON, THE SUIT COMES EQUIPPED WITH TWO WEAPONS. THE PRIMARY WEAPON IS A MOBILE RAIL GUN. THIS WEAPON HAS BEEN DEVELOPED FROM TECHNOLOGY PRESENTLY BEING DEVELOPED BY HUMANS. THE WEAPON WAS ORGINALLY SHELVED DUE TO A REQUIREMENT FOR A LARGE POWER SUPPLY AND THE RAILS NEEDING TO BE REPLACED TOO OFTEN. I HAVE COMBINED IT WITH THE TECHNOLOGY FOUND ON THE GRINGUN SHIP TO CREATE A SUITABLE INTERNAL POWER SUPPLY AND A HARDENED, HEAT-PROOF MATERIAL WHICH WILL REDUCE WEAR AND TEAR ON THE RAILS SIGNIFICANTLY. THIS REDUCES ITS EFFECTIVENESS SLIGHTLY, BUT IT STILL PACKS AN OVERWHELMING PUNCH WHICH WOULD MOST LIKELY KILL ANYTHING ANYWAY. IN ADDITION, THE SIZE HAS BEEN REDUCED CONSIDERABLY AND IT IS NOW SHOULDER-MOUNTED. THE WEAPON CAN FIRE SHORT ACCURATE BURSTS OVER DISTANCES OF UP TO ONE AND A HALF MILES. IT CAN ALSO BE USED ON SHORT DISTANCE TARGETS. IF THE WEAPON IS ACTIVATED AND THE OBJECT TARGETED IS SOME DISTANCE AWAY, THE VIEWER WILL AUTOMATICALLY SELECT SCOPE MODE. THIS WILL ENSURE ACCURACY OVER

LONG DISTANCES AND WILL TAKE ENVIRONMENTAL CONDITIONS INTO ACCOUNT. YOU WILL NOT NEED TO MANUALLY AIM THE WEAPON. ONCE A TARGET HAS BEEN SELECTED, THE WEAPON WILL AIM AND WAIT TO FIRE WHEN YOU ARE READY. LARGE-SCALE RAIL GUNS HAVE PROPELLED PROJECTILES AT SPEEDS OF UP TO TWENTY KILOMETRES PER SECOND. AS THIS IS MINIMISED CONSIDERABLY, IT WILL ONLY MANAGE SPEEDS OF UP TO TEN KILOMETRES PER SECOND.

THE SECONDARY WEAPON IS A MELEE WEAPON. THERE IS A RETRACTABLE CARBON STEEL ALLOY WRIST BLADE ON EACH WRIST. THE TWIN FORK DESIGN HAS BEEN MADE TO CAUSE MAXIMUM DAMAGE AND INCAPACITATE AN ENEMY AS QUICKLY AS POSSIBLE. THEY ARE MADE BASED UPON DESIGNS FROM HUMAN HISTORY.

"Lovely history you have, Jon," Wei says, sounding slightly sickened by the description. I allow the comment to pass.

PLEASE MAKE YOUR WAY TO THE WEAPONS TABLE TO COLLECT YOUR RAIL GUN.

We move to the table and look at the neatly arranged items. There are three rail gun packs and six twin-pronged blades in a perfect line. Carefully, I pick up the rail gun pack in front of me and turn it over in my hands, studying every angle of it. It has an elongated shape with two small prongs extending from the front and what look like heat dissipation grills at the back.

HOLD THE RAIL GUN IN YOUR RIGHT HAND WITH THE HEAT GRILLS TOWARDS THE BACK. PLACE IT ON YOUR SHOULDER AND THE SUIT WILL TAKE CARE OF THE REST.

I lift it to my shoulder and turn my head to look at what's happening. I rest the rail gun gently on my shoulder and wait. Moments later, the surface texture of the suit changes, forming weird tendrils. I watch as they practically ooze off the surface and attach to the bottom of the rail gun. The gun guides itself into place and locks in position with a soft click. The rail gun mount symbol on my viewer flashes a few times before changing from a dull grey to a vibrant, danger red. Without hesitation, I move to the line on the floor and face the targets. The viewer changes to scope mode as I focus on the small target ahead of me. The crosshair settles on the centre dot of the target. It's a bit like the targeting reticule on the HUD of fighter jets. I focus on other areas of the target, making the crosshair move from point to point. My focus returns to the centre of the target and I decide I'm ready to fire.

I feel a small tug at my shoulder and the target is utterly obliterated. Seriously, I didn't see any trails or anything. One moment I decided to fire at the target, the next there was no target. Oh, and when I say the target was obliterated, I really mean it doesn't exist anymore.

WELL DONE, JON, HICS says.

For the first time, I feel like I have really come into my own. Forrahh and Wei stare at me in stunned silence. Ignoring them, I move over to the table and pick up a pair of blades. I turn them over in my hands, careful not to hold them too firmly. It's obvious which way they connect in. I place the back of one of the blades to my left sleeve and watch as the weird tendrils ooze out from the sleeve. Almost as though they sense the blade being close, they search around for the connection like miniature blind snakes tasting the air for a fresh meal. As one finds the blade, the rest home in on the location. The blade is drawn into the sleeve and disappears from sight. I repeat the process with the right blade and watch as it retracts into the sleeve, too.

The weapons console on my viewer flickers as the left and right blade images appear in the same danger red.

THINK ABOUT USING THE BLADES, JON.

I do as I'm told. The blades slide out from the sleeve so fast, I could've been mistaken into thinking they were already there. I focus on only the right blade being visible. The left blade retracts, leaving only the right blade extended. I think about it being sheathed again and it disappears back into the sleeve just like the left one did.

The viewer shows some movement behind my EMO. As I turn, I see a target dummy rising from the floor.

ATTACK THE TARGET WITH YOUR BLADES.

I set myself into a crouch on all fours. I take a stance similar to a lioness preparing to pounce on its unsuspecting prey. Suddenly I launch at the target and land beside it. As my left foot hits the ground next to the target I slash out sideways, the right blade extending instantly and cutting a large gash in the target. My left hand swings round to stab into the target, followed by a final slash from the right blade to what would've been the neck area. The sheer power and aggression of the three consecutive attacks leaves the target in tatters. A stunned sound comes from Forrahh. Wei lets out a quiet whimper before he collapses to the floor and curls into a ball.

"Oh crap! Sorry, Wei. I didn't think!" There is no response from him. "HICS, is he alright?"

HE IS HIGHLY DISTRESSED, JON. THERE IS AN EMERGENCY EJECTION SYSTEM. ONLY TEAM MEMBERS ARE AUTHORISED TO ACTIVATE IT.

"How, HICS?" Forrahh commands.

THINK ABOUT LINKING TO THE TEAM. THE VIEWER WILL DISPLAY EACH MEMBER. Forrahh follows the instructions precisely. SELECT THE ONE YOU WANT AND A SERIES OF OPTIONS WILL APPEAR. THE LAST OPTION IS REMOTE EJECTION. SELECT THE OPTION AND CONFIRM IT.

Wei's suit straightens out and the front opens up to show Wei inside. "HICS, I need a table," I say urgently. As the table rises from the floor, I lift Wei carefully from the suit and carry him to it. I gently lay him down, step back and disarm my EMO. I step out of the suit. Forrahh has already exited hers and is standing beside Wei.

It takes almost an hour to console Wei. He eventually stops his incoherent mumbling and pulls himself up into a sitting position. He takes a few deep breaths before slowly lifting his head and looking at us.

"I do not belong here! This is not for me."

"It is just a minor upset, Wei," Forrahh explains gently. "It will get better soon. Besides, we are a team and we work best together."

"You don't understand. My people are not used to seeing such barbaric actions. I have been able to control myself till now because I have been around Jon for so long. I trust him implicitly. I know he will never try to harm me. Obviously, I have heard of the violence that Humans are capable of, but I never actually saw it before. I did not expect such capability for violence in someone so young!" He pauses to think for a moment and sighs as he reaches his decision. "I am not going to be of any use to you. Not in battle anyway. You see, I *thought* I could handle the violence, but if I go catatonic after seeing a simulated event, then how will I cope for real?

"No, it makes more sense for me to behave in a way that is natural to me. My people do not get involved in war because we do not have the temperament or the capacity for it. We share something in common with the Keteran males. This is why Humans are a necessary part of our alliance. Admiral Nique and I have already considered this as a possibility. And we knew it might become a necessity if I was unable to do this. I am truly sorry."

"But how will we cope without you?" Forrahh asks concerned.

Wei perks up a bit, "Your natural ability to communicate telepathically allows you to be highly efficient in all activities. I believe that teaming Humans and Keterans into pairs would result in a highly efficient fighting force. The Humans will lead the charge and the Keterans can pre-empt their next movements. Yes," he says thoughtfully, "this would work well. I have to admit, I had hoped I would cope with it, but that last display proved otherwise."

"But we want you as part of the team, Wei!" I say openly concerned. I even surprise myself with how much I want Wei there with me. I'm not sure why I need him there, but it seems important somehow. "There has to be something we can do. What if we don't mention this? You could keep out of the way when things turn nasty."

"Be sensible, Jon. Can you see that working? Besides, Admiral Nique and I have already considered our position in the battles. I do not know what I will be doing, but I am sure they will not split us up." He doesn't sound convinced to me. "Please do not worry, Jon. I won't leave you, I promise." I feel like a child who has been shown a glimmer of hope. "Let us see what everyone says when we tell them. Okay?"

Reluctantly, I nod my agreement.

"Okay. HICS, are there any other lessons we need to learn?"

NO. THESE ARE THE BASIC TECHNIQUES YOU ALL NEED TO MASTER. OVER THE NEXT FEW DAYS YOU NEED TO CONCENTRATE ON PERFECTING THESE SKILLS.

"Good." He turns to face us both. "Then for the next few days I will be working with you both, helping you to perfect your skills. Just warn me when you decide to work on your fighting techniques. That way, I can take a quick break or move into the other room and test my own skills. I must admit, though, I will miss using my EMO."

The rest of the day continues with Wei studying how we move and perform actions. Every now and then he interrupts with tips to help us learn the techniques and perfect our skills. Coming from someone standing on the side-lines, his tips are surprisingly helpful. There are also times when Wei leaves the area so Forrahh and I can practise actual battle techniques. While I was working on the military base, some of the combat trainers had taken a liking to me. During their spare time, they started my hand-to-hand combat training, even though I was officially too young to start. Apparently, I have a natural talent for hand-to-hand combat. The trainers were impressed at how easily I picked up the moves. Of course, being very agile from the start had to help a bit. I found this talent useful now. Anyway, while Forrahh and I are alone, I make an effort to teach her many of the techniques I learnt. I'm not too surprised to find she's an excellent learner and has a flexibility which most Humans could only wish for. This allows her to perform some manoeuvres more efficiently than even I can.

As the day draws to an end, we leave CB6 and head back to the MCC. We enter the perpetually busy circular room. The Admirals are standing before the raised platform. It looks like Enira is explaining something to Wesley and Nique. As we approach, we catch the end of a conversation about what is to happen when we land. We stop in front of the platform and wait to be acknowledged.

"So, how is the training going?" Wesley asks.

I don't have the courage to speak. Wei takes a step forward and quietly says, "We need to talk, sir. It is important."

Admiral Wesley's expression changes with the gravitas of Wei's voice. Nique and Enira look at us curiously. "Okay. Let's talk," Wesley says. He gestures to the meeting room.

We sit in the same position as we did the last time we were here. We are on one side of the table facing our respective commanders.

As the door closes, the din from outside dies down to utter silence, while the windows remain clear allowing people to still see inside.

"There is no problem here," Enira suggests. "Simply a misunderstanding and that is our fault. Forrahh has explained everything to me." She smiles gently to Wei. "It appears that Jon has taken to the weaponry training a little too well. This has had a negative effect on Wei." Nique sits back in his seat with an understanding look on his face. "Now Wei is assuming that he cannot perform his part in the team and will therefore have to leave his friends to perform other more mundane tasks. Wei, you were *never* going to be sent out into fighting environments."

Wei is clearly stunned by this information. "Then why was I given an EMO?"

"You will need the EMO to help investigate on some of the safer missions. When Jon and Forrahh are in fighting situations, you will be in constant communication with them... as their intelligence and strategy advisor from the ship. You will be tasked with providing them with the necessary information they need to complete their missions. You need to work with HICS to ensure all possibilities are considered. You all make for a great team and it would be a tactical mistake on our part to break that."

Wei relaxes with the news. I can now see what his involvement could be in the coming missions... and I like it. "I understand," he says, apparently elated at the news. "I have been unable to see my role in the team. When I received my suit, I thought that maybe I could get over my fears, but this is better, much better."

"Wei, you already know that each of our races has its own advantages. In fact, thinking about it, if there were one race with all of our traits, *that* is a race I would not want as an enemy. It makes logical sense for us to work together and rely on each other's talents. You already know this, though, don't you?"

"I do, but I think I lost sight of it," Wei says apologetically, "I'm sorry to have wasted your time."

"This is not a waste of time, Wei," Enira says. "We prefer that you come and speak to us." Nique and Wesley both nod in agreement. "We do need you all to continue training, though. HICS has been reporting back to us with your progress. It is impressive, but you have only a few more days before your first mission begins. We need to know that you will be ready by then. In addition, Wei, as you now know, you will not be involved in the fighting, but the Najess seem extremely proficient at creating battle strategies and attack techniques. When Jon and Forrahh are practising these techniques, you could maybe create some new strategies for them."

"Great idea!" I say. "Hey, that kind of makes you our coach!"

"He is right," Forrahh says laughing. "So what do we do now?" Suddenly there is a more upbeat feel to the room again.

Wesley responds to the question, "HICS has informed us that you have already learned the basic techniques. For the next few days, just keep working on mastering those techniques. Now, if that is all, we have a lot of work to get on with." We all nod to confirm we are done. "Excellent. Dismissed, people."

The next morning, HICS calls us to the MCC Meeting Room. We stretch as we get out of the bunks and prepare for yet another meeting. Personally, I just want to get back into my EMO.

Admiral Wesley is already in the MCC when we arrive. The seats have all been moved to one side of the room, creating an auditorium effect.

"Morning," Wesley says as we enter. "There is not much for you folks really, but I figured you could do with a break. And besides, it would be good for you to see some of the progress we have made in areas other than the EMOs."

He nods to Enira and the test pilots come into the room. Ten Keteran women, all smartly dressed with their long hair tied and pinned back, enter the room. They stand to attention in front of the commanders. They are all very young... in fact they appear to be around the same age as me and Forrahh. Nique and Wesley take their seats on either side of Enira.

"Please sit." Enira pauses while we all sit down. "We have been studying your progress with the interceptors. Exceptional, truly exceptional!" The three commanders all continue to study their paperwork.

"It would be useful if we could see something," Nique says,

still looking at the paperwork. "HICS, do we have any video footage of the prototypes?"

YES, SIR. THE FOOTAGE WILL BE DISPLAYED ON THE SCREEN BEFORE YOU SHORTLY.

We all look around confused and mumbling, "What screen?" to each other. As we look at the wall in front of us, expecting a screen to rise from the floor, the glass walls darken. The lights switch off leaving a large part of the wall dimly lit. A few seconds later, an image of the outside of the ship appears. The camera pans around as ten interceptors fly past at breakneck speeds. The camera continues to pan round, keeping them in view.

They are all in perfect formation and fly in a straight line. Suddenly they all change direction in unison and perform a steep climb. As they climb, the ships continue to rotate on their axes, until they flip over to face downwards while continuing their upward momentum. Suddenly the ships' drives kick in and they move back down towards the ship. As they approach, they continue to pick up speed and at the last second they turn sharply, skimming over the surface of the ship. The camera switches to a new view and we watch as the interceptors travel across the freighter before weaving skilfully in and out of the transports.

"The manoeuvres are so precise!" Wesley states. "I thought basic physics prevented these types of manoeuvres from happening. I thought it was impossible to turn that sharply in space. You would need the presence of air or some other resistance."

"That was my understanding, too," Nique says.

THE PHYSICS STATEMENT IS CORRECT. I HAVE DEVELOPED A NEW TYPE OF INERTIAL DAMPENER BASED ON THE ORIGINAL GRINGUN DESIGNS. THIS ALLOWS US TO COMPLETE THIS TYPE OF MANOEUVRE.

"How often do your pilots get to practise this back home?" Wesley asks Enira.

"Never!" Enira states proudly. "This is the first time they have ever tried this formation. Also, the way the ships react in space is very different to anything we are used to. You see, when the pilots are turning, the initial inertia keeps the ships travelling in the same direction. This means that they have to learn how to change direction. As we saw in the footage, the ships were able to travel upwards, but even when they turned the interceptors around they continued in their original direction. To change direction requires an additional burst of power in the opposite direction. This is where the inertial dampeners come in."

"I see. Well, it would seem that your pilots have already perfected that stunt." Nique seems impressed by the display. "But how would they cope in a battle situation?"

THIS IS DISPLAYED ON THE SCREEN NOW SIR.

We turn to the screen again to see the ships. The screen splits into two. The left screen shows the interceptors and the right screen shows a series of twenty drones heading towards the fleet. The interceptors all turn towards the drones simultaneously. They change direction holding their formation and accelerate towards the drones. There is absolutely no radio chatter the whole time. As the interceptors come within range of the drones they split apart. The drones react to this manoeuvre by splitting up and moving in to attack their targets two to one. The drones attempt to herd the interceptors, making it easier to target them. The pilots weave in and out of each other, evading the drones at every turn. Each weave brings a drone into the line of fire of another interceptor which releases a burst from its ion cannons until the last drone is destroyed without a single lost interceptor. The image freezes.

"I'd say you have proved your effectiveness," Wesley says. "Okay. You ten are the best that the Keteran forces could offer. You will each train ten pilots and they will train any that are left. Do we have any more interceptors ready, HICS?"

ANOTHER TWENTY INTERCEPTORS ARE READY AND MORE ARE IN PRODUCTION. I WILL INCREASE THE RATE OF PRODUCTION TO COPE WITH FUTURE DEMANDS.

Enira stands up and faces the pilots, "Excellent. HICS, please prepare the ships for take-off."

Without another word, the ten pilots stand up together and walk out of the room.

"What happened?" Wesley asks looking slightly confused.

"I told them to select the ten most gifted pilots and start the training. I also told them to get the twenty interceptors out there in the next thirty minutes."

"Wonderful! I don't think I will ever get used to the way you communicate, but it is wonderful nonetheless!" Wesley says sounding very impressed.

Enira smiles warmly at him. "I am sure you will get used to it eventually. Ah, good news! The new trainees have been selected and will be in the hangar within five minutes." She smiles smugly.

"Incredible!" Wei exclaims.

For the next couple of hours we sit with the commanders. My eyes are glued to the screen as we watch the pilots and their trainees perform unbelievable manoeuvres. It's almost like they're using a hive mind. They actually know what their partner is going to do before the manoeuvre even starts... and with total radio silence the whole time.

"What weapon is used on the interceptors, HICS?" Nique asks as a volley of shots hits a target.

IT IS A LARGER, MORE POWERFUL VERSION OF AN ION CANNON DESIGN BEING TESTED BY THE HUMANS. IT IS VERY EFFECTIVE AGAINST SHIPS. I WAS CONSIDERING USING A SMALLER VERSION ON THE EMOS ORIGINALLY, BUT FOUND THAT A SMALLER RAIL GUN WOULD BE MORE EFFECTIVE IN A BATTLE SITUATION.

"I can vouch for that," I say.

"They learn really fast!" Wesley says.

"The telepathy helps," Enira responds. "Using telepathy, all of the ten pilots are feeding information to the trainees at the same time. It is as though the trainees are downloading the information directly from the trainers. They also upload anything that they learn which the trainers do not know. It is a very effective way of learning."

"Evidently!"

I HAVE IDENTIFIED AN UNUSUAL SIGNAL.

The talking stops instantly.

I HAVE TRACKED A SIGNATURE WHICH HAS MOVED INTO OUR AREA. I BELIEVE WE ARE BEING WATCHED.

"Recommendations, HICS?" Nique asks.

SEVERAL SCENARIOS CALLED FOR SIGNAL JAMMING TO PREVENT COMMUNICATIONS. AS A PRECAUTION, I HAVE ACTIVATED JAMMING FOR ALL LONG-RANGE COMMUNICATIONS.

"Inform the pilots and prepare the fleet," Enira says. "If there is something there, I want to capture it. Primary objective: do not allow it to communicate; secondary objective: bring it in alive and, if possible, with the technology intact."

THE PILOTS HAVE BEEN INFORMED OF THE APPROXIMATE POSITION OF THE SIGNAL. THEY ARE MOVING TO FLANK THE TARGET LOCATION NOW.

We all watch the screen as HICS continues the commentary. FLANKING COMPLETE. PREPARING TO MOVE IN. NOTICE THE SHIMMERING AREA THEY ARE CONVERGING ON.

As I look closely, I see the stars in one area are shimmering. It's like looking through the heat haze rising off a barbeque.

The interceptors carefully approach the shimmering effect. As they get closer, it moves rapidly away and disappears. The pilots instantly shift direction. They increase speed and perform a series of erratic manoeuvres. HICS' camera follows the action closely. Suddenly, the interceptors drop back in unison. They open fire with a short ion burst in a random spread within a small area. Sparks appear and a strange blue haze forms around one small area.

A HIT.

The ship fades into view. It starts to increase its speed, but the interceptors keep up with it easily. Another interceptor opens fire. The ion bursts seem a bit slow. Another burst from an interceptor. This one hits the drives at the back of the scout ship.

THE DESIGN OF THIS SCOUT MATCHES THE ONES WHICH ATTACKED THE PLANETS. THIS IS A GRINGUN SCOUT SHIP.

Another volley from the interceptor and the scout comes to a complete stop. The lead interceptor pulls alongside the scout and another appears on the other side. A shield of energy emanates from both interceptors and envelopes the scout from the left and right. In unison, the interceptors rotate and head back to the freighter with the Gringun scout floating powerless between them.

The camera pans around, following the ships as they approach the cargo bay. The doors open and both interceptors move slowly in. The camera switches to the inside of the cargo bay. The three ships stop and hover over the floor. The extended shield shrinks back into the interceptors. They slowly back out of the cargo bay, leaving the Gringun scout floating on its own as the airlock door closes behind it.

"Should we get into the EMOs, sir?" Forrahh asks Wesley.

"Not necessary, Forrahh. We have made other arrangements. I suggest you all get back to your practice. I believe HICS has some zero G training for you to get on with. Stay prepared, though. If something happens, we may need you there sharpish."

We walk quickly to CB6 and enter the cargo bay, but I just can't think about the EMO right now.

"HICS," I say, "are you able to put up a view of the Gringun scout in here?"

CERTAINLY, JON. THE IMAGE WILL BE DISPLAYED ON THE FAR WALL.

We walk to the wall and the image shows the airlock doors as they close behind the scout. Gravity in the cargo bay is slowly restored, bringing the scout to a gentle rest on the floor. On the opposite wall to the airlock door is a clear window of reinforced glass. Laser cutter arms and clamps come up from the floor around the ship. The ones closest to the scout's main door begin to cut into the doorway. Vacuum clamps attach themselves to the door. The laser cutters make short work of the doorway and, as they complete their work, the clamps hold the door in place. The piece of hull is slowly detached and moved away, creating an opening. Everything stays quiet. No movement is detected anywhere inside the ship. The camera location provides a clear view into the ship. A shadow moves inside. In a blur of movement, a shape jumps through the small space created in the hull. It rolls to a stop, arms rising to firing position. The fingers are wrapped firmly around an object in its hands. It take aim at the nearby window, steadying itself. The nearby cutters lean towards the now crouched figure. Electrical bursts hit out at it until the lone figure is lying on the floor writhing in pain. Welts appear where the cutters made contact.

We keep watching the screen. A part of me feels guilty that I am not doing what I was told to do, but I can't shift my gaze from the image. The Gringun just lies there, chest heaving slowly with each intake of breath.

After ten minutes, the Gringun sits up. It carefully gets up from the floor and walks around, examining its surroundings. The cutters have now gone and they have taken the weapon too. It moves over to the wall and lays its hands on it. It's about five foot six inches tall judging by its height against the wall and quite broad, giving it an almost rectangular body shape. The legs are quite short too, but the body is long, giving it some extra height.

There's very little hair on its head and what there is has a yellowish tint to it. The skin colour is very pale with a hint of yellow as though it is jaundiced.

It studies the wall closely and then returns to the area where it was lying down. Slowly it lowers itself to the floor and waits patiently.

"We are not going to get anything like this," Enira says, sounding frustrated as she stares at the screen in the meeting room. "Where is it, HICS?"

HE IS IN CB3.

"So, it is male. Okay, I want a Human soldier to meet us there. Make sure he is armed."

I WILL MAKE THE ARRANGEMENTS, ADMIRAL.

Enira gets up from the chair. "Well, I cannot sit here anymore," she says to Wesley and Nique. "You are welcome to join me," she says as she strides purposefully out of the room.

Wesley gets up with a tired sigh, followed by Nique, and they follow her out.

As they arrive at CB3, the guard comes around the opposite corridor. Holstered at his hip is what looks like a small handheld weapon. "What is that, soldier?" Wesley asks.

The soldier looks down at the weapon. "It's a handheld ion blaster, sir. HICS provided them to all on-duty guards. It allows us to either stun or kill our target, so quite useful in a number of situations."

"Excellent."

They approach the heavily tinted window. The Gringun is sitting patiently facing them. The window tint reduces, allowing him to see through. We watch the events from the safety of CB6, prepared in case we are needed.

"Who are you?" Enira asks. The Gringun shows no reaction. "Why did you attack our home worlds?" Again no reaction. "HICS, does he understand us?"

IT IS HARD TO SAY. UNFORTUNATELY HE HAS NOT SAID ANYTHING SO I HAVE NOT BEEN ABLE TO UPDATE OUR TRANSLATORS. I HAVE BEEN STUDYING HIS READINGS, THOUGH, AND HE APPEARS TO BE RESPONSIVE TO YOUR QUESTIONS. I BELIEVE HE CHOOSES NOT TO RESPOND TO YOU.

"What about the data you translated from the other scout we captured?"

MUCH OF THAT DATA AND TECHNOLOGY WAS LOST DUE TO DAMAGE. LANGUAGE TRANSLATION ATTEMPTS HAVE NOT BEEN POSSIBLE SO FAR.

Enira sighs, "We need to make him talk."

A panel beside the Gringun opens and an arm rises from the floor. He looks at it, before returning to face the window. A small spark connects to his bare arm, making him jump slightly. He gets the message, though, and slowly gets to his feet.

He looks to the window and calmly walks towards it. Stopping in front of the window, he stares at the people on the other side.

"Who… are… you?" Enira speaks slowly, hoping he can understand her this time.

He mumbles something under his breath and shudders slightly.

"What do you want with us?"

More mumbling from the Gringun. His body shudders more aggressively this time.

Wesley steps closer to the window. "We can do this all day, you know."

The Gringun loses control of himself. He shouts out at them and stares aggressively at them all. Slowly, a smile creeps onto his face.

Enira and Nique crumple to floor, fingers tightly gripping their heads. Wesley ducks down to help them while shouting orders back to the guard, "WATCH HIM!" The guard winces briefly in pain and starts to reach for his blaster. The smile disappears from the Gringun's face. Enira and Nique relax slightly. He tilts his head to the left and steps closer to the window. He looks directly at the guard. His body instantly stiffens. His eyes roll upwards into his head. His legs give way and he slumps to the floor like a sack of potatoes. It was as though someone had reached in and placed a heavy weight upon his shoulders. The guard stands there staring at the prone figure on the other side of the window, unsure what just happened. Enira and Nique carefully rise from the floor using the corridor walls to balance themselves. "What happened, HICS!" Wesley shouts.

IT WOULD APPEAR THAT THE GRINGUN IS DEAD.

"Dead?" he says stunned, "But how? There was no-one in the bay with him."

IT IS HARD TO SAY WITHOUT FURTHER INVESTIGATION. IT APPEARS HE TRIED TO ATTACK YOU ALL AT THE SAME TIME. THE TELEPATHY IS SIMILAR TO THE KETERANS, BUT MUCH MORE POWERFUL AND ALSO SOMEHOW DIRECTED SIMULTANEOUSLY AT YOU ALL.

"Okay, okay," he says impatiently. "We can go into the details later. For now, get a medical team in here and arrange for the body to be moved to the medical bay… and do it quietly!"

YES, SIR.

Enira seems to be gathering herself again. "We need to look into this further," she says steadying herself against the wall. "I believe our mystery entity within has made another appearance. He really does not like uninvited guests, especially hostile ones! HICS, we are going to need a CT scan on the Gringun as soon as possible."

EVERYTHING WILL BE READY IN MEDICAL BAY 4.

"Thank you!" She looks to Wesley. "We should get back to the MCC. We need to look into these events. I don't think any of our scenarios refer to the Gringuns being telepathic."

"Agreed." He moves to where Nique and the soldier are crouched on the floor. "How are you feeling?"

"Fine," Nique says. "Just gathering my senses a bit. I have never felt anything like that before." The Najess commander attempts to stand up. Wesley takes his arm and helps him to his feet. "I'll be fine. We need to go. We have a lot to do."

As they move down the corridor, the medic and two orderlies carrying a collapsible stretcher walk quickly towards them.

"What happened?" the medic asks as the orderlies enter the cargo bay and open the stretcher. They carefully lift the dead Gringun onto the stretcher.

"Not sure," Wesley says assertively. "Get him to the medical bay right away. HICS needs to run some tests and I want the results ASAP."

"Yes, sir." He heads off down the corridor with the orderlies following closely and disappears around the corner. The soldier follows them out.

"HICS," Wesley says, "please ask Alpha Team to meet us in the MCC Meeting Room immediately. No need for the EMOs."

YES, SIR.

"Alpha Team?" Enira asks.

"I got fed up of listing their names every time. And let's face facts. None of us would consider breaking them up!"

The Admirals are already in the room when we walk in. We take our seats at the table.

Nique has an impatience about him I have not seen before. This is confirmed when he blurts out what's on his mind. "It looks like we have a functional scout! Well, almost. Some of the circuits are burnt out, but the rest appears in order. This could work out to be a great advantage for us."

"It could be useful if we ever want to enter any of their restricted space," Enira says more calmly.

"Maybe, but that would be some time away, if at all. No, I was thinking about something else actually. To start with, we have technology which was not available before. Much of the equipment on the previous scout was too heavily damaged for us to replicate it. In addition, we have something else that will be useful. We have new data on the scout's computers and the ability to read it."

"Indeed," Enira says. "HICS has been tasked with analysing the hardware and data on the scout. Do you have a progress report HICS?"

THE ANALYSIS HAS ALREADY STARTED, ADMIRAL.

"What about the Gringun?" Wesley asks.

"Well, what do we know?" Nique says rhetorically, "To start with, they look a lot like Humans and Keterans. Secondly, we believe they have telepathic abilities..."

"We *know* they have telepathic abilities!" Enira firmly corrects him.

"We will cover that shortly. Thirdly, they are going to be missing a scout soon! Is there anything you wish to add?" They both shake their heads.

"Okay, the first fact. If they look like Humans and Keterans then we may have a chance to infiltrate them at some point. It could also mean that they can infiltrate us. Based on their technology, we have to assume that they would be able to alter their appearance to some degree at least. There is something else that we have to consider, though."

"Which is?" Wesley asks curiously.

"We all look similar to each other and we think that that is a huge coincidence. How big a coincidence is it for them to look similar to us... and come from a different dimension?" Wesley and Enira don't look like they want to even think about this. "We have to consider the possibilities here. Assume that we are all in some way related. We believe that they have telepathic abilities and they have violent tendencies, too. Well, that covers two of our races." I could've taken that as a dig at Humans, but I figure it's best to just let it pass. "We would have to assume that they are intelligent, too. After all, they created the ships and technology which we simply copied." He looks at Enira. "You mentioned not wanting to meet someone with all of our traits? I think we just did!

"Second fact: what if they do have telepathic abilities? Enira, you say they *have* got these abilities. What makes you so sure?"

"The feeling in my head. I could feel him in there and could read his intention. He was focused on causing us pain. What was strange was that he forgot about us both when he realised that the Humans were not affected. I could sense his interest in you both."

"So did *you* do something to him? When he was distracted by us maybe?" Wesley asks.

"No, not me. I'm not sure what happened. I just know that when he noticed you both, the pain in my head stopped. I could feel his confusion. A Keteran's life begins with telepathy before we are even born. I know when someone is using it against me. Trust me… the Gringuns have telepathic abilities, and if we take this Gringun as a general sample, he was strong, too strong for me to fight off. Which means they are likely to be stronger than our strongest telepaths."

"A scary prospect," Nique comments. "I think you are right, though. All the evidence shows that they must have the ability and that they are powerful. What about the third fact?"

Wesley fields this question, "There are going to more scouts soon. They must have already tried to communicate with the scout. If they have, then we can expect more scouts – or larger ships – to arrive soon."

"True, but we are already a long way from there and they do not even know which way we went." Nique appears quite confident of this.

"Agreed, but if I was commanding them and I found one of my scouts missing without a reason, I would be sending more ships to investigate. Moreover, this is their home turf, which means that they must have sufficient people and ships to send to every planet and investigate. The cloaking device on that scout was a damn sight better than the one we have. How long do you think it is going to be before we are spotted? And that aside, they know this technology better than any of us here, including HICS."

There is an uncomfortable silence in the room as we absorb this information.

"Okay. So, what do you suggest?"

"What are we going to do when we get to the planet, HICS?"

FIRST, WE SHOULD STOP ALL INTERCEPTOR TRAINING. I WILL BUILD SIMULATORS FOR THE PILOTS TO TRAIN ON. ADDITIONAL UNCLOAKED FLIGHTS COULD GIVE AWAY OUR DESTINATION.

"Agreed," Nique says.

ON ARRIVAL AT THE PLANET, THE PLAN IS FOR ALPHA TEAM TO START THEIR FIRST MISSION. BASED ON THE NEW INFORMATION PRESENTED HERE, I WOULD SUGGEST WE BUILD AN UNDERGROUND BASE. I HAVE ALREADY IDENTIFIED THE EQUIPMENT WE NEED TO USE. IT IS BASED UPON A DESIGN FROM SOME EQUIPMENT THE NAJESS HAVE. IT WILL ALLOW US TO DRILL THROUGH AND CREATE SUBTERRANEAN CAVERNS. THIS SHOULD PROTECT US FROM A CURSORY SURFACE SCAN. OUR ONLY ISSUE IS THAT A THOROUGH SCAN WILL SHOW US BELOW THE SURFACE.

"What is the likelihood of a thorough scan of the planet?" Nique asks Wesley.

"Unlikely. Even if they have an abundant supply of people and ships, there are simply too many planets to investigate thoroughly. If we are below ground and able to hide our drilling zones, we should be okay. In addition, we are looking at a number of dead planets for our base. That should hopefully invite only a cursory surface scan. Does that make it any easier, HICS?"

IT DOES. I WILL BEGIN WORK ON THE EQUIPMENT NOW.

"Good," Nique says. "HICS, can you also find a way to help

us infiltrate one of their bases? At some point, we are going to need to visit them ourselves."

YES, SIR. I ALSO HAVE THE RESULTS OF THE CT SCAN ON THE GRINGUN.

"Excellent! That was faster than I had expected. What have you found?"

HE DIED OF A SEVERE CEREBRAL HAEMORRHAGE. THE RESULTS SHOW EXTREME TRAUMA CAUSED TO HIS BRAIN. HIS DEMISE WAS INEVITABLE. THERE WAS, HOWEVER, NO OTHER PHYSICAL DAMAGE TO ANY PART OF HIS BODY INCLUDING THE HEAD. THE TRAUMA TO THE BRAIN WAS CAUSED WITHOUT PHYSICAL CONTACT.

"What would you deduce from this, HICS?" Nique asks.

THE DAMAGE WAS CAUSED BY ONE OF THE TWO HUMANS IN THE VICINITY. I WOULD SAY THAT IT WAS THE RESULT OF A DEFENSIVE REFLEX AGAINST THE GRINGUN'S ATTACK AND WAS SIMILAR, ALTHOUGH CONSIDERABLY MORE SEVERE, THAN THE ATTACK ON NALONN. AS NALONN WAS NOT PERMANENTLY HARMED, THIS SUGGESTS THAT WHATEVER LASHED OUT, DID SO CONSCIOUSLY AND KNEW WHETHER TO INJURE OR KILL THE SUBJECT. IT IS POSSIBLE THAT THE HUMANS MAY HAVE THE MOST POWERFUL LEVEL OF TELEPATHIC ABILITY, ALTHOUGH WITHOUT THE ABILITY TO CONTROL IT.

"That, or the Humans are not meant to control it. Is there anything we can do about it?" Enira asks HICS.

NO. THIS IS SOMETHING BUILT INTO HUMANS. I CAN INVESTIGATE THE OPTION OF EXTRACTING IT, BUT I BELIEVE IT COULD HAVE LETHAL CONSEQUENCES.

"How so?"

BASED ON YOUR DESCRIPTIONS, NALONN'S AND

OF COURSE THE MOST RECENT EVENTS, I WOULD SUGGEST THAT THE ENTITY WITHIN THE HUMAN MIND IS HIGHLY INTELLIGENT AND PREPARED TO CAUSE AS MUCH DAMAGE AS NECESSARY. THE REAL ISSUE, THOUGH, IS THAT IT APPEARS TO HAVE A CONSCIOUSNESS ALL OF ITS OWN AND IT SELECTS ITS TARGETS VERY CAREFULLY. NALONN IS EVIDENCE THAT IT KNOWS WHO TO KILL AND WHO TO WARN.

"Investigate the options anyway, HICS," Nique suggests. "You never know when it could be useful." He addresses us now, "While HICS is investigating this, I suggest you go back to the cargo bays and practise using the EMOs again. Your first mission is imminent."

8

WELCOME HOME

The next stage of our training was kind of interesting. It was the first time we had been under pressure to complete our training, and pressure was not something I was used to. Wei did seem impresssed at how I handled myself, though. Then again, the Najess race is not exactly known for its ability to handle pressure. There was also my ability to rush into things without thinking first. This presented its own problems, which Wei happily pointed out was 'expected from someone who was both young and Human'.

Anyway, we have donned our EMOs and are gathered in CB8. There are several objects and barriers scattered around, forming a complicated maze or obstacle course. There is only one exit and this is the hole through which the three of us crawled to enter the room. I examine the contents of the room using the visor, while HICS details the next phase of our training.

CB6 WAS DESIGNED TO TEACH YOU THE BASICS OF USING YOUR EMOS. THE INTENTION OF CB7 WAS TO

TEACH YOU SOME OF THE ADVANCED FEATURES AND CONTROLS OF YOUR EMOS. CB8 IS THE LAST STAGE. THIS IS WHERE YOU WILL BE SPENDING THE REST OF THE WEEK. ALL OF THE SKILLS YOU HAVE GAINED OVER THE LAST FEW DAYS WILL BE REQUIRED TO MAKE YOUR WAY THROUGH THIS.

WHAT YOU SEE IN THIS ROOM IS A HOLOGRAM OF AN OBSTACLE COURSE.

"Cool, a real hologram?" I say, darting towards the nearest wall.

STOP, JON!

I reach out before I even come to a stop and put my hand through the nearest holographic wall. Sparks fly out as I my hand connects. "Arrrggghhh!" I shout in pain and surprise as the electric shock hits my arm. "What was that?" I cradle my right arm delicately in my left.

"The sound of a child running before he can walk!" Forrahh says. Wei sniggers at the comment.

I slowly walk back to them, still cradling my arm. I watch as the entire obstacle course sinks into the floor before rising again as a completely different course.

AS I WAS SAYING, HICS continues, THE COURSE IS A HOLOGRAM AND IS DESIGNED TO TEST YOUR SKILLS THOROUGHLY. TO COMPLETE THE COURSE, YOU MUST ALL MAKE IT THROUGH WHILE COLLECTING SPECIFIC TOOLS ON THE WAY. YOU NEED TO DO THIS WITHOUT BREAKING THROUGH ANY WALLS. TO ENSURE THAT EVERYONE KNOWS WHEN THEY HIT A WALL, A SMALL ELECTRIC SHOCK WILL HIT THE PART OF THE BODY THAT BREAKS THROUGH.

"Yeah, found that out!" I say, still slightly disgruntled.

THE COURSE MUST BE COMPLETED WITHIN ONE MINUTE TO PASS THE TEST. I HAVE CALCULATED

THAT YOU WILL HAVE TO TRAVEL CONSIDERABLY FASTER THAN YOU HAVE UP TILL NOW. IN ADDITION, THE COURSE WILL CHANGE EACH TIME ONE OF YOU ATTEMPTS IT AND FAILS. THIS WILL PREVENT ANYONE FROM MEMORISING THE ROUTE.

"Yup, saw that too," I say.

PLEASE COMMENCE TRAINING. I WILL BE MONITORING YOUR PROGRESS.

As usual, my impetuous nature takes control and I step forward first. "Easy! I can do this!" I prepare myself, check my map and spring into action. My EMO disappears from view. Forrahh and Wei track my progress on their maps as I leap over the first obstacle and past the next turning.

I spot the first object on the floor and sweep my right hand down low to grab it on my way. My hand grabs the box handle, and as I lift my hand it swings around grazing the wall. The course disappears and I roll to a stop clutching my hand. I walk back to my team as a new course rises out of the floor. "Someone else's turn! I might need to think this through!"

That evening, we walk back to the living quarters in silence. It has been a rough workout today and not too successful, either. We walk slowly through the unusually empty corridors.

"I need to get something done," Wei says. "I'll see you both at the living quarters in a few minutes."

I nod as Wei takes the next left while Forrahh and I continue our silent progress to the living quarters. We sit down and request our meals.

"I have a question for you," I blurt out between mouthfuls. "How come the Keteran males are not on this ship? I mean, you don't see them around anywhere."

"This is primarily a command ship, Jon. Most of the Keteran males are working on the other ships and mainly in the loading bays. They are considerably stronger than their Human counterparts but lack in initiative, so this is the best place for them."

"I can see how that makes sense. A slightly more personal question... How old are you? I tried to figure it out, but I just can't. You look my age, but your eyes tell a different story. There's something about your eyes, though."

"That is not personal, Jon. I have heard that some Humans are embarrassed about their age. My people feel that age brings respect and experience with it. We also tend to age slower than Humans. I suppose in Human years, I am about sixteen years old." I'm enjoying the chance to get to know something about her. It dawned on me that we had spent a lot of time together, but I knew nothing about her or her culture.

"So, what about traditions? My people have lots of traditions spread across many cultures and beliefs."

"We have our own traditions, too, although they are not diversified over different cultures. All of my people have the same beliefs and perform the traditions in the same way."

"Has it always been that way?"

"Yes."

That's when Wei returns and sits next to me. He orders his meal, obviously frustrated about something. "Do you think we will ever beat that course?"

"It will just take a little more practice," Forrahh says.

"I suppose so. I just don't see why *I* need to practise like this. It is not like *I* will be on any of these types of missions." I look up from my meal now and again as I listen to their conversation. Wei did have an issue with the electric shocks. I wonder if this is why he is so irritated.

"You will be providing us with support on some of the missions, Wei. We may have to get out quickly one day and this training will be useful."

"I know. I am just frustrated at how slow our progress was today."

"Don't worry, we will get there… We have to!" She turns her attention back to her food.

Two days later, we get the call we have been waiting for.

APLHA TEAM, PLEASE REPORT TO JOINT COMMAND IN THE MCC MEETING ROOM IMMEDIATELY.

We are out of our bunks and dressed in record time. We run down the corridors, trying to get there as soon as possible. As we enter, the commanders are sitting at the table waiting for us.

"Sit down, please." Wesley indicates the seats on the opposite side of the table. We sit down without saying a word. "Report please, HICS."

WE ARE APPROACHING THE PLANET NOW.

"Excellent," Nique says; "have the interceptors returned yet?"

YES, SIR. THEY HAVE SCOUTED THE PLANET AND RETURNED WITH THEIR FINDINGS ALREADY. THE PLANET IS RELATIVELY HOT. THE SURFACE IS BARREN AND DESOLATE DUE TO EXTENSIVE VOLCANIC AND SEISMIC ACTIVITY, AND THERE ARE NO LIFE SIGNS DETECTED ANYWHERE. THE SURFACE IS EXPECTED TO BE DENSE AS I AM UNABLE TO GET ANY READINGS BELOW THE SURFACE. THIS MAY WORK TO OUR ADVANTAGE.

"Sounds like a hostile environment! Maybe we made a mistake coming here," Nique says, sounding concerned.

I HAVE IDENTIFIED SOME AREAS WHERE WE COULD SET UP BASE. THERE IS A NEARBY RANGE OF DORMANT VOLCANOES APPROXIMATELY TWO KILOMETRES AWAY. THE INTERCEPTORS HAD TO FLY VERY CLOSE TO THIS AREA AS THEIR SCANNERS WERE UNABLE TO DETECT THE SURFACE DETAIL CORRECTLY. I WILL SET UP A BASE BELOW THE PLANET'S SURFACE AND THIS WILL SUFFICE UNTIL A BETTER OPTION IS AVAILABLE. THE TRANSPORT SHIPS WILL TAKE THE

PEOPLE TO THE SURFACE ONCE THE BASE IS READY. A WORD OF WARNING, SIR. ANYONE EXPOSED ON THE SURFACE FOR MORE THAN A FEW MINUTES WILL HAVE PROBLEMS BREATHING. ALTHOUGH THERE IS BREATHABLE AIR, IT IS TAINTED BY UNUSUALLY LARGE AMOUNTS OF HYDROGEN SULPHIDE AND SULPHUR DIOXIDE. THE TRANSPORT SHIPS HAVE HAD A DOCKING HATCH INSTALLED BELOW THEM. THIS WILL LOCK ONTO THE LIFT AIRLOCK. WHEN EVERYONE HAS DISEMBARKED, THE AIRLOCK WILL LOCK SHUT AND THE TRANSPORT WILL LEAVE.

"Do we have any more EMOs ready?" Nique asks.

YES, SIR. THERE ARE A FURTHER FIFTY SUITS READY FOR USE.

"And Alpha Team? How have they been coping with your obstacle course?" He looks to us but is obviously more interested in a report from HICS.

THEY COMPLETED IT A FEW TIMES THIS MORNING SO I GAVE THEM SOME TIME OFF TO RELAX. THEIR STRESS LEVELS WERE ELEVATED.

"Good. It won't be long before you are all going to be busy. How are you going to hide the ships, HICS?"

I HAVE PERFECTED THE DRILLING EQUIPMENT FROM THE NAJESS PLANS. THEY ARE READY FOR LAUNCH NOW. THE SCREEN WILL SHOW THE DRILL'S PROGRESS. An image of the planet is displayed on the screen. Moments later, a missile-shaped object is fired at it. The screen changes to show the view of the planet from the nose cone of the object. We watch intently as it approaches the planet at high speed and impacts the side of the volcano. Then the signal is lost and the image on the screen is replaced briefly by a snowy effect.

"I was expecting a bit more, to be honest," Wesley says frankly.

I HAVE LOST TRACK OF THE DRILL, SIR. THERE

APPEARS TO BE SIGNIFICANT INTERFERENCE FROM THE SURFACE OF THE PLANET.

"Do you have more drills?" Nique asks. Enira leans forward in her chair.

I HAVE A GOOD STOCK OF THESE DRILLS, SIR. I WILL SEND ANOTHER ONE. I WILL CONFIGURE IT TO CONTINUE WORKING EVEN IF WE LOSE CONTACT.

"Sounds like a plan, HICS. Proceed." We turn back to the screen and watch as another drill leaves the ship. As before, the image from the drill disappears when it gets to the planet.

THE DRILL WILL STILL BE ACTIVE. THE LIVING QUARTERS BELOW THE SURFACE WILL BE READY IN ANOTHER TEN MINUTES. WHEN ALL PERSONNEL HAVE TRANSPORTED TO THE BASE, I WILL MOVE THIS SHIP AND THE TRANSPORTS INTO THE VOLCANO RANGE BEFORE SEALING THE ENTRANCE FROM WITHIN. There is a brief pause. THE TRANSPORTS HAVE BEEN MADE READY AND I HAVE GIVEN THE ORDER FOR EVERYONE TO BOARD THEIR DESIGNATED TRANSPORTS. YOUR TRANSPORTS ARE ALSO READY AND WAITING FOR YOU. ALPHA TEAM WILL BE YOUR SECURITY DETAIL UNTIL YOU ARE ALL SAFELY BELOW THE SURFACE.

"Excellent. Where is the transport?"

PLEASE FOLLOW THE SIGNS TO CB1. THE TRANSPORT IS WAITING FOR DEPARTURE.

"Alpha Team, get into your EMOs. Your time has come," Wesley says. We stand and exit the room in silence.

LIVING QUARTERS ARE NOW READY. PREPARE FOR DEPARTURE. The announcement comes through the intercom system. The commanders are seated near the airlock to their transport, waiting for HICS to let them enter. We have arrived dressed in our EMOs and stand about ten feet behind the commanders.

HICS speaks over the CB1 intercom. THE VENTILATION SHAFTS SHOULD BE COMPLETE AND FUNCTIONING NOW. MEDICAL AND ENGINEERING TEAMS ARE ON THEIR WAY. PLEASE BOARD THE TRANSPORT.

The commanders rise from their seats and move to the airlock. As they approach the door, it slides upwards, allowing them to walk through the rear portal of the ship. The commanders sit in their allocated seats. We move to the back of the transport where specially designed seats have been installed to fit our EMOs.

With all harnesses securely attached and the transport ready for flight, we wait nervously for the order to be given.

MEDICAL AND ENGINEERING TEAMS HAVE LANDED. THE AIRLOCK HAS BEEN OPENED. THEY WILL NOW GO BELOW THE SURFACE AND ENTER THE LIFT. There is a brief silence. THERE APPEARS TO BE A PROBLEM.

"Explain, HICS?" Nique asks, controlling his obvious discomfort at the news.

THE TEAMS HAVE DISAPPEARED FROM MY SCANNERS. PLEASE WAIT… HICS TO MEDICAL AND ENGINEERING TEAMS, ARE YOU RECEIVING? There is no response. WE WILL NEED TO MOVE TO THE SITE AND CONFIRM THE SITUATION VISUALLY, SIR. I SUGGEST YOU ALL EXIT THE TRANSPORT. ALPHA TEAM WILL INVESTIGATE AND REPORT.

The commanders exit the transport, leaving us alone in the back. A screen switches on at the front of the bay area, displaying a view of the planet as we detach from our ship. It is a bleak, dull image with no notable features. As we move closer to the planet's atmosphere we catch a view of the incredible volcanic activity on the surface through a rare break in the cloud. Huge ranges of volcanoes are visible, spewing forth molten lava in all directions.

"Not possible," Wei says. "How are we supposed to live there?"

THE AREA I HAVE SELECTED HAS CONSIDERABLY LESS ACTIVITY. YOU WILL BE RELATIVELY SAFE THERE.

"Relatively!" Wei states sarcastically.

THERE ARE ALWAYS GOING TO BE DANGERS, WEI. I WILL ENDEAVOUR TO KEEP EVERYONE SAFE. WE ARE NOW ENTERING THE ATMOSPHERE. IT IS NOT AS DENSE AS EARTH'S ATMOSPHERE, BUT YOU WILL STILL FEEL SOME TURBULENCE.

HICS' timing is perfect this time. The moment he stops speaking, the ship begins to jump around. It lasts only a few minutes, but it is enough time for us to feel some concern and tighten our grips on the seats. I may have gripped mine a bit too hard… I left finger-shaped indentations in the arm rest.

We punch through and continue down to the planet's surface, where all we can see is more cloud cover. We continue our descent and soon drop below the clouds. The screen shows us the area ahead, but I can't see any clearing where we could land. I try to zoom in with my viewer, but the distortion on the screen stops me from seeing anything useful.

THE AREA YOU ARE LOOKING AT IS OUR LANDING ZONE. YOU WILL SEE A SMALL HATCH IN THE GROUND. THE TRANSPORT WILL BE LANDING ON TOP OF IT. THERE IS A HATCH IN THE MIDDLE OF THE TRANSPORT FLOOR. WHEN THE LIGHT ON THE HATCH CHANGES FROM RED TO GREEN, IT WILL BE SAFE TO OPEN IT. WE WILL BE LANDING SHORTLY.

The turbulence dies down considerably and Wei seems to be controlling his emotions now.

ONCE THE HATCH IS OPEN, MOVE INTO THE LIFT BAY AND TRY TO COMMUNICATE WITH THE TEAMS. IF THE SITUATION IS CONFIRMED OKAY, INFORM ME, AND THE TRANSPORT WILL RETURN TO COLLECT THE COMMANDERS.

I feel the ship slow down and the nose rise into the air as we approach the landing zone. It hovers briefly over the landing area before slowly dropping to the surface for a gentle touchdown. THE HATCH IS UNLOCKED. I HAVE NO LIFE SIGNS BELOW THE SURFACE. I SUGGEST YOU ENTER INDIVIDUALLY.

"Agreed," Wei states. "Okay, go through the lift hatch and confirm the situation. Radio contact at all times, understood?"

"Yes, sir," Forrahh and I chorus sarcastically as we release our harnesses and rise from the seats. We carefully move to the floor hatch and wait until it opens fully.

The door opens upwards and a rush of hot, stale air pours into the ship. My visor displays the air composition, highlighting it with an orange warning colour. "It's like we got dropped in a desert! I'll go first," I volunteer. They both step back to give me space. I stand over the hatch and look down into the darkness. I actually can't see a thing beyond the hatch. My visor's night vision activates automatically. Now as I look down, I can at least see the floor about ten metres down. I look back at my friends. "This is what we've been training for!" I state as I take a small step forward and fall to the floor, purposely avoiding the stepladder provided.

"What are yo…" Wei says. His voice cuts out just as my head drops below the surface level.

I bend my knees to lessen the impact as I land on the floor. "Weird!"

"Who's that?" The dismembered voice comes through my visor.

It's not a voice I was expecting, but I do recognise the voice! "Garry?" An image of him appears with his name below it. "Garry Ford? Is that you?" I knew Garry at the base on Earth. He always seemed to have a problem with me. There was something about me that really bugged him – at least, that's what people kept telling me – but I never said anything. I figured it was best to just keep my distance.

"Jon? That you?"

"Yeah! Are the others with you?" I notice Forrahh's marker moving towards me on my map. I step sideways and narrowly avoid being hit by her.

"… matter with you, Jon," Forrahh calls out. "Why didn't you answer?" I'm not sure if she's annoyed or worried.

"I lost communications with you."

"Jon," Garry says, "the others are here, too. We're all fine and real happy to hear your voices again. As soon as we got down here, we lost contact with HICS. By the time we realised, the transports had already left."

"Yeah, we know. It's okay. We're here now." I look up towards the hatch. "Forrahh, I'm going to head back up and let Wei know that everything's fine. I'll be back in a minute." I leap up and grab the hatch edge enough to get my head through. "Wei?"

"Yes!" There's relief in his voice. "What happened? How could you just jump down there? There is a ladder, you know."

"If I took the ladder, my weight would have broken it. I scanned the ladder before jumping. You need to trust me, Wei." I say smugly, realising that I had got one over on him.

"Fine. So, what happened?"

"No idea. As soon as I got down below the surface, I lost all communication with you. But we gained communications with the others below the surface."

"They are okay?"

"Yeah, they're fine. Just a strange communications blackout. It's one for HICS to figure out."

I SUGGEST WEI COMES BACK WITH THE TRANSPORT TO COLLECT THE COMMANDERS. YOU AND FORRAHH WAIT IN THE LIFT BAY. IF YOU REMAIN IN COMMUNICATION WITH THE REST OF THE PEOPLE, IT WILL KEEP THEM CALM.

"Sounds good," I confirm.

WE WILL MEET YOU BACK HERE IN APPROXIMATELY THIRTY MINUTES.

"See you soon, Jon." I detect a little nervousness in Wei's voice.

"Relax, Wei. It's only thirty minutes." He nods and I let go of the hatch ledge, allowing myself to drop to the floor.

I'd love to be as accurate as HICS with his timekeeping… Well, sometimes anyway. Almost dot on thirty minutes later, we hear a dull thud as the transport lands and the hatch above changes from red to green. It opens upwards and Wei's EMO looks down through the hole. I figure I still can't hear him, so I hold my right thumb up to indicate everything is okay.

Wei steps back and Admiral Wesley's face appears over the hatch, takes hold of the ladder and makes his way down into the lift bay. As his feet touch the last rung, a tentative-looking Admiral Nique looks down the hatch and, holding the ladder carefully, steps on the top rung of the ladder. Tentatively, he moves his legs down the ladder towards us. Last of all, Admiral Enira steps more confidently onto the ladder and lowers herself down to us. When we are all down below, a small metallic arm reaches over from inside the ship and closes the hatch, sealing us in.

I press my hand up against a plate on the wall. I expect this calls the lift. While we were sitting here waiting, we couldn't see any other buttons. While we wait, I look at Admiral Nique. His name and rank are displayed on my screen along with a series of other details including his heart rate which, according to the data, is going through the roof.

"Wei?" I say, switching to internal EMO communications. "Yes, Jon?" His voice is shaky.

"Calm yourself, Wei. I think Admiral Nique needs to know that you are not worried. His heart rate is too high."

Wei checks his screen data and confirms the information. I can hear him taking a few deep breaths to control his breathing. In a steady, controlled voice he says, "The rest of the group appear

161

to be in good spirits. I suppose that is a good sign. What do you think Admiral, Wesley?"

Wesley looks up at him. "Absolutely, Wei. I couldn't agree more."

I put my hand out and place my palm on the lift door. The image clears up on my visor screen and I see the lift cables moving on the other side. As I look down, I see a box-shaped object moving towards us with data readings beside it. "The lift will be here in another thirty seconds." The non-EMO-wearing group nods, but no-one says anything.

The lift door opens and I move inside first. It seems sturdy enough to carry us all… at first glance anyway. I give a thumbs up signal to everyone and they nervously follow me into the lift. I press the down button and wait while the lift door slides silently closed – none of this science fiction whooshing noise, just silence. It gently begins to move downwards, picking up speed as it goes.

"Garry? Are you there?"

"Yes, Jon, I can hear you."

"Excellent. We are on our way down."

"Juan Rios?" Forrahh calls out the name, pronouncing it perfectly. "As medic, how do you assess the living quarters? Are they suitable for long-term habitation?"

A tentative voice comes through the lift speaker system, "Er, yes? Do I know you?"

"No you don't, Juan. My name is Forrahh. Please answer the question."

Still nervous, he pulls himself together and responds, "Living quarters are actually quite good considering where we are and how quickly it was built. It is small, though, and probably only suitable for a few weeks." He takes a deep breath. "Why is the lift so heavy? The lift information panel is displaying weight warnings. I thought there were only going to be six of you."

"Of course!" She checks the visor data. "The lift will arrive in about ten seconds, Juan. When the lift doors open, do not be alarmed. We are wearing environmental suits provided by HICS. This is why you are seeing the weight warnings." The lift door opens as she finishes her explanation and we step out into the cavernous room. The walls appear to have been melted into shape by whatever tool HICS sent down here. We step out of the lift and into the midst of a large crowd of people.

"Oh cool!" One young Human walks up to me and touches the outside of my suit. I stand perfectly still, scared I might hurt him.

"Garry. It's me, Jon!" I say out loud.

Forrahh switches to internal intercom. "I suggest we open the visors so we can prove who we are. The Najess people appear to be getting agitated."

"Agreed," Wei says. I realise his voice is a lot steadier now.

"Okay." We open our visors and Forrahh speaks to the group, "Hello? Are you all okay?"

Another Human slowly steps forward. "I am Juan Rios. Are you Forrahh?" The initial shock of seeing three armoured suits approximately eight feet tall, entering this huge room was maybe a bit too much at first, but he seemed to have regained some control now.

"We were worried. We came down here and lost communication, so we thought something must have happened to the fleet. We could not leave the base as we did not know if there was a transport waiting on the surface."

"Don't worry, the fleet is fine. There just seems to be some interference down here which stops us communicating with the surface."

"And yet, we were able to communicate with you just as we lost contact with the fleet," Wei says, coming into his own again. "It would suggest that this may not be a natural phenomenon."

"I agree. We will have to investigate that after we have regained contact with HICS." Forrahh looks to the commanders. "I suggest you all get settled and in a few minutes we will go back up to the surface to communicate with HICS."

Wesley nods his agreement. Garry is still in awe over my suit, when a thought sets like concrete in his head. "Hey look, if you guys are going back up top, you may need more people... just in case something happens, you understand." Same old Garry looking to get his hands on a new toy. "Why not give me a suit and maybe I can help!"

"It's not that easy to use, Garry," I say politely.

"Well, you're doing it. Can't be that hard!" I bite my tongue and step back from him. "Not this time, Garry." I catch a glimpse of Forrahh's face. She doesn't seem too impressed by him so far.

ALPHA TEAM, ARE YOU RECEIVING ME?

"HICS," I say with relief. "What happened?"

ALL SYSTEMS ARE BEING CHECKED, JON. AS SOON AS THE SHIP ENTERED THE VOLCANO AND THE ENTRANCE WAS SEALED, I BEGAN TO RECEIVE COMMUNICATIONS FROM YOU AGAIN. BASED ON CURRENT INFORMATION, IT WOULD APPEAR THAT COMMUNICATIONS CAN ONLY HAPPEN WHEN BOTH PARTIES ARE EITHER ABOVE OR BELOW GROUND LEVEL. THIS DOES NOT APPEAR TO BE A NATURAL PHENOMENON.

"Now you sound like Wei. You two must have the most interesting conversations."

WE DO, JON. Changing the subject, he continues, I HAVE ALSO LINKED INTO THE BASE'S SPEAKER SYSTEM. THIS WILL ALLOW YOU TO COMMUNICATE MORE EFFECTIVELY WITH ME.

"Thanks, HICS," Forrahh says. "Right, people. We should get settled in."

The crowd disperses, with many of them still looking back for another glimpse of the suits.

Well, all I can say is this new base had best be a temporary solution. The main area is open-plan, which offers no respite from people you just don't want to meet... Garry and his inane questions about the EMO in this case. The only other place to have a little private time is in the sleeping quarters, a place which unbelievably is smaller than the one on the ship. Fact is, over the last hour we have realised that there is not enough bunk space for everyone, so some people are actually sleeping on the floor.

As time progresses, tensions start to increase, with a number of low-level arguments and fights breaking out. The commanders have been watching as the scene plays out, but without an alternative option or space to move anyone to they can only try to calm everyone down.

The relief is evident when HICS' voice comes through over the intercom soon afterwards.

ADMIRALS?

There is a sigh of relief from everyone, but more I think from the Admirals. Nique smiles openly and has to speak up to be heard over the commotion of the crowd, "Welcome back, HICS. What is your status?"

ALL SHIPS HAVE BEEN MOVED INTO THE CAVERNS BELOW THE DORMANT VOLCANO RANGE. WE ARE NOW COMPLETELY HIDDEN FROM AT LEAST A CURSORY SCAN OF THE PLANET. I HAVE PERFORMED ADDITIONAL TESTS AS THE SHIPS ENTERED THE AREA BELOW THE SURFACE. I CAN NOW CONFIRM THAT THIS IS NOT NATURALLY OCCURRING. ALSO, SINCE BEING BELOW THE SURFACE, I HAVE PICKED UP AN UNUSUAL ENERGY SIGNATURE FROM A NEARBY AREA.

"How far away, HICS?" Nique asks.

IT IS DIFFICULT TO SAY. IN THE SAME WAY THAT WE ARE HIDDEN WHEN BELOW THE SURFACE, THERE IS SOME DISTURBANCE CAUSING THIS TO BE HIDDEN, TOO. I CANNOT CONFIRM IF IT IS A BUILDING ON THE SURFACE – ALTHOUGH THAT WOULD BE UNLIKELY

– OR IF IT IS A STRUCTURE BELOW THE SURFACE. THE ONLY WAY TO KNOW WHAT IT IS WOULD BE TO PHYSICALLY TRAVEL THERE.

"And what do you expect to find there? Do you think there may be an indigenous species here? Maybe some structures?"

THAT IS ALSO UNLIKELY. IF THERE WERE BUILDINGS ON THE SURFACE, EITHER OUR INTERCEPTORS WOULD HAVE SPOTTED THEM OR, MORE LIKELY BY NOW, THE GRINGUN WOULD HAVE SEEN THEM AND MADE CLOSER INVESTIGATIONS OF THE PLANET.

"How do you know that they haven't already done this?" Wesley interjects. "What's to say that they are not down there waiting for us?"

IF THERE ARE ANY INDIGENOUS SPECIES ON THE PLANET, THEY ARE MOST LIKELY HIDING FROM THE GRINGUNS, AND SINCE OUR ARRIVAL THEY WOULD MOST LIKELY BE HIDING FROM US, TOO.

"Makes sense, I suppose! So, what's the plan?"

WE NEED TO SEND A TEAM TO INVESTIGATE. THE TEAM WILL CONSIST OF JON, FORRAHH AND FOUR OTHERS. WEI WILL BE REQUIRED TO HELP ME, SO WILL NOT BE ABLE TO GO. THE NEW OPERATORS NEED TO BE TRAINED IN THE USE OF THE EMOS. IT IS IMPERATIVE THAT WE UNDERSTAND WHERE THIS ENERGY SIGNATURE COMES FROM.

9

INVESTIGATIONS INTO DISAPPEARANCES

The nine Gringun assault frigates and sixteen scout ships de-cloak near where the allies entered the dimension. They slowly come to a halt, remaining in formation at all times.

"This is where the trace signatures are, sir," the sound comes through the radio in the lead scout ship.

"Do you know what it is yet?" the leader asks impatiently.

"It is distorted, but you would expect that after some time."

"You know my feelings about people who waste my time. If you want to live, you had best make yourself clear."

"Yes, sir! I believe it is a dimensional rift that has been left open. Someone has been very careless, sir. This incident has caused significant interference in the surrounding areas."

A shimmering patch comes to a halt near them and four scout ships de-cloak.

"We have a report, sir. The missing scout's drive signature has been located nearby, but the scout is still missing. There are also some other drive signatures, sir. They are very similar to ours, but with some unusual differences."

"How long ago was the rift opened?"

"At least a week sir."

The leader considers the information for a moment. *I do not remember the last time one of our people left a rift open like this. Something is not right here.*

The first scout speaks again, "Should I close the rift, sir?" There is a note of nervousness in his voice.

There is a short pause while the commander passes a few plans through his mind. "No, we need to find out where it leads. Flight Group 3, join formation and prepare the Dimensional Jump Drive. I want to know where this rift leads to and who opened it."

The four scout ships join formation with the other sixteen. No-one moves until the lead assault frigate begins to move forward. Then they all move, keeping the formation intact and turning towards the dimensional rift. As they approach, the leader gives them the signal and all of the ships jump through the rift with him.

10

DISCOVERIES

The next two days prove to be a difficult time for me. The four new people consist of two Humans and two Keterans – apparently we're better as a team – and it's down to Forrahh and me to train them. Under normal circumstances, I would have enjoyed passing my new-found experience to someone else, but this was different. Garry Ford was one of the two Humans. Great! I really didn't need to spend time with his royal smugness. He must have really badgered the commanders to get this mission. Anyway, they all paired up and we stepped into the lift to the surface for training.

We stand with our backs to the hatch, the four new EMO operators facing us and listening intently. "Normally, we would be able to communicate with HICS directly." I try to put a level of authority in my voice. "There will of course be situations where this is not possible. When this happens, we use P-HICS. P-HICS is a portable version of HICS, and although slightly limited it is still highly useful and you are unlikely to notice anything different. P-HICS will store all information until we are within transmission range with HICS and it can transfer the information.

"Right now, though, our job is to teach you the basics of moving. We would have wanted to teach you the more advanced techniques, but there is no time. For now we need to explain the layout of your visor interface and how to move around slowly. The rest will be taught as we travel. Is this understood?"

The four recruits chorus their acknowledgement.

"Excellent! Okay, let's have a roll call."

"*Private* Garry Ford!" Garry calls out, stressing the 'Private' as usual. He loves to remind me that I'm too young to have a rank or be officially enlisted.

"Welcome, *Private* Garry Ford." I emphasise the 'Private' to let him know, 'you're just a Private, mate! No big deal!' His stress levels increase… I guess I hit a nerve. Right, now that that's out of the way, it's time to get back to work. "You will all notice that as Garry began talking his icon highlighted on the visor display. At present, his icon and all others in the group are displayed in green. This shows that the individual is in good health. If the icon turns red, the person is in critical condition." I pause and speak more gravely, "A greyed-out icon means no life signs. In the event of death, the suit will self-destruct within sixty seconds. This is to prevent the capture of the technology and its use against us. Of course, this means that the body will not make it back to the base for a burial." I pause for a moment, allowing this to sink in. "So, who's next?"

With Garry on the far left, they chorus their names in sequence, "Private Anris, sir! I am partnered with Garry."

"Please don't call me sir. I'm not a commissioned officer yet." Private Anris nods her head.

"Private Andy Carmine!" I remember Andy from the base on Earth. We never really spoke, but he always seemed a likeable person.

"Private Entai! I have been paired with Andy."

"Excellent! Well, it's time you all got to know your EMOs

personally. For now, Forrahh and I will just watch while you start to get to know your suits. Try taking slow and precise steps. You have to concentrate on moving slowly. As you all progress, Forrahh and I will begin to explain the more advanced actions."

Forrahh takes a step forward. "We don't have much time, people. You need to learn how to perform a light jog by the end of the day. This will not be easy! We leave tomorrow morning… and trust me it is going to hurt tomorrow, so get finished as soon as possible today!"

We step confidently out of the hatch and into the barely lit morning, wistfully looking up at the thick layer of cloud obscuring the sun. I can clearly remember the bright, nourishing sun back home and wish I could see it now. I look back at our new recruits, their visors turned up to the sky like four sun worshippers searching for a sign of God. "I know what you're thinking," I say, fully understanding their loss. "But we really need to move. Let's go." I activate the maps on our visors and turn to face the flashing waypoint marker at the top of the display. Without another look back we step forward into a light-paced jog and move in the direction indicated. I activate the private communications between me, Forrahh and P-HICS. "HICS, how long until we arrive?"

AT CURRENT SPEED, IT WILL TAKE APPROXIMATELY TEN HOURS. YOU WILL NEED TO REST OVERNIGHT, THOUGH.

"That will not be necessary, HICS. I think we'll all be capable of travelling for ten hours."

THE DAYS ONLY LAST FIVE HOURS, JON, AND THE NIGHTS WILL BE TREACHEROUS EVEN WITH YOUR NIGHT VIEW ENABLED. I ADVISE YOU TO REST OVERNIGHT. I WILL BE MONITORING THE SURROUNDINGS AND WILL ALERT YOU IF I DETECT ANYTHING UNUSUAL.

I increase my speed slightly.

"HICS, how long is a full day cycle on this planet?" Forrahh asks.

THE DAYS ARE EIGHTEEN HOURS LONG, CONSISTING OF FIVE-HOUR DAYS AND THIRTEEN-HOUR NIGHTS. THE DAYS WOULD BE SLIGHTLY LONGER, BUT DUE TO THE EXTENSIVE CLOUD COVER IT GETS DARK VERY QUICKLY. I DO NOT ADVISE ANY MOVEMENT DURING THE DARK HOURS, DUE TO THE LOW VISIBILITY.

"Why not use the lights in the suits?"

LIGHTS COULD DRAW UNNECESSARY ATTENTION TO US. WE STILL DO NOT KNOW IF WE ARE ALONE ON THIS PLANET, FORRAHH.

"True. I suppose that makes sense." She increases her pace to match mine. "I guess a night out camping won't harm anyone."

As we jog towards our waypoint, we inform the team of what we have learned about the planet and we all decide to continue our run through the five hours without a break. With the EMOs on, it's really not that hard anyway. On the way, we continue to teach our new recruits some of the more advanced techniques. This includes a challenge of picking up specifically sized and weighted rocks without breaking their stride. The task teaches them how to use the scanners to detect the rocks and how to control the EMOs at the same time. We also learn how to select targets and allocate them to the team.

We make excellent progress by nightfall and settle down to rest. Garry, meanwhile, insists on looking for something to burn.

I DO NOT ADVISE LIGHTING A FIRE. IT WOULD NOT HELP ANYWAY. THE SUIT WOULD KEEP ALL THE HEAT OUT.

"The fire is for psychological purposes, HICS!" Garry says and then barely audibly he mutters, "You'd know that if you were even slightly Human!"

IT WOULD ALSO SERVE TO ALERT ANYONE OF OUR POSITION. THIS WOULD BE A MISTAKE. BESIDES, YOU WILL NOT FIND ANYTHING TO SET ALIGHT.

"Leave it, Garry," I say to him, "you know HICS is right. It's safety over psychology right now!"

Garry doesn't reply, but I can almost sense the hostility coming through his suit. He's going to make me pay for publicly taking HICS' side.

Forrahh wakes us all up bright and early the next morning – well, less bright, more early. We slowly get to our feet and stretch. It's quite an unusual sight really, a group of huge humanoid-looking creatures – totally black all over – standing up suddenly and reaching for the cloudy sky. Well, if anyone on this planet was watching us, that's what they'd have seen, anyway.

"I have to admit," Entai says in mid-stretch, "that was probably the best night's sleep I have had in months. These EMOs are great!"

I stretch and take a look at the surroundings. *Things look real different in the day,* I think to myself. I look out at the surrounding volcanoes, some of which still have smoke pouring out of the tops. The scene really is desolate, with no trees or wildlife anywhere. Just to be sure, I check for any life signs in the area.

AS I SAID BEFORE, JON, THERE IS NOTHING ALIVE HERE.

"I know… it just doesn't seem possible. The planet should be able to sustain some life at least, but nothing exists!"

THERE IS TOO MUCH VOLCANIC AND SEISMIC ACTIVITY ON THIS PLANET. LIFE MAY NEVER HAVE EXISTED HERE.

"And yet here we are, trying to locate an energy signature in the middle of nowhere. Defies that logic, huh?"

IT COULD BE ANOTHER CIVILISATION WHICH TRAVELLED HERE TO SET UP BASE. LIKE US, MAYBE IT IS SOMETHING THEY LEFT BEHIND.

"You have an answer for everything!" I switch back to the team. "Okay, people. I guess we can assume everyone knows how to use their EMOs now. There is something I have wanted to do since HICS first mentioned it some time back, and this is the first real chance I have had to try it."

"What are you planning, Jon?" Forrahh says tersely, a sense of foreboding creeping into her voice.

I twist my EMO boots into the dirt, firmly planting my feet into the ground, "Remember when HICS said that jumping would be the fastest way to get around?"

"Jon, HICS also said it was the most dangerous way to travel."

"Are you planning on living forever?"

"Five more minutes would be good!" she responds sarcastically. THIS IS TOO RISKY, JON!

"You *are* going to live forever!" The dirt beneath my feet compresses as I am propelled into the air and land in a small cloud of dust about two hundred metres away. The journey completes in seconds. "Wow! Now, that was awesome! And it was only a small jump, too."

As the dust settles around my feet I turn to face the team. The visor zooms in on them, and then tracks them as the two Humans bound into the air and land within five feet on either side of me.

"Nice jumping, lads!" I say, impressed with them both. A few seconds later the three Keterans leap into the air in unison, land in front of their partners.

"Rash," Entai states.

"Dangerous," Anris says sternly.

"And incredibly foolish!" Forrahh scolds me before she has even landed.

I knew she'd go into one. That's why I started scanning her

vitals while she was in the air. "Accelerated heartbeat, raised body temperature... You enjoyed that!"

She breathes slowly, calming herself before responding, "Okay, maybe a little. But it was still foolish!"

"But quick, right? And fun!"

"A little maybe." She leaps into the air and lands about four hundred metres away. "But you still have to learn how to do it right!"

"Highly unusual!" Anris remarks to Entai telepathically.

"I know. I have never seen her act that way. Come, we best keep up." They both jump to their partners and a moment later we are all leaping across the landscape.

"What do you think would make her act that way?"

"I have no idea, but her actions are very unusual. He appears to have influenced her in some way," Entai considers thoughtfully.

"Well, I like her better this way... less serious!"

Entai laughs as they continue to play 'Follow the Leader'.

The extra travelling speed allows us to arrive at the destination an hour earlier than expected. Forrahh and I try to look around and get some information on the surroundings, but the light levels are too low.

"What's happening, HICS?" I ask. "I thought you said we had made good time? I still can't see anything."

IT IS DUSK, JON. THE SUN IS STILL SETTING, BUT THERE IS INCREASED CLOUD COVER IN THE AREA DUE TO ADDITIONAL VOLCANIC ACTIVITY NEARBY. IF THERE IS A SETTLEMENT HERE, THE LOCATION MAY HAVE BEEN CHOSEN ON PURPOSE. IT IS MORE HIDDEN FROM ORBIT THAN MOST OTHER AREAS OF THE PLANET.

I switch on the lights around my visor, making me look more like an alien from a sci-fi/horror movie than anything we'd seen so far. "Well, that didn't help much," I say, thinking aloud.

175

"I do not see any buildings nearby!" Forrahh says.

"What mode are you using?" I ask.

"Try your night vision!"

"Now, why didn't I think of that?" I say as the night vision activates.

"I am assuming that was a rhetorical question?"

"Yeah. I get the feeling I wouldn't like your answer anyway. Are you sure this is the right place, HICS?"

THE LOCATION IS CORRECT. THE ENERGY SIGNATURE IS STRONGEST HERE. IT WOULD BE LOGICAL TO ASSUME THAT IF THERE ARE NO BUILDINGS AND THE SIGNATURE IS STRONG, THAT THE..."

"... Structure is below us!" Garry says, completing HICS' statement.

INDEED, GARRY. AS I SAID, IT WOULD BE LOGICAL.

"So, let's start digging!" I suggest.

"It's too late, Jon," Forrahh responds. "And besides, we don't know where to start. Tomorrow morning we can get up early and spread out. Let's get some rest for now."

I reluctantly give in and look for a flat area to lie down on for the night. "One thing I do like about this planet, though... you get plenty of sleep when you're outside!"

We all laugh as we settle down to a well-deserved rest while recounting tales of home.

Forrahh wakes us up just before daybreak. "I know it is early," she says, adding a commanding tone to her voice, "but we have plenty of work to get on with. Come on, people, get up!"

Grudgingly, we get up and carefully walk around the still dark area, getting our bearings. Over the next few minutes the sun rises over the surrounding volcanoes, brightening the area enough for us to see without the night vision activated... although barely enough light passes through the clouds to make a huge difference.

The area is much the same as anything else we saw the day before. There's just more volcanoes and dust in every direction.

"I already checked the ground with the sonar," Forrahh says. "There is definitely something down there. The structure seems quite big, but it looks like this is the only raised area. We should spread out. Maybe we can find a way in before nightfall."

Anris and Andy bend down, palms facing downwards to use their sonar on the ground. "That's really cool!" Andy says quietly to her.

"Good idea," I say. "Everyone, spread out and use the sonar to mark the outer edges. Once we have marked the outsides, we can start to move inwards. Hopefully we will find an opening somewhere."

We all move outwards, our hands facing down towards the ground, reading the structure below.

"It is metallic, but I have never seen anything like it," Anris says.

"I know," I reply, deep in thought. "Have you seen the thickness? If this is correct, our weight alone should've made us fall through."

"Whatever the material is, it is stronger than anything we have come across so far," Forrahh says. "Do you know anything about this material, HICS?"

I HAVE SEARCHED ALL DATA INCLUDING THE INFORMATION FROM THE GRINGUNS. THIS IS A NEW MATERIAL. IF POSSIBLE, PLEASE TRY TO GET A SAMPLE. I WOULD NOT ADVISE ATTACKING THE STRUCTURE, THOUGH. THERE MAY BE DEFENCE MECHANISMS IN PLACE.

I'm not sure how we're supposed to get a sample if we can't chip away at it! Anyway, we continue working in silence. When we reach the outside edges, we circumnavigate the structure and turn back inwards, mapping the outer edge as we go. As we slowly move to the centre, we continue scanning the surface and clear away the dirt down to the metallic structure. I'm not sure, but either the surface was designed to be the same colour as the dirt or it has been stained by it over the years. Either way, it matches almost perfectly.

It's about two hours of solid, hard toil – made considerably easier by the EMOs, of course – before Andy calls out to us, forgetting that the headset delivers his voice. "I'VE FOUND SOMETHING! Sorry," he says, realising how loud that must have been, "forgot about the headset."

Ignoring it, we move quickly to his side and bend down to the ground for a closer look. The otherwise smooth surface of the structure is interrupted by two indentations, side by side. The left indentation is shaped with an almost rectangular centre area. There is a deeper indentation coming from the top of the rectangle and down into the surface, almost curling back on itself like cracks in a rock face. Another indentation comes from the bottom right side of the rectangle, curving upwards towards the top of the rectangle. The second indentation is to the right and is a mirror image of the left one.

We brush away the dirt from the surrounding area but find nothing else of interest. I look around but can't find any images or symbols telling us what we need to do. Confused, we sit around staring at the indentations, trying to understand what they could mean.

Almost an hour goes by before I stand up and walk around to the other side of the indentation. I look at it again, a thought taking shape in my mind. I raise my hands and study them. My hands fall to my sides as I stand there considering the indentations again. Forrahh and the others got bored ages ago and started looking for something else. I guess they must think this is a red herring. All I can do is simply stare at the indentations and wonder why someone would put them there if they served no purpose. There has to be a reason.

"I have an idea," I say to no-one in particular. Forrahh returns to my side. *Only another hour of daylight left,* I think to myself as I look up at the sky.

"What are you thinking, Jon?" Forrahh asks, concern creeping into her voice again.

"You're going to think I'm crazy, Forrahh, but just let me try this, okay?" She considers this briefly, her concern growing before she grudgingly nods her approval. By now, Garry has also arrived beside us.

I stand on the opposite side of the indentation so the deeper grooves are above the rectangles. I join my fingers together on both hands, leaving the thumbs sticking out from the sides. "Here goes," I say looking at Forrahh. For once I wish she would stop me... No luck this time, though.

I concentrate on the EMO armour covering my hands and watch as they open up, exposing my hands to the blistering heat of the surrounding environment.

YOU MUST SEAL THE SUIT WITHIN TWO MINUTES TO PREVENT PERMANENT SKIN DAMAGE, JON.

Forrahh flinches at the words but restrains herself. Without saying a word, I bend to my knees and place my hands onto the indentations, inserting my fingers into the grooves and my thumbs into the side grooves. The metal is comfortable and surprisingly cool beneath my hands. Of course, the tops of my hands feel like they have been placed in an oven.

I grip the grooves and wait. Nothing happens.

"Yep, he's lost it!" Garry says.

"I've only just started." I curl my fingers deeper into the grooves and grip tight with my fingertips. Nothing happens. I was sure that was going to work. I try to pull my hands off the surface, but they feel like they've been glued in place. Something needle-like pricks my left and right index fingers. I pull my hands back harder this time. No luck. Panic sets in. "What the...? I... I can't get free." I stop resisting and allow it to finish what it is doing… If you can't beat 'em, join 'em. A few seconds later, the horrible glued sensation disappears. "What was that?" I say as I focus on my EMO armour covering my hands again. "Not exactly a friendly welcome!" I stand up straight and look impatiently at the indentations, waiting for something, anything, to happen.

"What a waste of time… and an unnecessary risk too, Jon!" Garry says, trying to make a point.

"Yeah," I say disappointed, "and all I got was this nasty pin prick in my finger. Hey, I hope it's not infected with something!"

There is a sudden whooshing sound like air escaping. A crack appears in the otherwise seamless surface. The area where the indentations were lifts up to show a hatch big enough for the EMOs to climb down. I lean over the edge and look inside. There is a light on in the entrance but no more the rest of the way down. I put my hand out and check the depth using the sonar. It's quite a cool gadget to have, actually. I wonder how many other gadgets there are in these suits that we haven't found yet. "It's about two hundred feet. I can make it."

"Oh no you don't," Andy says from behind me, "it's my turn for a little fun." I look at him.

"You sure you're up to it?" He nods and gives me the thumbs up. I step back from the edge as he lowers himself down the tube.

"Looks that way!" Forrahh says quietly.

"Sorry?" I ask, not sure what she means.

"Entai just asked me a question, telepathically of course," Forrahh says. "She wants to know if all Humans are so reckless!"

"Obviously, but that's why you guys are here… to be the voice of reason and stop us from doing reckless things!"

"They're not doing a great job!" Andy says as he looks down the hole. "I'm about to jump into a deep, dark hole. Can't imagine what might be down there."

"Would you listen to us?" Entai asks.

"Probably not," Andy responds. "So, can we get on with this? I'm getting old listening to you both!" I confirm with a thumbs up and he carefully lowers himself into the hole. As his feet go below the planet's surface, the next level of lights comes on. He looks down at the lights. "Well, that's promising!" he says.

"When you reach the bottom, try and communicate," Entai says. "There is a possibility that we will not be able to hear you, so flash your lights a few times and check the immediate area only. Get back to the tunnel within two minutes and flash your lights again if all is clear. If you don't flash your lights within two minutes, we are coming in to get you!"

"Yes, Mum," he says in a sarcastic but good humoured way. Then he lets go of the side and drops surprisingly slowly down the tunnel. "Hey this is great. It's like a low G fall."

"Not bad," I say, impressed already. "Activate the video footage. We'll be able see what you see."

"Nice! My YouTube ten minutes of fame starts now!" Our visors activate, showing us all peering over the top of the hole... and we do look a strange sight!

We watch as Andy slowly floats down the shaft. At each twenty-five metre interval, another set of lights activates below him, illuminating the path downwards. Not long after, the floor appears below him. A quick glance upwards confirms that we are still watching him float straight down like a bubble in a draught free room.

"Can you guys hear me still?" Andy asks. There is a slight nervousness to his voice.

Entai seems unusually concerned and responds before anyone else does, "We can still hear you, Andy."

His feet touch down gently. He turns to face a small opening in the shaft and peers into the gloom, but nothing is visible. "Can you hear me now?"

The image is difficult to see through the static and only a few garbled words can be made out. "... barely... you... osing com... Ent..." He looks up and sees us peering down at him. I get the feeling he's a bit scared, though he'd never admit it. He slowly turns back towards the opening and waves to confirm that he is okay instead of switching on his lights. His night vision activates and the map helps to provide an image of the room in front of him. It's larger than the entire cavern we have been living in over the last few days. The walls are perfectly smooth and seem to have been created on purpose. The visor – which is barely visible now – shows the statistics for the room. The first thing we notice is its right-angle alignment, which appears to be exactly ninety degrees.

"Anything here, HICS?"

Clear as day, HICS' voice comes through the headset. THERE ARE NO LIFE SIGNS ANYWHERE. THE ENERGY SIGNATURE EMANATES FROM THIS ENTIRE AREA.

"Well, here goes… One small step for man," he steps into the room, "one giant leap… Well, you know the rest!" I see some lights flicker as he steps inside. Then the image turns to snow and we lose contact with him completely.

A few seconds later he is back in the shaft, the lights from inside the room reflecting off him. "ome… am… municati… Niq… fe." He desperately tries to convey his message to us, signalling us with his hands while he speaks.

I step towards the tube, but before I can jump Entai has stepped straight into the shaft and started floating down to the bottom. I shrug – no easy feat in an EMO, trust me – and allow her to go next. Garry waits patiently for us all to get down there and signal that it is safe. Some things never change!

One by one we all drop into the shaft and float down to the floor below. As I step into the cavern, I can see exactly how big it really is. The video image on the visor didn't do this place justice.

Andy is excitedly recounting to Entai what happened, "… and as I stepped into the room, all of the lights activated right to the end and that's when Admiral Nique…"

I look away from him and study the room as Garry finally makes his way in. There are tables and chairs all lined up everywhere. "I guess this was a communal area, then."

"Jon? This is Admiral Nique. Are you receiving me?"

"Sir, where are you?" I ask looking around for him.

"We are still in the main base, but we picked up your transmission."

IT SEEMS THAT WHEN YOU ARE BELOW THE SURFACE, COMMUNICATIONS ARE ACTIVE AGAIN. I AM FORWARDING YOUR VIDEO FEEDS TO THE MAIN BASE.

"Okay. Let me know if there is anything you specifically want us to look at," I say as I walk around the room.

Forrahh walks to one of the tables and wipes her finger across the top of it. She looks closely at the finger. "It is like someone has been keeping this place clean!" She continues to look around the rest of the room.

"Status report, HICS?" I ask.

ALL OF YOUR CAMERAS ARE ON. THE COMMANDERS ARE MONITORING YOUR PROGRESS. IT WOULD APPEAR THAT THE RANGE OF ALL COMMUNICATION EQUIPMENT BELOW THE SURFACE IS AUGMENTED SOMEHOW. THIS WILL BE HELPFUL. IT WILL ALLOW US TO COMMUNICATE MORE EFFECTIVELY. I HAVE BEEN STUDYING THE VIDEOS SINCE YOU ALL ENTERED THIS ROOM. YOU WILL SEE THAT THERE ARE FIVE EXITS FROM THIS ROOM. ONE OF THESE WAS THE SHAFT YOU ENTERED FROM. I NEED YOU TO SCOUT THE REMAINING AREAS. I HAVE ALREADY IDENTIFIED SOME OF THE ADJACENT ROOMS AND ADDED THESE TO YOUR MAPS. I WILL CONTINUE TO UPDATE THE MAPS AS YOU PROGRESS, HIGHLIGHTING ROOMS WHICH REMAIN TO BE EXPLORED.

"Okay, HICS. Leave it to us," I respond. I turn to the team.

"You heard the orders, people. We travel in our designated pairs at all times. Identify the rooms and check for life signs, past or present, as you go."

We all form up with our partners and begin to move to different areas. I switch to private communications with Forrahh. "Did you tell them to do that? They all moved to separate exits at the same time."

"Yes," she says as we move to the exit in front of us, "we communicate about everything, Jon. This is why Humans and Keterans make good teams."

"It must be good to communicate like that, but what if you wanted to keep something to yourself sometimes?"

"When you are born to telepathy, you grow up reading people and of course being read. It does not occur to you to hide anything. Secrets are actually alien to us. Our people confer about everything." We step into a wide corridor with doorways at regular intervals all the way down. Each doorway opens into a room which could easily be made into living quarters if required.

"I guess it makes things more efficient at least." We peer in through each doorway as we walk past. HICS then maps the room and identifies anything inside which may be interesting. We continue until we reach the end of the corridor where it splits into a T-junction. "Left or right?" I ask, deferring the choice to Forrahh.

"Left this time."

"As you wish!"

"The right attitude; keep it up!" Even through the EMO, I can tell she is smiling as she says this. We turn left into the corridor.

A couple of hours go by before I feel it's time to contact the team. "Okay, people. It's time for a break. Meet back at the main area."

We arrive back at the entrance and I feed back our progress – or lack of, in this case – to the others.

"We haven't found anything either," Garry says sounding dejected. "Just a load of barely furnished rooms."

"We found some large rooms surrounding a central, circular hub room," Entai says. "HICS said it could act as a good command centre. The rooms surrounding it could also act as conference rooms. We suggested that we could set up the circular room in the same format as the MCC. I think HICS liked the idea. Something about making it easier for everyone to adapt."

"Anything else?" I address the rest of the team, but there are no further suggestions. "Commanders, are there any particular rooms you need us to investigate further?"

"No, Jon." Nique replies. "Your team has done exceptionally well. Good job."

JON, I HAVE DETECTED A CHANGE IN THE LIVING CONDITIONS IN YOUR AREA.

There is a moment of unease. "What kind of change, HICS?" I ask.

PLEASE CHECK YOUR VISORS. IT WOULD APPEAR THAT THE TEMPERATURE HAS INCREASED AND THE QUALITY OF THE AIR HAS ADAPTED TO YOUR REQUIREMENTS.

I say nothing for a moment before exposing my hands to the air and stretching my fingers. "It's warm. Not too hot, just comfortably warm." I raise my visor and cautiously take a shallow breath in. "Seems fine." A deeper breath now. "Yep, definitely fresh air!" The rest of the team raise their visors and take deep breaths of clean, fresh air.

YOU MAY REMOVE YOUR SUITS IF YOU WISH. THE BASE APPEARS TO BE PERFECTLY SAFE, AND LIVING CONDITIONS ARE OBVIOUSLY ADAPTABLE TO YOUR NEEDS.

"But who made the change, HICS?" I ask.

THAT IS NOT CLEAR YET, JON. IT WOULD APPEAR THAT THE BASE YOU ARE IN MAY HAVE ANALYSED YOUR REQUIREMENTS THROUGH THE EMOS AND CHANGED THE ENVIRONMENT TO MATCH YOUR

NEEDS. ALTERNATIVELY, THE BASE MAY HAVE TAKEN A SAMPLE OF YOUR BLOOD FOR ANALYSIS WHEN YOU OPENED THE BASE.

"Yeah, forgot about that," I say nervously as I remember the pin pricks on my fingers earlier. "We will probably spend the night here, Admiral," I state, pulling myself together. "Is there anything you need us to do before we leave tomorrow?"

"Actually, Jon, we have decided that your present location will make a better base for us. You are to stay there. HICS is preparing a few transports to take us to you tomorrow morning. The space issues over here are already causing problems."

"Understood, Admiral. We will prepare the area for your arrival."

Transporting people between bases turned out to be a much greater task than expected. HICS decided that as we were trying to keep a low profile on the planet, we should use only two large transports to ferry people to the new base. This decision cost us a couple of extra days before we got everyone here. The good thing was, as we were the first to arrive, we had our own choice of rooms. The commanders arrived the next day and they took up the rooms closest to the new Command Centre. Slowly, the remaining people arrived at the base and selected their rooms. Some settled down and started working, while others explored the rest of what turned out to be an immense complex. The Command Centre – CC as everyone started referring to it – was made to look exactly like the mobile version.

We had exited our EMOs and stored them away in the corner of a nearby store room. After this, the three of us found we had some free time and made the most of it by exploring the base a bit further.

Many of the new arrivals were investigating the new rooms and informing HICS when they found anything unusual. As they finished investigating an area, HICS told them where to go next.

The base was huge and I got the feeling this was going to take a while.

That's when Forrahh walked into the living quarters, giddy as a schoolgirl. "They found something! Andy's on his way there now. Let's go." She takes my hand, practically dragging me out of the chair and into the corridor.

As we speed walk through the numerous corridors, she continues to tell me what little she knows until we arrive at the room and stop by the doorway.

A crowd of people has already gathered in the doorway. Inside, a Keteran girl is already reciting her tale to the guards, "No, I was about to leave when I noticed a small marking on the wall. I thought it was just a blemish, but none of the other rooms had any markings. The other rooms appeared so perfect, this actually looked out of place. That is why I reached out to see if it was just dust or something. As I rubbed it, the wall above the marking moved in slightly. Then it slid right to show that space in the wall." She points at the alcove in the wall.

Forrahh pushes through the doorway for a closer look. I follow through the wake she creates to stand right behind her. The crowd is increasing rapidly as news of the discovery spreads.

"Do you know her?" I whisper to Forrahh.

"We all know each other, Jon. Her name is Nuada." She stops and listens as HICS begins asking questions.

DO YOU REMEMBER DOING ANYTHING ELSE, NUADA? ANYTHING WHICH MAY HAVE CAUSED THIS TO HAPPEN?

"I do not think so. I just rubbed the mark on the wall and the alcove appeared."

AND THE METAL BLOCK IN THE ALCOVE?

"It was there when it opened."

PLEASE DESCRIBE THE BLOCK IN MORE DETAIL.

An eerie silence creeps into the room as people lean in to hear the description of the strange block. Nuada looks at the object more carefully and starts to describe it, "It appears to be relatively nondescript except for one simple marking on the top. The marking looks like the one on the wall. Do you want me to touch this one, too?" she says enthusiastically.

NOT YET. A MEMBER OF THE SECURITY TEAM AND A LIAISON WILL BE ARRIVING IN A FEW SECONDS.

As usual, HICS is spot on. After just a few seconds, Private Andy Carmine and a huge Najess male enter the room.

Andy approaches Nuada and extends his hand to her. "Nuada?"

"Yes," she responds.

"Hi, my name is Andy Carmine and my friend here is Peryt." He notices the object in the wall behind her and cocks his head to the right to look around her. Nuada takes the hint and shifts to her right slightly. "What do we have here?"

"I am not sure."

He smiles. "Rhetorical question. Was it just there in the open like this?"

"No, there is a marking on the wall below the alcove." She seemed to be getting annoyed at repeating herself for everyone. I suppose telepaths would find this repetitiveness highly irritating. "I rubbed the marking and this part of the wall appeared. Before that, you would not have known there was a sliding section there. It was seamless."

Peryt looks at the symbol and extracts a small camera from his pocket.

He leans in close to the wall and starts to take pictures of the symbol. Andy meanwhile examines the rest of the room.

"I was trying to think back to the other rooms I have been in," Nuada explains. "I do not remember seeing these symbols in any other rooms. I would have noticed them."

"I think I have another one here," Andy calls over from the opposite side of the room. They both move to his side and look closely at the symbol. "It's different, though. You said you just rubbed it? Did you press it at all?"

"No, I just gently rubbed it. I did not want to damage it in case it was something important."

Andy extends his index finger, hesitating before gently rubbing it. The panel above it slides away to reveal another metallic block. He examines the block carefully without touching it. "Just the one symbol on top." He looks to Peryt who nods his approval. "Here goes." He rubs the image on the top of the block. He pulls his hand away quickly. "Its temperature is changing!" He looks like he is expecting something horrible to happen as a thin slice of metal below the symbol rises, lifting it from the main block. When it is about two centimetres high, the symbol tilts forward to balance on its edge on the small pedestal. We all watch amazed as the pedestal sinks back into the block again. I resist the urge to get involved… This is officially Andy's find after all. We wait, patiently anticipating another event, but nothing happens.

Peryt clears his throat, "I believe that is it."

Nuada is still looking at the block. "There has to be something else," she says, frustration creeping into her voice.

"I agree," Andy says more calmly. "It's just a puzzle… and it needs solving." He gently bites his upper lip as he mulls over the puzzle before him.

"We have found two symbols on the walls," Peryt thinks aloud, "so we can assume there may be more."

"They are both at the same height on the wall. A clue?" No-one needs any further instructions, they just start looking at the walls, and in moments, another four symbols have been found.

"Anymore?" Andy asks.

"No," Nuada says, "that is it."

Andy looks around the room, pointing at each symbol in sequence. "Six symbols. Can you see any relevance to the number, HICS?"

THERE ARE NO SPECIFIC REFERENCES TO THE NUMBER SIX IN MY DATABASE.

"Okay." Andy scratches his head as he turns around looking at all of the symbols. "Which one did you find first, Nuada?"

"That one there," she says, pointing to the symbol on the far wall.

"And the one I found was on the wall opposite. When I touched the block, it activated and then went dormant again."

Peryt raises his head. "Either this is a waste of time, or we are missing something." He pauses. "Maybe there is a sequence they need to be opened in?"

"Possible," Andy replies. "But what are they for? I wonder…" He walks to the doorway and looks into the corridor. He looks left and right and then walks to the next doorway on the right, counting each step as he goes. "That's twenty-five full paces." He enters the room, stands with his back to one wall and counts the paces to the opposite wall. "And that's fifteen paces. Noticing anything here?" He stops and bites his lip thoughtfully. "Hold on, there was a symbol by the doorway, right?" Nuada nods. "Activate it, please."

Nuada steps over to the block. She gently rubs the symbol on top and steps back as the symbol rises and stands on edge. This time, though, the symbol stays standing.

Andy moves in for a closer look. "I thought so. Look at the symbol. It's angled slightly."

Peryt looks at it before taking another picture. He lowers his head to the height of the symbol and turns to face in the direction it is facing. "That one," he says pointing at the symbol to the left on the opposite wall.

Andy rubs the symbol on the block. Before the panel has slid away fully, he impatiently rubs the top of the block and steps back.

The symbol rises and stands on edge. A narrow beam of light shines from the first symbol to the second, hitting the symbol perfectly in the centre. We all wait, but nothing else happens. Peryt checks the angle of the symbol and points to another symbol across the room. Nuada goes there and activates the block. The light connects with the symbol. "The fourth symbol is on the wall opposite the doorway," Peryt says. "And I think it points to a fifth symbol on the second wall."

"That leaves one more," Andy says, pointing out the obvious. He walks over to the block, activates the symbol on it and steps out of the way. The beam of light hits the sixth symbol. A soft humming sound emanates from the wall. One by one, starting from the sixth symbol and working back, the symbols collapse back into the blocks and the light drifts back the way it came until it disappears into the first symbol Andy activated. The centre part of the wall behind the block shifts backwards as though someone had pushed on it. It stops briefly and then slides to the right, revealing a small hidden room.

Andy walks inside first, with everyone else following him at a slight distance. The lights switch on as he steps inside. The room is only about three metres deep and five metres across. In the centre there is what appears to be a waist high metallic block with lots of symbols engraved on it. The walls are covered with similar symbols.

Andy walks over to the centre block and wipes his hand across it. Nothing happens. Peryt walks around the room, snapping away with the camera like a photographer looking for a Pulitzer. "Any ideas, HICS?" Andy asks.

I BELIEVE THIS MAY BE A LANGUAGE. I FIND MINOR REFERENCES TO THESE SYMBOLS IN MY DATABASE, BUT NOTHING THAT WOULD EXPLAIN THEIR MEANING. DECIPHERING IT WILL NOT BE POSSIBLE. I WOULD SUGGEST THAT THIS WAS DESIGNED TO BE A SECRET MESSAGE. THERE IS LIKELY TO BE A MESSAGE HERE, BUT IT IS INTENDED FOR A SPECIFIC AUDIENCE.

"What does that mean, HICS? You figured out the Gringun language."

THAT WAS DIFFERENT, ANDY. THE SYMBOLS HERE REQUIRE A SPECIFIC KEY SYMBOL TO DECIPHER THE LANGUAGE. THIS SYMBOL IS EITHER HIDDEN HERE SOMEWHERE OR IT WAS NEVER PROVIDED. I BELIEVE IT IS THE LATTER. WE WILL HAVE TO FIND SOMEONE WHO KNOWS AT LEAST THE BASICS OF THE LANGUAGE.

Andy chews his lip again before grudgingly accepting the explanation. "Okay, HICS notify the commanders of the find. Then send a team here to cordon off the area. I don't want anyone in this corridor for now."

I WILL MAKE THE ARRANGEMENTS NOW.

"Thanks, HICS. Alright, folks, I suggest we make our way out of here for now. Thanks for your help." They all leave the room. Andy takes one last look at the room and leaves with everyone else, smiling at me as he passes.

"What do you make of that?" I ask Forrahh.

"We do as HICS says," she says in a matter of fact manner as we walk down the corridor.

"What, we just leave it to the commanders and do nothing else?"

"No. We find someone who can read the symbols. Keep your eyes open, Jon."

11

DISCOVERED, THE TRAP IS SET

The small formation of uncloaked ships slowly glide through the dimensional rift, reducing speed until they come to a gentle halt. They remain in formation, the lead frigate heading up the pack.

"We have arrived, Commander Torzden." The reprimand delivered to the scout pilot earlier is making him nervous – more so than he usually is with the Commander.

"You are still stating the obvious, Lieutenant Morkal?" The irritation is evident in his voice. "Say something of consequence before I kill you for endangering my team through idiocy!" He is losing control of his temper again.

"Sir... yes, sir." He goes quiet.

"I need information, fool!"

"Sir..." He is shaking uncontrollably in his seat. The fear increasing until he is unable to talk. "I... er, I, sir..." He fumbles with the controls.

Torzden activates the control screen in front of him and begins tapping on it. Moments later, the cover over Morkal's cockpit lifts and his harness releases itself. His pained scream is cut short as he floats out into the dark emptiness of space, the vessels in his body enlarging until they ooze through his skin. Torzden continues tapping the screen, bringing the scout ship in to dock with the frigate. A new pilot nervously enters the cold, still craft and takes his place in the seat.

"Pilot Engek, you just got promoted. I hope you can provide me with something useful."

"I have checked the star charts, sir. This is Dimension Thapa, the test zone. This dimension was used to develop test races long ago. According to the database, the area was recently visited by our people. They located some previous test races which had not been exterminated. They proceeded to cause as much devastation as possible before returning. The High Command has now designated this as a low priority. An extermination team will be despatched to complete the work soon."

"Good work, *Lieutenant* Engek. Try not to fail me as your predecessor did." He checks his screens again. "Where were the races they found?"

"There were three races on three different planets, sir. They are highlighted on your screen now."

Torzden checks his screen and examines the information. "You said they were test races. Is there any more information about them?"

"Well, there is something else interesting, sir. It seems these races were failed candidates for the warrior race. They could have been the Umach."

Torzden's interest peaks. "Well, well, I had heard rumours of these races. Yes, they were supposed to be exterminated as failures. It looks like something went wrong." He thinks aloud, "The potential warrior race… Ha, no wonder they were discarded. Look at them. Even a small contingent of light craft devastated them."

He activates two of the ships on his screen. "You two, go back through the rift and send a message to the High Command. Inform them that we are investigating a dimensional rift which has been left open. We will investigate the planets further, and on their command we will complete the extermination."

"Yes, sir."

"And *don't* mention anything about the potential Umach. I want to deal with this infestation myself!"

"Yes sir." Both ships turn around and disappear through the rift.

"You are Attack Group 1," he says, as he activates three frigates and another six scout ships on his screen. "Head towards this planet and await my orders." He highlights the Najess planet. "Do *not* allow yourselves to be seen.

"You are Group 2," he says activating the next three frigates and six scout ships, "head to this planet." He highlights Earth.

"Lieutenant Engek, you and everyone else will come with me to the last planet," he says indicating the Ketera. "Stay hidden. *No-one* is to be detected at any time."

"Yes, sir!" they all say in unison, and their ships move towards their destination, activating the cloaking devices as they go.

In the High Command Central Chamber, the council members lounge on their ornate, high-backed chairs debating the menial issues of state.

Moments later, their attention is diverted to the large doors at the back of the room. With great effort, the doors laboriously swing open, revealing a diminutive figure.

The frail looking Gringun stumbles nervously into the huge, daunting room, his head bent low as he makes his way to the large pedestal at the opposite end. He keeps his head down, avoiding all eye contact, and awaits permission to talk.

The Council members see him bent before them, the pressure on him evident.

"Ignore him for a moment," the head Council member commands telepathically.

"Why?"

"Why not? Look at the peon. I despise these people. I want him to suffer."

"They are of the same race as we are."

"Yet they allow themselves to be ridiculed, treated like dirt. They should stand and fight like we would!" The Gringun's back is beginning to hurt, but he has trained all his life to ensure this type of thought never enters his mind. *"Despicable creatures!"*

"Maybe, but I still prefer them to the scientists. I actually pity them for their weakness."

"Pity, mercy… these are weaknesses not befitting our greatness. Only the strong need survive. It is true, though. They are more tolerable than the scientists."

"I despise the way the scientists hold themselves. They have no self-respect!"

"Of course they don't. We took that away long ago!" This memory obviously pleases them both considerably.

The Council member in the middle turns his attention back to the small Gringun before them. *"Speak, fool!"* The voice appears to boom at him from all directions, but the messenger has been here before and knows it is an implanted thought. The weight of the command still takes its toll on him, though.

He clasps his hands together behind his back, wringing them together to take his mind off the voices. "I have a message from Commander Torzden of Flight Group 3," he says, forcing confidence into the words. Weakness at this point would result in extreme punishment. "He has found where the missing scout was, but has not been able to locate the craft itself.

"He wanted to inform you that he has also located a dimensional rift in the area which has been left open. It is believed that this may have caused the communication issues with the scout. The Commander has now travelled through the rift and is investigating."

"The Umach test subjects!" His thoughts are now focused on all but the messenger. The rest of the Council members have sat

upright and are taking an interest in the proceedings. *"Do you think there are many survivors?"* He is more concerned than curious.

The other Council members add their opinions. *"Not likely. The report stated they were devastated in the primary attack."*

"A recent flight group discovered them."

"I remember. They launched a surprise attack on the three planets, but the force was not large enough to complete the task."

"When was this?"

"Some months back."

"We have an extermination request open?"

"Yes, we do. It has been set to low priority."

"Raise the priority. Inform Commander Torzden that he is to collect information about the planets. A separate task force will be sent to exterminate all life in Thapa Dimension."

"Why? Is there a threat?"

"We are missing something here. Something very important."

"Which is?"

"The dimensional rift was left open. When was the last time that happened?"

"We do not remember it ever happening." The statement is thought by all, stated by one.

"Which means that someone else left it open. Torzden found no wreckage from the missing scout. More importantly, not all of the original attack craft made it back from the Thapa Dimension."

"You believe they have done something with the downed scouts?"

"It is the only explanation. Who else would leave the rift open? We must allow the Commander to gather information."

"Should we not let him complete the extermination of life in Thapa Dimension? He will already be in position. It will be quick. It will be decisive."

"No. That it is what he wants. I do not want him to have the pleasure."

"Understood. Should we provide him with information about the Umach test subjects?"

"It is Commander Torzden we are discussing. He neglected to mention the Umach, but do not underestimate him. He will be planning on surprising us with the knowledge. Notifying us of the Umach test subjects right now is not part of his plan."

He turns his attention back to the hunched-over Gringun. "Do you have the location of the scout before it disappeared?"

"Yes, sir."

He returns his focus back to the Council members. "When the Commander has completed his task, we will have him locate the path from the rift to where the scout was when it disappeared. This should tell us the general direction they were travelling."

"Agreed!"

"Inform the Commander of the plan."

"Yes, sir." The messenger gratefully stumbles away from the High Command and out of the great hall, allowing the huge doors to close behind him.

"They are here!"

"You are concerned?"

"I was not when we first attacked, but they can travel through the dimensions now."

"You believe they reverse engineered our technology. Is this possible? They should not be capable of that even."

"What should we do?"

"Remember what the scientist said before the alteration, '… they have potential!' They are here now and they are busy." There is a pause as they consider the information. "There will be an attack on one of our planets. It will be soon. We will be prepared. This will show us where they have set their base."

"We need only wait patiently. We will prepare all bases around the last known location of the missing scout."

12

MAKE OR BREAK TIME

The CC is literally buzzing with activity. Word spread like wildfire that the next mission update was imminent. By the time we got there, the commanders had taken their positions in front of the platform. Meanwhile, the teams were slowly assembling and sitting in the chairs. Luckily, we got in early enough to grab three front seats. Well, I didn't want anyone blocking my view!

I lean closer to Forrahh. "They look tense," I say looking at the commanders as they huddle together.

"Looks important. Must be something to do with the new mission."

"Hopefully something interesting for us to do! I'm tired of sitting around here."

"Why must you always wish for trouble, Jon?" Wei whispers from Forrahh's right.

"It's not that I want something bad to happen. I just hate all this sitting around. It bores me!"

"I have to admit," Forrahh responds, "even I want something to happen. I want to get into my EMO again."

"Yeah, me too. Weird, isn't it? I'm always thinking about it," I say. "I almost regret it when I have to get out."

"I know. I have been having dreams about mine recently. I wonder if it is a side—" Nique starts talking, cutting her off mid-sentence.

"For those of you who are new, welcome to the new Command Centre, affectionately known as the CC. For now, this will be our base. It is where we will update you all on the mission status and activity updates.

"The first item on the agenda is the cordoned off corridor in the North Wing. There have been many rumours about this area. HICS will hopefully put these to rest now. Go ahead, HICS."

THANK YOU, SIR. AS YOU ALL KNOW, THIS BASE WAS NOT MADE BY US. I HAVE BEEN CO-ORDINATING THE DISCOVERY EFFORT TO MAP THE SITE. THIS IS NOW COMPLETE AND I HAVE DETERMINED THAT THIS WAS MOST LIKELY USED AS A BASE OF OPERATIONS – MUCH LIKE WE ARE DOING NOW.

THE ONLY AREA OF INTEREST FOUND IS THE CORDONED OFF CORRIDOR WHICH YOU HAVE ALL BEEN TALKING ABOUT. I CAN CONFIRM THAT WE HAVE LOCATED SOME ALIEN SYMBOLS IN THIS AREA AND THAT THESE REVEALED A SECRET ROOM. THE ROOM IS COVERED IN ALIEN SYMBOLS WHICH I HAVE NOT BEEN ABLE TO DECIPHER YET. THE SYMBOLS APPEAR TO FORM A MESSAGE. HOWEVER, WITHOUT A SPECIFIC KEY SYMBOL, I WILL NOT BE ABLE TO UNLOCK THE LANGUAGE AND CONFIRM THIS. I CAN CONFIRM THAT THE KEY SYMBOL WE NEED IS NOT LOCATED ON THIS SITE. I EXPECT THIS WAS DONE ON PURPOSE.

Some minor whispering breaks out in the room, quietening down as HICS begins to speak again.

I BELIEVE THAT THE ALIEN RACE WANTED

SOMEONE TO FIND THEM. ASSUMING THEY ARE STILL ALIVE, WE NEED TO BRING THEM BACK TO THIS PLANET TO HELP US DECIPHER THE SYMBOLS. UNFORTUNATELY, WE DO NOT HAVE ANY DATA TO CONFIRM WHO MAY HAVE MADE THESE SYMBOLS AND WHAT HAPPENED TO THEM.

A Najess male sitting in the back row asks, "How can you be sure they are still alive? It seems that they left a perfectly good and well-hidden base. It is possible that the symbols are a warning about something else."

THEY APPEAR TO HAVE LEFT THE BASE IN AN ORGANISED MANNER. THIS WAS A CALCULATED DEPARTURE AND, AS THERE HAS BEEN NO EVIDENCE OF ATTACKS ON THE SURFACE OF THE PLANET, WE CAN ASSUME THAT THEY LEFT THE PLANET VOLUNTARILY. IT IS OF COURSE POSSIBLE THAT THE SYMBOLS ARE A WARNING BUT, BASED ON THE EVIDENCE AVAILABLE, IT IS LIKELY TO BE SOMETHING MORE POSITIVE. UNTIL WE LOCATE THE ALIEN RACE THAT CREATED THIS BASE, WE WILL NOT KNOW FOR SURE. The explanation seems to satisfy the Najess male for now. He nods his agreement.

"Thank you, HICS," Nique says, stepping forward to the platform in front of them. As he approaches it, the local star chart appears above it, rotating slowly. "This brings us to our mission requirements. Based on the analysis results provided, we have located a few planets which are of interest to us." The map zooms in to a small group of planets on the outskirts of the Gringun space lanes. "These are the closest inhabited planets to us. They will give us an opportunity to study the Gringuns up close."

A Human male raises his hand briefly. "Sir, are you saying that we are going to actually land on the planet?" There is a definite note of excitement in his voice even though he tries to hide it.

"Yes, but we will discuss that soon." A planet highlights on the three-dimensional image before him. It shrinks slightly and planetary statistics appear beside it. "This planet is the one we have chosen. As you can see, there are significant resources available on the planet. In addition, there is evidence of significant travel to and from the planet. Based on the data from the captured Gringun scout, we can confirm that the planet appears to be of some importance to the Gringuns and we need to find out what that importance is."

Wei raises his hand. "Sir, the information shows the importance levels, but I am confused about the defensive levels for this planet." The panel shows hardly any defensive activity. "Has this data come from the scout ship, too?"

"No. You will notice an asterisk beside the data values. This denotes real-time data. HICS has located some long-range scanners in the base here and activated them. They are allowing us to monitor some of the closest planets without detection."

"Then the data concerns me, sir. Your data shows that the planet is important and yet they have decided to leave it almost completely undefended."

"Remember, they have no enemies here, therefore no need for excessive defensive measures. Besides, the planet is on the outskirts of their area. How important could it really be?"

"And yet, we have to assume that the missing scout has raised some questions. We did our best to hide our presence, but that does not mean that they did not investigate thoroughly. What if they found evidence of the use of energy weapons?"

IT WOULD BE PRUDENT TO ASSUME THAT ANY PLANET OF SIGNIFICANCE WOULD BE DEFENDED. IF THE MISSING SCOUT HAS RAISED ANY CONCERNS AND THEY LOCATED OUR ENTRY POINT INTO THE DIMENSION, WE CAN ASSUME THAT THEY MIGHT KNOW THE APPROXIMATE DIRECTION WE TRAVELLED. I WOULD NOT EXPECT THIS PLANET TO BE COMPLETELY UNGUARDED.

"What about the larger planet further in?" I ask.

The map zooms in to the planet. Nique checks the data as HICS highlights it. "It has possibilities, but is there enough there to warrant risking exposing ourselves? At the moment, they might have a clue that something is wrong, but if we get caught then there will be no doubt. Is it worth the risk?"

"You said that we want to use this as an opportunity to study the Gringun up close. This would give us the opportunity."

Nique considers this briefly. "What do you think, HICS?"

IT SEEMS TO BE MAINLY AGRICULTURAL, BUT THERE ARE A NUMBER OF SMALL CITIES ON THE PLANET. SOME OF THESE HAVE BEEN MENTIONED CONSIDERABLY IN THE DATA FROM THE SCOUT. AS THE PLANET IS FURTHER INSIDE THE GRINGUN AREA, THEY WOULD NOT EXPECT ANYONE TO GO THERE FIRST. IN ADDITION, AS THE CITIES ARE SMALL AND FAR APART, IT WOULD BE EASIER FOR A SMALL TEAM TO BLEND IN.

ONE CITY HAS BEEN MENTIONED MORE THAN MOST, ALTHOUGH I CANNOT ASCERTAIN THE REASON FOR THIS. THIS WOULD BE A GOOD CITY TO START WITH. IT IS SURROUNDED BY LARGE PLAINS AND FARMS, WHICH WILL MAKE IT EASY TO LAND WITHOUT DETECTION. THE PLANET HAS A LOW DEFENSIVE RATING AND TRAFFIC TO AND FROM IT IS MAINLY FOR RAW MATERIALS AND PRODUCE. VISITING THIS CITY WOULD ALLOW US TO UNDERSTAND WHY THE GRINGUNS FIND THIS PLANET IMPORTANT AND HOW WE COULD USE THIS IN THE FUTURE.

"Excellent! Looks like we have identified our planet and city. Now we can turn our minds to blending in. We are going to need some disguises."

I HAVE BEEN WORKING ON THIS ALREADY. IT IS

AN UNTESTED METHOD, BUT I BELIEVE IT WILL
WORK. I HAVE FOUND SOME GENETIC ALTERATION
RESEARCH BY THE NAJESS. THEY WERE NOT ABLE TO
COMPLETE THE WORK, BUT I BELIEVE I MAY HAVE
FILLED IN THE GAPS IN THEIR RESEARCH.

"Genetic alterations?" a Human male on the right voices his
concerns. "That sounds pretty dangerous. Especially as you say it's
untested."

IT WILL NOT BE WITHOUT RISK, BUT I AM VERY
CONFIDENT THAT IT WILL WORK. The Human does not
seem particularly impressed by HICS' confidence. I WILL BE
USING THE DNA FROM THE GRINGUN TO PHYSICALLY
CHANGE YOUR APPEARANCE. THIS WILL ONLY
BE TEMPORARY. WHEN YOU RETURN FROM THE
MISSION, I WILL RETURN YOU TO YOUR ORIGINAL
FORM. THERE REALLY IS NO OTHER WAY FOR YOU TO
BLEND IN AND STUDY THEM UP CLOSE.

"Okay, HICS has determined that this is the best method of
entry and that is good enough for me." Admiral Nique steps back
and sits down. "Right, you all know where we are going. Now
for the mission. First, we need to understand some important
details about the Gringuns. We need to know how many Gringuns
there are, how many ships they have and how spread out they
are. Identify any information possible about other bases in this
dimension, including troop numbers in those areas and any other
relevant strategic information. We are going to need to observe
them for a short while and learn something about their ways. If
we're going to beat them, we need to know them first!

"The first stage is getting there. Admiral Enira will take you
through this." He backs away while Enira stands and walks to the
platform.

"Good morning, people. The Keteran pilots will fly the team
to the planet aboard a transport ship. Now, HICS has managed to
reverse engineer the cloaking device we found on the scout ship

we captured recently and retrofit it to an existing transport. The existing weapons systems are too weak, though. They are going to be almost useless to you. HICS has however modified the boosters so that the transports are considerably faster than they were before.

This additional speed, and of course the new cloaking device, should get you out of any trouble relatively fast! Of course, the aim is that you should not be seen and therefore you will not need to get out fast. There will be a team of nine people made up of five Keterans, three Humans and one Najess. Two of the Keterans will act as pilot and co-pilot during the mission. They and the Najess will remain on the ship during the entire mission. The Najess will be the lead on the mission. The other three pairs will be the usual Human and Keteran teams. All must wear their EMOs during the flight until the ship lands – that does not include the pilots of course. The pilots will land in a small area some distance outside the main city. HICS has the co-ordinates programmed in and will guide you there. The ship must remain cloaked throughout the duration of the mission. If you are detected at any point, the mission will be regarded as a failure and you are to evacuate immediately. Admiral Wesley will talk you through the rest of the mission."

As she steps back and sits down, Wesley rises from his seat and moves to the platform. He claps his hands together, rubbing them in eager anticipation. "Right, now for the guts and glory!" The Najess in the room wince at the expression, but the Humans are clearly aroused by it. "Once the ship has landed, the ground team are to leave the landing zone carefully and ensure they are not seen at any point." The planet above the platform zooms in on the area where the ship is set to land. A dotted line extends from the ship image towards the main city. "You are to travel in this direction until you reach the vicinity of the city. Once there, you will hide your EMOs somewhere safe and then find a way into the city. Keep in mind, you will have your disguises but it's your mannerisms that will give you away, so try to keep out of the way of any Gringuns until you have had enough time to study their behaviour. Your primary objective is a large tower located in the centre of the city." The map zooms in to the city and circles around to show the surroundings, finally focusing on the main tower. "The tower seems to be where the activity is centred. HICS…"

THANK YOU, SIR. IT IS LOGICAL TO ASSUME THAT THIS TOWER WILL HOUSE A FEW TERMINALS AND THERE WILL BE SOME DATA ON THESE WHICH WE CAN USE. THE DEVICE WHICH WAS USED TO CONNECT TO THE COMPUTERS ON THE HUMAN HOME WORLD WILL BE USED HERE AGAIN. I HAVE REDUCED ITS SIZE CONSIDERABLY, SO IT IS EASILY CONCEALED IN A SCANNER-PROOF ORGANIC MATERIAL. THIS IS DESIGNED TO BLEND IN WITH YOUR SKIN, OR THE GRINGUN SKIN IN THIS CASE. DEPENDING ON THE QUANTITY OF DATA TO DOWNLOAD, IT WILL TAKE UP TO TEN MINUTES TO COMPLETE THE DATA TRANSFER. OUR INTELLIGENCE SHOWS THAT VIDEO SURVEILLANCE ON THE PLANET IS RELATIVELY LOW. THE ONLY PLACE YOU NEED TO WORRY IS IN AND AROUND THE TOWER. THIS SHOULD MAKE ENTERING THE CITY VERY EASY. SIR…

"Make your way inside the tower and find these terminals. Connect the device and wait for the data to download. When the data has downloaded, get to your EMOs and get out of there as quick as possible and without being seen.

"The teams will consist of Jon and Forrahh, Andy and Anris, Garry and Entai. You have all been chosen because of your exceptional performance in locating this base and the teamwork you all showed. Wei will be the mission leader." Wei starts twitching until Forrahh lays a reassuring hand on his arm. Wesley must have noticed this as he turns his attention to Wei. "Don't worry, Wei. Remember, you will not be leaving the ship. You are expected to be the voice of reason and logic.

"Okay," Wesley continues, "it's time for a little surgery. Get to your bunks and relax yourselves. HICS will be in touch when it's time. You have now all been designated to Alpha Squad. Best of luck, Alpha Squad. The rest of you need to start preparing your analysis. Dismissed!" They all get up and move to their workstations.

Garry and Entai are the last to walk into the lab and take their places. The looks on their faces tells the story of us all. The room we are in is large, rectangular and very, very white, with a number of screens around. Six operating tables are lined up in a row, with a number of robotic arms beside each. They have the spotless look of any item you would expect in a medical facility. HICS explains the process to us and informs us that there are name tags on each operating table.

IT IS IMPERATIVE THAT YOU ALL USE THE CORRECT TABLE.

One by one we all check the name plates and lie on the correct table. Thanks to HICS' consideration, we find ourselves lying next to our partners.

THE INITIAL SENSATION WILL BE SLIGHTLY UNCOMFORTABLE. THIS WILL PASS QUICKLY AND YOU WILL DRIFT INTO A DEEP SLEEP. YOU NEED TO UNDERSTAND THAT WHEN YOU WAKE, YOU WILL MOST LIKELY FEEL STRANGE. THIS IS BECAUSE THE DNA WILL HAVE STARTED TO AFFECT YOU. YOUR SKIN COLOUR IS LIKELY TO CHANGE FIRST AND MAYBE YOUR APPEARANCE. THE COMPLETE METAMORPHOSIS IS LIKELY TO TAKE A COMPLETE DAY, DURING WHICH TIME YOU MAY EXPERIENCE SOME DISCOMFORT. LIE BACK AND MAKE YOURSELVES COMFORTABLE. I WILL BE ADMINISTERING THE ANAESTHETIC SHORTLY. THE PROCEDURE MAY TAKE SLIGHTLY LONGER FOR THE HUMANS – EXCEPT FOR JON – AS WE WILL

ALSO BE INTRODUCING AN IMPLANT INTO YOU. THIS IMPLANT HAS BEEN TESTED ON A COUPLE OF HUMANS, INCLUDING JON.

"And that didn't go entirely perfectly, HICS. Are you sure this is the right thing to do?" I'm concerned that we are about to go on a mission with these chips in everyone. How would we cope if something happened when we were on the planet?

THE JOINT COMMANDERS HAVE SEEN THE MEDICAL EVIDENCE GATHERED FROM YOU AND ROBERT. THEY HAVE NOT SEEN ANY OTHER SIDE EFFECTS. WHILE YOU ARE AWAY, THE IMPLANT WILL BE INSTALLED FOR ALL OTHER HUMANS, TOO.

"Guys, are we sure this is the right thing to do?" Garry asks. "What does it do anyway?"

"It helps you to communicate with the ship telepathically," I say.

"Sounds kind of cool actually."

"I'm sure the commanders will have checked everything out before agreeing to this," Andy says reassuringly. Admittedly, it does seem to have the desired effect on Garry, but I still have my doubts, and by the looks of it so does Forrahh.

OKAY. LIE BACK AND RELAX.

I lie back and try to relax. Actually, I feel like I'm in a trance. Metallic arms move simultaneously towards the tables. Each arm adjusts itself to the height of the neck and a needle approaches the skin. I feel the needle slowly puncture my skin, forcing the viscous, blue liquid into my blood stream as the plunger sinks deeper into the syringe. Then it simply retracts back into the metallic arm. Seconds later, I feel my eyes begin to close. I try to fight it, but I can't. It's like being a passenger on a long car journey. Your eyelids feel so heavy, you can't stop them from closing. As I drift off, I glimpse through half closed eyes the metallic arms morph into hand-like shapes before I close my eyes for the last time…

Entai is the last of us to wake up the next morning. Her eyes flit open and close again as she battles to pull herself from the deep sleep. Groggily, she sits up and rubs her eyes. She blinks a couple of times trying to adjust.

Garry steps up behind her. "It won't change," he says to her. She starts to turn around, but he stops her. "Wait. I don't want you to be alarmed. Things have changed a bit while we were asleep." His voice sounds slightly different, but she can tell that it is still him. "We slept through the entire change. Brace yourself and expect the differences, okay?" It's the first time I've seen him worried about someone other than himself.

She nods and waits a moment to gather herself. "I know I feel different," she tries convincing herself, "which means you probably look different, too?" The statement comes out as a question.

She slowly turns her body towards him. As the rest of Alpha Squad come into view, she cannot help the shocked intake of breath. I remember the same sensation when I woke up. Garry is standing beside her and is looking at her gently.

"Relax," he says to her, "you're with friends."

She keeps looking into his eyes as he slowly walks around the table to stand in front of her.

"When you try to stand, it will feel a little strange. It's easier to balance if you put a little extra weight on your toes."

She looks down at her legs, which are slightly shorter than before. Slowly, she shifts her legs over the edge of the table and lowers herself to the floor. She takes a moment to balance herself before looking up from her feet. She sees the full-length mirror on the wall across the room and takes her first shaky steps. "It does help to put my weight on my toes." She adjusts her weight forward again and takes another few steps until she reaches the mirror.

"Seems strange, right?" Garry says from behind her.

"Strange, yes, but somehow it is also a little familiar." She looks at herself in the mirror. "The shape is so strange and these wisps of yellow hair!" She looks down to where the rectangular body leads to a pair of short, stunted legs. With the rectangular upper body creating an almost top-heavy effect the whole image seems comical. At least the jaundice-tinted skin matches the yellow hair, though.

"Why has my hair colour changed, HICS?" she asks.

I HAVE STUDIED THE GRINGUN DATA AND ALL REFERENCES SHOW THAT THIS IS THE HAIR AND SKIN COLOUR FOR ALL GRINGUNS.

"And my voice sounds different?"

I HAVE INSTALLED A SPEECH CHIP INTO YOUR THROAT. IT WILL BE REMOVED WHEN YOU RETURN FROM THE MISSION. IF YOU ARE CONFRONTED BY GRINGUNS, IT WILL HELP YOU TO COMMUNICATE WITH THEM. WHEN YOU ARRIVE ON THE PLANET, MAKE YOUR WAY TO THE MAIN CITY AND LOCATE A BUSY AREA WITH PLENTY OF PEOPLE TALKING. THIS NEXT PART WILL BE DANGEROUS. YOU NEED TO STAY THERE FOR APPROXIMATELY ONE HOUR WHILE THE SPEECH CHIPS LISTEN AND LEARN THE LANGUAGE. THE CHIP WILL VIBRATE ONCE WHEN THE TRANSLATION SOFTWARE HAS BEEN UPDATED. YOU WILL THEN BE ABLE TO COMMUNICATE. PLEASE BE CAREFUL. YOU MUST TRY NOT TO COMMUNICATE TOO MUCH OR YOU MAY BE DETECTED.

Entai turns to face us. She smiles and steps more confidently in our direction. "Good thing this is only temporary. It is an awkward posture to walk in. Any idea when the changes will revert back, HICS?"

I HAVE NO PREVIOUS DATA TO DRAW FROM. ALSO, YOUR PHYSIOLOGIES ARE SLIGHTLY DIFFERENT, SO THE EFFECT MAY BE DIFFERENT FOR EACH OF YOU. I EXPECT THE EFFECT TO LAST APPROXIMATELY TEN DAYS, BUT THIS IS ONLY AN APPROXIMATE FIGURE. THERE IS ONE MORE CHANGE. WHILE INSTALLING

THE IMPLANT FOR THE HUMANS, I WAS ALSO ABLE TO INSTALL IT FOR THE KETERANS. THIS WILL ALLOW YOU ALL TO COMMUNICATE TELEPATHICALLY WITH ME. THE IMPLANT WILL ACTIVATE SOON. I APOLOGISE FOR NOT INFORMING YOU ALL OF THE CHANGE; HOWEVER, THE ADMIRALS WERE MADE AWARE AND AGREED TO THE CHANGE OF PLAN.

"That's okay, HICS," I say. "So, what do we do now?"

THE TRANSPORT IS READY. IT WILL TAKE A FEW DAYS TO TRAVEL TO THE PLANET. I SUGGEST YOU BOARD THE TRANSPORT RIGHT AWAY. YOU WILL NEED ALL THE TIME AVAILBLE TO COMPLETE YOUR MISSION BEFORE THE DISGUISE WEARS OFF.

"Sounds like a plan. Right, folks, let's get moving." We walk swiftly to the hangar, prepared to face our first real mission.

We walk through the doorway into the hangar, chattering excitedly to each other. Forrahh and I lead the group. As we approach the transport ship, a panel opens on the side with a gangplank sliding down to our feet. We step into the ship and onto the metal decking, still laughing at how we look and walk. The metal flooring inside the large transport ship clanks under our footsteps.

I glance around the interior. There is another door towards the front of the ship – the flight deck, I guess – and a second doorway towards the rear. Confused, I move to this second doorway and open it. The back of the transport opens into a spacious rear activity section. The ship didn't seem this big from the outside. There is a padded area in the entrance and all of our EMOs have already been placed there.

"Is this a training zone, HICS?"

YES, JON. Forrahh comes to a stop beside me.

"Something has been bugging me, HICS," I say. "Will the EMOs work for us now? I mean, you said that they were directly linked to our DNA. And you also said you have altered our DNA. Won't that affect things?"

NO, JON. THE EMOS HAVE A LEVEL OF INTELLIGENCE TOO. THEY STILL KNOW YOU EVEN THOUGH YOUR APPEARANCE AND DNA HAVE ALTERED SLIGHTLY. I HAVE COMMUNICATED THE TEMPORARY DIFFERENCE TO THE P-HICS UNITS ON BOARD EACH SUIT.

"Okay. So, why the training zone? I thought we had covered everything we would need?"

NOT YET. THERE ARE STILL OTHER THINGS YOU NEED TO KNOW. ON THIS TRIP, I WILL BE INTRODUCING YOU TO ZERO G EXERCISES. THERE MAY BE OCCASIONS WHERE YOU WILL HAVE TO FIGHT IN THESE CONDITIONS. YOU WILL NEED TO KNOW HOW TO PROPELL YOURSELVES EFFECTIVELY.

"Interesting. Right, back to the flight deck, then. Are we ready to go, HICS?"

ALL CHECKS HAVE BEEN MADE, JON. JUST GIVE THE WORD.

"Cool. Let's go for it."

13

A FORAY INTO ENEMY TERRITORY

It takes a few days to arrive at the planet, but none of it was boring. Initially we needed to get used to walking round in our new bodies. That was awkward at first, but when you got used to how to balance on your toes, it kind of made sense. Once we had mastered that, HICS started our zero G training. This included learning to negotiate turns and twists in zero G. Actually, that was pretty good fun. Aside from learning something new, there was a familiar, comforting feeling when I was in my EMO. I'm not sure why, but I'm always happiest when I'm in my EMO.

Gringun communications were patchy and infrequent until we started to break through the atmosphere. We were hoping to get a head start on setting the speech chips, but most of the communications were encrypted. As this meant we could only sit and wait, we started to get dressed into our Gringun clothes while HICS landed us gently into a large field.

THE AREA IS LARGELY UNINHABITED, JON, HICS

confirms. THERE APPEARS TO BE A SMALL SETTLEMENT APPROXIMATELY TWO KILOMETRES AWAY. I WILL MARK IT ON YOUR SCANNERS. IT APPEARS TO BE A SMALL UNINHABITED FARM, HOWEVER I STILL RECOMMEND YOU TRY TO AVOID IT IF POSSIBLE. YOU MAY LEAVE THE SHIP WHEN YOU ARE READY.

Wei inhales sharply, reminding us that he is there. He must have been really nervous as he had hardly said a word all day. Forrahh approaches his EMO and lays her armoured hand on his arm. "Relax, Wei," she says. "Stay in your EMO until we return. And I promise we will return safe and sound to you!" She turns and follows me off the ship.

I activate the waypoint markers and our target flashes, showing our destination clearly on the map. *YOUR DESTINATION IS HIGHLIGHTED, JON.* Thanks to the implant, the voice appears directly in my head. *I HAVE ALSO ADDED SEVERAL OTHER WAYPOINTS ON YOUR MAP. IT IS NOT NECESSARY FOR YOU TO FOLLOW THESE, HOWEVER THEY WILL AVOID ANY INHABITED AREAS.*

"There's another marker flashing, HICS. What is that one for?" I respond using the implant. May as well get used to it. We'll be using it throughout the mission.

I HAVE SUGGESTED THIS LOCATION AS A GOOD PLACE TO REMOVE THE EMOS AND HIDE THEM. THE AREA APPEARS TO BE LARGELY UNTOUCHED AND THE FEW SETTLEMENTS NEARBY ARE PRACTICALLY UNINHABITABLE.

"Right. Let's move, people. We have a lot of ground to cover."

The area HICS suggested for the EMOs is perfect. The tall grass and weeds are everywhere and it looks like no-one has been here in ages. The only minor signs are in a ruined settlement a short distance away.

214

"What about the EMOs, HICS?" Andy ask. "It will look kind of obvious leaving six large humanoid suits in the middle of the field. Someone's bound to notice."

THERE IS A SMALL BUTTON ON THE BACK OF EACH SUIT. YOU WILL FIND IT BETWEEN THE SHOULDER BLADES. ONCE YOU ARE OUT OF THE EMO PRESS THE BUTTON AND STEP BACK.

I exit my EMO and follow the instructions. It's the coolest thing! The EMO collapses into itself until it is the size and shape of a large suitcase... It even has wheels! The whole process takes about fifteen seconds.

"Nice!" Andy exclaims. "I want a go." He gets round the back of his EMO and presses the button.

While the EMO collapses onto itself, something occurs to me, "Er, HICS? What happens if someone is inside the suit when that button in pressed?" They all stop suddenly as the gruesome prospect dawns on them.

DO NOT WORRY, JON. I HAVE KEPT YOUR SAFETY AS MY HIGHEST PRIORITY. THE BUTTON IS NOT VISIBLE AFTER YOU GET INTO THE EMO AND, AS A SAFETY PRECAUTION, IT IS ALSO DEACTIVATED. IT CANNOT BE ACCIDENTALLY PRESSED. A feeling of relief washes over me.

The rest of the team collapse their EMOs and hide them with a layer of the tall grass. When we are all ready to go we start walking towards the main city which we can see a few kilometres away across the fields.

As we near the city gates, I take the opportunity to go over the mission with everyone. "We will be entering the city soon. I think we should follow HICS' instructions and find a place with a lot of people first." After gaining agreement from everyone – even Garry agrees without an argument – we move through the large gates and into the city.

The first thing I notice is the technology. This may be a 'backwater', but the technology available for use is incredible. Considering the run-down fields and buildings we left outside the city walls, this place has everything. There are computer terminals at every corner, with people accessing information on demand. Strange box-shaped vehicles seem to float silently through the air in perfect formation towards, around and into towering buildings so high you can't see where they end.

There are a few guards here and there too, but they don't seem too bothered about anything. Generally, the Gringuns wander through the streets, occasionally disappearing into shops. It would be like a quiet little town if not for the sheer size of the place. We move further into the city, making sure to communicate using the implants only. The market centre has a few areas where people are seated on benches. No-one talks on the benches. The only talking seems to be with the people interacting with the shopkeepers. There are a couple of the benches further along the square which are empty. I walk towards them and sit down. The others follow me and find some empty ones nearby. We relax after the long tiring walk through the grass and watch the Gringuns go about their business. It helps to study some of their customs from a distance.

THE TRANSLATION PROCESS HAS STARTED. I WILL NOTIFY YOU WHEN COMPLETE.

"*Thank you, HICS,*" I think, remembering not to speak out loud.

It felt like the slowest hour of my life, but the chip eventually vibrated in my throat causing me to cough slightly. Looks like the same happened to the rest of the team as they all clear their throats at the same time.

TRANSLATION HAS COMPLETED. THERE IS A LARGE STRUCTURE IN THE MIDDLE OF THE CITY. THIS IS YOUR TARGET DESTINATION. MOST OF THE TERMINALS WILL

BE LOCATED THERE. ALL OF THE TERMINALS YOU SEE
HERE ARE DIRECTLY CONNECTED TO THAT BUILDING.
"Why do we have to go in there, then?" Garry asks. "Surely it
would be safer to find a terminal out here than risk entering the
building."

"If anyone sees us connecting a device to a terminal out here,"
Andy responds, "it will immediately raise suspicions. We can check
inside for a terminal which is out of sight."

"What if there isn't one?" Garry says argumentatively. Entai
elbows him, signalling him to back down.

"Then we come out and follow your plan," Andy responds calmly,
ignoring the attitude.

HICS continues the instructions. PLEASE PROCEED TO
THE BUILDING. ONCE INSIDE, CONNECT TO ONE OF
THE TERMINALS AND GATHER THE DATA.

We walk for about five minutes before we arrive at the building. A
few shopkeepers along the way try to entice us into their stalls to
sell us their wares. I expect this means the disguises are working.
We manage to avoid them and continue without having to say
anything. The first thing we learn is that instead of holding your
hand out to say 'no', you simply turn your head in the opposite
direction. It seems rude at first, but it seems to mean a categorical
'no,' as the shopkeeper tends to leave you alone after that.

The first thing that occurs to me when we enter the building
is the lack of security. It's as though the Gringuns have no worries,
no enemies. The general public just walks in off the street and into
the building. Some of them wander through, while others take a
place at one of the many terminals. The place actually reminds me
of a library, only much, much quieter.

We continue walking, looking for a quiet place to start work.
As we move through the aisles, keeping our distance from each
other, we notice another race walking through the corridors. There
are very few of them and they are dressed in torn, dirty rags. They

are small in stature unlike the Gringun and their bodies look weak and tortured. It is as though they have been bred that way or maybe evolved that way after a long time under the forced will of another.

We turn a corner into a secluded area with a few terminals close together. *"These ones,"* I think to the team as we arrive at the bank of terminals. I pull up a chair and sit down, with Forrahh sitting beside me. The others mingle around for a bit keeping a lookout for anything that might cause a problem, and then sit at other terminals. I reach into my pocket to retrieve the small device. The tiny, black, metallic object touches my hand.

THE DEVICE IS PROXIMITY ACTIVATED, JON, AND SHOULD ATTACH TO ALMOST ANY SURFACE. HOLD IT IN THE PALM OF YOUR HAND AND MOVE IT AROUND THE UNDERSIDE OF THE TERMINAL UNTIL IT VIBRATES GENTLY. THEN ATTACH IT TO THAT AREA.

Again, I do as I am instructed… Well, things always seems to work out when I follows HICS' directions. Around the centre point of the terminal, the device vibrates. As I move my hand upwards, it attaches itself silently to its underside. *"I guess we just wa— Trouble, guys,"* I think to the team.

They all look back in time to see one of the feeble looking creatures hobble towards us.

He approaches us slowly, his backed hunched and a pronounced limp on his right leg. At least I think it is a 'he'. Having not seen the females, I could be mistaken.

"May I bring you some beverages, sir?" Thankfully, the chips translate the question. Now we have to hope it translates the other way successfully too. "Some beverages, sir?" he repeats, the question and I realise I have not responded to him yet.

I look at him spellbound, wondering how to answer the simple question. Luckily, Anris responds for me, "No, thank you," she says and turns her back on him.

He remains standing behind us, not moving an inch.

Anris turns around to face him. "No, thank you," she repeats herself.

I look back at the screen and realise that he has not left. We both turn to look at him. "Can I help you?" I ask slightly more sternly than Anris.

He seems to think about this for a moment before responding with a terrifying question, "Who are you?"

I can't think how to respond and I can see that the others are as stumped as I am.

"Something is wrong here," the strange creature states. "Maybe I should get help," he says thoughtfully. He turns to call for help, but Entai is already behind him. She catches him off guard, shocking him into silence as he sees her standing resolutely before him.

"Can you read his intentions?" I ask through the implant.

"I should be able to," she says.

The creature tenses before turning to look more closely at us all. "No," he says thoughtfully, "not who are… What are you?" He turns back to Entai. "You are not like the others. You look Gringun, but… Imposters?"

Forrahh takes a risk, "Wait. Do not call for help. We mean you no harm." She looks around, searching for something. "Is there somewhere we can talk privately?"

He considers the question. Our appearances are obviously clouding his thoughts. The Gringuns must have treated his people very badly to instil such fear. "You are not like them, are you?"

Forrahh shakes her head before realising that it may not mean the same thing here. "No," she says adding clarification.

"My people are not like Gringun either," the creature says in a low enough whisper for us all to hear. "Come with me."

I feel nervous. We know nothing about their affiliation with the Gringun. He may be walking us into a trap. I look at Forrahh, hoping for some guidance, but she looks as unsure as I am. We both reluctantly get up and follow him. On the bright side, he looks very feeble and malnourished, so it should be easy to quietly overpower him if need be.

As the others start to follow, he turns to them, "Not all of you. It would be suspicious. We only need to talk. I promise no harm to them." Reluctantly, we follow him out to a small room, leaving the rest of our team with the terminals.

The dimly lit room is obviously rarely cleaned. The floor is littered with wrappings and there are no tables or chairs anywhere. There is a smell of decay coming, I guess, from remnants of food in the wrappers on the floor. Who knows how long things have been left rotting in here.

He shuts the door behind us. "Please. Who are you? And remember, I only need to shout and the guards will come," he says, trying to mask his fear. I guess he is still perturbed by our appearance. It must have taken some bravery on his part to make it this far.

I look to Forrahh and she nods her agreement. "Who do you think we are?" I ask, attempting to hide what I can until I really know his intentions.

"I know you are not who you look like. *What* are you?" he asks, keeping his distance and changing the question. "You look Gringun, but there are differences."

"Are you saying we are not Gringuns?"

He flinches slightly at the question before gathering himself. Again using every bit of bravery he can muster, "I do not know what you are, but I believe you are not Gringun."

I feel really nervous now, until Forrahh lays her hand on my arm to calm me down a bit.

He smiles suddenly and starts to rock back and forth excitedly. "I was right!" he exclaims, his voice rising in pitch with excitement.

Forrahh decides to bring this conversation to an end. "Assume we are not Gringun," she says. "What would you do next? What would you expect us to do?"

"But you are not Gringun. You just proved that!" His smile fades. "Could it be?" he asks himself as he looks at the floor thoughtfully, "What else could it be?" He looks back at us. "First – and remember this when we leave here – you must *never* make physical contact like you just did. No Gringun ever touches another unless intending to cause harm. Second, I would ask you to do something for me. I need to meet you later tonight. There is a better place for us to talk further. Somewhere safer for me too. There I can explain who I am and how I can help you."

"Thank you. I know this must be dangerous for you," Forrahh says.

"Oh no. You must never thank one of my kind. No Gringun ever thanks the Aneesh. Worse still, never apologise. This would give you away immediately. Gringuns are never kind to us. Never." He takes a deep breath before continuing, "Tonight, when it is dark, go to the south side of the city. When you leave the gates, keep walking southwest until you arrive in a dead field. There will be only rocks and dirt. Nothing can grow there now. At the far side you will see a small building with very few windows and a single door. Knock four times on the door and we will open it for you. There we will talk further.

"And remember this, when you leave the gates, look for guards. If you see them on the inside of the gates, do not say anything. As you walk towards them, you must point your right hand in the direction you are travelling, your hand clenched tight into a fist. They should let you go without saying anything. Try not to leave in a big group either. If the guards stop you, remember that Gringuns speak very little to each other. They prefer to use telepathy, but they will not do this without cause."

"Based on what we've seen so far, they best not try that either," I mumble to myself.

"My name is Haslyyn," he says without extending his hand or any other gesture of greeting. "When you arrive at the building, tell them you want to speak to me and they will understand.

"Now, this is very important. When we leave this room, you must leave ahead of me and at no point should you turn to look at me. I will pretend to be under some strain as I walk. You will not see me leave you, but I will see you tonight. Until then, try and avoid contact. Your gestures give you away. I suggest you try to sit somewhere quiet and do nothing."

Forrahh nods and thanks him for his help before realising that this would be one of those give-away gestures. I walk to the door and open it. We step out of the room and back to the terminal where the others are waiting for us.

"Where did the creature go?" Andy asks me telepathically.

"No idea," I respond, resisting the urge to turn around.

"Your information transferring device thing buzzed."

ANDY IS CORRECT, JON. THE DEVICE HAS COMPLETED THE TRANSFER. YOU MAY DISCONNECT IT FROM THE TERMINAL NOW.

"It's good to hear from you again, HICS."

I HAVE BEEN MONITORING YOUR PROGRESS, JON. THE MISSION HAS PROGRESSED WELL.

I remove the device from the terminal and we slowly leave the building. We locate a small square a short walk from the building where there seem to be less Gringuns. We stop there and I relay the events from the room to everyone.

"And he just disappeared?" Garry says. *"Jon, you really should have been keeping an eye on him. Tonight is likely be a trap to capture us all."*

"I know it could be a trap too, Garry," I say slightly defensively. *"But they are a new race we knew nothing of before. There could be some important information we need. And that reminds me. HICS,*

check your database for any mention of the Aneesh, please."

"Jon's right," Andy steps in. *"We may have mission objectives, but they didn't take this turn of events into consideration. We have to take the risk."*

"Agreed," Wei says, his words shifting seamlessly into my head.

A smile creeps across my face before I realise that Gringuns rarely smile. *"Wei. Great to hear from you. Are you okay?"*

"I am fine, Jon. I have been listening in to everything. You need to go to that meeting, but you should take every precaution to make sure you are safe. I suggest you leave the city now. Head back to the EMOs and take them with you."

THIS IS MY RECOMMENDATION TOO, JON. TAKE THEM WITH YOU AND BE PREPARED TO USE THEM IF REQUIRED.

"Okay. We will leave soon. Let's have a quick update first, though. How do I get the data we have retrieved to you and when will you have time to analyse it?"

THE DEVICE HAS BEEN TRANSMITTING THE DATA SINCE YOU LEFT THE BUILDING AND I HAVE COMPLETED ANALYSING THE DATA. THE TECHNOLOGY ON THIS PLANET IS CONSIDERABLY AHEAD OF WHERE WE ARE EVEN NOW. SOME OF THE TECHNOLOGY CAN BE ADAPTED TO OUR CURRENT SHIPS. WHEN WE GET BACK TO THE BASE I WILL BEGIN TO IMPLEMENT THESE IMPROVEMENTS ON EXISTING AND NEW TECHNOLOGIES. THE CHANGES IDENTIFIED SO FAR WILL INCREASE THE DEFENSIVE CAPABILITIES OF THE SHIPS.

"Do you have anything for the weapons systems?" Andy asks.

I WILL REQUIRE FURTHER DATA ON THEIR WEAPONS SYSTEMS BEFORE DECIDING WHAT IMPROVEMENTS CAN BE MADE, BUT I AM UNABLE TO IDENTIFY A SUITABLE SOURCE FOR THE INFORMATION.

"What about this new alien race… the Aneesh?" I ask.

IT IS POSSIBLE THEY WILL BE ABLE TO HELP, BUT JUDGING BY THEIR POSITION IN SOCIETY, THEIR HELP MAY BE VERY LIMITED.

"Agreed, but it is still worth asking. I will bring it up if I get a chance."

IT IS WORTH ASKING. I RECOMMEND YOU LEAVE SOON, THOUGH. YOU HAVE A LOT OF WALKING TO DO.

"I'm still not sure about this meeting. It just seems too risky to me." Garry says, voicing his concerns again.

"It is possible that this is a trap, Garry," Wei responds, *"but in this case it warrants the risk."*

"Easy for you to say. You're safe in the ship, dressed in an EMO," he remarks scornfully.

"Garry," Anris responds angrily. *"That is completely unfair!"*

He shuts up instantly. The looks he is getting from the rest of the team probably have something to do with it.

"I agree that I am relatively safe here, Garry," Wei continues unperturbed, *"and that is why I have advised precautions. The EMOs will help if you are detected."*

"Let's get to the EMOs now," I say, closing the conversation down. *"It is a good distance to the building from the EMOs and they are going to be heavy to transport. If we leave now we should get to the building just after sunset."*

AGREED. THE LOCATION STATED BY HASLYYN IS NOT FAR FROM HERE, BUT YOUR EMOS ARE SOME DISTANCE AWAY.

"The detour may also prevent anyone from discovering your eventual destination," Wei says.

"Okay. Is there a quick way to the EMOs?" Forrahh asks.

UNFORTUNATELY NOT, FORRAHH. IF YOU LEAVE RIGHT NOW, IT WILL TAKE AT LEAST THREE HOURS TO TRAVEL THE TOTAL DISTANCE REQUIRED.

"At least?" Garry asks, obviously irritated at having to travel the distance by foot. *"But those EMOs weigh a ton."*

"Regardless, I'd rather have mine and not need it, than need it and not have it," Andy remarks philosophically.

"Enough talking," Forrahh says. *"We need to leave now."* We stand up and follow her out of the city, towards the EMOs.

Walking slowly and in pairs to avoid looking too suspicious, we eventually make it to where we left the EMOs. The small carry handles on the sides make it easier to pull the EMOs, but they are still heavy, and pulling them through the tall grass doesn't help much. I can't remember the last time my body got a workout like this. Actually, I do… it was when we first used the EMOs.

On HICS' advice we locate the short-range scanners on the EMO boxes and activate them. The scanners apparently allow HICS to monitor the surroundings and warn us of anyone coming in our direction. On Wei's advice, we also carry some of the foliage we used to cover the EMOs. Combined with HICS' help, the scanners and the foliage, we managed to avoid detection on more than one occasion. As always, there's a bright and a dark side to everything: bright side – we got a rest every time HICS detected someone; dark side – the journey took another hour to complete. I'm telling you… I was shattered when we got to the building in the early evening. So much for checking the area out!

The two windows on this side of the building are dimly lit with what seems to be candlelight. A single solitary door is barely visible in the darkness. We trudge carefully through the dead fields towards the building, HICS still monitoring the area.

STILL NO MOVEMENT OUTSIDE THE BUILDING, JON. I CAN DETECT A SMALL NUMBER OF PEOPLE IN THE BUILDING, BUT I CANNOT CONFIRM IF THEY ARE THE ANEESH. IT WILL NOT BE SAFE FOR ANY OF YOU TO STAY OUTSIDE FOR MUCH LONGER. YOU ARE LIKELY TO BE DETECTED AND QUESTIONS WILL BE ASKED.

"What do you suggest, HICS?"

THERE IS A FENCE AROUND THE OUTSKIRTS OF THE BUILDING. ONE PART OF THE FENCE IS APPROXIMATELY TEN METRES FROM THE DOOR. LEAVE THE EMOS THERE AND TWO OF YOU GO TO THE BUILDING. IF THIS IS A TRAP, THE OTHER FOUR CAN GET INTO THE EMOS WITHIN THIRTY SECONDS AND ATTEMPT A RESCUE OR AT LEAST GET AWAY SAFELY. IF IT IS JUST THE ANEESH IN THE BUILDING, THEN ALL OF YOU NEED TO GET INSIDE AND TAKE THE EMOS WITH YOU.

"Sounds like a good idea," Andy says.

I pick up my EMO, move forward, and when I reach the fence I drop it carefully to the floor.

"I'm coming with you, Jon," Forrahh whispers to me. I have to admit, it's good to hear her voice rather than feel it in my head. Since we arrived, we have had to keep quiet so we don't give ourselves away. I had no idea I would miss hearing a voice so much.

I climb over the fence and into the mud on the side. I don't know what the situation is, but either the Aneesh choose to live in squalor or they have no choice. Either way, I'm sure we'll find out eventually.

I hold my hand out and help Forrahh over the fence – not that she needs it, she's more agile than I am, even if I am faster in a sprint.

"When we enter, can you use your telepathy to read their intentions?" I ask her. We walk up to the door together and I knock on it four times as instructed.

After a bit of shuffling around inside, a lock is released and I am greeted by the face of another malnutritioned member of the Aneesh race. He studies my features for a few seconds before speaking, "Sir? Can I help you?"

In a quiet, almost inaudible whisper, I say, "We are here to see Haslyyn. He is expecting us."

He looks at us again as though he is unsure whether to trust us. After considering the matter briefly, he opens the door and gestures for us to come in without saying a word. I look for signs of Gringuns, but there is nowhere they could hide in here. The Aneesh male begins to shut the door.

"Wait, we have friends outside. They need to come in, too," I say as I call to the others using the implant.

More nervously now, he pulls the door open again and allows the others in. Andy and Garry carry in the extra two EMOs while Forrahh and I step inside the dimly lit room.

Another quick scan of the room shows there are several Aneesh people in here. They are all huddled in a corner of the room looking very scared. The floor of the room is clean and tidy with any rubbish neatly pushed into one corner. I notice some more people sitting on the floor in the opposite corner. Not a voice or sound can be heard in the room. I wonder if they have the same telepathic ability as the Gringuns?

I hear the door close behind us. Looking around, I notice that Haslyyn is not in the room. "Where is Haslyyn?" I ask the Aneesh male who let us in.

He looks to the first group of people in the corner of the room. They move aside, revealing a dusty patch of floor. One of the females pulls a small device from her clothes and waves it over the area where they were sitting. As it passes over the floor it suddenly gets pulled from her hand and attaches to the flooring. That's when I realise that the object has small finger grips on it, allowing it to be used as a handle when it attaches to the floor.

One of the males grips onto the handle and pulls it upwards with surprising ease. As it lifts, I see the underside of the slab. What at first glance appears to be a solid concrete slab is actually a wooden hatch. It's a nice way to hide something you don't want found! The Aneesh male who allowed us in climbs down through the hatch, gesturing for us to follow him.

I look back at the others and shrug my shoulders. "We're here now. Let's see what he has to offer."

I get to the hatch and look down into the dimly lit area below. A small, rickety ladder leads down. I carefully step onto the first rung and slowly apply my weight to it… It's tougher than it looks. I lower myself down the few steps to the room below and look around to make sure everything is okay. One by one, the team follows through the hole.

This room is much bigger than the one above and a lot cleaner too. There is no rubbish, but there are a number of other people. The two closest to me include the Aneesh male who opened the door and Haslyyn. Other than the people, there is a single table with ten chairs scattered around the room. Several of the people gather the chairs and move them to the table.

"Welcome to Raoca Dimension," Haslyyn says. "Please sit down. We have much to discuss."

The other male whispers something to Haslyyn. So much for the telepathy theory! I sit down as requested but keep an eye on them all. Forrahh takes the seat next to me and after a few seconds the others take their places at the table.

Haslyyn waits for us all to be seated before sitting down opposite us. He examines us all carefully but takes a particular interest in the Keteran women.

"You are telepaths?" he asks them.

"How did you know?" Forrahh responds. "You are not telepathic." This is a statement rather than a question.

"That is correct, but we have a strong ability to detect and even resist telepathy. We know when it is being used against us. My brother here detected your intrusion much like I did in the council building earlier today." He pauses as he considers his next statement. "Your intrusion was not aggressive, however. It was more… inquisitive. Very unlike the Gringuns. It is what really gave you away."

"We use our telepathy for information gathering and communication," Forrahh explains. "We do not have the ability to use it as a weapon."

"That is the sense we have had so far. But this is a conversation for later. We have other more important things to discuss, including who you are and where you have come from… and of course how you come to look so much like the Gringun, yet are so different."

14

SOMETHING IS WRONG

The debate in the Gringun High Command continues in the usual silence. With telepathy being the far more efficient method of communication, it makes sense for them to continue that way.

"No," the Gringun High Commander considers thoughtfully, *"something feels wrong about this. They should have arrived there by now. Assuming these creatures did arrive in the Raoca Dimension, we should have detected them already. No, something else has happened."*

Another member of the High Command interjects, *"With all due respect, Emperor Ullank, the presumption that they have even arrived could be incorrect. We have no evidence that—"*

"The evidence is obvious," he comments, closing the conversation down immediately. *"A dimensional rift has never been left open! All who manage the rifts know the punishment for not completing their tasks correctly. Besides, we know we have lost a scout too. There are too many coincidences. No, one of the races has made it through and... I think I may even know which one."*

"Really?"

"There is only one which has the ability to understand our

technology. The reports we had from the scout group said that the technology on one planet was very advanced compared to the others. I think it is that cowardly, pathetic race." His thoughts carry with them enough venom that the others can feel his total revulsion for the race. *"They are here and they are hiding somewhere. Arghh, they were a complete waste of our time and resources. What I can't understand is how they would have found the courage to attack one of our scouts?"*

"Perhaps they had it outnumbered. Enough maybe to feel confident of victory."

"No. That is not it. You do not know them the way I do. Even thinking about it will have them cowering on the floor. Acting is not one of their strengths. They like to debate and argue over things."

One of the other members of the High Command who has been listening intently during this time leans forward in his seat. *"With this in mind, can we still expect them to fall into our trap?"* he asks the leader of the High Command, ensuring he holds the respect in his voice. *"Surely the fear would get the better of them, forcing them to stay hidden?"*

"A possibility, but there is still the questions of where they are now and what they are planning. They may be cowards, but they are cunning!"

"Yet there are others who have our telepathic ability and others who have our strength. Could it be one of them who has managed to push them to go further into our territory?"

"Unlikely, Latlac. I have already considered this. There would have to be a significant amount of courage on their part to simply visit that planet. With the technology the Najess already possessed, I am positive they have been monitoring the Human and Keteran races and have decided – over decades of debate, no doubt – to keep their distance forever."

"Yet it could be prudent to consider that they have done so and that, maybe, at least one of the races has joined with them."

Ullank does not like his tone, but he can see where the

questioning is going. *"Agreed, and it is likely that they will have contacted the Keteran race first. They are the weaker and more civilised race in that dimension so it would go with their cowardice to make first contact with them for protection.*

"So, on the assumption that this is the case, and all of the races have arrived here, would they be capable of causing us a problem?"

"You tell me, Latlac," Ullank redirects the question back at him. *"The scout group was under your command!"*

Slightly flustered, Latlac gathers himself before responding, *"The small group of scouts devastated them on their home worlds. These races are not capable of causing us any issues. It will be many years before they become a problem for us. In that time we will have flushed them out and exterminated them, Lord."*

"Excellent," Ullank says, pleased with the positive stance. *"Now all we require is to understand why they have not shown up on our scanners. Are the ships in place?"*

"Yes, My Lord," Suzmac replies. *"The net has been in place since you requested it, but there has been no sign of them around the planet."*

"Is it possible that they have already got past the net?" Latlac directs the question to Ullank, but everyone else heard it too.

"Are you implying that I failed in my task, Latlac?" Suzmac responds strongly to him.

"I am simply inferring that it is possible the net was not as tight as it could have been."

"The net is as tight as required. They are not on the planet, but I believe there is another possibility. We have not considered Amerang."

"Really?" Ullank states questioningly. *"Latlac, you did not mention Amerang in your analysis of possible locations. What do we have there of importance?"*

"It is a farming planet, Lord. The defences are low and it is mainly used for research projects. We do not place much significance on this location. Also, it is too far within our area. Even if they attempted such a risky excursion, they would have been spotted by now."

"Not entirely true, Latlac," Suzmac says, *"The research done there*

includes some weapons research too. They may go there for information gathering purposes."

"Aside from landing undetected, they would need to access the terminals and we would know if that happened, Suzmac. Your statement is wholly inaccurate. Besides, it would be foolish of them to go so far into our dimension on their first excursion." His temper begins to get the better of him as he applies more pressure on Suzmac. *"They will not risk a journey such as that. You are simply scaremongering now."*

"Being prepared is not scaremongering, Latlac." The calmness of his voice is annoying Latlac now. *"We should continue to monitor other locations. It is obvious that they are not going through our net. Either they have seen the problem or, more worryingly, they already have access to some intelligence on Raoca Dimension. Maybe they know where they can get some useful information from. As you like to put it, Latlac, 'on the assumption that this is the case,' should we not place some guards around Amerang?"*

"If you insist on guarding a planet with little or no interest to us, let alone anyone else, then so be it, but I will not suggest moving too many of our ships to the planet. In my opinion, this is a complete waste of time and resources."

During this whole conversation, Ullank has been listening intently as the rivalry builds. *"I believe 'prudent' was the word used earlier. We will send a small contingent of craft to this planet. I am a bit concerned that intelligence relating to the research done on the planet was not mentioned when we were planning the location of the net. We need to eliminate these insurgents before they become a problem. Latlac has been insistent that Amerang is of little importance, so we will do as he instructs and send only a small contingent of craft. Had I known of the lack of general protection around the planet, I would have posted some of our ships there earlier."* Latlac prepares to say something but is cut off immediately by Ullank. *"If I were to put myself in their place, my first foray into a foreign land would be to the least protected location, not somewhere which appears to be buzzing with activity.*" He pauses briefly before giving the final command, "*Inform the fleet commander to dispatch some ships to Amerang and immediately begin surveillance on the planet. I want to know of anything out of the ordinary.*" He dismisses the topic and turns his attention to other matters of importance to the Gringun Empire.

15

A HISTORY LESSON

Sitting opposite Haslyyn in the still dimly lit room, I get my first good look at what the Aneesh look like. They all look very similar in appearance with none of the variances you get in Human people. The hair, eye and skin colour appear almost the same for all of them. Obviously, age brings about some differences and this is visible in a few of the people in the room. Their hair is a tangled, muddy brown colour. The pupils of their eyes are perfectly black without a hint of any colour in them. The lips are thin and have a similar dark brown colour to the hair. Even the young appear to have stress lines and wrinkles across their faces, although this is much more visible in the older ones. Haslyyn is slowly drumming his three thick, stubby fingers thoughtfully on the table.

After a few quiet seconds, he takes a deep breath in. "Well, you know who I am. Who are you?"

I realise the lapse in etiquette immediately. Entai sits bolt upright and apologises for the mistake, before introducing our small party.

Following the brief introduction, Haslyyn starts to recount

the tale of his people. "My people are called the Aneesh. We are a very old race of people who came to this dimension a long, long time back. Recent centuries have felt longer and more painful, though. Many of our ancient histories have been lost to us now."

"How were they lost?" Forrahh asks softly.

"Anything documented was destroyed over the initial years. We tried to remember as much of what we knew through speech and tales to our children, but there are very few children and too many tales for them to remember."

"You have yourselves hidden down here very well. Could you not write the histories down and hide them here now?"

"We are not allowed to buy anything, not even food and water. What we are given is what we are allowed to eat. You have seen the field outside. The Gringun did this to prevent us growing any extra food. Tools for writing and learning are completely banned for us. Even the raw materials for making writing tools are banned, to prevent us from making them ourselves."

"And the Gringuns did this to you?" I ask.

"Yes. Over time we have taught our children what we can through word of mouth… and even that was banned when they found out. We have almost lost the ability to read and write the ancient language now. Those who know can only read the basics and we fear that the next generation will lose even that ability. You see, they are afraid of what we might become. Long ago we were an old and powerful people, but we believed in peace and tolerance of all people and their ways. We trusted people easily and this was our downfall."

"Which is when the Gringuns came?" Forrahh asks.

"Came? No. They did not come. We found them in this dimension. They were a young race with a very low level of technology. We could see their destructive instincts immediately, but we thought we could tame those instincts and help them to better themselves.

"It all started off so well. In the beginning they were eager to learn our ways, our technologies. Over time we started to realise that our ways and teaching were becoming less and less important to them. They hungered for technology and the ability to create new technologies, but their minds were never capable of understanding it. Oh, they were incredibly adept at assimilating technology and converting it to their needs. In fact the only thing they did better than that was realising how even the most peaceful technology could be used for domination and destruction. No, they abhor weakness and view kindness as a form of weakness. Of course, they always kill the other races they come across."

"You mean genocide?"

"Yes."

"How many times has it happened?"

"Many races have been lost and almost all of them have been peaceful. Some we are better off without, believe me, but most had beautiful histories.

"You know, we collected histories back then. We were known as 'The Guardians of Knowledge' and we devoted our lives to finding intelligent races, to sharing knowledge with them. We would learn from them and they learnt from us. Obviously, we knew the dangers involved in this, but we were naive too. There was always that chance that we would meet another race which would be more powerful than us and would attack us before we could explain why we were there. The problem was, we had become complacent. We honestly believed that we could convince any race that we meant them well and that we came in peace. We always believed that knowledge was power and that the power of knowledge should be shared. We would travel the dimensions, seeking out intelligent life, and when the races we discovered were capable of interplanetary travel we introduced ourselves. You see, that is the dangerous time for the races. After travelling to other planets for the first time, interplanetary technology improves at a dramatic rate. That is when we intervene and teach them about the other races. It is like moulding a child's mind at an early age.

"In all cases we were capable of teaching the races we met. We gave them the technology to travel through the dimensions and we would meet regularly to discuss new races we had found and any new knowledge we had gained. They were great times!"

"Were there many races?" Entai asks for the first time.

"More than you would believe."

"And dimensions?"

"In thousands of years, we still had not visited them all. Some races became so technologically advanced that they found us first. The few that did were always peaceful."

"So, are you the oldest of the races?" I ask.

"Of the ones we have found, yes."

"And how long ago did you invent the dimensional drives?"

"Oh, we did not invent them. The drives were part of the knowledge given to us when we first travelled between the planets."

The look on my face alone must have said a thousand words, but I couldn't help adding a few more, "So, who gave them to you... and how old were they?"

"Oh, they were an ancient race. Old enough, in fact, that we were never able to understand how old they were. But they were a good people. Did you know, we were the first intelligent race they discovered? It was a matter for pride for them as well as us," he says, the pride brimming over the full vessel of his voice. "They also found many who had potential, but we were the first. After giving us the knowledge to use their technology, they showed us how to find new races. Then, one day, they left. All they said was that it was now our duty to 'enlighten' the other races when they matured and that their time here was finished. Then they left and we never heard from them again."

This story was actually getting interesting. "So, what happened next?" I found myself leaning forward, my elbows on the table in an excited childlike pose, desperate to hear more of the story.

"Over time, we found many wonderful races. We were working well, our mission a success. Then one day we found the

Gringuns. They were the last of the races the Aneesh found. As I said, things started well, but we soon realised that something was different with them. They were not interested in tolerance. It was just another word for weakness. They wanted to know how to destroy their enemies in the most devastating manner possible. They were always hungry for war.

"Initially, the Gringuns followed the rules and mixed with the other races well. Everyone accepted them like an adult accepts the actions of a child. You accept their errors as a learning experience. This continued for over one hundred years. At no point did they show their true selves. Everything they wanted was for the betterment of our great mixed society.

"After some time working together with the other races, a few of the Gringuns appeared as spokespeople for the race. They called gatherings with all of the elders and stated that they had now understood their place in the society. They said they were going to create a fleet of ships. These were to be medical and scientific vessels with great technology, allowing them to travel great distances very quickly. The vessels would be used to transport the Gringuns to areas where they could provide the best medical services on distant planets. They would provide aid to planets devastated by natural disasters. When not in use, the ships could be used as mining vessels and would therefore by outfitted with mining equipment.

"It was wonderful. They had finally found their place. We had no reason to suspect our friends. They had been with us for so long. Some of the races did still harbour doubts about the Gringuns, but no-one took these doubts seriously. After all, when the battle instinct is suppressed for so long, the future generations start to see the benefits. Of course, we never understood the true extent of their nature. They were keeping their battle instincts honed, and in secret they used the knowledge and technology they were introduced to for development of bigger and better weapons.

"When the ships were ready, the Gringuns departed and started mining for rare minerals and metals. They said they were testing for more beneficial properties. They wanted to give back to the community. We only got to see some of what they found, of course. The other materials they hid from us, the ones with mainly military benefits.

"After some years, their fleet of vessels grew to enormous proportions, but they always responded to natural disasters in other dimensions and provided excellent medical care even if their level of medical technology never appeared to increase.

"It later became obvious that they were waiting until their fleet was large enough to suit their own personal agenda. They co-ordinated their efforts over a period of a few weeks, ensuring they were all in specific locations. They positioned themselves in orbit around the planets where the other races were. No-one thought anything was strange about this. Why should they? In a single co-ordinated attack they wiped out everything on the planets. Even though a few managed to send out a distress call, no-one was in a position to respond. The Gringun ships were inside our planetary boundaries already. We were all defenceless. Of course, they left us till last. For some reason we were the ones they hated the most… the ones who found and taught them. They had something special planned for us.

"First they held us captive but not incapable of hearing the occasional distress call. They ensured that there was a single, small ship holding the portal open at all times, allowing them to keep the communication lines open. We got to see the devastation on all of the planets as they beamed the images throughout the dimensions. A group of ten Gringuns were based on our central home world. They were tasked with co-ordinating the attacks and they were the ones that planned everything, right down to what would happen to the Aneesh people. They later became the High Commanders, and of the original ten only four remain. As their bodies grow old, their consciousness is transferred to a new one.

"So, we got to watch as they killed everyone on the other planets and then destroyed all historical traces of the race. They set up identification zones and located anyone who was off world at the time. They were killed too, but at least they had a quick death.

"The attacks took a day to complete, in which time hundreds of races were terminated and removed from history. When only we, the Aneesh, were left, they turned their attention to us. They made us watch as they killed our families, leaving such a small number of us on each planet that any uprising would be impossible. Then we were delivered into servitude. We were forced to live in large groups in small buildings such as this. Procreation is allowed, but once a child gets to six years old it is taken away from the parents. We never see them again."

"Do you know what happens to them? The children, I mean," Entai asks.

"All we know is they are flown off world to labour colonies where they are forced to work for the Gringuns. Every now and again, when one of us dies, another is brought here to replace the dead. Occasionally, a direct descendant of our home world arrives here. They are kept safe, as the Gringuns like to torture them more than most. The sad thing is, now we have to remember our home world through stories. We have nothing else available to us, no pictures, nothing."

"Do you know how to get to your dimension again?" Forrahh asks. "I mean, if you could get you off this planet? Could you then?"

"No. The route to our dimension is complicated. That is why the Gringun still search for it, but there are too many dimensions to count. Finding our home would be pure luck. Besides, they do not want to be found, which makes this dimension our home now.

"It is a shame really. We wanted only the best for the Gringuns. Do you know that we had adopted a planet in this dimension as our own? You should have seen the structures we built." Haslyyn's eyes almost glaze over as he pictures the images placed in his head from childhood. "They rivalled the ones on our home world. So much so, that many came to see the spectacular buildings we had made."

"Did you see them yourself?" I ask him. I figured it was a stupid question but, trust me, the way he said it, the remembering stare, everything shouted out that he had seen this with his own eyes.

"No, Jon. We were told these things as stories. None have seen the planet for so long now. We have not found anyone in centuries who can even remember where it is."

"Maybe we will find the cities on one of the planets as we pass through. Do you know anything about the planet?"

"Unfortunately not! You see, when the Gringuns turned their attention to us, they took what remained of our people into orbit around the planet. They knew the pride we had in our new home. That's where they struck us. They forced our ancestors to watch as they razed the cities and killed those left on the planet. Even the rubble was disintegrated to make sure no-one could discover the cities again. They were thorough! Nothing was left alive and I believe nothing has lived there since. It is a dead planet now.

"There were stories of another planet, hidden from view. It had an underground base and there were some of our people in there at the time. They were all scientists, and the base was used to store the DNA of all of the wildlife on the planet. We were always worried that something we invented might harm the indigenous wildlife, so we ensured their safety by keeping their DNA coding. At least we would have a chance of bringing them back to life. And on the off chance that we damaged the planet too much, the DNA was stored on small ships which could be prepped for flight in a short time. There was no need to inform anyone else about this. This was something we did which affected no-one. We do not know if the stories are true but, if they are, we hope they got away safely. Our people knew how to take routes through dimensions the Gringuns had not investigated yet, uninhabited dimensions. We are sure that if they had been caught the Gringuns would have taken great pleasure in torturing them in front of us. But nothing was ever heard from them or about the planet. That is why so few believe the stories now."

"No news is good news," Andy mumbles to himself.

"I suppose it is," Haslyyn says, nodding his head.

"Are you sure you do not know where the planet might be?"

"We lost that knowledge long ago and we have not talked of it for a long time. We dare not in case someone should hear it and investigate the planets again. No, they believe they have found everything and destroyed everything. It is better that way. There are technologies on that planet which you would not believe. Should the Gringuns know of this information, they would surely seek it out. Their technology has remained almost stagnant since we stopped helping them. Their scientists are not gifted with innovative thought. Finding that planet would give them an unbelievable advantage over anyone else. That technology was given to us by the ancients, and we vowed never to tell anyone how to recreate it. At first we kept the secret so we could tell it to those who would come, but that was so long ago that we have now forgotten where the planet is."

"You said 'those who would come'? Who will come?" I ask him, regretting it as soon as the words leave my mouth.

"You, of course. You are our saviours. It was prophesied that you will come, you will deliver us from this evil. You will defeat the Gringuns. The technology the ancients created was peaceful, but as with anything of great power its ability to be used for peace is only matched by its capability for destruction."

"Wait, saviours? We can't be your saviours!"

"How do you know, Jon?" Enira asks me.

"She is right, Jon," Forrahh says. "We do not know that. Maybe with Aneesh help we will be able to defeat the Gringuns. Besides, we came here looking for information and allies. Maybe we have found them."

"We may have got more than we bargained for," I respond.

"And I can't believe you're all fine with this." I turn my attention back to Haslyyn. "So, what is this prophecy you are talking about?"

"We do not know where the stories came from, but we know that they have been passed down through the generations. At first they were whispered rumours kept from the Gringuns, but now they are tales told to our young to give them the hope they need. Many of our stories tell of how wonderful things were at first. How beautiful the cities were on our planet. But this was not enough. The young needed to hear that there was hope out there too. The prophecy came from nowhere, but it spread hope among the Aneesh. We knew that we would have to wait a long time, but it would be worth the wait if freedom was the reward."

"Hold on," I say, shaking my head a little too vigorously perhaps. "You have this all wrong! We are not chosen ones. We didn't even know you were here. We came here for information on the Gringun technology. We need something to fight them with."

"We have already said that we know of great technology. We know how to use it for peace and we understand how it could be used for war, but if you are looking for help in making weapons of war, we cannot help you with this."

"Do not worry. The Humans can do that better possibly than the Gringuns," Anris mumbles loud enough for all to hear. The concern on Haslyyn's face is evident – they have been here before!

"You need not worry," Forrahh says, noticing the change in emotions around the room. "The Najess are also with us. They would take an interest in any technology with a medical or scientific usage too. Without weapons to use against the Gringuns, what use would we be?"

Completely missing the explanation, Haslyyn hooks onto something we hadn't expected. "You are all different races? Which is Human and which is Najess?"

We all look at each other and Forrahh nods to me to explain.

"I and the other males are Human. The females in our group are Keteran. There is a third race called the Najess. They are great thinkers. One is with us on our ship."

"And you are all from the same dimension?" Haslyyn asks.

"Yes," I reply innocently to the question.

Haslyyn turns to look at his people who have been quietly listening to the conversation. They all shift and whisper nervously before settling down again.

"Is there a problem, Haslyyn?" I ask him.

"No, no problem at all."

I know he is hiding something, I can sense it, but it's not the right time to bring it up. Time to bring in Wei I think. *"Wei? Should I ask about the technology? I don't want to scare them off or anything, but I think we need any help we can get."*

"This is the right time, Jon. Ask them if there is another way to locate the planet and gain access to the technology."

"You mentioned that you had forgotten the location of your planet and that there was a great power source and technology there. If we help you to find the planet, will you help us with the technology?"

"As I said before, we can help with the technology, but we do not know how to create weapons of destruction."

"We will not need you to do that. Our concern is if we will understand how the equipment works."

"We may be able to help with that. You must understand, I can offer no guarantees to you. There is hardly anyone left who even remembers the old stories. Understanding the equipment may also take time and may not even be possible. If you are still willing to try, then so be it. We will offer any help we can."

"Excellent. In that case, let's talk about the planet and how to get there."

Another male sitting in the back of the room speaks up. "There are other stories. They tell of how to find our true home."

Haslyyn looks back at him. One of the younger Aneesh males

pulls a chair to the table while another gently lifts an almost impossibly old Aneesh male from the floor and helps him to the chair.

"This is Tefaaz," Haslyyn says. "He is the oldest of us. He has been hidden in this house for many years now. All of our elderly are killed when they cannot work any longer. It saves the Gringuns some rations." He gestures to Tefaaz to continue.

"There was one story from when I was a child," he retells his tale in a broken and weak voice. "It tells of another planet, much smaller than ours was. It was a deadly planet and one where none could ever live. Beneath the surface was a power source, similar but smaller than the one on our home. This planet was a starting point for us. Because it was already dead, we used it to test new inventions and ideas. The power source on the planet was a prototype for the real one we made later. If it works as well as the next one we made, it will still be active even after all of this time."

"If you have not been to the planet for so long, how can you be sure?" Forrahh asks.

"Because the Gringuns stole the designs from us and installed them on all their planets. As you can see, even with the power being used constantly, they are still active."

"Are you saying they never changed or charged them in all this time?" Garry always had a strangely compulsive interest in technology. "How did you make them? And what keeps them active for so long? Oh, and what materials were used?"

"We do not know," Haslyyn states bluntly but politely. "You forget, we do not even remember where we come from."

"Oh yeah, sorry," he responds, dejected and for once apologetic.

"We only know," Tefaaz continues, "that the planet was small and barren. There was no evidence of life having ever existed there, which is what made it a good option for testing. It was said that first the power supply was installed into the planet." He thinks for moment, struggling to remember something from his distant past. "There was something about the power supply linking to the planet's core." He shakes his head, giving up the attempt to remember any further information. "When the power supply proved successful, plans were made for DNA storage bases and a small craft hangar. These were created beside the power supply, below the planet surface." He thinks about this again. "Yes, that's right," he says almost to himself now, "the base was originally intended to be used above ground, but the planet was uninhabitable on the surface. There were volcanoes everywhere. It was taken as an opportunity to test a hidden underground base... There were some of us who were still very nervous about the Gringuns."

I exchange a glance with Forrahh as he describes the planet. We turn back to Tefaaz as he continues unaware of what just passed between Forrahh and me.

"A small base was created out of the planet's own materials. It was supposed to be protected from heavy bombardments, which is what allowed them to remain safely undetected when the attacks came."

"How would they have remained hidden from deep scans?" I ask, hopefully giving nothing away.

"Well, that was the point. It was designed to prevent being scanned. Remarkable, really. There was a problem of course. I do not remember the details, but I think people on the planet could not communicate with those below. They had to create a rudimentary warning system which would tell those below if an attack came. Yes, something like that. Why do you ask?"

TELL HIM, JON.

"Are there many planets similar to this in this dimension?"

"We cannot be sure," Tefaaz replies thoughtfully, "but I believe there may have been a few. But none had the volatile surface of this planet or the hidden base. This one was special."

"I see. Well, and we can't be sure it's the same, but we found a planet similar to the one you describe. It's devastated by constant volcanic eruptions. There are no signs of life and a strange communication problem between the surface and the construction below the surface. We also found a base there and we managed to enter it."

Haslyyn speaks up excitedly, leaning across the table, desperate for the information. "Where? Are you sure it is the same one?"

"As I said, I can't say for sure." I am trying to contain his excitement. "It matches your description, but that doesn't mean it is the same."

"But you said that you found a base?"

"Yes, we did."

Haslyyn leans in to Tefaaz and starts whispering to him, quietly enough that even with augmented hearing I can only pick up a small amount of the conversation. I get the idea that they are more encouraged by our news than I am.

Haslyyn looks to the back of the room, and a few of the other Aneesh gather around him, getting involved in the conversation while we sit there quietly waiting for the outcome.

"We believe you have found the planet. We do not remember tales of any planet like this in this dimension. Tell me, did you find anything unusual on the base?"

We look at each other before I offer the information, "Yes, we did. There was one room with some small symbols on the walls. When activated in the correct sequence, they opened a hidden doorway into a small room. There were symbols written everywhere. The walls, floors, ceiling, everywhere, but we could not decipher them."

"You needed a key," Haslyyn offered, "or at least someone who could read enough of the writing to give you a start."

"That's right." Now he had my interest and he could tell the rest of us were interested too.

"It is the right planet."

"So, you have the key?"

"No. We would not even know how to find it."

"Then the language. You have someone who can read it?"

"Not really. As I said, much of that knowledge has been lost over time."

"Then how does it help us?"

"I do not know," Haslyyn says, thinking as he speaks. "Tefaaz here is the oldest amongst us, though. Do you think you could read the symbols, Tefaaz?"

"I am not sure." The old man seems more alive and energised now. "I remember some of them. Maybe if I see them, some of them will make sense."

JON, YOU NEED TO TAKE HIM WITH YOU.

"*It's a risk, HICS. We will have to get him out of here without being seen.*"

YOU CAN TAKE HIM WITH YOU TOMORROW EVENING UNDER COVER OF DARKNESS. THAT WILL BE SAFEST. IN THE MEANTIME, YOUR PRIMARY OBJECTIVE IS NOT COMPLETE YET. THE DEVICE FAILED TO DOWNLOAD EVERYTHING FROM THE TERMINALS. YOU NEED TO CONNECT TO ONE AGAIN SO I CAN GATHER INFORMATION ABOUT THE GRINGUN PLANS.

"We will take Tefaaz with us tomorrow evening when it is dark. Will you be able to travel, Tefaaz?"

"You are taking me away from the Gringuns. I will travel anywhere you want me to."

"Good. Then we will need to rest somewhere this evening. Tomorrow morning, we need to locate a computer terminal so we can gather information about the Gringun plans."

"You can stay here underground tonight," Haslyyn offers. "It will be safe for you here. There is a terminal in the main city where you can connect and download your plans in the morning."

"Is there nothing outside the city?"

"There are a few, but if you use them to access the information you need it will set off alarms. It is necessary for you to do this from within the main city where I first met you. On the ground floor, there are four terminals in a corner of the room. The Gringuns rarely go there. How long do you need?"

"About five minutes will be enough," Forrahh says.

"That should be okay. You can go there tomorrow morning, complete your work and then come back here. Tefaaz will be ready to go when you arrive, but you will be able to hide down here until the evening. For now, I suggest you rest."

"That sounds like a good idea," I say to him.

Haslyyn nods to the people in the back of the room and they start to gather some bedding for us to sleep on. When everything is set, some of them climb back up, leaving a few, including Haslyyn and Tefaaz, with us. The cover is replaced above us, sealing us back in again. I have to admit, with the cover closed I felt a bit nervous that this might be a trap, but I also have this feeling that we can trust them. Still, even though I am tired, sleep comes with difficulty.

I am the first to wake up the next morning… kind of surprised myself really. I sit up and consider what we have to do today, quickly forming a plan in my head. For some reason I feel kind of queasy this morning, as though I have eaten something I shouldn't have. I think back to what I ate last night, but I figure if it was going affect me, it would have done so overnight, not now. It's probably only a case of nerves, anyway. We have a big day ahead of us, after all.

Garry wakes up a few minutes later, yawning loudly and stretching his body. He obviously aches as much as I do, but he looks strangely better this morning. I suppose the rest did him good. Slowly, everyone else wakes up looking slightly more rested than the night before.

"Morning, folks. How is everyone today?" I ask them, looking for a positive answer.

"Yeah, not too bad. I feel a little weird today, though," Garry says rubbing his head. Andy reiterates the response moments later.

I look at Forrahh, hoping it is just the Humans, but I guess it's not my lucky day. She shakes her head in silent protest to how she is feeling.

"HICS? Any ideas? Could it be the food from last night?"

I WILL DO SOME TESTS, JON. TRY TO RELAX FOR A FEW MINUTES.

"Okay, HICS. Thanks."

A few minutes later, HICS responds with our results. *ALPHA TEAM. THIS IS AN URGENT WARNING. YOU MUST COMPLETE YOUR MISSION THIS MORNING AND LEAVE THE PLANET AS SOON AS POSSIBLE.*

"What's happened, HICS?"

YOUR DNA RESEQUENCING IS REVERTING BACK TO ITS ORIGINAL STATE EARLIER THAN EXPECTED. YOU WILL HAVE NOTICED THAT YOUR SKIN TONE HAS CHANGED, AS WELL AS THE NAUSEA YOU HAVE BEEN FEELING. THE NAUSEA IS DUE TO YOU BEING AWAKE DURING THE CHANGE PROCESS.

"Which explains why we were made to sleep through it before. Okay, so how long do we have before it is obvious we're not Gringun?" I ask.

IN APPROXIMATELY FOUR HOURS, THE CHANGES WILL BE NOTICEABLE ON CLOSE INSPECTION. A FURTHER TWO HOURS AND IT WILL BE OBVIOUS FROM A DISTANCE.

"But that means we will have to leave here early... very early... in daylight, in fact," Andy says.

IT IS IMPERATIVE THAT YOU LEAVE THIS AREA BY LATE AFTERNOON. IF YOU ARE SPOTTED, YOU WILL BE EASY TO TRACK FROM ORBIT. IN ADDITION, THE SHIP IS LOCATED ON A FLAT PLAIN.

"So ground forces will be able to see us for a good distance," I murmur to myself. "We are going to have to go directly there after the mission is complete. Evasion won't be possible, so a direct route will *have to do. How long will it take us to travel the distance from here to the ship, HICS?"*

USING THE EMOS, THE JOURNEY SHOULD ONLY TAKE A FEW MINUTES. I HAVE FACTORED IN THAT YOU WILL BE CARRYING TEFAAZ WITH YOU.

"Will it be safe to take him?" Garry asks.

"It's necessary to take him," I respond while straightening and dusting off my clothes. I don't even have time to turn and face him. "Are there going to be any other symptoms for the DNA change, HICS?"

THE ONLY SIDE EFFECTS ARE NAUSEA AND SOME MILD PAIN. IT WILL BE A BIT LIKE MUSCLE ACHE TO BEGIN WITH. THE EMOS DELIVER A MILD ANAESTHETIC WHEN YOU GET INTO THEM. THIS WILL HELP TO CONTROL THE MAIN PAIN WHICH WILL FOLLOW. ONCE YOU ARE IN THE SHIP, I RECOMMEND YOU SLEEP THROUGH THIS CHANGE.

By now almost all of the Aneesh have woken up and are watching us as we all get ready to leave. It is the total silence which gets Haslyyn, though. Especially when he sees Andy and Anris just stare at each other silently before getting back to the packing.

Carefully he approaches me. "Was I wrong? Are you all telepathic?"

I turn to face him and smile. He takes a step back from me, but I don't notice it right away. "No. We have an implant installed which allows us to speak to our ship. The Keterans, though, they really do use telepathy. We were being informed of the results of some tests the computer has run on us." I pause as I look at his face and realise what must have upset him. "Oh, of course! Our faces have changed slightly. It's okay. As we said, we are a different race to the Gringuns, so we had to have our appearance changed to allow us to blend in with them."

He accepts the explanation pretty quickly and comes closer for a look. "They will notice this. Do you feel okay?"

"Yeah. It hurts a bit, but I'm okay. We have another problem, though. We will be looking very different in a few hours, so we need to get to the city right now and complete our mission. Then we have to leave with Tefaaz in daylight. The computer said we need to get back to our ship before nightfall."

Haslyyn pauses to think for a moment before looking at a young male sitting in the corner. The male stands up and leaves the room. "He will prepare the terminals area for you right away. You can leave when you are ready. By the time you return, Tefaaz will be ready to leave with you. In the meantime, the best advice I can give you is to avoid any contact with Gringuns. From a short distance, there is nothing to see, but close up they may suspect something."

"Thank you, Haslyyn. Really… thank you for your help."

"You can thank us by looking after Tefaaz. He is the oldest and wisest among us. It would be a great loss to us if something happened to him."

"His safety is as important to our future as to yours," I respond honestly to him.

None of us talk much as we walk to the central building for the second time in two days. I try to create a plan in my head as we walk, but for some reason I can't stop thinking about our changing appearances. And of course my thoughts often wander to Tefaaz and what he will be leaving behind. It's kind of like what I – we – had to leave behind, I suppose. We left our home planets, we left our families – what was left of them – we left everything we knew and understood. I, for example, left my parents lying under the rubble in the catacombs. My otherwise steady and focused steps falter briefly, but I don't think anyone else notices. But the question still remains… Should I have tried to pull them from the rubble? My dad would have said it was a bad idea, I think. He would have wanted me to get out, to get away. Or maybe I'm just trying to convince myself that I did the right thing? Some way of removing the guilt I feel about leaving them there. One thing's for sure, though… time doesn't heal all wounds. Almost a year on and I can still feel the stabbing, painful emptiness when I think about them.

"Almost there," Andy says out loud, thankfully breaking my depressing train of thought. It is the first thing anyone has said since we left the Aneesh house. The towering building we are heading for is clearly visible in the bright, clear day, which means that we would be clearly visible too… especially when we run to the ship later today.

"Right," I say, forcing myself out of my depression. "We need to head straight there and get into the building without being seen by any Gringuns. Haslyyn said that some of the Aneesh in the area are aware of our presence and will try to help if required.

"Once inside the building, we move to the location described by Haslyyn. Andy, when we arrive, use the link device to download the data," I say as I hand him the small device. "We will keep watch and warn you if anyone comes."

"Sounds like a plan!" Andy replies, obviously happy with his role in the mission.

We walk through the gates and move towards the building, avoiding any Gringuns. Luckily, it is still quite early, so there are not too many people around. Minutes later we arrive and enter through the main doors into the lobby area. There are very few people here, but we still keep away from the few we do see.

We move forward vigilantly, until a young Aneesh male appears from behind some large bookcases. After checking he is not being watched, he beckons for us to approach him. I carefully lead the way forward, aware that anyone could be an enemy here. As we approach, he disappears around the back of the bookcase. I carefully step around the corner, wary of an ambush, until I see him standing there waiting for us.

He smiles and quietly whispers to us, "I am so honoured to meet you. You do not know how wonderful it is that you are here. Even with all of the stories I was told as a child, I still never believed it would happen." He struggles to control the excitement in his voice. He seems completely overjoyed to have met us. For a moment, I actually feel like a hero. "Come, your terminals are this way. I have prepared everything for you."

"How did you recognise us? Was it something we did?"

"You all look lost, and no Gringun is lost here. Also," and this was the bit I was hoping he would not say, "your skin colour is slightly different from normal Gringuns."

"Be careful, guys," I say to everyone else. *"Make sure you keep your distance… and try not to look lost, I suppose."*

"Never thought I would miss my EMO so much," Andy says. *"Bet I wouldn't look lost in that!"*

"I know what you mean," I say. Then to the young Aneesh, "Let's get to the terminal. Lead the way, please."

He turns and walks around the back of the next bookshelf towards the corner of the large room with us all following behind. Luckily the area is empty, so hopefully no-one can see us here.

We round the last bookcase and enter a small area where a bank of four terminals are set near a wall and completely hidden from view.

"You're up, Andy," I say to him.

"It's about time, mate," he replies, smiling as he removes the small metal device from his pocket.

"Alright, I want everyone else on lookout." They all disperse in different directions to cover the exits, reporting back when in place.

When they are all ready, I give Andy the go-ahead and he attaches the device to the underside of the terminal just like I did yesterday.

DOWNLOAD COMMENCING, ALPHA TEAM. ESTIMATED COMPLETION IN FOUR MINUTES.

"So, what do we do now?" Andy asks.

"Wait, I guess."

HIGH LEVEL DOWNLOADS ARE COMPLETE. ESTIMATED COMPLETION IN THREE MINUTES.

"*Hmm, time really does go slow when you watch the kettle boil.*"

"*You going to keep talking, Andy?*" Garry asks.

"*Was thinking about it!*"

"*Tell me there's a way to get him out of my head, HICS,*" Garry implores.

"*Tell me there's a way to get them both out of my head, HICS,*" I implore more.

MID LEVEL DOWNLOADS COMPLETE. STARTING LOW LEVEL DOWNLOADS. ESTIMATED COMPLETION IN TWO MINUTES.

"*Thanks, HICS.*" Now we wait in silence, the tension level getting higher all the time. I really hate waiting for things to happen.

ESTIMATED COMPLETION IN ONE MINUTE.

"*Nearly there, Andy.*" I am missing the sound of talking, or at least some noise. It always gives me a sense that things are okay and people are around me. That is of course until I heard the sirens ringing out throughout the building. Now, silence would be great!

"*What's happening, HICS?*"

SOME OF THE LAST FILES WERE HEAVILY ENCRYPTED. THE DOWNLOAD MUST HAVE TRIGGERED AN ALARM. DOWNLOAD WILL COMPLETE IN TWENTY SECONDS.

Officially the longest twenty seconds of my life, but if they bothered to encrypt the files there must be something important there.

DOWNLOAD COMPLETE.

"*Guards!*" Entai says as she briskly walks back to me. "*They are almost here.*"

The young Aneesh male pushes Andy off the seat he is sitting on, toppling him heavily to the floor. He sits down and starts activating the touchscreen terminal. "Please, you must do as I say!

Shout at me. Tell me to stop immediately." He unplugs the device and throws it to me, forcing me to rush the catch, almost dropping it in the process.

Andy clambers clumsily to his feet as I jump in front of him to cover his actions. "Get off that terminal, scum!" Anris shouts as the guards appear around the corner. They ignore us in the commotion, charging past us and hitting him hard across the side of his head. He collapses to the ground and lies there, not moving, his heaving chest the only thing showing he is alive.

We watch in silence as they lift him off the floor, giving him the occasional kick for good measure.

Forrahh takes my arm and pulls me away from the area. *"We have to leave the area, Jon. If they see us, they will ask questions."* I come to my senses and follow her out to the main area as they drag the bewildered Aneesh male away. She releases my hand when we get to the central lobby again and we spread around the room. We wait patiently until they leave the building, dragging the Aneesh male behind them. I lock eyes with Forrahh and somehow I think she understands what is going on in my mind. *"Our primary mission is complete, Jon. He chose pain now so we could help him to freedom later. But we cannot do him any good if we are captured."*

I take a deep breath and wait until the gathered crowd disperses before exiting through the main door as any Gringun would have done.

"Come on, Jon. It's over now. We still need to get to the house and leave with Tefaaz." I can feel a powerful nausea taking hold of me, wrenching at my stomach. Is it the change or the events?

I force myself under control and nod. *"Okay. Remember, though, no more physical contact,"* I say, indicating the arm she used to drag me out of there.

She smiles. *"Yeah, I forgot."*

"Where are the others?"

"They left already. I told them it would be more obvious if we were in a big group."

"Makes sense. Come on, let's go." I lead the way out of the door and into the main courtyard with Forrahh beside me. There are a lot more people in the courtyard now. They are crowded round in a circle like schoolchildren watching a fight in the playground. I see through the gaps as we walk and catch a glimpse of the Aneesh boy. He is kneeling on the ground, his left eye fully closed from the beatings, and judging by the way he is balancing himself his left arm has been dislocated too. One of the Gringun guards moves behind him. The other hits him across the right side of his face with a stick. I watch as a couple of teeth fly out and land beside him. The Gringun standing behind him takes hold of his hair, pulling his head back and preventing him from falling to the ground. With a single devastating move, he slams his hands onto either side of his head. He holds him there for all to see, before twisting the head sharply left until it faces backwards, hanging down at an awkward angle. He slumps to the ground, dead before he hits it.

I stand there paralysed. *"We have to go, Jon. Everyone's attention is in that direction now. If they start to disperse, our skin colour will stand out too much. They will know!"*

Reluctantly, I start to walk with her, picking up pace the further away we get from the body. *"You couldn't have done anything to save him, Jon,"* she tries to reassure me.

"But we can try to save the rest of them!" I say quietly.

Her steps falter as she walks. *"What do you mean? We have to discuss this with the commanders first."*

"No. I have made my decision already. I will not leave them to suffer like this forever."

"I know you want to help them gain their freedom, Jon—"

"What freedom, Forrahh? Will he be free? I don't even know his name!" My pace increases as we leave the city confines and turn in the direction of the Aneesh building. *"You said it yourself. He chose pain in exchange for his freedom. I don't see how he is going to get that freedom! I really don't, but if you do, let me know because I really need to understand!"* I pause. *"I never even knew his name!"*

Her head hangs down as she walks beside me, and I realise my mistake. *"I'm sorry, Forrahh. It's not fair to take it out on you."* I look back at the city as we walk across the countryside. The alarms can still be heard in the distance, but I figure we are far enough away from sight so I take hold of her hand and I gently squeeze it reassuringly. Luckily, she squeezes it back. *"I promise I will speak to the commanders first. Right now, though, we need to get Tefaaz off this planet."*

We pick up the pace a little more. The others are a little way ahead of us, but I figure it makes sense for them to get there before us. At least they can ensure Tefaaz is ready. We need to get out of there pretty quick.

The door to the building is already open and as we enter I hear the commotion inside. Tefaaz is standing in the middle of the room waiting for us. A group of Aneesh people are gathered around him saying their goodbyes and wishing him a safe journey. Many actually look like they would happily exchange places. Based on what I've just witnessed in the city, I don't blame them. A part of me wants to take an extra person per EMO, but I know that's not really possible. We need to ensure the safety of Tefaaz first and foremost.

"Are we ready to go?" I ask as I walk to my EMO which has been moved back into the room for us. I notice the rest of the team is milling about. "Guys, what are you doing? Get into your EMOs!"

"We are ready," Haslyyn says, "but there is problem. One of my people has overheard something. The Gringuns have sent a small group of ships to this planet. They are looking for intruders here."

"The alarm!" I say as it dawns on me what has happened.

"Yes. They must know that you are here now. We have not had an alarm activated here in many decades. And the Gringuns do not subscribe to coincidence."

"Then we had best move quick."

"We're still leaving in broad daylight?" Garry asks in disbelief.

"We have to, Garry. If we stay here any longer we might be found and if we are found here, then I fear the outcome for these good people will not be pleasant." I wait for any further objections before continuing. "I'll take Tefaaz with me. Garry, you lead the way to the ship… No detours please, directly there. Andy, bring up the rear. If they open fire, do what you must to get rid of them. And if I fall, someone else takes Tefaaz the rest of the way. He's mission critical now, so get into your EMOs and prepare for evac!"

They move in unison to their EMOs and gather their things together. At the same time, I move to my own EMO and, with a shade of happiness, get in.

A couple of minutes later, we are all ready to go. I stand before Tefaaz, who looks a little daunted suddenly. I suppose I can understand where he is coming from. Two minutes ago, he was standing before a group of people who looked a lot like his worst enemy. Now he is standing in front of a group of enormous creatures the likes of which he has never imagined before. I kneel down slowly, trying to remember what it is like to be in the EMO whilst hoping being a bit smaller will help him get over his fear.

"Okay, Tefaaz. There is nothing to worry about. This is going to be a bit uncomfortable, but hopefully it should only last a few minutes. We need to move as fast as possible to get to the safety of the ship. The journey should only take a few minutes. Are you ready for this?"

He gulps down a lungful of air before nodding tentatively.

"We should jump our way there, Jon," Garry says. "It would get us there a bit quicker."

"We can't risk it, Garry. We may not feel the landing so much, but someone being held in my arm is likely to feel the full force of the impact."

"But it will get us to safety faster!"

I switch to internal team communications, "I'm not going to argue with you in front of the Aneesh, Garry. We are running to the ship, you are taking the forward position, Andy takes the rear guard and the Keterans will act as a guard for me and Tefaaz. Is that understood or do you need me to explain it further?" The frustration is evident in my voice.

"Hey, have it your way, but I like the way you've surrounded yourself with guards and left everyone else in the open."

A part of me wants to get up and smack him one for that remark, but I figure it just shows his own cowardice. There were always times in the past when I saw him stand back from situations where he could have hurt, but now was not the time to bring it up. "Do you want to take Tefaaz yourself, Garry?"

"Yeah, why not!"

"Fine. Change of roles, people. I'm taking the front and will guide you all to the ship."

I get a series of affirmatives from everyone except for Garry. Forrahh's voice cuts in on a private channel, "You handled that well, Jon. I know you were protecting Tefaaz. We all do."

"Thanks, Forrahh."

I switch back to external communications. "Tefaaz, there has been a slight change of plans. Garry will carry you back. But I will be with you the whole time, okay?" I say reassuringly.

Still obviously daunted by us, he nods his agreement again. I turn to look at Haslyyn. "We have to leave now. If they find us here, it won't go well for you all."

"Agreed. Whatever the outcome of this, thank you for your help, Jon," Haslyyn says. "Thank you all."

"I'll do my best to get you all out of here, Haslyyn, I promise."

JON. THE SCANNERS ARE PICKING UP SOMETHING IN THE CITY. I CAN ONLY GET PARTS OF IT, BUT I THINK THE GRINGUNS ARE AWARE OF YOUR GENERAL LOCATION NOW. YOU NEED TO LEAVE IMMEDIATELY.

"No time like the present. Garry, pick up Tefaaz. Take care Haslyyn. I will see you soon."

With that said, I turn and leave the building, stooping to exit the door without breaking the doorframe.

The moment we exite the building, the scanners go crazy. There are hundreds of objects moving towards us. Most are moving slowly, on foot I guess, but a few were travelling pretty fast. These are the ones I am most worried about. Judging by how fast they are moving, it looks like they might even be able to keep up with us. What I can't figure out is how they knew where we were. The only thing I can think of is that we were seen walking in this direction. Regardless of how they found us, we need to get out of here and we have to do it quick.

The team falls into formation behind me. I check my scanners and wait until we are settled and ready to move. Garry confirms that Tefaaz is tucked securely under his right arm and ready.

I take my first slow steps, gradually picking up speed. I can see everyone on my scanner. Andy is still holding formation at the rear. Some way behind him there are a number of red dots closing in fast.

"Let's pick up the pace a bit, people," I say, using the internal communications. "Andy, watch your back. They're gaining on us."

Andy checks his scanner quickly. "Man, what are those things?"

"Whatever they are, they're quick. If they get too close, Andy, open fire, but don't fall too far behind. We only need to slow them down a bit."

"Easier said than done, Jon. What do we do if they're flying?"

I look up and behind as we run. I can't believe it. A couple of scout ships have punched through the atmosphere and are heading straight for us. The green cross on my scanner shows our destination and the ETA... just over two minutes. "Forrahh, take the lead. I'm going to help Andy guard the rear."

Without another word said, I see Forrahh increase her pace

and come up alongside me. Entai and Anris change formation slightly to fill the gap Forrahh has left around Garry.

"Andy, activate weapons," I say, activating mine at the same time and dropping back to his position in time for the scouts to do a quick flyby… I guess they needed to identify us as the target, because they turned right around and opened fire. Luckily they rushed their attack and all the shots missed the target – namely us.

Almost in unison, Andy and I separate, turn and shoot at the two ships, barely missing them. They must have seen us attacking and decided that we were the bigger issue. They turn around, pick one of us each and strafe the ground on the run up to us. Dirt flies into the air, creating swirling clouds of dust spiralling in the air behind us. We roll to the sides in mid run and get up to continue our attack. I launch a volley of shots at the ships, but they are too manoeuvrable. One of my shots barely scratches it and that's the best I get. Andy does little better himself. It sure is different from the training exercises! These ships are incredibly fast.

"HICS? Can you adjust the targeting sensor so I don't have to aim ahead of the target?" I hear Andy ask hoping for a positive answer. "I want the target to be highlighted when my shot is likely to hit. Adjust for atmospherics and speed and stuff."

ADJUSTMENTS COMPLETE.

Well, that was quick! We both dive to the side again, rolling to an upright running position. Mid roll I catch a glimpse of the area behind us. The ground vehicles are closing in. We have to end this quickly. If we have the ground and air vehicles to deal with, this isn't going to work out well for us.

One of the ships passes directly overhead as I get back to my feet. It travels a short distance forward before turning around to attack again. As before, it flies directly towards me. Out of the side of my visor I see Andy's gun raise and a volley of shots are released, punching holes in his target's hull several times before it disappears from view behind us. My attacker flies in low, firing a torrent of shots at me. Change of tactics! This time I launch myself straight up, not to the side. The scout sees this too late and tries unsuccessfully to veer out of the way. I close in fast, data flashing across my visor showing the strength of the ship's hull and the impact point. I pull my right arm back as I approach it and punch my clenched fist forward as hard as possible, hitting it on the side of the hull near the small left wing. My fist goes straight through the hull and I grab hold of anything I can inside. Part of me wants to inflict as much damage to it as possible. The other part of me is holding on for dear life as the small ship veers in all directions trying to shake me off.

With my left hand, I punch another hole in the hull and grab hold of anything I can inside before ripping it all out with one mighty pull of my arm. The ship shudders severely and starts to roll out of control. Ripping out whatever I'm holding onto with my right hand, I remove the contents from the ship and drop to the ground, rolling as I land to break my fall, before turning to watch the destruction I have caused. The wreckage of both scouts is lying close by each other, with smoke and flames pouring out of them.

A cheer rises from the others, with Andy's the loudest by far, "Ho-ly crap! That was awesome. I gotta try that next time."

"That was so cool," is all I can say. The adrenaline rush has not left me yet, but I can feel a certain clarity return to my thoughts and senses. There are other vehicles and a number of them are approaching fast. "Let's go, Andy. The others are still running. Pick up the pace!"

"Yes, sir," he replies good-heartedly, and we both hit a sprint immediately. "How did you know you could do that?"

"Don't know how I did it, let alone know I could." According to the scanner we are catching up with the others, but they were almost at the transport now. The ground vehicles are not making any ground on us now, but we still have to get the ship ready. It would have been good to get a little extra speed out of the EMOs, but it wouldn't make a huge difference.

"We are prepping the transport, Jon," Enira says. "You boys might want to show us some more of those tricks."

I zoom my visor onto where the cloaked ship should be. The side door opens as the ship turns to face side on to us. "You ready, Andy?"

"Oh, yeah! I want some of this!" He chuckles like a boy jumping a stream on his bike. Then we prepare ourselves for what's next.

We leap into the air together, arcing through the air like arrows at a target, landing as gently as possible on the deck of the ship. There's still an almighty thump when we land, though, and the ship tips slightly while it tries to compensate.

We are greeted by a round of applause from the rest of the team which, let me tell you, is loud when clapping in an EMO. HICS closes the door behind us and I feel the ship move forward instantly. I take a bow to acknowledge their greeting.

"How's Tefaaz?" I ask getting straight to business.

"He is in the training area at the moment," Entai says. "HICS had it converted into a medical and rest area after we left. He was a bit shaken up when we arrived."

"Okay, let him rest for now, then. How's the cloak holding up, HICS?"

THE CLOAK IS ACTIVE, JON. WE HAVE NOT BEEN DETECTED YET.

"Yet?" I ask. "You expecting trouble?"

A BLOCKADE OF SHIPS HAS ARRIVED IN ORBIT AROUND THE PLANET. THEY ARE SCANNING THE ENTIRE AREA. THEY KNOW WE ARE HERE.

"You sure they can't track us?"

THERE ARE NO COMMUNICATIONS WITH ANYONE OUTSIDE THIS SHIP, SO THEY CANNOT DETECT US THAT WAY. SO LONG AS WE KEEP OUR SPEED LOW

UNTIL WE CLEAR THE BLOCKADE, THEY WILL NOT BE ABLE TO DETECT ANY HEAT SIGNATURES OR DISTORTIONS FROM US.

"Well, we're putting our faith in you, HICS. If you say it's safe, then it's safe."

EXITING THE ATMOSPHERE NOW.

16

HOMEWARD BOUND AND ONTO THE NEXT PHASE

It's almost an hour before we manage to navigate our way through the mass of ships orbiting the planet. HICS kindly provided us with some comfortable seats to relax in during this time. We stowed our EMOs out of the way in the corners of the room before sitting down. We figured it would help Tefaaz to adjust if he saw us outside the EMOs again. Of course, once we exited the EMOs we noticed the change in skin colour and that our faces were a slightly weird shape now thanks to the DNA changes. The shape change explained the aching in my jaw at least. The nauseous feeling was much stronger now too, and I really felt like sleeping it off. For now, though, we all sat down and enjoyed a well-earned rest while we recounted some of the recent events. One subject we kept revisiting was Andy and me taking out the ships… especially my attack manoeuvre.

Not long after leaving Amerang behind, Tefaaz walks in, slightly more refreshed and a bit stronger too. "Welcome, Tefaaz," Forrahh

267

says, trying to smile warmly, but the changes in her appearance make the smile look almost menacing. "Please, sit down. Can I get you a drink?"

Gingerly, Tefaaz sits down on the seat which rises from the floor for him. "I have just had a drink. Your computer has been very helpful, thank you."

"How are you feeling?" I ask.

"I am slightly bruised," he says, "but I will be fine. Your suits are very powerful. They are very impressive."

"Thank you. They were designed by HICS, our computer. Are you sure you would not like something to eat or drink? HICS should be able to formulate anything your body requires."

"No, thank you. What I am interested in, though, are the symbols which you say you discovered."

"Fair enough. HICS should be able to help there."

WE FOUND MANY SYMBOLS ON THE PLANET, BUT THE SYMBOLS ARE NOT LOGICALLY LAID OUT LIKE A LANGUAGE, OR IN WHAT WE WOULD TERM AS SENTENCES. THEY ARE NOT TELLING A STORY IN ANY WAY, WHICH MAKES IT CONSIDERABLY MORE DIFFICULT TO DECIPHER THE LANGUAGE.

"Are you able to describe the images?" Tefaaz asks.

IT WOULD BE BETTER TO SHOW THEM TO YOU. A panel in the floor moves apart, and a device similar but smaller than the holographic imaging device in the MCC appears. All of a sudden, one of the symbols shimmers into view and hovers above the surface.

"I'm concerned," Garry says to me using the implant. *"I'm not sure we should be showing him so much, Jon. We have only just met the Aneesh and I'm not sure I trust them yet. You have to admit, the Gringuns turned up pretty quick when we were on the planet."*

I glance at Tefaaz who is already taking a real interest in the symbols appearing before him. *"I know where you are coming from,*

Garry, but you didn't see what I saw there. The way they were treated was shocking. I do trust them, but I will err on the side of caution for now. We do need him to work on the symbols, though. Would you agree with that?"

"Agreed."

I have to admit, I thought that conversation was going to be a lot worse. Although I do get the feeling that Garry harbours some ill feeling towards this race for some reason. I'll just have to watch them both for now. Personally, I trust the Aneesh, and it will be interesting to see if they really can help with the symbols.

"Excellent," Tefaaz says, breaking my chain of thought. "Wonderful!"

"Do you see anything you recognise?" Anris asks expectantly.

"No. But I vaguely remember descriptions of some... I think! Are there more?" HICS cycles through the symbols one by one every three seconds until Tefaaz suddenly sits bolt upright. "That one," he says, his voice oozing positivity. "I recognise it. I remember my grandfather describing it to me."

"Great," Garry mumbles sarcastically. I stare at him reproachfully.

"It means... I think it was... path. Yes, that is it... I think. Yes, path, but not in the sense of the right path to take in your life. No, it means the path that you follow to a destination."

I look at the others. "Carry on, HICS."

The symbols shift through again until Tefaaz sees another. "Yes, this one too. This is the symbol for safety. Oh, it is all coming back to me."

A few more symbols later. "Wait!" Tefaaz exclaims, a stunned look on his face. "Can it be? But this is not a word. It is a name."

"For what, Tefaaz?" I ask, leaning forward in my seat now.

"For a planet. In fact, if this is correct, then you have found... you have found the test planet. It is where we tested all of our technology. Wait, I remember something about this, something about a pattern… no, a formation linked to the symbol." He thinks quietly for a moment and none of us dares to distract him. "HICS? Do you have a picture of all of the symbols? I mean from the entry point into the room?"

A new three-dimensional image shimmers into view and Tefaaz cocks his head to one side, then to the other. A smile slowly spreads across his face.

"What do you see, Tefaaz?" I ask, barely able to wait any longer.

"I never thought I would live to see this day. But here I am. And I am the one who found it. I was always told I was going to do something wonderful for my people, and I have you all to thank for this."

"Tefaaz, I can barely control my own curiosity," I say. "Please, what have you found?"

"In the beginning, I could not understand why you could not decipher the symbols yourself. Then I met this computer of yours and then I really could not see the reason. Now, though, now I understand. A computer would not think like a person trying to hide something. It is not capable of innovative thought… No offence, HICS," he corrects himself. "HICS, take the centre symbol, the one which looks like a broken bridge. Simulate the properties of a huge gravitational force, something like a small black hole. Make the symbol the focal centre of the force and the other symbols all around it as objects."

The broken bridge symbol highlights and the rest of the symbols around begin to move towards it as though it had a gravity of its own.

"Stop," Tefaaz says. The symbols remain frozen where they are, in a spherical shape around the centre symbol.

"What is it, Tefaaz?" Andy asks.

"A map of the planets in this dimension, of course. This is how my ancestors hid our planet."

"So, which one is it?"

"Well, that is the easy question. It is the one in the middle. What we need to find out is, which one is the planet we will be starting from?"

"Okay, so how do we find that planet, then?"

"That is where your computer, HICS, can help."

"HICS? What do you think?"

COMPARISON OF THE PLANETS AGAINST THIS STAR MAP SHOULD BE COMPLETE BEFORE WE ARRIVE AT OUR DESTINATION.

"Excellent," I say yawning. "Right, now I intend to get some sleep."

THERE IS SOMETHING ELSE, JON. I WILL NEED TO COMPLETE SOME TESTS ON YOU ALL WHILE YOU SLEEP. I HAVE CHECKED MY DATA AND CAN CONFIRM THAT THE DNA CHANGES MADE TO YOU ALL SHOULD NOT HAVE REVERTED BACK WITHOUT ME TRIGGERING YOUR ORIGINAL DNA SEQUENCES AGAIN. THE FACT THAT THEY DID AND THAT IT HAPPENED SO SOON NEEDS TO BE INVESTIGATED. WE ALSO NEED TO UNDERSTAND WHY IT HAPPENED TO YOU ALL TOGETHER.

"Why should that make a difference?" Garry asks.

"You are all essentially different races, Garry," Wei says. "Your DNA may be unusually similar, but the changes should not have happened at the same time. Metabolic rates should have played a part in this at least."

"Understood, Wei," I say. "Run the tests and let us know the results when we wake up." The last bit trails off a bit as I yawn loudly.

"Yeah, I'm bushed too!" Garry states while stretching his arms out wide. "And I really want to get past this feeling that I'm going to throw up!"

We all get up except for Tefaaz. "Do you mind if I stay for a bit and talk to HICS?" he asks without taking his eyes off the changing symbols. "I have already had my sleep and am a bit excited at the moment."

"That's fine, Tefaaz." I know that will annoy Garry, but I couldn't care less at this point if he stays up or not. I really do feel dead tired and really sick. All I need right now is to sleep. Aside from Forrahh, the rest of the gang has already made their way into the sleeping area. She waits for me to finish my conversation before walking back to the bunk area with me. We don't say a word to each other, but it feels good that she waited... like she is saying that I have her support.

You know when you wake up in the middle of the night after a nightmare and someone – occasionally you – is screaming, but then you realise that it was all in your head? Well, this was not one of those times. I wake up fresh, adrenaline coursing through my body as the sound of the alarm screeches through my unwilling eardrums and into my confused brain.

I swing my feet out of the bunk and hit the floor in a standing position. I look around and absorb the situation as quickly as possible. Our Keteran entourage are all beside Andy and Garry, watching over them. I sprint the short distance to their bunks shouting to HICS on the way, "What happened, HICS?"

THE IMPLANTS ARE REACTING LIKE YOURS DID.

"Bring up the scans, HICS!" I have to shout the order over the alarm system. "And please shut the alarm off. I think we are all awake now."

Thankfully, the alarm switches off immediately and I wait impatiently for the scans to complete. The screens behind their bunks flicker and the brain scans appear. I look over at the large screens, trying to make sense of the information displayed.

"What am I seeing here, HICS?"

"These look the same as yours did, Jon," Forrahh says as she arrives at my side.

FORRAHH IS CORRECT, JON. THE IMPLANTS ARE REACTING EXACTLY LIKE THEY DID WITH YOU.

"I thought they were tested?" I say, realising that I had guaranteed them all that it was safe. "But they didn't react that way on Russell. Why would that be?"

I DO NOT HAVE SUFFICIENT DATA AVAILABLE YET. THERE IS A FURTHER PROBLEM, THOUGH.

"Which is?"

ASSUMING EVERYTHING WENT AHEAD WITHOUT DELAY, ALL HUMANS WILL HAVE HAD THE IMPLANTS INSTALLED BY NOW. IT WAS DUE TO HAPPEN WHILE THIS MISSION WAS IN PROGRESS.

"What do you think will be the outcome?"

BASED ON WHAT WE HAVE SEEN HERE, THEY WILL BE SEEING A SIMILAR REACTION IN THE COMING HOURS. THERE DOES NOT APPEAR TO BE ANY NEED FOR EXCESSIVE CONCERN, THOUGH. ANDY AND GARRY HAVE NOW SETTLED DOWN EXACTLY AS YOU DID. THE SCANS SHOW THAT THE IMPLANT HAS LINKED ITSELF DIRECTLY INTO THEIR BRAINS AND IS FULLY FUNCTIONAL. I BELIEVE THIS WILL BE THE SAME FOR ALL HUMANS AFFECTED.

"But what is causing it in some and not in others?"

WE WILL ONLY BE ABLE TO DETERMINE THAT WHEN WE ARRIVE AT THE PLANET AND SEE WHO ELSE HAS BEEN AFFECTED.

That, I guess, makes some sense to me. I just hope it does not affect too many people. For now, though, we are going to have to monitor our friends and make sure they don't have any other side effects.

The rest of the journey home – well, new home, anyway – went relatively uneventfully. The guys woke up the next day, not understanding what all the fuss was about. As they had their seizures during their sleep, we had to explain to them that they had actually lost a day. Funnily enough, this upset them more than the seizure. For the rest of the journey, we kept a close watch on them, but nothing unusual happened.

The transport hovers momentarily over the hatch before gently landing and closing the seal with a hiss. We jump down, suited and booted in our EMOs, and carefully lower Tefaaz down from the ship. He looks up as the hatch closes above, leaving us bathed in a dull yellow light. A low rumble can be heard as the now heavily used lift makes its way up to us. When it eventually arrives, we step inside with the very nervous Aneesh elder following us. The doors close behind him, sealing us in the now crowded lift.

What we didn't know was that we would be missed so much. As the lift door opens, half the base has congregated in the main entrance to greet us. Trust me, this is a much better surprise than you would believe.

I deactivate my visor allowing everyone to see my face. Tefaaz understandably has a severe case of the nerves and is now trying to hide between us… possibly one of the more dangerous moves he could have made.

"Hi, folks," is all I can think to say. I honestly never expected anything like this.

THE COMMANDERS ARE WAITING FOR YOU ALL IN THE CC.

I can't believe it. We just walked in! "Do we have ten minutes to change, HICS?" I ask sarcastically.

I WILL INFORM THE COMMANDERS.

"It would have been nice to relax a bit first," I whisper over the din to Wei.

"We need to debrief while it is all clear in our minds, Jon," Wei says. "Come on. We should get ready."

"I suppose," I reply as I carefully pick a path through the crowd.

Dot on time, we arrive at the CC. As we enter the large circular room, we see the joint commanders enter the meeting room and sit down. I lead the way inside and sit down at the table opposite the commanders. The rest of the team – including Tefaaz – sits down on both sides of me, making me the centre of attention for the commanders... Thanks guys!

Wesley barely acknowledges us. Instead, he simply flicks through a new tablet he seems to have acquired.

"So, it appears you had a somewhat successful mission." He is looking at me directly, giving me the feeling that he expects me to respond on behalf of everyone else.

"Yes, sir. Having landed..."

"HICS has explained the key events already, Jon. No need to go over everything again." He continues examining the tablet before looking up again. "Okay. Let's cover a few updates first. HICS has been analysing the data retrieved from the planet. The initial higher level data is giving us a good idea of the troop numbers and the ships they have. HICS, show some of the information you have on the ships, please."

A holographic panel rises from the centre of the table. THE DATA DOWNLOADED FROM THE GRINGUN TERMINALS SHOWS THE TYPES OF SHIPS THEY CURENTLY HAVE.

A ship flickers into existence and hovers over the raised panel. Based on the scale bar at the bottom, it looks to be about the same size as the flagship we arrived on. It has a large body with a streamlined front end and a boxy rear where the thrusters are.

THE SHIPS LISTED IN THESE FILES REFER TO A RANGE OF CRAFT FROM SMALL SCOUTS AND FIGHTERS TO LARGE CAPITAL SHIPS. IT APPEARS THAT THE ATTACK CRAFT THEY PREFER TO USE INCLUDE THE SCOUTS WHICH WE HAVE ALREADY SEEN AND A BOMBER CLASS ATTACK CRAFT.

THE NEW INFORMATION WE NOW HAVE ON THE SCOUTS WILL ALLOW US TO TAKE THEM DOWN MORE EFFECTIVELY. WE ALREADY KNOW THEY ARE FAST AND HIGHLY MANOEUVRABLE. THEIR WEAPONS SYSTEMS ARE LIGHT BUT HAVE A HIGH RATE OF FIRE, ALLOWING THEM TO CAUSE SIGNIFICANT DAMAGE TO LIGHTLY ARMOURED GROUND TARGETS AND OTHER SMALL SHIPS. HOWEVER, THEY ARE UNABLE TO BE EFFECTIVE AGAINST LARGER, MORE HEAVILY ARMOURED SHIPS AND BASES. THE SCOUT ARMOUR IS LIGHT, THEREFORE A COUPLE OF DIRECT HITS TO THE HULL SHOULD BE ENOUGH TO REMOVE THE ARMOUR AND DESTROY THE SHIP ENTIRELY. THIS MAKES THEM ALMOST USELESS AGAINST CAPITAL CLASS SHIPS, AS THE HIGH DAMAGE RATING OF THE EXTERNAL CANNONS MEANS THEY ONLY NEED TO BE HIT ONCE.

THE BOMBERS ARE VERY DIFFERENT. THEY ARE MUCH SLOWER AND THEREFORE EASIER TO HIT, ALTHOUGH BRINGING THEM DOWN IS A DIFFERENT MATTER. THEY ARE GENERALLY USED TO ATTACK CAPITAL CLASS SHIPS. THEY UTILISE TWO METHODS OF ATTACK. FIRST, THEY ATTACK USING AN ELECTRICAL CHARGE. THIS IS A NEW WEAPON WE HAVE DISCOVERED. ITS EFFECT IS SIMILAR TO AN ION BOMB WHICH DELIVERS A LARGE ELECTRICAL CHARGE TO A SPECIFIED AREA OF THE TARGET. ION BOMBS, HOWEVER, REQUIRE A LARGE PROJECTILE SUCH AS A MISSILE WARHEAD TO CARRY THE ELECTRICAL CHARGE. THIS WEAPON IS DIFFERENT. IT IS CAPABLE OF GATHERING THE ELECTRICAL CHARGE INTO A SMALL BALL AND FIRING IT OUT TOWARDS A TARGET. AS THERE IS NO PHYSICAL PROJECTILE USED HERE, THE BOMBERS CAN CREATE

HUNDREDS OF THESE CHARGES WITHOUT TAKING UP ANY ADDITIONAL SPACE ON BOARD. THIS ALLOWS THE BOMBER TO REMAIN RELATIVELY SMALL. THE DISADVANTAGE, THOUGH, IS THAT THE PROJECTILE IS RELATIVELY SLOW AND THEREFORE EASY TO EVADE. DUE TO THE NATURE OF THE WEAPON, IT REQUIRES AN ELECTRICAL CHARGE TO BE FORMED, MEANING THAT THE RATE OF FIRE IS VERY LOW TOO. THE ELECTRICAL BOMB IS USED TO INITIALLY DISABLE SMALL SEGMENTS OF THE SHIELDS – NAMELY THE AREA WHICH THEY HIT. A SECOND WEAPON TYPE HAS ALSO BEEN DISCOVERED. AFTER THE ELECTRICAL BOMBS DISABLE THE SHIELDS, THESE NEW WEAPONS ARE USED TO PUNCH A HOLE THROUGH THE HULL AND EXPLODE WITHIN THE SHIP CAUSING MASS DAMAGE. THESE BOMBS ARE SIMILAR TO MISSILES CREATED BY HUMANS EXCEPT THAT THEY HOME IN ON THE AREAS OF THE SHIELDS WHICH ARE DISABLED. THIS MAKES THEM INCREDIBLY DANGEROUS. THEY WILL NEED TO BE DESTROYED BEFORE THEY HIT. AS THESE ARE PHYSICAL WEAPONS, THE BOMBER CAN ONLY CARRY A LIMITED NUMBER OF THEM – APPROXIMATELY TWENTY PER SHIP. A LARGE NUMBER OF THESE BOMBERS CARRYING THIS COMBINATION OF ELECTRICAL CHARGES AND MISSILES WILL BE CAPABLE OF BRINGING DOWN A CAPITAL CLASS SHIP, THOUGH.

"Are you able to replicate this technology, HICS?" Nique asks.

BOTH WEAPONS CAN BE REPLICATED, BUT I HAVE BEEN CONSIDERING ONE SIGNIFICANT CHANGE. SOME OF THE SECONDARY HOMING MISSILES CAN BE USED TO PUNCH THROUGH THE TARGET'S HULL AND DELIVER AN EMP BLAST TO THE ENTIRE SHIP.

THIS WILL DESTROY SOME OF THE INTERNAL SHIP SYSTEMS BUT LEAVE THE MAIN SHIP INTACT. WE MAY BE ABLE TO LEARN SOMETHING FROM THESE SHIPS IF WE DO NOT DESTROY THEM.

"True, but what about the people on board?"

UNFORTUNATELY, IT IS LIKELY THAT THEY WILL ALL DIE, AS THE LIFE SUPPORT SYSTEMS WILL ALSO BE DISABLED.

"Can the blast not be directed to avoid these systems?"

NO. THIS IS A WEAPON DESIGNED BY HUMANS TO BE USED ON EARTH. IT IS NOT DESIGNED TO BE USED OFF WORLD AND THEREFORE THE CONSIDERATION FOR HUMAN LIFE WAS NOT CONSIDERED, JUST THE ABILITY TO REUSE THE NATURAL RESOURCES IN THE AREA ATTACKED. IT MAY HAVE BEEN POSSIBLE IF THE EMP BLAST WAS LIMITED IN STRENGTH SO IT AFFECTED A SMALLER AREA, HOWEVER THIS WOULD LIKELY ALSO LEAVE SOME WEAPONS SYSTEMS ACTIVE TOO. I DO NOT RECOMMEND THIS APPROACH.

"What about the other ships?" Wesley asks.

THESE ARE THE CAPITAL SHIPS. MOST ARE APPROXIMATELY THE SAME SIZE AS OUR FLAGSHIP, BUT A FEW, ONE IN PARTICULAR, ARE CONSIDERABLY LARGER. An image of their flagship appears, with our much smaller flagship beside it.

THIS IS JUST AN EXAMPLE OF THEIR FLAGSHIP. THE ACTUAL SHIP WILL BE DIFFERENT BUT WILL HAVE BEEN BUILT FROM THESE ORIGINAL DESIGNS. AS YOU CAN SEE, THE GRINGUN FLAGSHIP IS APPROXIMATELY TWENTY-FIVE PER CENT LARGER THAN OURS. HAVING STUDIED THE RANGE OF WEAPONRY FITTED ONTO THIS SHIP, I CAN CONFIRM THAT ONLY ANOTHER CAPITAL SHIP WILL BE ABLE TO BRING IT DOWN. SMALLER, MORE MANOEUVRABLE CRAFT WILL BE

ABLE TO AVOID THE TURRETS FOR A SHORT PERIOD, BUT THEY WILL NOT BE ABLE TO DELIVER ENOUGH FIREPOWER TO DAMAGE THE SHIP.

I look around the table and see what I expected to see… I am not the only person in awe of this new ship.

"Every ship has a weakness, HICS," Wei states.

THE ONLY KEY WEAKNESS IS SPEED. THE SHIP IS SO LARGE THAT THE ENGINES TAKE TIME TO BUILD UP ENOUGH POWER TO SPEED UP OR SLOW DOWN. THERE IS ANOTHER VULNERABILITY. DUE TO ITS SIZE AND SPACIAL DISPLACEMENT, THE SHIP CANNOT JUMP INTO A LOCATION TOO CLOSE TO ANY OTHER SHIPS OR PLANETS. THIS PROBLEM DOES NOT MANIFEST ITSELF WITH THE SMALLER SHIPS, THOUGH.

"How is that possible?" Wei asks. "My understanding of the jump window is that it is just a fold in space to travel through. There should be no displacement."

THE DISPLACEMENT OCCURS WHEN THE WINDOW IS CREATED. ALTHOUGH THE WINDOW APPEARS TO BE INCREDIBLY THIN, IT CREATES AN ELECTRICAL CHARGE IN THE IMMEDIATE AREA. THIS CHARGE COVERS AN AREA THE SAME SIZE AS THE SHIP ENTERING IT. ANY ELECTRICAL DEVICES IN THE VICINITY ARE IMMEDIATELY DRAINED OF ALL ENERGY – I NEED TO STRESS THAT IT DRAINS *ALL* ENERGY FROM ANYTHING IN ITS VICINITY.

"Interesting," Wei says. "So that means the ship is unprotected when it jumps into a new location. We could lie in wait if we knew the entry point."

TRUE, BUT ANY OF OUR SHIPS IN THE VICINITY WOULD BE DESTROYED AS IT ENTERED. THE ELECTRICAL STORM CREATED WOULD BE DEVASTATING.

"Can this not be used as a weapon?" I ask.

IT ALREADY IS A WEAPON. WHEN THE SURROUNDING ELECTRICAL ENERGY IS DEPLETED, THE LINK IS NOT SEVERED. AS THE SHIP EMERGES THROUGH THE WINDOW, IT CAUSES THE ENERGY TO BE TRANSFERRED BACK TO THE SOURCES IT CAME FROM, CREATING A MASSIVE ELECTRICAL CHARGE WHICH EXPLODES WITH ENORMOUS POWER. THIS IS HOW THEY ORIGINALLY DISCOVERED THE ELECTRICAL ENERGY WEAPONS AND DEVELOPED THEM TO WHAT I DESCRIBED EARLIER.

AS MENTIONED, THERE ARE SEVERAL DIFFERENT TYPES OF CAPITAL SHIPS. THE FLAGSHIP IS BY FAR THE LARGEST, WITH THE OTHERS BEING SLIGHTLY SMALLER THAN OUR OWN FLAGSHIP. THESE SMALLER SHIPS TAKE THE FORM OF LIGHT AND HEAVY ASSAULT FRIGATES. THEY CAN BOTH BE TAKEN DOWN BY THE BOMBERS, BUT THE HEAVY FRIGATES HAVE CONSIDERABLE ARMOUR. THEY WILL TAKE A SUSTAINED ATTACK FROM BOMBERS BEFORE THEY CAN BE DESTROYED. THE LIGHT FRIGATES ARE OBVIOUSLY FASTER DUE TO LESS ARMOUR, BUT THE WEAPONS ARE ALMOST AS EFFECTIVE AS THEIR HEAVIER VERSION. THESE SHIPS CAN ALL TRAVEL THROUGH THE WINDOW AND APPEAR IN THE MIDST OF THE FLEET WITHOUT ANY PROBLEMS, MAKING THEM A DEVASTATING FORCE TO CONTEND WITH.

"Excellent information, HICS," Wesley says, looking longingly at the assault frigate rotating in front of him. "When can they be ready?"

WE HAVE THE NECESSARY RESOURCES FOR A COUPLE OF FRIGATES ALREADY.

"Excellent. And the weapons?"

AS MENTIONED, ONLY A COUPLE OF FRIGATES CAN BE MADE RIGHT NOW. THESE WILL NOT BE

PARTICULARLY EFFECTIVE IN BATTLE ON THEIR OWN. A GROUP OF THEM TOGETHER, HOWEVER, CAN BE DEVASTATING. ADDITIONAL SUPPORT CRAFT, SUCH AS INTERCEPTORS, WILL NEED TO BE MADE TO PROTECT THEM FROM THE BOMBERS. IN ADDITION, I HAVE USED THE DESIGNS WE GATHERED ON THE LAST MISSION TO CREATE DESIGNS FOR OTHER CRAFT.

"Really?" Nique asks. "Like what?"

ACTUALLY, SOMETHING THE NAJESS WILL BE VERY HAPPY ABOUT. THE FIRST OF THE VESSELS I HAVE BEEN CONSIDERING IS A SCIENTIFIC RESEARCH VESSEL. I HAVE CONSIDERED THIS VESSEL AS THERE MAY BE OCCASIONS WHERE WE IDENTIFY SOMETHING OF INTEREST ON A MISSION. THE MOBILE RESEARCH FACILITY – MRF FOR SHORT – WILL HAVE A DUAL PURPOSE. THE FIRST IS TO RESEARCH NEW TECHNOLOGY OR MATERIALS ON THE MOVE. THE SECOND IS TO ASSIMILATE NEW TECHNOLOGY IDENTIFIED ON MISSIONS. THE MRF IS A LARGE CAPITAL CLASS VESSEL.

THIS BRINGS ME TO THE SECOND OF THE SHIPS. THESE ARE SALVAGE VESSELS. THEY ARE SMALL, LIGHTLY ARMOURED VESSELS WITH NO ARMAMENTS. USING ONE OF THE DESIGNS I HAVE STUDIED ALREADY, I HAVE CREATED A NEW DEVICE WHICH WILL ALLOW THE SALVAGE VESSEL TO PUSH OBJECTS TOWARDS THE MRF. THE MRF IS BIG ENOUGH TO ASSIMILATE THE SMALLER CAPITAL CLASS SHIPS LIKE THE FRIGATES. THE EMP WEAPON WE WILL BE USING WILL DAMAGE MANY OF THE COMPONENTS ON THE SHIP; HOWEVER, THE TECHNOLOGY WILL STILL BE SALVAGABLE. WITH THE ENGINES DISABLED, THOUGH, THE SALVAGE SHIPS CAN

ATTEMPT TO SALVAGE THE ENEMY VESSEL. SMALL SCOUTS OR FIGHTER CRAFT CAN BE HANDLED BY AN INDIVIDUAL SALVAGE VESSEL. LARGER SHIPS SUCH AS THE FRIGATES WILL REQUIRE TWO OR THREE SALVAGE VESSELS. THE ASSIMILATION PROCESS WILL BE ESTIMATED TO TAKE APPROXIMATELY THREE DAYS DEPENDING ON THE COMPLEXITY AND SECURITY OF THE ON-BOARD SYSTEMS. DURING THE PROCESS, ANY ORGANIC MATTER ON BOARD WILL DIE IF IT DOES NOT LEAVE THE SHIP PRIOR TO ENTERING THE MRF. ONCE A SHIP HAS BEEN ASSIMILATED, THE TECHNOLOGY AND DESIGNS WILL BE AVAILABLE TO US AND WE WILL BE ABLE TO COMMENCE CONSTRUCTION IMMEDIATELY.

THE NEXT SHIP TYPE IS THE RAPID MINING VESSEL, OR RMV. WE WILL NEED TO HAVE AT LEAST TWO OF THESE AVAILABLE AT ALL TIMES. THEIR PURPOSE IS TO GATHER RAW MATERIALS FROM NEARBY PLANETS AND BRING THEM BACK TO THE BASE FOR PROCESSING AND CONSTRUCTION. WE ARE ALREADY RUNNING VERY LOW ON RESOURCES AND WILL NEED THESE VESSELS URGENTLY. THE RAW MATERIALS GATHERED WILL ALSO BE USED TO DEVELOP THE NEW WEAPONRY I DETAILED EARLIER.

"The MRF sounds interesting. Do we have enough to build one of those?" Enira asks.

CURRENT RESOURCES WILL BE ENOUGH TO BUILD THE MRF, HOWEVER THERE WILL NOT BE ENOUGH TO COVER FUTURE REPAIRS AND MAINTENANCE. WE ALSO HAVE ENOUGH RESOURCES FOR A FEW SMALL INTERCEPTORS AND FUTURE REPAIRS IN CASE OF ATTACK. THE RMV CAN ALSO BE BUILT. IT WILL BE RELATIVELY QUICK AND ABLE TO OUTRUN THE LARGER FRIGATES DUE TO ITS LACK OF WEAPONRY,

BUT GROUPS OF SCOUTS AND BOMBERS WILL BE ABLE TO TAKE IT DOWN EVENTUALLY. AS THEY ARE EXPECTED TO TRAVEL SOME DISTANCE, IT IS ADVISED THAT A GROUP OF INTERCEPTORS ARE PROVIDED AS A DEDICATED GUARD FOR THE SHIPS. THESE SHOULD BE KEPT CLOAKED AT ALL TIMES AND ATTACK ONLY IF THE RMV THEY ARE PROTECTING IS ENGAGED. THE RMV IS A LARGE SHIP, BUT IT IS NOT A FRIGATE CLASS VESSEL.

"So, what do we build first?" Wesley asks, confused by the abundance of information. "We could do with the frigates for firepower, but one or two won't make a difference and more interceptors will hardly make a dent on the Gringuns."

MY RECOMMENDATION IS TO DIVERT OUR EXISTING RESOURCES TO THE RMV. WITHOUT THEM, WE WILL NOT BE ABLE TO CREATE ANY OTHER SHIPS, AND TRADITIONAL RESOURCE GATHERING METHODS ARE INEFFICIENT AND WILL GIVE AWAY OUR POSITION.

"Agreed," Nique says. "We need to be sure that we have enough to build more vessels for as long as possible. I suggest we allocate a contingent of our existing interceptors with the cloaking device and send them with the RMV at all times. How can we increase production of ships, HICS?"

AS MENTIONED, THE RMV IS A LARGE VESSEL AND WE NEED TO RESERVE SOME RESOURCES IN CASE WE ARE ATTACKED. BASED ON THIS INFORMATION, WE ARE ABLE TO BUILD ONE RMV. WHEN THE FIRST RESOURCES ARRIVE, WE CAN START CONSTRUCTION ON THE SECOND RMV AND ANOTHER SMALL CONTINGENT OF INTERCEPTORS.

"Can the RMV not be fitted with a cloak?" Enira asks.

YES. ALTHOUGH THE RMV IS LARGER THAN MOST SHIPS, IT IS NOT CLASSED AS A TYPICAL CAPITAL

CLASS VESSEL. CAPITAL CLASS VESSELS ARE TOO BIG FOR THE CLOAK AT PRESENT. I AM WORKING ON A NEW MODEL OF THE CLOAK WHICH MAY BE USED ON CAPITAL CLASS VESSELS IN THE FUTURE. ALSO, DUE TO THE POWER REQUIREMENTS TO ACTIVATE THE CLOAK, IT MUST BE DISENGAGED BEFORE MINING CAN COMMENCE.

"Well, that helps us to travel back and forth without being seen," Wesley murmurs to himself, "but it doesn't help much when mining starts."

IT IS THE BEST WE CAN DO FOR NOW AND THIS IS WHY WE NEED THE CONTINGENT OF INTERCEPTORS.

"The interceptor pilots will be defending the RMV some distance from the base," Enira says. "What if one of the interceptors is damaged? Is there a way they can get back to us?"

AS INTERCEPTOR PILOTS ARE NOT GENERALLY REQUIRED TO ENTER INTO MELEE COMBAT SITUATIONS, I HAVE ALREADY BEEN ABLE TO MINIMISE THE SIZE OF THE EMOS FOR THEM. THE NEW EMOS WILL GIVE THEM THE SPEED AND AGILITY THEY REQUIRE TO LEAVE A DANGEROUS SITUATION QUICKLY. TO ALLOW THIS TO HAPPEN, THEY WILL ONLY HAVE ACCESS TO HAND-TO-HAND WEAPONRY FOR THE TIME BEING.

"You mean the blades?" I ask, causing Wei and Nique to flinch.

YES. IN EXCHANGE, I HAVE BEEN ABLE TO SEAL THE SUITS COMPLETELY IN CASE THEY NEED TO EJECT DURING SPACE COMBAT. THE SUIT WILL SUSTAIN LIFE FOR A COUPLE OF DAYS AT MOST IF THE PILOT IS ABLE TO KEEP CALM AND CONTROL THEIR BREATHING. ALTHOUGH THIS DOES NOT SEEM LIKE A LOT OF TIME, THESE SUITS ARE EQUIPPED WITH SMALL THRUSTERS IN THE SOLES OF THE FEET. THESE

WILL ENGAGE AUTOMATICALLY WHEN THE SHIP IS DESTROYED AND WILL TAKE THE PILOT BACK TO THE NEAREST SHIP OR BASE OUTSIDE THE COMBAT AREA.

"Sounds cool," Garry says. "Can we have those?"

THE PROPULSION SYSTEM COMES AT THE COST OF THE ADDITIONAL WEAPONRY. I CAN PROVIDE IT FOR YOU, BUT YOU WILL NEED TO LOSE EVERYTHING EXCEPT FOR THE BLADES.

"No, thanks," Andy says. "Those I like!"

"Tell me about it!" I reply.

"I heard you both had some fun out there," Wesley says. "We will have to talk about that later." I notice a sly smile creep across Andy's face. Out of the corner of my eye, though, I catch a furtive glance between Garry and Entai. They don't look so impressed.

"Do you have a planet in mind for mining, HICS?" Enira asks.

THERE IS A PLANET NEARBY CALLED RISTEN. THE GRINGUNS HAVE IT MARKED AS A PLANET WITH PLENTIFUL RESOURCES. THESE RESOURCES HAVE BEEN RESERVED FOR EMERGENCIES. ONCE THEY REALISE THE EXTENT TO WHICH WE ARE IN THEIR DIMENSION, I BELIEVE THEY WILL START TO MINE THIS PLANET. ALTHOUGH THERE ARE SEVERAL OTHER PLANETS WE COULD USE, THIS IS THE CLOSEST AND WILL DELIVER THE MOST RESOURCES AT THE FASTEST PACE. I SUGGEST WE MINE THIS PLANET FIRST.

"Agreed," Nique responds. "Okay, any other business to discuss before we turn our attention to our new friend?"

"The implants, sir," I say. "They malfunctioned again."

"Yes, I heard. We were of course glad to hear that they malfunctioned on the way back. In fact, you probably haven't heard about the effects back here."

"We assumed they would have malfunctioned here, too," I say. "I thought they had been fully tested before we left, sir?"

"They were tested, but I believe HICS knows what has happened."

I HAVE BEEN ABLE TO MAKE A COMPARISON OF THE PEOPLE WHO HAS BEEN AFFECTED SO FAR AND HAVE FOUND SOMETHING UNUSUAL. NONE OF THE PEOPLE AFFECTED HAVE BEEN OVER EIGHTEEN YEARS OLD.

There is a moment of total silence in the room. A part of me doesn't really believe it. For the first time, I wonder if HICS has made a mistake… Well, there's a first time for everything.

I AM NOT SURE WHAT THE REASON IS FOR THIS YET, BUT I WILL BE INVESTIGATING IT THOROUGHLY.

"What percentage of the Human population has received the implants?" Forrahh asks.

EIGHTY-NINE PER CENT HAVE ALREADY RECEIVED THE IMPLANT. AS IS COMMON IN HUMANS, THE YOUTH ARE VERY IMPULSIVE AND DRIVEN BY TECHNOLOGY… ALL HUMANS BETWEEN THE AGES OF TWELVE AND EIGHTEEN HAVE RECEIVED THEIR IMPLANTS. WHERE PARENTS WERE PRESENT, IT WAS DONE WITH THEIR CONSENT, AND AFTER THE RESULTS APPEARED PROMISING OTHERS STEPPED FORWARD.

Another stunned silence.

"Really? All the parents gave their consent?" Forrahh remarked.

AFTER THEIR QUESTIONS WERE ANSWERED AND THEY HAD HEARD ABOUT THE ADVANTAGES, ESPECIALLY AROUND SAFETY AND BEING ABLE TO MONITOR THE HEALTH OF THEIR CHILDREN, THEY ALL AGREED.

"So," I ask, hoping for an answer I actually want to hear, "how many of them were affected by the implants?"

ALL OF THEM. THEY ALL RECEIVED THE IMPLANTS

OVER A FEW DAYS AND THEY ALL SUFFERED FROM THE SEIZURES.

"What was the time interval between receiving the implant and seizures?" Wei asks.

THAT IS THE STRANGE THING. SOME PEOPLE WERE OBVIOUSLY EARLY ADOPTERS TO THE TECHNOLOGY AND HAD THE IMPLANT EARLY. OTHERS WAITED TO SEE THE OUTCOME AND HEAR ABOUT HOW IT WORKED BEFORE AGREEING. BY THE END OF THE WEEK, ALL HAD AGREED AND WERE SCHEDULED IN. THE EXPECTATION WOULD BE THAT EVERYONE WOULD SUFFER THE SEIZURES AFTER THE SAME AMOUNT OF TIME HAD ELAPSED. INSTEAD, THEY ALL HAD THE SEIZURES AT THE SAME TIME.

"Wait, HICS," Forrahh says. "Are you saying that the early and late adopters all had the same problems at the same time, regardless of when their implants were installed?"

THAT IS CORRECT, FORRAHH.

The Keterans glance at each other before Enira comments, "This would imply some level of telepathy in the Human youth."

"I agree," Wei says. "This warrants further investigation."

ASSUMING SHE GIVES HER CONSENT, I SUGGEST NALONN MAY BE ABLE TO HELP WITH THIS. SHE ALREADY HAS EXPERIENCE AND KNOWS WHAT TO EXPECT.

"Agreed, but not right now, though," Nique says, checking the small tablet in his hand. "I think it would be best to allow her some time to prepare herself mentally for this task. We know how it hurt her last time."

"That would be good," Enira replies. "I will discuss this with her when we have finished here."

"In the meantime," Wesley says, laying his tablet on the table as he leans casually back in his seat, "I suggest we hear more about these combat tactics you and Andy have been using." Andy and I exchange glances and I nod to him to continue.

It's obvious that Andy is taking a huge amount of pleasure in recounting the tale. Somehow he manages to add an extra twang to everything that happened, making it all so much more interesting. I was never any good at telling stories. My dad always said that my problem was I thought about reading the words too much. He believed you had to feel each word and sometimes that meant reading a little slower and imagining the words being spoken by the character. I guess now he's gone, I'll never fully understand what he meant.

And that's when I realised that I needed to concentrate on Andy and his story before I fell into depression again. I swear, sometimes I have a really short attention span.

Anyway, Andy goes over the details of how we got the data and how we escaped. Every now and again someone else adds something, but on the whole they let him tell the story. The 'wow factor' moment is when he goes to the escape and how the two of us fought off the two scout ships. What we did not know was that HICS had been recording the whole event using our visors. As Andy went over the details, HICS put it onto the screen. It was like Andy was narrating a movie sequence to everyone. The image would switch from my view to Andy's throughout this time, allowing us to see the events from the other person's point of view. It was like watching a movie with audio descriptions. The funny thing was, when I saw myself jumping up to the airborne scout through his eyes, it looked a lot more amazing than I remembered it.

One thing I noticed about Andy, though? He was a thinker. Before opening his mouth, he knew what he should and shouldn't say. He conveniently left out the bits about Garry refusing to take the position assigned to him. He just didn't make a big deal out of it.

So, after the events had been recounted and we were all laughing and joking about our new moves – and I mean all of us were laughing, even Wei and Nique – our Joint Commander presented us with another task. While plans were set and building started – specifically on the RMV – we had to train a group of people in how to fight using the EMOs. From what we were told, these would be the best people we had from all of the races, including the Najess, but they would be young too. In fact, the strange thing was, only a third of the Humans were over eighteen years old. It turns out that not only do the implants cause seizures in all Humans under the age of nineteen, but they also work better after the seizure. That's another thing HICS is trying to figure out without much success. We asked why they hadn't brought in Nalonn yet, but we were told they wanted her to be the last resort. I suppose it makes sense not to risk her anymore. Last time she tried, it almost killed her. Whatever it is living in our heads may not be so merciful next time.

Anyway, the fact is, we were tasked with training the troops over the next few weeks while the plans were set and HICS tried to figure out some of the more intricate issues which always seem to surround humanity. Between the six of us we had thirty people. Twenty of them were under nineteen years old. They were instructed to learn everything they could from us. The remaining ten were the best of the group. They were in their late twenties, early thirties. They were calmer and better at taking instructions – which I later found out was because they were the remnants of elite armed forces from around Earth. The others – well, the Human others anyway – had a tendency to mess around a lot more and always seemed to think they knew better than us. They probably didn't like taking instructions from someone three years younger and not even commissioned into the forces yet. Luckily, they seemed to take a shine to Forrahh and the other Keterans, which made them behave a little better. The group was split into teams of ten and we trained them together. So, Forrahh and I trained one group of ten Human and Keteran pairs, Anris and Andy the next, and Garry and Entai the last group. The idea was, we would train this group who were handpicked by someone up above and were supposedly the most promising people we had. They would in turn train another group, and so on down the line until we had a large army of highly trained individuals who were not only capable but highly effective in combat situations. As you can imagine, the Najess soon opted out when they realised what was expected of them. The team allocated to Forrahh and me were mainly the highly trained, ex-special forces people. That made it a lot easier to train them. Of course, age was a factor. As time went on, I could see that their EMOs did react slightly slower to their commands than the younger people on the team. This did not appear to be a problem for the Keterans, so I figured this was a side effect of the implants. Even so, it was amazing what the elite forces people could do with their EMOs. Some of the moves made my stunt with the scout look childish. By the time we had shown them how to use their EMOs, they were teaching me and Forrahh a load of moves we had never known were possible. I actually learned how to do flips and, let me tell you, they look spectacular in an EMO.

About a week after the training started, we were called into the CC again. For some reason, I thought HICS' voice sounded tense when giving us the orders, but I knew that could only be my imagination.

We enter the meeting room. The commanders are sitting in their usual places behind the table. Tefaaz is sitting beside them with his hands on the table. The atmosphere seems more tense than usual. You can feel it in the air. Something is definitely wrong. We sit at the table and wait patiently for someone to speak. I guess everyone else senses the same tension in the room too, as we all sit in total silence.

Seconds later, Nique clears his throat and begins, "As you are all aware, HICS has been examining the documents you managed to get from the planet. The primary task has been to find out some information about what we are up against. The data does not fill us with a great deal of confidence. We are incredibly outnumbered." We remain silent, waiting for the commanders to provide the data we have all been secretly dreading. "The data shows that we are currently outnumbered by about one thousand to one."

"Wait," Garry interrupts, breaking our silence, "wait, are you saying that for every Human, they have one thousand Gringuns?"

"That is correct, Garry."

"There's no way that can be right. The planet we just came from had hardly anyone there. The planet was practically empty. The only normal place was the main city and that wasn't exactly teeming with life."

"Don't exaggerate, Garry," I respond to his childish reaction to the news.

"Chill out, *hero*," he says, stressing the 'hero' sarcastically.

"People," Wesley steps in, instantly cooling down the situation. "We are not going to let this get in our way and we will not let this news leave this room. Is that understood?"

We both nod our heads and Nique continues. "In addition to the troops outnumbering us one thousand to one, they have approximately ten thousand ships of differing classes. This may seem like a tremendous number, but keep in mind that, from what we have seen, our ships are considerably more powerful, faster and better armoured than theirs. In addition, Tefaaz has been extremely helpful to us. With his help, we have been able to translate more of the symbols in the room than we previously thought possible. I will detail these findings shortly.

"First, we need to discuss the Gringun troop and vessel numbers. I know these numbers look daunting, but we have the advantage of knowing their current technological level and, thanks again to Tefaaz, their potential too."

This last statement confuses me. "What do you mean by 'potential', sir?"

"Tefaaz pointed out something vital to us. The Gringun scientists are much like our own scientists. They belong to a faction of people who are generally peaceful by nature. The problem is, they insisted on doing things in a way that went against the Gringun High Command. Eventually, the High Command took matters into their own hands." He pauses while he considers his next words. After a deep breath, he continues, "The High Command permanently changed their DNA and using telepathy, altered their minds. They changed them so that that they were unable to stand against the High Command. They removed their ability to think about opposing them without affecting the intelligence of the scientists." Andy prepares to say something, but Nique raises his hand to stop him. "There was an unexpected side effect, though. It also removed their ability to problem-solve. They are still capable of learning and absorbing massive amounts of information, but they are incapable of putting the theory to practical use. This is what we mean by knowing their potential."

"We know who the High Command are," Andy says. "We have heard mention of them a few times. But what makes them so special?"

"They are the leaders of the Gringuns and the strongest of them," Tefaaz answers. "Their telepathic ability is unmatched by any others, including other Gringuns. This is the talent which Gringuns place above all other talents and it is this which has allowed them to be accepted into the High Command."

"But surely other Gringuns must be born with a greater talent?"

"There are many born and tested every year, but few truly have the gift. The lower orders of the High Command change every decade or so. As someone with a greater talent is discovered, their natural instinct takes over and they challenge the one above them. Sometimes this is successful and the new Gringun moves up the ranks. Other times, it is not successful."

"What happens to the unsuccessful ones?" Andy asks.

"The telepathic battle is a lot like a challenge for superiority between animals. One is usually wounded during the show of strength. In the case of Gringuns, though, the damage is done directly to the brain. A Gringun knows if they are going to win or lose in the first few seconds. If they win, they ascend the ranks to the High Command. If they lose, they suffer a major brain haemorrhage resulting in death. The High Command itself only ever has ten members at any one time. Between them, they run the empire in a truly malicious manner and it is these rulers who decide how a race will die. Aside from my race, none were allowed to live."

You can feel the tension in the air. Everyone is silent, but I can see Forrahh and Enira having a conversation between themselves.

Wei's voice cuts through the tension, making us jump back to reality, "Based on the numbers we have been presented with today, combined with the technology they have already, are we sure we can do this?" I can hear the nervousness in his voice and I'm sure everyone else can too.

"We will need help if we are going to stand a chance against those numbers," Wesley answers, "but we will go over that later with everyone else. As for the technology, I believe with HICS managing our technology we will have a few tricks up our sleeves. Besides, we already know that the technology we have developed recently and the technology being developed currently is already better than anything they have."

"What about Nalonn?" This was the question I was hoping Wei would not bring up.

"She is willing to perform the probe again," Enira replies. "She is nervous about it and still fears what she saw last time."

"So, when do we do this?" I ask, resigned to the fact that she will risk her life again to take a look inside my head.

"Not yet," Wesley says. "We have another mission for you all before that happens."

We look up in unison, surprised at the statement.

"What mission?" Forrahh asks.

"This is one of Wei's ideas," Wesley says. I look at Wei, not understanding why he didn't say anything to us. He had plenty of opportunities. I guess my expression must have been like a book or else Wesley has learned to mind read better than the Keterans. "Wei came up with the plan but was instructed not to mention this to any of you."

"It was not easy, Jon," Wei says apologetically. I nod, but I can't help myself wondering if he is hiding anything else from us. I shake it out of my head, realising the stupidity of this. Wei would tell us if he could and if it were important.

"Once your mission is complete, Nalonn will be asked to attempt another mind probe on you, Jon," Enira continues. "We do not want to risk anything prior to an important mission. I hope you all understand."

I figure Nalonn would be happy to put it off for as long as possible too.

"Right," Wesley says as he fiddles with the tablet in front of him, "if you are all done, I believe it is time for a briefing on the next mission."

Nique clears his throat and presses an image on the table in front of him. A small planet appears, with a strange mess of indiscernible objects floating above it. "You are looking at a new planet we have discovered. The orbiting object you all have taken an interest in is a junkyard for wrecked ships."

There are sounds of agreement from us all as it dawns on us what the objects are – pieces of ships floating in orbit.

"Although we have some interesting data regarding this planet, there is a lot we do not know about it. We are interested in it, though, because the data you captured recently refers to this planet for some of the designs for the capital ships and the weapons we need to develop."

"I thought HICS was able to create these already?" Garry pipes up. "If that's the case, why do we need to go there and get more data?"

"HICS will be able to build the ships, but there are some areas, particularly around the shielding and weapons, which will take longer to develop. If HICS had access to the data, it would mean that the additional research would not be required." Garry does not seem too pleased with the response but decides not to go on about it any further.

"What's the planet called?" Forrahh asks.

"The planet is called Sidarack," Nique responds. "We need you to go there and remain undetected for as long as possible. Your teams are required to go down to the planet and steal any plans you can regarding capital ships and weaponry. In addition, you need to return with any pieces of ships you can carry back from the orbiting junkyard."

Wesley takes over from Nique, "Your transport ships have already been modified for this mission. The cloaking device installed on your previous transport has been improved, as have the engines. You can now travel faster with less fear of being detected. The hull has also been improved considerably, allowing you to take a few direct hits if required. This is only a few hits, mind you… Try not to get hit at all, please."

Nique continues again, "HICS has upgraded all of the long range scanners, both on the ships and on the base. We have run some extensive tests and have confirmed that even with one of our ships in orbit around the planet, no life signs or communications are detectable. Tefaaz has explained that he remembers stories about this planet and this was one of the technologies the Aneesh were testing here. During the long range scanner tests, HICS detected a lot of movement emanating from one of the central and more heavily guarded planets… the Gringun home world. Communications and ship movements have increased significantly since your last engagement and it looks like they have started searching all of the planets in this dimension, starting with their own.

"Now, they have a long way to go yet, but they will get here eventually. We think they tracked your trajectory when you took off from the planet and have started travelling in this direction now."

"Sneaky," I say partially to myself. "That's a lesson learned."

"Indeed, but it is not worth the trouble if it means endangering your lives. Where possible, leave the planet and circle around again if it is safe to do so. Back to the Gringuns now. We expect them to arrive here at some point, but hopefully our existing protection offered by this planet will keep us hidden. In case it doesn't, though, we are going to put another plan in motion. You will not be using your cloaking devices the whole time."

"Ah, yes of course. Well, that's easy for you to say," Garry responds angrily. "You're sitting back here with all the protection you need provided by the planet. We are the ones putting our lives at risk."

I can't believe I'm thinking this, but a part of me has to agree with him… at least a small part does, anyway. It does sound like a suicide mission. And besides, how are we supposed to make our way to the planet without being seen if the cloak is off? We'll be surrounded before we even arrive. The fact is, though, I know we need to do this. In fact, there isn't anyone else who can, and Garry should know this by now. Before I can say anything, though, Andy confronts Garry directly, "You need to calm down, Garry. You know this has to be done, and I'm sure there is not only a good reason but also a contingency plan to keep us safe. Admiral Nique has always tried to keep us safe."

The look on Garry's face is a picture I won't forget in a long while. I'm not sure who he dislikes most now, me or Andy.

Nique continues, ignoring the outburst from both of them, "As mentioned earlier, HICS has redeveloped the long range scanners. What we did not mention was that we have also found a way to detect cloaked ships. Using the long range scanners, you will be able to travel at maximum speed to your target and only slow down when another cloaked vessel has been detected. This will ensure maximum efficiencies for speed and cloak effectiveness. You will have two groups of five ships. Each group will travel to the same destination using a different trajectory. When you leave here, you will both be using the cloak and will travel to the highlighted planet." A path appears on the holographic image floating above us and connects our planet to a new one we have not been to before. "This is a barren and desolate planet much like this one, only Tefaaz has confirmed there is no technology there. It used to be the home of another race that was wiped out by the Gringuns. You will be travelling to this planet first. Both groups of ships will then disengage the cloak and travel using this path for a short distance."

Another trajectory path appears, dotting its way in a long curve away from the planet and towards our destination. A number of small red crosses appear along the path, preceded and followed by a small blue dot.

"The distances travelled are exactly the same and, travelling at a uniform speed, you will both arrive at the same time. The small red crosses represent listening posts which the Gringuns have recently activated. When your ships enter scanner range for the listening posts, you will disengage your cloak and briefly travel at a reduced speed. You will then engage the cloak again when you have left the area and accelerate to maximum speed again. The small blue dots show where you will disengage and engage the cloak. Hopefully, this will confuse the Gringuns enough to make them split their search party and delay how long it is until they reach this planet.

"Following the plan and the flight path at the correct speed is vital to the success of the mission. It is imperative that you all arrive at the target together. If you can arrive as quickly as possible and without detection, it should hopefully convince the Gringuns that we are occupying a planet somewhere near there. Remember, you are not able to communicate until you are all in close vicinity to each other. At no point can you use any communications channels."

"So, how do we co-ordinate the attack with each other?" I ask.

"That is our area of expertise," Enira responds. "We are able to communicate over short distances telepathically. So long as the ships are within a mile of each other, we will be able to communicate without alerting the Gringuns. HICS has been given the exact co-ordinates and will guide the ships to their destinations. Once there, your attack on both locations must be synchronised, and the only method of communication will be your Keteran team members. You will be split into two teams called A and B. Team A will infiltrate the planetary base and extract information from the computer systems in much the same way as you did on Amerang. Based on what we have discovered from the data you previously captured, we believe the base holds the plans for several of their capital class ships, including the frigates we plan to make next.

"Team B will be travelling directly to the shipyard. You may have noticed during the training exercises that half of the people you were training had a very different skill set. Although these people are adept at fighting, this is not their key skill. This group of people are capable of identifying items of value. Their mission will be to scour through the shipyard and identify anything that may be of technological importance to us. If they find something useful, they will inform the pilots. The pilots will then manoeuvre the ship to it and gather it into the cargo bay. The primary stage of their mission is to dock with the orbiting station located in the shipyard and take control through any means necessary. We have already seen that the Gringuns use a highly aggressive form of telepathy as their primary weapon. You will understand when I say that the team has been ordered to shoot first and search later. We need to avoid casualties, please."

"Who is leading this mission?" I ask.

"You and Forrahh proved highly proficient as team leads in your last task, Jon," Enira says. "For this reason, we have decided to give you both the opportunity to prove yourselves again. As the mission is more complicated and will require some planning experience, your second will be Major Jim Clarke. He is highly experienced at managing dispersed teams and can help you to learn how to do this."

"Wouldn't it be better for him to lead the mission, then? I can shadow him and learn that way."

"If you want to learn," Wesley interrupts, "then this is the mission to learn from. Troop numbers will be low, and communication will be minimal. This is possibly the only chance you will get to train on the job like this."

Easy decision really, especially when your commander puts it to you like that. "Yes, sir."

"Good," Wesley continues, "then let's go over some logistics. First, we know that troop numbers will be low because of the communications we have intercepted and the data we got from Amerang. Tefaaz has also confirmed that the rumours he has heard over the years point to this being a planet of minimal value to the Gringuns. The area is used to occasionally build ships and pieces of equipment, but as conflict has been at a minimum for a long time there are very few fully functional ships in the vicinity and none in the immediate vicinity. This is why the area has been used as a junkyard.

"Based on this information, you will be leading a force of one hundred people to the planet. This will still leave you slightly outnumbered, but a combination of a surprise attack and a dual location attack should allow you to overcome this disadvantage. There will be ten ships altogether, five per team, and each ship will hold ten people. Garry and Entai will be leading Team B in the shipyard." Garry lets out a hissed victory yelp and quietly murmurs something to Entai. I get the feeling he wants me to look in his direction... not that I'm going to give him the satisfaction, of course. "Gather any items of value and make the most of your limited cargo space. HICS will help your team to identify items. It will be up to you to target the items, and HICS will work with the pilots to pick them up.

"On the ground, Team A is expected to land close by and approach the base. There is only one way in and out of the base, and the main airlock doors are heavy. You will have to figure out how to access the base when you get there. All images for the base will be available for you to plan your entry point during your trip. I suggest you gather your troops and board your ships immediately. The timeframe for arriving at your target is approximately four days, which should give you some time to plan and some to relax. Make the most of the relaxation time you get. You need to be in good spirits before the assault begins. Brief your teams while travelling to save time and, remember, there are no communications allowed once you breach the surface of this planet. Best of luck, people, and keep safe! Dismissed!"

17

SURFACE ASSAULT 1

Leaving the base was getting to be a habit for us now. I gathered the few things I liked to take with me – toothbrush; toothpaste; a book to read – and boarded the ship without thinking about it too much. Garry attempted to wind me up about not being the only one leading a mission. I felt myself rise to it on one occasion, but then I managed to control myself. Not long afterwards, Jim Clarke gave me a gentle nudge in the ribs and told me I had handled the situation well.

It had been about two hours since we had taken off. We had all removed our EMOs and stashed them within easy reach. Then we relaxed by lounging around on the comfortable chairs which seemed to rise out from anywhere that we decided to sit. This theory needed testing. Either HICS was omnipresent and knew what we were going to do before we did, or he really could make seats appear anywhere.

While I was considering how to test this theory, Jim leaned over the back of my seat making me jump half out of my skin. "It's time,

Jon," he said in his heavy Alabama accent. "You're probably best getting the mission briefing done early. Give them some time to understand the mission and rest a while before jumping into action."

I nod and, remembering not to use the implant until we landed, hailed HICS, "HICS, please notify the crew that we have a mission briefing in fifteen minutes. Prepare the room for the briefing… and where is Forrahh?"

FORRAHH IS IN HER BUNK, JON. I WILL NOTIFY HER THAT YOU NEED TO SPEAK TO HER. THE ROOM WILL BE READY IN FIFTEEN MINUTES.

"Thanks, HICS. Oh, and what about the other ships? How far away are they from us? I will need Forrahh to set up a telepathic link to relay the briefing to the other ships."

THEY ARE CLOSE ENOUGH FOR HER TO COMMUNICATE WITH THE OTHER KETERANS, JON.

"Excellent." As if on cue, the door to the sleeping quarters slides open. Forrahh walks in rubbing her eyes and combing the knots out of her hair with her fingers.

"Hey, Jon."

"Hey. Jim suggested we get the mission briefing done early and I need you to relay the briefing to the Keterans on the other ships."

"Okay. We have about fifteen minutes, right?"

"About that, yeah. Would you mind signalling the other ships first to prepare for the briefing?"

"Sure." She thinks for a moment before responding. "Done. I need a glass of water. I will be back in a couple of minutes." As she walks away I realise how much I want to be able to do that.

ATTENTION, ALL CREW. The announcement goes out around the ship. MISSION BRIEFING WILL BE HELD IN THE MAIN LIVING AREA IN THIRTEEN MINUTES. ANYONE CURRENTLY USING THE LIVING AREA WILL NEED TO STAND FOR THE NEXT FIVE MINUTES. THANK YOU.

As one, they all stand and congregate in one corner of the room. Forrahh returns with a glass of water and actually looks a lot better for it.

"Okay, Jon, the Keterans on the other ships are ready and will repeat everything you say to the rest of the team."

"Excellent. Jim? Any suggestions?"

"Unless you were told to keep anything to yourself, just tell them everything the Joint Commanders told you. Oh, and relax. It's just a speech."

I take a deep breath and watch as all the seats in the room sink under the floor and new seats appear in a semi-circle facing me. A table and two seats appear at the front of the room facing back to the semi-circle. I guess those are mine and Jim's. I look at Forrahh.

"It is time, Jon," she says, gesturing towards the chairs.

"You're going with him Forrahh," Jim says.

She looks at him astonished. "But I thought you were helping Jon with this mission?"

"I may be training Jon, but I'm not his right hand. You both proved yourselves as a team last time. Now go do it again."

I feel a sudden burst of positivity as the tension washes away. Although I had been happy to have Jim helping me, I missed having Forrahh to confide in. Somehow, I could sense that she was not happy either.

I notice a slight smile on Forrahh's face as she walks with me to the seats at the head of the room. Jim follows us and stops behind us. As I sit down with Forrahh to my left, he leans forward and speaks quietly to us both, "Now, I'm not so sure about the Keterans, but most of the Humans you have here don't have the longest attention spans, so keep it short and keep it sweet. Y'all just tell 'em what they need to know and that'll do just fine!" He slaps me on the back and moves to the back of the room, ignoring the seats at the front.

"The other ships are ready, Jon," Forrahh confirms. "It is time."

I take a deep breath and start to speak, "Okay, people." I feel like something is stuck in my throat, and my heart's thumping so hard the whole room must be able to hear it. I look around at the familiar faces in front of me. There seem to be more than just eight other people on this ship. And of course, there's the people on the other ship too. Everything I say will be repeated to them. I gulp as my throat constricts even more. This isn't going to work. I look to the back of the room for encouragement. Jim is right there trying to signal me. He's moving his hands up and down, gesturing something… both hands turned upwards… stand up? Stand up! Got it! I stand up and take another look at everyone. I clear my mind and surprise myself as the words begin to flow on their own, "Our destination is a planet called Sidarack." HICS produces an image of the planet above the table. "There are two areas of note here. One is an old shipyard in orbit around the planet. The other is a base on the planet. As you already know, there are two parts to this mission. We are focusing on the base on the surface of the planet." The image zooms further into the planet, clearly showing the base.

"We are required to infiltrate this base through any means necessary, locate the central terminal and download the data. Intelligence shows minimal resistance from ground and air forces. We will still be outnumbered, but we will have surprise on our side and the EMOs will give us a strength and speed advantage over the Gringuns. Surprise will be our greatest ally in the beginning.

"The only entrance is through the main airlock door." The camera pans around the image and shows the door. "The door is heavy, but calculations show that with the combined force of the EMOs we will be able to get through it. Once inside, we need to investigate the building. We already know there is a central terminal holding all the data. There are satellite terminals, but these will only get us in part of the way, so our primary mission is to locate where the central terminal is.

"Following base infiltration, we will need to investigate any rooms and corridors we come across to map out the area. HICS will let us know when the terminal has been located. In the meantime, no-one travels alone, and where possible the team stays together. When the terminal has been located, HICS will activate a waypoint marker on your visor. Disengage from any enemy forces as soon as possible and make your way there. To add to everything else, we have a time limit over our heads. Enemy forces are about three hours away at maximum speed. As soon as we start the attack the alarm will be raised and they will know where we are. At the two-hour mark, all ships will take off and anyone remaining will be left behind. After we leave the planet, all remaining EMOs will self-destruct, so it is imperative that you are not late. The data transfer is estimated to take approximately three minutes. Once complete, we all leave the base together and go into orbit. Team B should finish its mission at about the same time and both sets of ships will travel back together at maximum speed.

"When we land, two people will need to be nominated from each ship to remain on-board and keep the ships prepped for take-off. I suggest you choose who they will be now so there is no confusion later. That about covers the mission requirements.

"For now, HICS is providing additional EMO training in the cargo bay. We will be arriving in just over three days. I suggest you all have a good rest the day before we arrive. Above all, though, people, watch your backs. Watch your partners' backs. Keep heroics to a minimum. And please keep safe! Dismissed!"

The image of the base disappears and I practically crumple into my seat. I lean back and take what feels like my first deep breath since I started talking.

"You did that perfectly," Forrahh says quietly. "The other Keterans have confirmed the message got through to them and they relayed the message without a hitch. It has been received very well by everyone on the other ships and spirits are high."

"Thanks. I feel drained. How do people find that so easy?"

She chuckles, "Who said they find it easy? Maybe, just like you, they found a way to distract themselves."

Before I can respond, another Human and Keteran pair approach me. "Hi, Jon. I'm not sure if you remember me. It's Marc Foster? And this is Terrera."

I can remember discussions about Marc Foster, but I can't quite remember why. I remember some major incident surrounding his name.

As though she read my mind, Forrahh cuts in, "You were with the Gringun we captured from the scout ship when we entered this dimension."

"That's right," I blurt out loud as I remember the incident. "Apparently it died when it tried to mess with your mind."

"That's me," he says grinning broadly.

"Wow, how are you feeling? I heard you were suffering from headaches for a while."

"Just for a few hours, but then something strange happened. It was like the wiring in my head was all twisted around. I felt him in my head and the painful confusion it caused. Then it just felt like something else in my head did something. Within seconds the pain went away. But the weird thing is, I felt like my thoughts were clearer suddenly, clearer than ever before. As though someone had rewired my brain to be more efficient. Not that I'm complaining, of course. Anyway, I'm sure you're busy. We just came over to let you know that for a first briefing that was pretty damn good! If you need me for anything, just shout."

"Thanks, Marc. I appreciate that."

He nods, and as they walk away I see Jim standing behind them waiting for me.

"Well," I ask, "how did it go?"

"Excellent. There's a natural in you, Jon. Now, if you both have some time, let's go over some of the finer points of the mission and I'll give you both a heads-up on managing your teams."

The next couple of days go relatively slowly with little for us to do other than relax and train. Jim passes over some good management techniques which Forrahh and I take on board immediately. After HICS announced our imminent arrival, the pace picked up a bit. People were rushing around getting into their EMOs and preparing for the attack.

Within forty-five minutes, we arrive in orbit and communicate with the other team through the 'Keteran Network'. Our metaphoric watches are set and it is agreed that the attack will begin in thirty minutes. That gives us enough time to land near the entrance and prepare to rush the base.

I feel the ship shudder slightly as it enters what was left of the atmosphere after the original Gringun attack. The ship slows gently and lands with barely a bump. I activate the EMO internal communications.

"Get ready, people. When the doors open, we rush the base. Forrahh, please notify the other ships to prepare to attack. The signal will be the doors opening. They are to rush the base airlock and apply as much pressure as possible. The attack will begin in thirty seconds. I don't want to give them too much time to find us."

"They have been informed, Jon. The crew is ready and waiting.

Twenty seconds to go… our first major mission… Fifteen seconds to go… it best go right or it will be our last… Ten seconds… best get to the front, I need to be seen to be leading the attack… Five seconds… almost there, Forrahh's at my side now, I'm low to the ground ready to burst into action when the door opens… the door silently slides open and I roll out onto the dusty, arid ground as soon as it is clear.

I roll back onto my feet and start the sprint to the base doors right in front of me. I can see the other EMOs running alongside me and Forrahh right behind me on my scanner.

Information about the airlock door ahead of me flickers onto my visor, showing me the strength and thickness of the material. The centre point is the weakest and most likely to give with enough pressure. I turn my shoulder towards the door as I approach it. Two seconds later I barely feel the jarring action of my shoulder hitting the centre of the door, but I can now see a gap between both doors. An alarm sounds and lights start flashing above the door as a sudden rush of air escapes.

Forrahh's EMO crashes into the other half of the door, forcing the gap to open enough for us both to get our fingers in. We push at the sides of the doors. The others bang into doors, forcing them to creak under the continuous pressure. The door's tensile statistics vary wildly as we apply more pressure and it starts to creak under the immense pressure. Just a little bit more. I can see the corridor within. A different alarm sounds now… They must know they are being attacked by now… Only two hours before we must be out of here… Come on, Jon, open the door already!

With a final push on the door, it opens enough for us to get in. I quickly lean out and back to check the corridor is clear beyond the doors. I take a deep breath before I charge through the gap between the doors, stopping about five metres down the corridor. The scanners show no movement ahead. I start to edge down the corridor. New green dots are appearing on my scanner showing the team as they file into the complex and take their positions behind me. My map shows that the corridor splits ahead of me.

"Which way, HICS?"

YOU NEED TO SPREAD OUT AND SEARCH THE COMPLEX, JON. I HAVE NO INTELLIGENCE ON THE LOCATION OF THE TERMINAL. I WILL KEEP MONITORING THE VISORS AND NOTIFY EVERYONE WHEN THE TERMINAL HAS BEEN LOCATED.

"Thanks, HICS," I say as I check the distance to the next turn. *"Okay, people. They know we are here, so get in there and locate that terminal. Travel in groups and make sure you don't get hit. Radio silence is no longer an issue. Use the implants for faster comms."*

They rush past me and slide acrobatically around the corners heading both right and left. Forrahh and I follow them and make the next left turn into another corridor. This one appears to end with a doorway. *"Sensors are picking up movement,"* I say to the team. *"Be careful when you open the door. Looks like some of them are hiding behind objects."*

I crouch down against the corridor wall and wait while one of the EMOs up front blows the door away leaving a gaping hole in the far wall. Well, that was one way to open the door!

Weapon fire erupts from the room as the first of the EMOs charges in. I take a moment to gather myself before charging in too.

I burst through the new hole in the wall, my visor highlighting the targets. At first glance I can see thirteen Gringuns hiding behind objects in the large oblong-shaped room. Projectiles are flying in all directions. I dodge right to avoid incoming fire and roll to a crouching position behind a pillar. I quickly poke my head around the side to take a quick look and pull back in. That's five to the right and nine to left of the pillar. They are all a dull red colour, showing that they are not in line of sight… yet.

"Jon, get ready to move," Forrahh says. *"I'll cover you!"*

"Great. I've got a few targeted already."

"Three… two… one… GO!" she shouts as a volley of fire launches from the EMOs in the room.

I roll out and all the visible targets turn a bright, vibrant red. My shoulder-mounted rail gun bursts into action, disintegrating the barricades and knocking the Gringuns across the room. What's left of them is not worth describing! I roll back behind the next column and catch my breath.

"I count four down. Confirm!"

"Confirmed!" Marc says from other side of the room. *"Cover me, it's my turn!"*

I stick my shoulder out and fire a volley in the approximate direction of the Gringuns. A further volley comes from across the room as Marc opens up on them and then ducks back down.

"I count seven. Guess that puts me in the lead!" he says laughing. *"Still teaching you young pups new tricks!"*

"Confirmed!" I call back to him. The two remaining Gringuns open fire. As soon as they stop, Forrahh stands up and dispatches the last of them, leaving a nasty, gooey mess on the back wall.

The ten of us in the room stand up and look around for any signs of the terminal. I'm hoping it's not in here, though… Based on the state of this room, the chances of anything surviving are relatively slim.

"Is the terminal here, HICS?"

NO, JON. THERE IS ANOTHER DOORWAY ON THE FAR SIDE OF THE ROOM. PLEASE CONTINUE THE SEARCH. I AM MONITORING THE PROGRESS OF THE OTHERS.

"Okay, HICS. Come on, people, time to move out."

We move into the next corridor elated at how well the suits are performing in combat. The excitement of the recent close quarters battle is still giving me a real buzz. The pace picks up and we speed walk down the corridor… Trust me, speed walking in EMOs is pretty fast going. The lights are flickering as we walk along, watching the corridor carefully.

We take the left turn at the bottom of the corridor, covering each other as we go. The heat signatures for four more Gringuns appear on the scanners moving carefully down the corridor on the right.

"Targets around the corner. Prepare yourselves!" Marc says. Forrahh and I are up front. We leap into action and charge down the corridor simultaneously. We round the corner using the walls to launch us down the corridor. Forrahh's MRG opens fire twice, knocking out the Gringuns on the left. My wrist blades flick out with a 'snick' sound as I skim past them. The two Gringuns raise their weapons, but their throats are sliced open cleanly before they can do any more than that. I land triumphantly behind them in a crouched position.

"Oh yeah, my turn next!" Marc shouts out behind me as I stand and take a bow. Even Forrahh nods appreciatively.

I continue down the corridor with Forrahh beside me, both of us checking behind us and laughing as we go. We are all having a great time as we turn into the next corridor in time to see the heat signatures ahead of us. I guess we must have been making a fair amount of noise. Their weapons are already raised and ready to fire. I hold my left arm out, forcing Forrahh to stop in her tracks. With a sudden push I shove her to the floor shouting aloud to everyone, *"GET DOWN!"* The Gringuns open fire and a volley of shots are propelled towards us. The drugs they pump into us when we get into the EMOs obviously help the reflexes. They all hit the deck like dominoes while looking towards the Gringun guns. The shots stream over our heads as we hit the floor. Looking up, I target the Gringuns ahead of us and loose a torrent of shots down the corridor. Marc's green icon starts to flash on my scanner as the Gringuns hit the back wall.

"Check those Gringuns are dead," I shout to the team. *"I want everyone else guarding both directions. If another Gringun appears, blast it! HICS? What does the flashing icon on my scanner mean?"*

"Oh God! Oh God, I didn't see them!"

I spring up to my feet, turn and see Jim kneeling beside Marc. He is checking the chest area on Marc's suit.

"Never mind, HICS. What happened, Jim?" I shout as I clamber over the others.

Jim is talking calmly to Marc, *"Can you breathe properly, Marc?"*

"Yes," he says between panicked breaths. *"Yes, I can! I didn't see them in time!"*

"It's okay, Marc. Your suit is damaged, but the life support systems appear to be working. Can you move your arms and legs?"

"Yeah, but with difficulty. My legs were the worst hit."

"And the targeting systems? Can you target me?"

A brief pause. *"No! Targeting systems are shot. The scanner is flickering wildly."*

"Okay, let's get you up on your feet." He gets his hands under Marc's arms and pulls him to his feet. *"Can you balance?"*

"Yeah, I think so. Let go and we'll find out." Jim tentatively lets go and waits while Marc steadies himself. *"I think that's about right. Give me some space. I'm going to try and walk."*

Jim steps back from him, but stays ready to step in if required. I stay right behind him, ready in case he falls backwards. Marc steps forward. I can see he is struggling to keep his balance. He takes a second unsteady step.

"It's a little different. A bit like learning to walk in the EMO again, but I think I've got it now."

"Okay, but you best stay between us," Jim says. *"Your suit's functioning, but its ain't battle ready, son!"*

"Yeah, sounds good, 'dad'!"

JON. THE TERMINAL HAS BEEN LOCATED. I HAVE ADDED A WAYPOINT MARKER AND A ROUTE TO YOUR SCANNERS. THE DATA DOWNLOAD HAS BEGUN, BUT THE SECURITY SYSTEMS ARE CONSIDERABLY MORE SOPHISTICATED.

"How long till it completes?"

THE DOWNLOAD WILL TAKE ALMOST TWENTY MINUTES.

I do the calculation in my head. That leaves us with about thirty minutes to leave the planet. "Okay, HICS. Tell the team we are heading that way now." I pat Marc reassuringly on the back and we follow the waypoint at a slower, more sober pace. *"Eyes peeled, people. Once bitten, twice shy!"*

18

SURFACE ASSAULT 2

We arrive at the waypoint within ten minutes. The rest of the team are already crouched down, watching the exits to the systems room. Terrera is crouching beside a terminal, monitoring the device attached to the side.

"How much longer?" I ask her.

"About ten minutes."

"How many exits?"

"Only these two," she says indicating the one we came in from and the other one. "We checked the rest of the room. There is nothing else."

"Any movement in the corridors?"

"Nothing anywhere. Looks like we must have got them all."

"I guess, but..." I turn and look around. I don't know. Something stinks about this. There's a nagging feeling in my head, a voice telling me something's wrong. *"Jim, Forrahh, we need to talk,"* I say privately to them. *"Something's wrong here. I know intelligence said there would be minimal resistance, but this just seems too easy!"*

"You have good instincts. It feels like a trap to me too." He turns and points to the two exits, *"Stand your guards at the two doorways. Watch for any movement. The surprise advantage has gone now, but we still have the EMOs and that should be enough. Hopefully we have done enough to also have a numbers advantage over them now."*

I allocate two people to each corridor using my HUD. They respond instantly and move to their new positions.

"Excellent, Jon," Jim says. *"I suspect the Gringuns..."*

A crackling sound comes from both corridors. The four EMOs guarding the corridors stagger backwards, their EMOs jerking like body poppers. Communications from them are garbled and barely comprehensible.

"What the... Heads up, people," I bark out at them. *"Looks like a new weapon."*

They all jump for cover as another round of static fizzes down the corridor and harmlessly hits the back wall. Sparks crisscross around the area where it hit, leaving a small burnt area before fizzing out a few seconds later. "What is that, HICS?"

IT APPEARS TO BE A MOBILE ELECTROMAGNETIC GUN. IF ONE OF THESE PROJECTILES HITS ANY PART OF THE EMO, IT WILL TEMPORARILY DISRUPT ALL ELECTRICAL SYSTEMS.

"Temporarily?"

THE CHARGE IS JUST LARGE ENOUGH TO DISRUPT, NOT DESTROY. YOU MUST AVOID ANY CONTACT WITH THE PROJECTILES.

"You heard that, people. Stay behind cover and duck out only when ready to fire." I open a private channel to Jim and Forrahh. *"Looks like we lost our EMO advantage!"*

"MOVEMENT, north corridor!"

"South corridor too."

"They're co-ordinated!" I say to Jim and Forrahh.

"They must be using telepathy to communicate," Forrahh responds.

"Great, another advantage gone."

Several shots fizz through the corridors. They're getting closer now. I can hear the fizzing sound start from closer down the corridor. Long shadows appear and disappear with the flickering lights. Another volley of shots. The team is nervous, I can feel it. They know their advantage has gone.

"CONTACT!" one of them shouts as he jumps out from cover and blasts the Gringun backwards. Unfortunately he does notice the second one. The second Gringun opens fire as his partner is propelled backwards. The shot knocks the hapless Human to the floor. His Keteran partner standing next to him leans over to pull him back. The next shot hits her arm, the electrical sparks shooting all over her. I can see the Gringun right through the barricade. His shape is lit up bright red on my scanner. I lock the target from behind the column and feel the MRG start to track him. With a burst of courage from who knows where, I stick just my shoulder out, launch a couple shots and get back behind cover. The briefly pulsing red shape on my HUD launches backwards and slams against the back wall. We still have one advantage!

More Gringuns pile into the room, raging screams emanating from their mouths, guns pointing forward, firing aimlessly in all directions.

"It's now or never, people! GET IN THERE AND TEAR THEM TO PIECES!" I shout out loudly to them all over the external speakers. It is the first time the Gringuns have heard us say anything out loud. It has the desired effect on two counts. First, their charge falters thanks to the bellowing voice from my EMO. Second, it buys enough time for our team to gather themselves and charge the stunned Gringuns.

What follows is total carnage. On the one side, fizzing static shoots around the room. EMOs are lying on the floor, shaking uncontrollably, sparks skimming over them. On the other, there are dismembered Gringuns lying everywhere on the floor. You read about these things, but it never truly prepares you for the truth about war. The battle continues for a few minutes, with the Gringuns trying to hold their position against an already angered allied contingent. I now know why Forrahh says that Humans are dangerous. Under normal circumstances we fight like our lives depend on it... when cornered, we fight because there's nothing else left! The Gringuns who survived the initial retaliation regret their survival soon after. While the Keterans co-ordinate the attacks using the implants, the Humans employ a truly vicious streak which completely throws the Gringuns off guard, causing desperate confusion amongst their ranks. The Human-occupied EMOs are propelling off the walls and streaking across the rooms at ridiculous speeds. We have even stopped using internal communications. Our ecstatic screams can be heard by all and if they worry the Keterans watching from behind cover, we terrify the Gringuns who have nowhere to run. Worse still, my Human counterparts have stopped using our MRGs... we are toying with them now! We streak through the air slicing Gringuns en route to the other side of the room before returning. It would make for an elegant dance if not for the gruesome aftermath we leave behind.

Not long after it starts, there are only EMOs left standing. Nothing else even twitchs a muscle. Part of me is elated by the adrenaline rush and want to rejoice in our victory. It would have been a truly glorious moment were it not for what I see next.

Lying in the middle of a pile of Gringun bodies is an EMO. Sparks are still dancing around the chest cavity. Without looking at the greyed-out icon on my HUD I know who it is. It looks like one of the Gringun rounds had hit Marc's already badly damaged EMO in the chest... exactly where it was damaged already. I stand there looking down at the broken EMO, knowing that Marc's body is in there. I try to repress the memories of my parents, but it doesn't work and, try as I might, I can't turn away either. Relief washes over me when Jim and Forrahh arrive at my side.

"I saw him go down," Jim says thoughtfully. "He joined the battle knowing that his EMO wasn't battle ready. One shot hit him square in the chest. The shock was too much for him. Looks like it shorted out his suit completely."

This is all too much for me, to be honest. I hadn't considered losing someone on this campaign. I mean, I know we are going to lose friends at some point, but not so soon and not under my command.

"You need to understand, Jon, this is no game. There are expected to be injuries and deaths. Do not be fooled. This is war and we are fighting for more than just our lives... We are fighting for our right to exist as Humans, Keterans and Najess. Now, there are people out there, waiting for you to tell them what to do. They will follow your commands if you show you are willing to make the decisions."

"But I don't know what to do."

"Yes you do. Take charge, Jon, and remember it's all about the way you say it."

I nod, *"Okay."* I switch back to group communications. "HICS, are there any areas left for the Gringuns to be hiding?"

IT IS UNLIKELY, JON, BUT I WOULD USE CAUTION REGARDLESS.

"Thank you, HICS. Okay, folks, well done, but we're not out of the woods yet. I want the injured and damaged to go back to the ships. Watch your backs the whole way and keep the ships ready. We are heading home as soon as the download is complete."

A large group starts to walk out of the room towards the ships. The rest hold their position and guard the exits from the room.

"Download update, please."

"Two more minutes to completion," Terrera calls out, clearly trying to hide her inner feelings.

"HICS, what about Marc?"

HE DIED ALMOST INSTANTLY WHEN THE SUIT OVERLOADED.

"Is it safe to take him with us?"

"We can't take him, Jon," Forrahh says from behind me.

FORRAHH IS CORRECT JON. THE EMO IS ALREADY SET TO SELF-DESTRUCT.

Of course, I forgot about that. I remember now that the EMOs were set to automatically self-destruct when the owner died. In a few minutes, there will be nothing left of Marc. I guess it is not too dissimilar to many cultures where they burn the dead.

Resigned to leaving Marc where he is, I pull myself together and focus on what needs to be done. "Pick up one of the guns the Gringuns were using. I want it taken back for analysis. We need to know what they are and how to defend against them."

A Keteran reaches down and picks up one of the weapons which is not covered in Gringun goo.

"Download complete, Jon."

"Excellent. Let's get going. Plot the fastest way out of here, please, HICS." The path appears on the HUD, and the five of us start walking back, keeping our eyes peeled for any more Gringuns.

We move at a good pace to the exit. After a few turns we feel the corridor shake… Goodbye, Marc. Moments later, the lights flicker again. I look up and see cracks appear in the ceiling. I instantly regress back in time to the catacombs in Italy. I remember the lights flickering in the same way and the dust falling from the ceiling… I can see my parents, my fear reflected on their faces. Realisation dawns on me. The others are shouting for me to move.

We break into a run before stopping suddenly as the ceiling caves in ahead of us. Just before it collapses fully, I see the heat signatures of two Gringuns in the background. Luckily the ceiling collapses on them.

"Another way out, HICS, quick!" The path appears on the HUD.

We break into a run, following the path which should hopefully lead us to safety.

BE ON YOUR GUARD, JON. PART OF THIS ROUTE IS UNCHARTED. THERE MAY BE GRINGUNS AROUND.

"Team A, this is Jon. Do you read?"

"Yes, Jon, where are you? It is almost time to lift off."

"Our exit route got blocked off. We are on our way now, but it will take another twelve minutes to arrive."

"Okay, it's cutting it close but we'll wait."

"No, wait only while it is still safe. If you need to leave, do so and get the cloak activated."

There is a short silence before the sombre response, "Okay, Jon."

We run through a maze of corridors looking for an exit we never noticed on the intelligence images. HICS is positive it's there; the terminal had it listed as an exit. We take the next turn, desperate to get out of here. At no point do we see any Gringuns in our path, but we see a few through the walls, so we know there are some still alive. All of us have the targeting systems on full alert and the MRGs are primed and ready to fire on a moment's notice.

We round the next bend and come face to face with a large door big enough for an ogre to fit through. There are no heat signatures showing on the other side, but the energy signatures are off the chart. Staying alert for anything, I press the button on the side panel. Nothing happens. I put my weight against the door and gradually apply pressure until it gives way. As it opens, we are presented with a huge hangar with numerous ships of all shapes and sizes. The area is spotlessly clean with nothing moving anywhere. The deathly silence is unnerving, and as I take my first steps inside the sound of each step echoes back and forth throughout the cavernous room. Lines upon lines of ships are on display.

"Are all of these functional, HICS?"

"Jon, do you read me?"

"Yes, what's the matter?"

"There's movement, Jon. Gringun ships are entering the area. We are engaging the cloaks now, but HICS will be adding a beacon for each ship to your HUD. Get moving, though. We need to leave real soon."

"Understood. Let me know what happens, but if you have to leave us, then do so."

"Yes, Jon."

"HICS?"

THIS HANGAR AND THESE SHIPS DO NOT APPEAR ON ANY INTELLIGENCE INFORMATION WE HAVE, JON, NOT EVEN ON THE DATA JUST RETRIEVED. THE ENERGY READINGS IN THIS ROOM, HOWEVER, ARE INDICATIVE OF ACTIVE SHIPS. THE LARGEST READING IS COMING FROM THE LARGE SHIP AT THE BACK.

I zoom in on the ship while walking forwards, magnifying it enough to see some extra details. "What type of ship is that, HICS?" Readings are flitting all over the HUD as I focus on different areas of the ship.

BASED ON THE DESIGN AND SIZE, I WOULD SUGGEST THIS IS AN ASSAULT FRIGATE, ALTHOUGH THE DESIGNS ARE VERY DIFFERENT FROM THE ONES WE VIEWED DURING THE MISSION BRIEFING.

"A prototype maybe?" Forrahh says coming up alongside me.

IT WOULD APPEAR THAT WAY.

"I wonder if we could fly it out of here," I think out loud. "It would be more likely than us getting back to the ships. I'm guessing the large doors at the back are the way it came in too. They look about the right size."

"Fly it out, huh? It could work," Jim says from behind me, "and it'd be one heck of a trophy for the cabinet! What d'ya think, HICS?"

IF THE SHIP SYSTEMS FOLLOW A SIMILAR FUNCTIONAL DESIGN AND STRUCTURE AS THE

SCOUT, THEN IT MAY BE POSSIBLE TO FLY THE SHIP. YOU DO NOT, HOWEVER, HAVE A PILOT AMONGST YOU, WHICH WOULD REDUCE THE POSSIBILITY OF SUCCESS DRAMATICALLY.

"True," I say arriving at the ship. "Team A. Do you read?"

"Yes, Jon. What do you need?"

"I need a pilot… the best available, please."

"That would be Saliin. Where do you want her to meet you?"

"HICS, add a waypoint for Saliin on the other side of the hangar doors. Jim, find a way to open the doors. Forrahh, come with me. We need to find a way to get into the ship."

SALIIN HAS THE WAYPOINT, JON. SHE WILL BE OUTSIDE IN TWO MINUTES.

"Thank you, HICS."

Forrahh and I approach the large assault frigate standing apart from the other ships and dwarfing everything in the hangar. It is raised up on several strong looking legs which appear to come from holes in the bottom of the ship. The sleek curved design somehow makes it look like it just needs some 'go faster' stripes to complete the look. There were turrets on the side and bottom of the ship which remind me of the ones we saw on the images before leaving the CC a few days back. I guess there are some on the top too, but it is far too high to confirm that.

Finding a way to enter the ship is pretty easy too… The door is open and the gangway lowers allowing us to walk on-board with minimal fuss. I am still checking my scanners constantly for any Gringuns hiding somewhere, but nothing appears. It's strange how the ships are left unguarded like this. Then again, based on the intelligence, this hangar and this ship don't exist.

I walk on-board first, making my way through the large open doorway. The room is large and open-plan, allowing us to see through to the far end. Bits and pieces of material and equipment are lying on the floor. Four exits are visible on all corners of the room. They appear to run around the ship following the contours

321

of the hull. I turn towards the front of the ship and walk down the corridor. Minor information points are lined up along the corridors. Forrahh stops to examine one, while making sure not to touch anything just yet. "I wonder if these are connected to the primary terminal in the cockpit."

THEY WILL BE CONNECTED, BUT THESE TERMINALS ARE ONLY FOR INFORMATION PURPOSES. FOR VESSELS OF THIS SIZE, THE TERMINALS ARE NECESSARY TO KEEP THE CREW INFORMED.

"This way, Forrahh," I call back to her. "I've found some stairs leading up."

Seconds later, she is climbing the stairs right behind me. As my head clears the top of the metallic steps, I see another corridor with additional rooms coming off at regular intervals. I continue walking and realise that these must be conference rooms. There are two large rooms with the doors open and a large metallic table fixed in the middle, a series of chairs surrounding it. Another larger door is visible at the end of the corridor.

As we approach the door, it slides silently open, revealing the spacious cockpit within. The four seats are turned towards the main entry door we are standing in.

"I'm in position, Jon," Saliin says.

"Excellent. Wait there. Jim, how's it going with those doors?"

"I've found the main control panel. Opening the door now."

"Great. When you get in, start searching the interior for life signs. I don't want to find any stowaways on the ship. Saliin, head to the largest ship in the hangar. Enter through the side doorway and move along the corridor towards the front. HICS will add the route to the cockpit to your HUD."

I look around the cockpit. "I don't get it. If this is the cockpit, where's the front screen?" There's just metallic walls all around us. Maybe the terminals provide the view outside and the walls are for extra protection against hull breaches. It is an assault frigate, after all. The readout on my HUD confirms the walls are made from an extremely dense metallic material. Anyway, that's something to worry about later. "HICS, is the terminal here?"

THE PRIMARY PORTAL IS THE LARGE PANEL AND SCREEN LOCATED ON YOUR RIGHT. THE SCREEN WILL BE OFF AS THE SHIP IS IN A SHUT DOWN STATE AT THE MOMENT.

I locate what looks like the screen HICS described and lean over the chair in front of the instrument panel.

THERE IS AN EMPTY AREA BELOW THE SCREEN. LAY YOUR RIGHT HAND ON THIS AREA AND WAIT. I WILL ATTEMPT TO ACTIVATE THE SCREEN.

I carefully place my right hand on the area as instructed and wait.

YOU WILL FEEL A TINGLING SENSATION IN YOUR WRIST AND THROUGH TO YOUR FINGERS.

"Yep, got that!" The screens flickers, as do the lights in the cockpit. The screen burst into life and strange characters start streaming across it.

PLEASE KEEP YOUR HAND IN POSITION, JON.

I do as I'm told and a few seconds later the characters on the screen pause in position, before the screen goes blank again.

"Can I remove my hand now, HICS?"

NOT YET, JON, I AM ALMOST DONE.

The screen flickers back to life again and this time the characters are all in English allowing me to read them... Of course, it still makes no sense to me, but the characters being legible provide me with some comfort at least. One by one the lights on all of the consoles come to life and a soft vibrating humming sound, like the purr of a sports car engine idling on a driveway, emanates from the ship.

ALL SHIP FUNCTIONS HAVE BEEN RESTORED, JON. YOU CAN REMOVE YOUR HAND FROM THE CONSOLE IF YOU LIKE.

"Huh?" I realise my attention was thoroughly caught by the

consoles all coming to life. I remove my hand and walk to the front console where, I presume, the pilot would sit.

Saliin enters the cockpit and gasps at the sight. "Wow," she exclaims. "Now, this is a ship! Are the life support systems active, HICS?"

ALL SHIP SYSTEMS ARE ACTIVE AND FUNCTIONING WITHIN NORMAL PARAMETERS.

"Now, that is what I wanted to hear." She deactivates her EMO, climbs out and takes her place in what I figured was the pilot's seat. She is perceptibly excited about the prospect of flying this ship.

"How are you supposed to see out?" I ask.

VIEW SCREEN ACTIVATING NOW, JON.

As if by magic, the metallic front of the ship fades out, allowing us to see the hangar and the open hangar doors to the outside.

"Now, that's impressive!" I say.

Ignoring me, Saliin continues talking to HICS about the ship.

"Jon, come in, Jon?"

INTER SHIP COMMUNICATIONS HAVE BEEN ACTIVATED TEMPORARILY.

"Thank you, HICS. Yes, I'm here."

"We are picking up a massive energy signature from your area. Is everything okay?"

"You wouldn't believe what we have found. How are we doing for time?"

"None left. We have to leave now. The Gringun ships are almost on us."

"Take off now and don't wait for us. We will meet you back at the base if we can."

"Understood, Jon. Good luck!"

"Saliin, get us out of here. You can play with your new toy later."

She doesn't ignore me this time. "Yes, Jon. HICS, activate ship engines and prepare the thrusters."

SHIP ENGINES ARE ACTIVE, SALIIN. LET ME KNOW WHEN YOU ARE READY TO LEAVE.

"Engage the thrusters, HICS, and guide us out, please."

The ship gently rises and I hear what I can only guess are the legs the ship was sitting on lift back into the base of the ship.

THE SHIP'S DATABASE HOLDS SOME INFORMATION ABOUT THIS HANGAR, JON. IT APPEARS THIS IS A PROTOTYPE SHIP. IT IS A TOP SECRET PROJECT WHICH HAS BEEN COMPLETED RECENTLY TO DEAL WITH OUR INTRUSION INTO THE GRINGUN DIMENSION. ONLY THE PEOPLE BASED HERE KNOW ANYTHING ABOUT THIS BASE AND THE SHIPS BEING DEVELOPED HERE. ALL OF THE SHIPS IN THE HANGAR ARE PROTOTYPES AND DUE TO BE THE BASIS FOR ALL FUTURE SHIPS BUILT BY THE GRINGUNS.

I watch as the ship narrowly but expertly clears the hangar doors. "Are you saying that the only people who know how to build these ships are based on this planet?"

YES, JON.

"And your strategic recommendation is?"

THIS BASE MUST BE DESTROYED ALONG WITH ALL GRINGUNS STILL ALIVE.

"I knew you were going to say that." I can see Forrahh's heart rate increase on my HUD, but I know what needs to be done. "See to it, HICS. How long till the ship clears the hangar doors?"

NINETEEN SECONDS, JON.

"Are the ship's weapons functioning?"

THEY ARE FULLY OPERATIONAL.

"No time like the present, then. Destroy the base once we are clear. Then check for life signs and destroy anything living."

YES, JON.

"Is there a cloaking device on this ship?"

THERE IS, JON. IN FACT IT IS AN UPGRADED

VERSION OF THE ONE ON OUR OWN TRANSPORTS. IF WE LEAVE IN THE NEXT FEW MINUTES, WE WILL BE ABLE TO ACTIVATE THE CLOAK AND MEET WITH THE OTHER TRANSPORTS EN ROUTE. WE WILL BE ABLE TO DO THIS WHILE MAINTAINING AN EFFECTIVE CLOAK DURING THE JOURNEY.

"Excellent."

WE ARE CLEAR OF THE BASE, JON. ATTACK COMMENCING.

"The ship is clear, Jon," Jim says as he enters the cockpit. "There's no Gringuns anywhere. What's happening?"

"HICS says that these ships are all prototypes. We need to destroy the base along with the other ships and any Gringuns left behind."

He shrugs his shoulders. "Makes sense to me." I get the feeling the Keterans in the room are having a hard time dealing with how relaxed we are about this.

With the ship clear of the base and weapons primed, HICS targets the base. Targeting reticles appear on the screen and lock onto multiple key areas of the base. A small spinning circle revolves around the targeted area before changing to a solid red disk when the weapons fire. The base bursts into flames, blasting debris in all directions. Flames engulf the base before dying out quickly in the minimal atmosphere. The base is reduced to nothing more than rubble. Any ships inside are now scrap for the junkyard above.

THE CLOAK HAS BEEN ACTIVATED, JON. IT IS IMPERATIVE WE LEAVE HERE IMMEDIATELY. A GRINGUN STRIKE FORCE HAS APPEARED ON THE SCANNERS. IT WILL BE HERE IN A FEW MINUTES.

"Okay, HICS. Leave now and head back following the same course as the others. Let's see if we can't arrive before them."

As we turn to leave, HICS changes the view to the rear. In the distance we can see a number of bright objects which appear to be getting larger in the distance… The ships are almost here. The assault frigate accelerates, leaving the devastated Gringun planet behind. I take a deep breath as I contemplate the events which have taken place over the last few hours. That's when it dawns on me… we just suffered the loss of our first comrade.

19

THE RETURN HOME

Well, this was another uneventful journey back. Not that I wanted something to happen, of course. After the recent events, it's nice to have a little peace and quiet. It gave me time to think about what happened on Sidarack, especially about Marc dying. Of course, we also have this new ship which has to be explored. That's helped to take my mind off things for a while. The skeleton crew we had was not really enough to manage such a large ship, so we were kept busy the whole trip back. It did limit how much time we really had to explore what the ship was really capable of, though. HICS managed the ship where possible, but every now and then we were instructed to go to a different area and examine a room or move some equipment. This kept us busy for most of the time. I hated having time to myself. It gave me too many opportunities to think and that just depressed me. I figured it was best to just keep busy, so where possible I was helping HICS to manage the ship. Forrahh must have figured something was up, and she stayed with me most of the time. That was something I was glad for. I got the feeling that she really wanted me to confide in her, though, but I didn't feel ready for that to be honest.

HICS spent some time running tests on the new cloaking device. Forrahh and I helped with preparing for the tests while we were travelling. The idea, apparently, was to see how fast we could go before the effects of the cloak diminished. I'm sure HICS could have done this without us, but it kept me busy so I didn't ask questions.

It took us about the same amount of time to get home as the others. Strange to call this home. I guess I've started to see the CC as my home now. Anyway, the assault frigate has better engines and a better cloaking device, allowing us to arrive slightly ahead of the others. We still had to slow down to keep the cloak at its most effective. And of course there were the tests HICS wanted us to run. These slowed us down too.

That was about the most excitement we had. After we arrived we could not communicate with anyone below the surface and they could not communicate with us. On top of that, we turn up in an enemy ship, flying the enemy banner and, as if that was not enough, the ship drops us off right by the hatch and heads straight to the volcano where the other ships are based… It's as if the Gringuns know everything now. In their position, I'd have figured that we had been captured, tortured and given up everything we knew. Luckily, HICS had that covered and once the codes had been entered and the ship was below the surface, it was communicated that everything was fine.

As the lift doors opened, everyone welcomed us back home. The best sight I had was Wei standing at the front of the crowd. Even with the EMO on he seemed to know which one I was. He smiled and led me to the living quarters.

After exiting the EMOs and helping ourselves to a well-deserved drink of water, we collapsed on the bunks.

"Do not get too relaxed, Jon," Wei remarks. "I realise it has been tiring, but you need to be debriefed first."

I hate it, but I know he's right. "I know, Wei. Don't worry, I'll be there." Forrahh arrives and sits on the bunk opposite us.

"Good. So, tell me what happened."

"Really, Wei? We have to debrief anyway."

"That is not the same. It is too formal. I want to know where this ship turned up from."

"Long story, Wei."

"Well, we do not have much time, so give me the condensed version. You know you are desperate to tell me everything anyway."

He was right actually. Of all the people here, he was the one I wanted to speak to, so I started to spill the beans and tell him what had happened. I purposely left out the bit about Marc... I only wanted to say that bit once.

The CC Meeting Room was set up in the usual way. As we walked in, Tefaaz smiled broadly, showing off his blunted front teeth. The commanders looked up, smiled and went back to their discussions.

I led the way to the chairs and sat down, Forrahh and Wei taking their places on either side of me. Garry and his team had not returned to the planet yet, which was a good thing. I didn't need him revelling in my failure. Jim was already sitting at the table in Garry's place. I could tell he had already been talking to the commanders before we arrived. I wasn't sure if that was a good thing or not, but I guess I was about to find out.

Wesley, sitting directly opposite me, flicked through his tablet, his expression never changing as his eyes flitted from side to side. Without looking up, he addressed us all, "Welcome back, team. It is good to see you all again. I realise you will all be tired, so I hope to keep this as short as possible.

"Before we begin, though, I need to speak privately with Jon." I feel everyone's eyes on me as they realise what this must be about. I can't bring myself to look at them. All I can imagine is the shame of having lost someone during one of my missions. I can hear them as they stand and walk out, but I still can't muster the courage to look them in the eyes. Even the other commanders leave, with Jim close behind. What did Jim say about the mission?

"Jon, look at me, please. I have cleared the room for your benefit. There are things you need to understand. Casualties are a part of war. You are still terribly young and yet have managed to do incredible things. I honestly see great things for you." Great things, huh? Well, I sense a 'but' coming. "You just have to understand that you were always going to lose someone eventually and believe me, Jon, this is just the beginning. There are going to be many more coming and some you lose may be closer to you than Marc was.

"You did an excellent job on this mission and Jim has told me how you managed to control yourself under extremely difficult circumstances. He has huge respect for you, Jon, as do I. Losing Marc was very unfortunate for us. He was a good man and will be honoured for his part in this, but he is gone and you need to come to terms with the fact that this was not your fault." I can feel a lump rising in my throat. Images of my parents lying under rubble. Guilt at not trying to dig them out, leaving them there to rot. They're probably still there now. I shake my head. I must get control of my thoughts. I'm not listening to what is being said anymore. Wesley's voice drifts back in again. "Will you be able to manage another mission, Jon? It's yours if you want it?"

Stunned that he still wants me to do this, I stutter my response, "M-M-Me? You want me to do this?"

"Of course, Jon. You have gone through and survived a tremendous ordeal and still come out on top. We need good people. People like you, Jon. You already know that the implants do not work as well on anyone over eighteen. This is all about the EMOs and the implants, Jon. After the age of eighteen, the EMOs are just not as responsive. This can be compensated for by experience, of course, but it is not the same. The problem is, we still do not know why the implants stop working after this age. You see, communication is the key to any successful mission. Without these implants, our enemies would have a huge advantage over us. And one day, Jon, your ability to communicate with HICS will diminish too."

This had never occurred to me and the shock the sudden realisation causes is evident.

"You have a few years yet, Jon. Hopefully, we will be able to fix it by then. Anyway, we have a lot to do. Please call everyone in HICS."

Seconds later they all file into the room, returning to their seats again.

"Right, HICS," Wesley says, "what have you learnt?"

THE ASSAULT FRIGATE RECOVERED BY TEAM A HAS PROVED TO BE AN ENGINEERING MASTERPIECE. I AM CURRENTLY RECREATING THE DESIGNS FOR ALL OF THE SHIPS, TO INCORPORATE THE NEW DESIGN. SEVERAL OF THE SHIP'S FUNCTIONS ARE CAUSING ME DIFFICULTIES, BUT WITH WEI'S HELP WE SHOULD BE ABLE TO OVERCOME THESE. ONE OF THESE FUNCTIONS IS THE NEW CLOAKING DEVICE, WHICH IS BEING WORKED ON AS A MATTER OF PRIORITY. THE NEW CLOAK SHOULD BE READY IN ANOTHER TWO DAYS.

THE ASSAULT FRIGATE IS CAUSING SIGNIFICANTLY MORE PROBLEMS, THOUGH. AT PRESENT WE DO NOT HAVE ENOUGH RAW MATERIALS AVAILABLE TO BUILD ANY MORE SHIPS.

"I thought you had some raw materials left over," Andy says.

ALL EXISTING RAW MATERIALS WERE USED TO BUILD THE RMVs.

"Would it not have been better to use the materials for additional interceptors or equipment like the cloaking devices? We could have kept collecting resources in the meantime."

COLLECTING RESOURCES SPORADICALLY FROM PLANET SURFACES IS VERY INEFFICIENT. ALTHOUGH

USING THE MATERIALS TO BUILD THE RMVs SLOWS US DOWN NOW, IT WILL INCREASE OUR PRODUCTIVITY ONCE THE FIRST LOAD RETURNS. THIS IS ONLY A SHORT-TERM SETBACK, ANDY.

"How long will it take to complete the build work on them?" I ask.

THEY ARE ALREADY COMPLETE JON. THERE WERE NOT ENOUGH RESOURCES TO BUILD THE RMVs, SO I SALVAGED SOME OLD PARTS FROM OTHER SHIPS AND CONVERTED TWO OF THE NAJESS SHIPS INTO RMVs. THEY ARE READY TO DEPART.

"So, why haven't they been sent out yet?"

WE HAD TO WAIT FOR THE MISSION TO COMPLETE. THE CLOAKING DEVICES ON THE RMVs CAN ONLY FUNCTION WHEN RESOURCE HARVESTING IS NOT TAKING PLACE. THIS MEANS THEY NEED TO AVOID BEING SEEN BY GRINGUNS AT ALL COSTS. THE RMVs HAVE MINIMAL ARMAMENTS AND SHIELDING AND WOULD THEREFORE BE EASY TARGETS FOR THE GRINGUNS. A SMALL FORCE OF INTERCEPTORS HAS BEEN PREPARED AND WILL BE ON ESCORT DUTIES.

"This highlights one of the key successes of the mission," Nique says. "As you know, the Gringuns were searching all planets in this direction and were closing in on us. We know it is highly unlikely that they would find us below the surface; however, we have performed numerous training exercises on the planet surface recently and it is possible that we left some evidence of these somewhere.

"Your mission was to infiltrate the base on Sidarack and gather the data stored on the computers. This was successful. The secondary objective was to lure the Gringuns into thinking we were somewhere closer to the planet. This was successful too. Our long range scanners have shown that, although they have widened their search, they have left this area of the dimension for the time being and are now searching other areas. This includes the location of the hidden Aneesh planet."

"But they'll find the planet before us, then."

"Apparently not. At some point in the last millennium they would have sent ships in that direction. Something must be blocking them from detecting it. The chances are it will also prevent us from detecting it, so we need to be alert to anything unusual. The good news is we are safe for the short term. It does, however, mean that we must make preparations to leave this planet soon. They will return to search this area at some point."

"We are bound to run into Gringuns while we travel," Forrahh says.

"That is why we will be gathering our things and a leaving in approximately one month."

That was the first time I had heard one of the commanders being so vague about a timescale. "Why not a specific departure date, sir?" I interrupt him, curious about the reason.

"It all depends on what the Gringuns discover and what they do. If they move away from the area where we believe the planet to be, we will go there. If they locate the planet, we will need to find an alternative planet as our destination or stay here. For now, we watch and learn from them. When we leave here, we will travel through the areas they have already been to and left. This should allow us to avoid contact almost entirely. We will be completely cloaked during the journey. Communication will be through telepathy only, so the ships will have to travel in close formation during the whole trip."

"Will the entire fleet be going there?" Andy asks.

"No. A part of the fleet will be sent back to Thapa, our home dimension. We are going to need all the reinforcements we can get. The team will help to build additional transports which will be used to bring everyone else to this dimension. At the same time, the rest of us will leave for our new home. Everyone else will meet us there when they return to this dimension."

"But you're saying that there may be issues locating the planet. Once they are gone, they will not know how to find us."

"The analysis team has come up with a suitable solution for this. Do you remember when we first came to this dimension? We came across a cloaked scout. Because it was so still, we barely noticed it was there. It was only when the scout attempted to communicate that we located it. We are going to use a similar strategy. A few interceptors will be placed at specific locations. Before the team leaves here, the first location will be fed into their navigation system as a waypoint. When they re-enter this dimension, they will travel there with their cloak fully active and come to a complete stop. The interceptor will be piloted by a Keteran and she will communicate telepathically with the Keterans aboard the transport ship. The new waypoints will be provided, along with any additional information, and will be provided verbally to HICS at that point. If anyone can see any issues with this procedure, this would be a good time to speak."

I had to admit it sounded pretty spot on to me, and as I looked around the room everyone else appeared to be in agreement.

"Good. Then we will continue as planned."

Forrahh clears her throat before continuing, "Going back to the RMVs, when will they be sent out and where are they going exactly?"

Enira responds to her question, "It is a planet called Scoveris, located near here. Intelligence shows that it has many of the raw materials we are going to need, although not in great abundance. There is another planet which is much closer to the Aneesh home world. Although intelligence shows that this planet has nothing of importance to it and hardly any raw materials, the Aneesh texts translated from within the map room show that the planet has a great deal of resources below the surface. Tefaaz cannot be sure, but he believes it is possible that the Aneesh elders may have hidden the resources below this planet too. Why they would have done such a thing is unknown, but we have decided it is worth the risk to find out if there is something there."

"So, how much can these RMVs bring back?"

"In what terms, Forrahh?"

"I mean, what will we be able to make from the resources gained when the RMVs return? I want to know when we can stop justifying using valuable resources on non-military equipment at a time of war."

This was the first time I had actually seen Forrahh get this agitated about something. The strange things was, for once I didn't feel the way she did about this. I honestly felt we needed to focus on gathering resources for now. "I'm not so sure, Forrahh," I comment. "Having two more assault frigates is not going to make a massive difference if we are attacked. I think using the resources to help gather additional resources faster is the right decision." Judging by the look on her face, this was possibly the wrong time to not take her side in the debate!

Luckily, Nique continues to answer her, "Two RMVs will be sent to Scoveris, and each is capable of carrying enough resources to build two complete assault frigates. Jon is correct, however. We know we need more attack craft, but we also need the ability to research and design new weapons and craft. The future is just as important as the present. The resources from the second harvester will be used to build a few more interceptors to cover the ones used for escort duties. The rest of the resources will be used on building science vessels. Does this sound acceptable?"

I had to admit, it sounded like they had covered all bases and were diverting resources in all directions. Eventually Forrahh nodded her agreement. "It sounds fair. I am just concerned that we are ignoring our military needs."

"We will not ignore them. As Jon said, if we are involved in a battle en route, two additional assault frigates will not help."

"Agreed. So, how long will they be gone for?"

"They are due to leave the base today and, if HICS' estimates are accurate, they will return in three days. The journey should only take a day each way. The resource harvesting itself will take a further day to complete. These journeys to Scoveris and back will continue until we leave."

"And the construction on the new assault frigates?"

"HICS has located an area of the volcano where the ships are currently docked. This is where construction can take place. It is currently being outfitted with machines which will be controlled by HICS. These will build the ships faster than any of us can. We expect the first assault frigate to be ready within two weeks. The second ship will be on a staggered construction plan running about one week later. We will aim to leave here when both ships are ready."

"Are we happy with this information now?" Wesley asks, sounding slightly bored by the subject.

"I believe so," I respond, hoping to cut everyone else off. I'm starting to know when Wesley is getting irritated with a subject… A handy skill to have.

"Excellent, then I suggest you get some rest. You will have plenty of training exercises over the next few weeks. Based on the coming relocation mission, HICS has designed some new training for you. Dismissed."

As I stand up, the rest follow my example and we file out of the room in total silence.

The next couple of weeks were a little boring. Garry and his team returned the next day without any losses and went straight into debrief just as we did. Forrahh was still angry with me and had not really spoken to me properly since the meeting. That's when I had my first confrontation with Garry since we returned. I was standing with Forrahh, Wei and Jim in the communal living quarters when Garry came out of the meeting room. My back was turned to him so I didn't see him coming. I just felt him as he 'accidentally' bumped into me while walking past. He had Enira and another Human-Keteran pair flanking him.

"Oh, sorry, Jon. I didn't see you there," he said smiling smugly. Jim nudged his way in front of Forrahh to make sure nothing happened. Personally, I decided this was the best time to ignore Garry.

"I heard about your mission. It's a real shame about Marc." I could hear the smugness in his voice. He didn't really care and had no idea what was going on. "You'll have to tell me what happened one day. Not now of course, I'm far too busy. The commanders have given me the mission to return to Thapa Dimension for reinforcements. I knew they would recognise my abilities eventually. I'm sure it's got nothing to do with me not losing someone on my watch, of course... Must be a coincidence!" He's too busy gloating to see my hands clench into fists, but as the tension continues to build I notice Jim slowly shaking his head, silently telling me not to rise to the taunts. "Not to worry, though," he continues regardless, "you just have to work a little harder while you relocate to the new base. The commanders will be able to look over you and make sure you don't trip up again, but I'm sure they will give you another small mission at some point." He turns and continues walking without acknowledging anyone else, his entourage chuckling at his jibe.

"You did well, Jon," Jim says. "Ignoring him was the right things to do. I know what the commanders have in mind going forward and they have a lot of respect for what you did out there. Keep ignoring him. Now, come on, I think it's time for more training."

The additional training HICS had in store for us was about as boring as you could imagine. About the only good thing was that we had to wear the EMOs the whole time. It was all about how to lift heavy objects and utilising the strength of the EMO. There were some small cranes and digging equipment in the area and we had to learn how to lift these, which was kind of fun, but it just wasn't combat training.

What was surprisingly good was that I found out Jim was a martial arts expert. Of course, the moment I found out, I started asking all sorts of questions. It was so obvious that I was interested and missed the training I received back home on Earth. Anyway, as he was mentoring me anyway, he decided to give me additional combat training too. After a full day training in the EMOs on the construction zones for both extreme and low gravity situations, Jim and I would take time out to spar with each other and he would teach me how to handle myself in close quarters combat situations. He also showed me some amazing moves he had learnt in the EMO. It made sense really. The likelihood would be that most – if not all – of our hand-to-hand combat would be in the EMOs, but I always seemed to think of it as unarmed, close quarters combat. That's when Jim explained to me that the EMOs were like an extension of us being unarmed. I took this on board and saw an immediate improvement to the skills and the speed at which I could perform them. Amazing how you don't see things that are right in front of you. This additional training also helped me to keep my mind off the things which were bothering me, things like why Forrahh was still so angry with me and how I missed Earth so much… and why I had to lose my parents. That one never left me.

Time continued to pass as normal, some days quicker than others. Overall, though, time was moving faster than I liked. The inevitable departure date was closing in on us and the preparations never seemed to end. I had no idea what to expect of the new planet… or even if we would make it there. The plan HICS had put into place seemed sound, but who knew what events were lurking around each of time's corners. Progress on the two assault frigates was going well and we were expected to depart on schedule. That meant we had only a few more days on the planet and that meant that HICS would be contacting us soon.

And that's how we found ourselves back in the CC Meeting Room again. The usual setup and usual suspects were all in their places. This included Garry, as expected, and Tefaaz as the advisor.

Nique was in control of the meeting again today. "Welcome back, folks," he started by saying. "I hope you have all had a little rest since your last mission. We have a few things to talk over today. These include areas such as the journey to the new planet, the journey to Thapa dimension to gather up the rest of our people and of course the analysis of the data you brought back from your last mission. HICS will start by detailing the data collected and what we now know."

THANK YOU, SIR. AS YOU ARE ALL AWARE, THE APPROPRIATION OF THE ASSAULT FRIGATE FROM SIDARACK WAS A HUGE BONUS FOR US. IT HAS HELPED US TO UNDERSTAND SOME OF THE NEW TECHNOLOGIES WHICH WE COULD NOT RECREATE, AND I EXPECT TO HAVE PLANS FOR THESE TECHNOLOGIES BY THE TIME WE ARRIVE AT OUR NEW HOME. IN ADDITION, I HAVE MADE SOME CHANGES TO THE CLOAKING DEVICES ON OUR SHIPS BASED ON THE NEW CLOAK INSTALLED ON THE ASSAULT FRIGATE. HAVING SALVAGED PARTS FROM SOME OF THE OLDER, MORE OUT-OF-DATE NAJESS SHIPS, TWO NEW ASSAULT FRIGATES HAVE BEEN BUILT SUCCESSFULLY. IN ADDITION, DESIGNS FOR THE SALVAGE SHIPS HAVE BEEN COMPLETED, AND BUILD WORK WILL COMMENCE ONCE ADDITIONAL MATERIALS HAVE BEEN HARVESTED.

BASED ON THE DATA RETRIEVED FROM THE PLANET, WE NOW ALSO HAVE THE INFORMATION NECESSARY TO BUILD CAPITAL SHIPS. THIS WILL NOT

BE POSSIBLE UNTIL WE HAVE GATHERED A LARGE QUANTITY OF RESOURCES, SOME OF WHICH WE KNOW MUST EXIST BUT WE DON'T KNOW WHERE YET. TO LOCATE THESE RESOURCES, SCOUTS HAVE ALREADY BEEN DESPATCHED IN PAIRS TO SEVERAL PLANETS. ONCE THE REQUIRED RAW MATERIALS HAVE BEEN LOCATED, THE RMVs WILL BE DESPATCHED AND WILL COMMENCE EXTRACTION.

THE WEAPONS AND ARMOUR ON THE ASSAULT FRIGATE ARE HEAVY AND THE VESSEL IS CAPABLE OF TAKING OUT MOST CAPITAL SHIPS, ALTHOUGH THE WEAKNESS WILL ALWAYS BE THE SMALLER, MORE MANOEUVRABLE INTERCEPTORS AND ESPECIALLY BOMBERS, SUCH AS OUR OWN. THE DESIGN OF THE ASSAULT FRIGATE LEAVES A BLIND SPOT FOR THE GUNS RIGHT BEHIND THE ENGINES. IF A BOMBER GETS INTO THIS BLIND SPOT, IT COULD TAKE DOWN THE FRIGATE.

"Could the design not be updated to remove the blind spot issue?" Entai asks.

"No," Wei says. "Covering the blind spot would result in other areas becoming more vulnerable. Consider the assault frigate as a knight on a chess board. Like the knight, the frigate can be a deadly weapon, but it is vulnerable too. If, however, you protect it using some of your smaller ships, it has the ability to create a hole in the enemy defence and still make its way out of danger again. I am sure the attack on Sidarack will prove to be a huge blow to the Gringuns, particularly as they had started using the base as a build location for prototype equipment. This ship would have been one of their best yet. Now, I think that about covers the ships. HICS, please continue with the other plans."

WITH TEFAAZ'S HELP WE HAVE NOW UNLOCKED SOME VITAL DATA SURROUNDING WHAT WILL BE OUR NEW HOME FOR THE FORESEEABLE FUTURE.

AS WE ALREADY KNOW, THE PLANET IS COMPLETELY HIDDEN FROM OUR SCANNERS.

"So, even the new scanners will not be able to pick up the planet when we are close?" I ask.

IF THE TEXTS ARE ACCURATE, WE WILL NOT EVEN SEE THE PLANET WHEN WE ARE CLOSE.

"It appears to be a test of faith, Jon," Wei interrupts. "The planet will be completely hidden from view. We believe it has never been found because the area where the planet is supposed to be will show a unique space phenomena, but this is speculation of course. We cannot say what shape this potential phenomena will take; however, based on the suspected location of the planet and some of the archived documents recovered over the last two missions, we know that something is in that location. The Gringuns know about it too and they avoid the area completely. No records are available to detail why they avoid the area, we just know they do."

WHAT THE SCANNERS HAVE DISCOVERED IS A CHANGE IN THE GRAVITATIONAL FORCES IN THE AREA. ALTHOUGH WE HAVE NO VISUAL CLUES THAT THE PLANET STILL EXISTS, WE KNOW WE HAVE TO GO THERE. THE GRINGUNS HAVE NOW CHANGED THEIR SEARCH PATTERNS AND ARE LOOKING IN OUR DIRECTION FOR ADDITIONAL PLANETS TO SEARCH. THEY ARE NOT LEAVING ANY PLANETS OUT. THE NEW PLANET IS CALLED BINTEEP AND, ASSUMING IT IS AS WELL HIDDEN AS WE ARE LED TO BELIEVE, IT COULD BE THE PERFECT LOCATION FOR US TO HIDE.

ALL EQUIPMENT AND MOST OF OUR RESOURCES AND SUPPLIES WILL BE LOADED ONTO THE WAITING CARGO SHIPS. THESE WILL BE TAKEN TO BINTEEP WITH US. THE REMAINING RESOURCES AND SUPPLIES WILL BE LEFT BEHIND FOR THE REST OF THE

COLONISTS FROM THAPA DIMENSION. I WILL LOAD THE WAYPOINTS ONTO ALL OF THE SHIPS PRIOR TO DEPARTURE, ALONG WITH THE TIME THEY ARE EXPECTED TO ARRIVE. THIS WILL ENSURE WE ARE ALL TRAVELLING CLOSE TOGETHER. PLEASE REMEMBER THAT ALL OF THE SHIPS WILL BE VERY CLOSE AND CLOAKED. THIS WILL MAKE IT ALMOST IMPOSSIBLE FOR US TO TRACK EACH OTHER. TO ENSURE WE DO NOT LOSE ANY SHIPS, WE WILL HAVE SINGLE POINT OF CONTACT KETERANS ON EACH SHIP. THEY WILL BE TASKED WITH MAINTAINING TELEPATHIC CONTACT WITH THEIR COUNTERPARTS ON ONE OF THE OTHER SHIPS. THAT WAY WE WILL KNOW IF CONTACT HAS BEEN BROKEN FOR ANY REASON.

SHOULD ANY SHIPS BE LOST, CONTINUE TRAVELLING TO THE NEXT WAYPOINT. THE FLEET WILL BE WAITING FOR YOU THERE. TRAVELLING UNDER CLOAK IS STILL SLOW, BUT WITH THE NEW CLOAKS WE SHOULD MAKE CONSIDERABLY BETTER TIME. ASSUMING NO PROBLEMS, WE SHOULD ARRIVE AT BINTEEP WITHIN THREE WEEKS.

"Three weeks?" Andy says louder than he probably wanted to. "Why so long?"

THE ROUTE WE ARE TAKING IS LENGTHY IN ORDER TO HIDE OUR TRUE DIRECTION AND DESTINATION. IF THE GRINGUNS HAVE FOUND A WAY TO TRACK US, THEN OUR MOVEMENTS SHOULD CONFUSE THEM A BIT. IN ADDITION, ONE OF THE WAYPOINTS PASSES THROUGH THE CENTRE OF AN ANOMALY. MY READINGS SHOW THAT THIS AREA OF SPACE IS COMPLETELY UNREADABLE DUE TO HIGH LEVELS OF RADIATION. OUR SHIELDS WILL PROTECT US FOR A SHORT TIME, SO WE WILL BE USING IT AS A GATHERING POINT. WITHIN THE ANOMALY, WE

WILL BE ABLE TO COMMUNICATE FREELY SO LONG AS WE ARE CLOSE TO EACH OTHER, BUT WE ARE GOING TO HAVE TO MOVE OUT AGAIN SOON AFTER. A SMALL GROUP OF SCOUTS WILL LEAVE THE FLEET WHEN WE LEAVE THE ANOMALY. THEIR TASK WILL BE TO RECON THE AREA AHEAD, FOLLOWING EACH WAYPOINT. THEY WILL BE CLOAKED BUT WILL STILL BE ABLE TO TRAVEL MUCH FASTER THAN US. WHEN THEY ARRIVE AT THE DESTINATION, THEY WILL BE LOOKING FOR ANY SIGNS OF THE PLANET. IF THEY DETECT AN AMBUSH OR SOMETHING ELSE, THEY WILL RETURN TO INFORM THE FLEET AND WE WILL CONSIDER RETURNING TO THIS PLANET FOR THE TIME BEING.

"Do we have any information about the planet we are going to?" Forrahh asks.

UNFORTUNATELY NOT. THE MAP ROOM DID NOT HOLD ANY INFORMATION RELATING TO WHAT THE PLANET WAS FOR OTHER THAN IT BEING A HIDDEN BASE FOR THE ANEESH. IT IS LIKELY TO BE SIMILAR TO THIS PLANET – DEVOID OF RESOURCES TO ENSURE NO-ONE EVER TAKES AN INTEREST IN IT.

"Okay," Garry interrupts rudely, waving his hands frantically to get everyone's attention, "so everyone else will be going to Binteep; I get it, I'm sure that will be wonderful. But what about the mission to Thapa Dimension?"

YOU WILL BE LEADING THE TEAM BACK TO THAPA. YOUR MISSION WILL BE TO VISIT ALL OF THE THREE HOME WORLDS IN THE DIMENSION AND TO GATHER ALL THE PEOPLE WHO ARE WILLING TO LEAVE. YOU WILL NEED TO INFORM THE INCUMBENT GOVERNMENTS ABOUT THE NEED FOR ADDITIONAL PEOPLE. YOUR TEAM WILL CONSIST OF NAJESS, KETERAN AND HUMAN PEOPLE TO ACT AS ENVOYS

FOR EACH PLANET. YOU WILL ALSO HAVE SEVERAL TRANSPORTS TO BRING THE ADDITIONAL PEOPLE BACK WITH YOU.

FOLLOWING YOUR DEPARTURE FROM HERE, YOU WILL ACTIVATE YOUR CLOAK AND TRAVEL TO THE LOCATION WHERE WE ENTERED THIS DIMENSION. ONCE THERE, REOPEN THE RIFT AND TRAVEL THROUGH TO BEGIN YOUR MISSION IN THAPA. YOUR MISSION TIME WITHIN THAPA IS EXPECTED TO LAST APPROXIMATELY TWO MONTHS. WITH THE NEW ENGINES INSTALLED ON THE TRANSPORTS THE TRAVEL TIME MAY REDUCE FURTHER, BUT YOU ARE EXPECTED TO TRAVEL UNDER CLOAK FOR THE ENTIRE JOURNEY UNTIL YOU REACH EACH PLANET.

AS WE NOW HAVE THREE ASSAULT FRIGATES, ONE WILL BE GOING WITH YOU TO PROVIDE PROTECTION IF NEEDED. YOU WILL ALSO HAVE A SMALL CONTINGENT OF INTERCEPTORS FOR ADDITIONAL COVER. ONCE YOUR MISSION HAS BEEN COMPLETED, RETURN TO THIS DIMENSION AND HEAD BACK TO THIS PLANET. IF ALL LOOKS CLEAR, SEND A SMALL TRANSPORT TO THE SURFACE AND ARRANGE FOR THE REMAINING EQUIPMENT AND RESOURCES TO BE MOVED ON BOARD... LEAVE NOTHING BEHIND.

AFTER THE TRANSPORT HAS REGROUPED, YOU WILL NEED TO FOLLOW THE WAYPOINTS. AT THE THIRD WAYPOINT, THE ANOMALY, A CLOAKED FRIGATE WILL BE WAITING FOR YOU. IT IS IMPERATIVE THAT YOU ARRIVE AT THE EXACT DESIGNATED POINT BEFORE ATTEMPTING TO COMMUNICATE. COMMUNICATIONS WITHIN THE ANOMALY WILL BE ALLOWED FOR A SHORT PERIOD, BUT YOU MUST LEAVE IMMEDIATELY AFTER TO

AVOID EXCESS RADIATION. OUTSIDE OF THE ANOMALY, ONLY TELEPATHIC COMMUNICATIONS WILL BE ALLOWED.

WHEN YOU MEET YOUR CONTACT IN THE ANOMALY, ANY NEW INFORMATION AND WAYPOINTS WILL BE TRANSMITTED TO YOU. THIS WILL ENSURE YOU ARE ABLE TO LOCATE US. IF THE CONTACT IS NOT WAITING FOR YOU, YOU MUST ASSUME THAT THEY HAVE BEEN DISCOVERED OR WE HAVE NOT BEEN SUCCESSFUL IN OUR MISSION TO LOCATE THE PLANET.

"How will I know which of the two it is?"

THAT WILL BE FOR YOU TO DECIDE. I SUGGEST YOU INITIALLY SCAN THE AREA FOR SIGNS OF COMBAT – DISCHARGE OF CHARGED WEAPONS, DEBRIS, ETC. IF YOU FIND SIGNS OF COMBAT BUT NO SIGNS OF THE FLEET, IT IS LIKELY THAT WE LOST THE BATTLE. UNDER THESE CIRCUMSTANCES, I SUGGEST YOU EITHER HEAD BACK TO THAPA OR YOU FORM A BASE ON THIS PLANET.

I believe this is where Garry realised that he may not have the best end of the deal. "So, you're saying that we may represent the last remnants of our races?"

"Of course, Garry," Wesley states in an obvious manner. "Your task is not without peril. You are expected to manage your team and ensure their safety through good decisions." As I steal a glance at him, I see his Adam's apple bounce once as he swallows hard… Impressive that that is the only tell-tale sign he gives away, though. "I hope you have been training well for your mission. You are going to need to have your combat skills honed."

I of course know he has been relaxing, assuming that his mission would be the easiest one going. It is sad to say it, but it looks like the commanders know it too.

I decide to break the tension in the room and buy Garry some breathing space. "So, when do our missions start?"

BOTH MISSIONS, KNOWN AS THAPA MISSION AND NEW ALLIES MISSION, WILL BEGIN IN TWO DAYS.

This time, both of our Adam's apples bounce.